BASI AND CO

Cheers

Ken Saro-Wiwa

Lagos 13690

BASI AND COMPANY
A Modern African Folktale

Ken Saro-Wiwa

Saros International Publishers

Saros International Publishers
Saros Plaza
33 Aba Road,
P.O. Box 193
Port Harcourt, Nigeria

48 Aragon Avenue
Ewell, Epsom
Surrey KT17 2QG
England

First Published in 1987
© Ken Saro-Wiwa

British Library Cataloguing in Publication Data

Saro-Wiwa, Ken
  Basi and company: a modern African
  folktale.
  I. Title
  823[F]   PR9387.9.S3

ISBN 1 870716 00 0

All rights reserved.
No part of this publication may be reproduced, stored in a
retrieval system or transmitted in any form or by
any means, electronic, mechanical, photocopying,
recording or otherwise without the prior permission
of the copyright owner.

Typeset by A.K.M. Associates (U.K.) Ltd.,
Ajmal House, Hayes Road, Southall, London, Great Britain
Published simultaneously in Nigeria and the United Kingdom

For Nomsy and the children

Author's Note

Nightfall. A moonlit night. In an African village playground, children sit in a circle and listen enthralled to a narrator tell folktales. In virtually all the stories, Kuru the Tortoise is present, either tricking others or himself at the receiving end of tricks. His is a world of animals with human attributes and of human beings. From the stories, the children gain an insight into the tortoise's world; they learn lessons from the moral of each story and go to bed well-entertained and educated at the end of the session.

I retain nostalgic memories of those story-telling nights. But of course the world has changed. As an adult, it has dawned on me that the form in which we heard the exploits of the Tortoise is very much of the genre of the television series. Consequently, in transforming the folktale into a contemporary idiom, I adopted the format of the television comedy series, and it is no wonder that *Basi And Company* first appeared as such.

In presenting it in book form, I have maintained this format in the belief that this accords better with African narrative methods than the European novel with its flashbacks, psychological analyses and progressive development of character, although elements of the latter are not entirely absent from my narration.

Missing, though, are the delightful, haunting songs which the listeners joined the narrator in chorusing. I have tried to make up for this by including repetitive slogans which appear like refrains through the stories.

All the stories but one are told by a narrator. In the one story, however, the narrator becomes a listener, just as it happened when, as children, we told our stories in relays and a narrator of one became listener to the others.

Folktales were always "the wisdom of the elders" told to the young for their instruction. *Basi And Company* as a television comedy series has, happily, appealed to both young and old in Nigeria. I hope that the same audience and more will find further enjoyment in this book.

Ken Saro-Wiwa
Part Harcourt, 1987.

Contents

Adetola Street	1
The Transistor Radio	26
A Company is Formed	39
A Shipload of Rice	50
The Mattress	63
The Vendor of Titles	75
The Contract	89
The Bank Loan	104
Countertrade	117
The Candidate	135
The Party Secretary	152
An Efficient Company	173
The Ghost Workers	187
The Proposal	201
Glossary	216

Adetola Street

My uncle, Mr Adetola, was the first man to build a house on the Street. So naturally, the Street was named after him.

Rumours have it that the matter was not that simple. Some have said that Madam the Madam, the First Lady of Adetola Street, completed her house long before my uncle started building his, and so hers was the first house on the Street. Consider therefore Madam's rage when, one day, she found that there was a sign at the beginning of the Street. It read simply, "Adetola Street". It was made of cardboard paper pinned to a twig buried deep into the earth. Madam the Madam uprooted the twig and tore up the paper. She did not bother to find out who had erected the sign.

When my uncle found that his sign had been torn down, he was naturally quite upset.

'Some goats have taken to eating cardboard signs,' he said. 'There is nothing the goats in this city won't do. Next time a goat eats my sign, I will kill and eat the goat.' He was firm in that resolution. Then he wrote another sign and pinned it, this time, to a mango tree somewhere on the street. He pinned it quite high up the trunk of the tree, way beyond the reach of all mischievous goats.

'We'll see if goats climb mango trees,' my uncle is rumoured to have said.

Madam the Madam, who was on the lookout for any obstreperous signs on the Street, quickly spotted it and destroyed it. She tore the cardboard paper into tiny little shreds and, for good measure, burnt the shreds into ashes. And lest there should be any mistake as to her intention, buried the ashes.

'We go see if de paper go commot from de fire,' declared Madam the Madam with immense self-satisfaction.

My uncle did not yet live on the Street. He came daily to supervise the construction of his house. He had laid the foundation thereof many years earlier, which was the reason he laid claim to the Street. Indeed the foundation of the house had been laid long before someone thought of laying a road in the middle of that wilderness so that people could build houses on either side of the road and so make a street. That was the fashion in those days. My uncle was very proud of his achievement. So, when he arrived to find that his sign had disappeared, leaving no trace behind, he did not waste his tears or time. Nor did he look for stray goats on the Street. He was a man of strong resolution, a man who stood on his honour, by his word, a proud man. And when he saw his resolve, his honour, his pride threatened, he knew precisely what to do. He hired a carpenter and a signwriter and had a proper sign made. White characters on a black background, and under his close supervision, the sign was dug into the earth at the beginning of the Street. He then went home, not to his new house which was only being painted, but to our old residence in the quagmire of Lagos Island.

Madam returned that evening from her business journey to central Lagos and found her Street properly labelled in traditional style, but with the wrong name. Her heart sank. Could the sign be authoritative? Had the Municipal Council sanctioned that name for her Street? She decided to test the will of the sleepy Council, and dug up the signpost. She did not destroy it, lest she fall foul of some unknown law. The way she threw down the post, it might have been the work of the wind. She felt satisfied with her handiwork. The Street was now nameless.

Then a great idea occurred to her. She ought to name the Street after herself. It took well on three days to make the Street sign bearing her proud name because she insisted on the way the letters should be carved or otherwise. She tortured the poor signwriter who complained bitterly. But to all his complaints, Madam had only one answer: 'It's a matter of cash!' Reminding the miserable fellow that she was paying the piper and she would dictate the tune. Before which wisdom, the signwriter reeled powerlessly. He finished the sign to Madam's satisfaction on the third night and dutifully delivered it.

In those three days, Mr Adetola was busy on other matters and did not go round to inspect either his new house or his new Street. When he finally showed up, he found his cherished signpost lying on the ground in utter abandonment.

'The wind has desecrated my signpost,' moaned my uncle. And he fell to re-establishing his name and authority on the Street. He re-erected the signpost properly. And went away.

When Madam the Madam returned that evening armed with her signpost, she found Mr Adetola's resolve flying bravely in her face. She looked about her furtively, removed the "ADETOLA STREET" sign and replaced it with hers which read simply, "MADAMS AVUNEU".

Then she retired to her house with immense satisfaction.

Early next morning, before the hour of eight, she took an unaccustomed walk to the beginning of the Street. Her sign stood there in the morning sun, proudly designating the "Avuneu" as hers. She laughed softly to herself and went back home to a hearty breakfast. When she went off later that morning to her daily routine, the sign was still there. She was happy as a lark.

Mr Adetola returned that afternoon to find his Street renamed "MADAMS AVUNEU". He went livid with rage.

'What illiterate nonsense!' fumed he. 'Avuneu! What's an "avuneu"?' He dug up the sign and replaced it with his signpost. He inspected his house which was rapidly nearing completion and went away, casting a satisfied glance at the street name.

Madam the Madam returned that evening, and we all know what she did. The next day when Mr Adetola showed up, he did what he had to do. And the evening of that same day, Madam did what she had to do.

Things went on in this way and would have gone on in the same way for much longer if Mr Adetola had not hit on the brilliant idea of stationing a security guard by his signpost.

The security man was called Amodu. He had been given strict instructions by my uncle. He arrived at his duty post armed with a bow and a quiver of arrows. Poisoned arrows. And sat beneath the sign. He waited all day for the robbers. They did not turn up. All he saw was a plump, black lady who refused to answer him when he threw her a cheery greeting, 'Good even, Madam!' which was about all he could say in the English tongue.

The object of this sincere adulation ignored him pointedly and said to herself:

'Security guard, ehn? We go see if you no go sleep dis night.'

Promptly, at dusk, the security guard withdrew. Promptly, Madam the Madam replaced "ADETOLA STREET" with "MADAMS AVUNEU".

The next morning, Amodu reported for duty faithfully and sat blissfully beneath Madam's sign. So was it that when Mr Adetola showed up at midday, he found his security guard watching over Madam's sign. Abomination.

'You fool,' says my uncle, 'do I pay you all that money to watch over another person's name? Is that why I hired you?' He stamped angrily on the ground.

Amodu did not understand what my uncle was so upset about. The sign was erect and safe. Which is what he had been hired to ensure.

'Which sign?' asked Mr Adetola.

'This one,' said Amodu, pointing to "MADAMS AVUNEU".
'This is not the sign I asked you to watch over.'
'It is.'
'It's not.'
'It is.'
'It's not,' said Mr Adetola in a voice that thundered.
'How should I know?' asked Amodu innocently.

My uncle was in despair. He knew it would serve no purpose arguing with Amodu. Or being angry with him. So he picked up the "ADETOLA STREET" signboard, asked Amodu to remove Madam the Madam's treasured sign and fell to erecting his proud name in the midday warmth.

'This is the signboard I pay you to watch,' said he to Amodu. 'This other one which you have just removed is bewitched. Don't touch it! Don't touch it! And don't allow anyone to touch it. It's an evil sign.'

Amodu looked at Madam's signboard with fear and trepidation. He began to shake like a wet dog. This pleased my uncle very much.

'Illiterate fool,' muttered he under his breath. Then he made to go. Suddenly, a thought came to him. His adversary was working by night when witches were known to operate best. So he told Amodu that he would have to keep watch at night also.

Amodu protested. He could not work day and night. My uncle insisted. Amodu pleaded. My uncle was adamant. It was either a full day's work or no work at all. Amodu needed the job. So he asked to be paid double the agreed stipend. My uncle said he would double Amodu's salary but he would have to prove himself an efficient guard.

'How?' asked Amodu.

'Keep watch tonight. If tomorrow the sign is still there, I will hire you for a whole day and pay you double.'

Amodu was mollified and signified his content by nodding vigorously several times.

'Don't leave this place for one moment,' my uncle warned. 'Let's see by what magic my signboard will be removed.'

'But I have no food to eat. And no torch to use at night,' protested Amodu.

'Wait here for me,' said my uncle. And he went off.

He soon returned armed with some roasted plantains and groundnuts in one hand, and a lantern and a box of matches in the other. Amodu thanked him with a smile and they parted company.

Amodu kept watch all day. When Madam the Madam returned in the evening, she found the security guard contentedly sitting underneath the "ADETOLA STREET" signpost and chewing gleefully away at his roasted plantains and groundnuts. As usual, he threw her a cheery "Good even, Madam". As usual, she ignored him. Her eyes coolly picked out the "MADAMS AVUNEU" signpost lying desolate beside Amodu.

Later that night when Madam, armed with a torch, turned up to do what she had to do, she found Amodu fast asleep on top of her signpost. A lantern burned brightly beside him. Madam was at a loss what to do. She could not retrieve her signpost without waking the nightguard. And Amodu awake was as dangerous as the poisoned arrows of his quiver.

Madam saw she was about to lose the war. She was not going to do so without a flourish. Amodu snored on musically. The lantern burned more brightly. Madam swooped down, took the lantern and walked away briskly, triumphantly. Amodu snored on, oblivious of his loss. Madam had won a trophy from her undeclared war with Mr Adetola.

The lantern was to hang in Madam's dining room for a long time. Later, she sent it into her kitchen. She refused to tell anyone exactly how she came by it, but most people knew the secret anyway.

Amodu woke up early the next morning and was gratified to find that the "ADETOLA STREET" sign was still standing erect. But fear stabbed his heart when he found that Mr Adetola's lantern had disappeared. He scratched his head hard and long until it bled to find the answer to the riddle of the missing lantern. Neither blood nor head could tell him what had happened to the lantern.

Later that day when my uncle appeared on the scene, he was pleased to find that his sign still stood on the Street. He did not worry about Amodu. There were other things on his mind. He had arrived with a lorryload of his possessions. His wife and I arrived in tow. He had decided to occupy his new house so he could keep a vigilant eye on his signpost. The painters had not completed their work on the house. But my uncle did not worry. There were more important things on his mind.

We had stayed in the new house for one week when Amodu turned up to ask for his salary. It was month-end. My uncle paid him happily. And thereafter, Amodu disappeared. He left a half-empty box of matches on our front door. My uncle knew immediately that Amodu had resigned. But where, he wondered, was the lantern? He searched Amodu out and questioned him. Amodu confessed to the loss of the lantern. My uncle accused him of having stolen it. Amodu swore that he had lost it.

'You can't lose a lantern just like that, man,' said my uncle.

'It disappeared,' said Amodu.

'Nonsense! Lanterns don't just disappear. Tell me where you kept it. It's my property. I will give it to the next nightwatchman I employ.'

Amodu swore he had lost it. So my uncle asked him to pay double its price for it.

Amodu complied and my uncle duly declared himself satisfied. The street sign still stood on the Street undisturbed. There was now no need to employ another nightwatchman to guard it.

As a final mark of the everlasting quality of the street name, my uncle had inscribed under the sign the words "BY ORDER M.M.C.", by which he meant that the Mushin Municipal Council had authorized him to name the Street after himself.

I believe Madam the Madam was fooled by that last addition. Rumour has it that she interpreted "M.M.C." to mean "Madam the Madam Consent", which interpretation assuaged her anger. The name stood without molestation for all time.

Thus did we become residents of Adetola Street. Thus was meanness established as a hallmark of the Street.

In those early days, living on the Street was not easy. For one, we were surrounded by a bush. A few more houses were under construction on either side of the road. There was no electricity and no water.

My uncle said he did not worry much about electricity. We could do without it. But water was a bother. My aunt, his wife, worried him no end about water. So he finally decided to dig a well at the back of the house.

That proved a great tribulation which was to keep my uncle in a permanent state of distress for a long time. This is what happened:

My uncle invited a man called Adisa one day to our house to discuss the matter of well-digging. Adisa had been highly recommended as a contractor well-versed in the matter of well-digging. He was said to have a nose that could discern the smell of water under the ground. And he had workers whose spades were so sharp they got to the water-level in a matter of days.

When Adisa called upon my uncle, he justified in words all that had been said of him. He examined the backyard with the eyes of an eagle. He rejected the spot which my uncle indicated to him as the position where he wanted the well established. He said he was sure there would be no water there. He moved five feet therefrom and said he was sure water would be found in the new spot. My uncle gave him the benefit of the doubt.

Then they started to haggle over the matter of costs. Adisa said he wanted one thousand naira. My uncle said he would pay a thousand one hundred and one naira. Adisa said he wanted one thousand five hundred.

Adetola Street

My uncle said he would pay one thousand six hundred and six naira.

'That is not good,' said Adisa.

'It is a lot of money,' said my uncle.

'Do you know how much Mr Adetoro of Brown Street paid me only last week to dig his well?' asked Adisa.

'No.'

'Go and ask him. He will tell you.'

'I don't want to ask Mr Adetoro,' said my uncle.

'Just go and ask him. He will tell you. And the soil here is harder than the soil on Adetoro Street.'

'So?'

'You should pay more.'

'How do you know the soil here is harder than that of Adetoro Street?' asked my uncle.

'I can see it. Once I see the soil, I know.'

That appeared to be an incontrovertible fact. Because my uncle did not dispute the matter any further.

'Exactly how much do you want?' asked my uncle of Adisa.

'Two thousand naira,' replied Adisa.

'Right. I will pay you two thousand,' agreed my uncle.

'No. That's too little,' said Adisa. 'I have several workers. We will do the work quick quick. You have to pay two thousand five hundred naira.'

My uncle thought over that for a long time. I imagine he came to the conclusion that since he could not dig the well himself, he might as well accept whatever Adisa wanted. So he accepted Adisa's quotation.

Adisa immediately raised the ante. He demanded that my uncle give the workers one meal a day for seven days. My uncle said he would pay money because he could not undertake to feed the workers.

'Impossible!' said Adisa. 'The workers must eat. Otherwise they cannot be able to work well from morning to night.'

'But they can use the money I give them to buy food,' reasoned my uncle.

'Impossible!' said Adisa. He lapsed into a long silence.

Stalemate ticked away.

My uncle accepted Adisa's terms. Again the latter proceeded to lay some more conditions.

'The food you will give them is *eba*. They must have two two pieces of meat everyday, Monday to Saturday. On Sunday, you will give them three three pieces of meat.'

'Why should there be more meat on Sunday than on all other days?' asked my uncle of Adisa.

'Sunday is holy day,' answered Adisa.

My uncle appeared to think that that was reasonable. So he accepted Adisa's terms. Adisa did not leave the house.

'Anything more?' asked my uncle.

'The workers will find the water on Sunday night,' said Adisa.

'That is good.'

'When they get to the water, you will kill one goat and two chicken.'

'One goat and two chicken!' echoed my uncle. 'Whatever for?'

'That is the rule,' replied Adisa coolly.

'Wonderful!' said my uncle.

'It's not wonderful,' Adisa replied. 'Go and ask Mr Adetoro of Brown Street. I complete his well only last week.'

'So what will happen if I do not slaughter the goat and chicken?'

'The well will dry. The water will not flow.'

'Nonsense!' said my uncle.

'It's not nonsense. Go and ask Mr Adetoro of Brown Street. 'It's true.'

I could see that my uncle had lost his temper. Adisa had succeeded in wearing him down. He would have loved to get rid of the man. But he needed him. So he said, 'Agreed, Adisa, I will provide the goat and chicken as soon as your men strike water.'

'Thank you, sah,' said Adisa, genuflecting gracefully. Then he sat back in his chair.

'Anything else?' asked my uncle, after a long pause.

Adisa sat in his chair, unmoved, unflappable.

'I need advance,' says he.

'You want me to pay you in advance?' asked my uncle.

'Yes sah. Go ask Mr Adetoro of Brown Street. I complete his well only last week.'

'How much do you want?' asked my uncle.

'One thousand naira only.'

My uncle quickly went into his bedroom and returned with a wad of notes which he made over to Adisa. The latter grabbed at it with quick hands. Then he counted and pocketed it. And now he stood up to go.

'When do you start?' asked my uncle.

'Maybe in two or three week,' Adisa replied, nonchalantly.

'Why?'

'I'm going to burial of my uncle's wife. She die three months now. But we have to keep the dead body till now so that we can be able to give her proper burial in her own house.'

My uncle opened his mouth in disbelief. He had, in fact, funded the burial carnival of Mr Adisa's relation. That was the last thing he wanted to do. So he demanded that Mr Adisa return the money he had just paid him.

'Why?' demanded Adisa.
'Because you are not ready to start work. You get paid when you start.'
'But I'm ready. Very ready. Ah-ah. I'm very ready.'
'So when are you going to start?'
'Immediately. After the burial of my uncle's wife.'
'Good. So you return my money now and you have it back immediately after the burial of your uncle's wife.'

That being the case, Adisa decided to start work immediately. He brought in a number of scrawny labourers who did not look like they could dig a flowerbed, much less a water well.

They lazed around for a whole day doing precious little. Adisa himself disappeared soon after they arrived, and both my uncle and his wife were not at home to supervise the workers. At six o'clock, the workers dispersed, having succeeded in making a drawing on the ground indicating the circumference of the well.

That was the last we saw of Adisa and his workers. They did not turn up the following day or the day after or ever. My uncle was mad with himself. He did not understand how he had trusted Adisa with one thousand naira. He laid a complaint against Adisa with the gentleman who had first introduced him to Adisa. The gentleman apologized fulsomely. He promised to send a more reliable contractor. One whose relation would not die without the permission of my uncle.

I think my uncle had had enough. He spurned all help from friends, relations and well-wishers and went out on his own to look for the men who would dig him his well.

He scoured the hovels of Isalegangan, the slums of Oshodi and the rubbish dumps of Isolo. Until he finally stumbled on a gang of workers who were pleased to be hired directly by the client. They said the contractors always cheated them. 'Monkey dey work, baboon dey chop,' they alleged, implying that they were monkeys who worked hard and contractors like Adisa were baboons who reaped where they did not sow.

Mr Adetola agreed with them on the status of Adisa and his kind. They were real baboons. He said he would see if the workers themselves were truly the monkeys they claimed to be.

This time, my uncle made no mistakes. He bargained with the workers the day they came to work. After the usual haggling, the sum of one thousand naira was agreed upon. Mr Adetola said he would pay nothing in advance. He would only pay for work done, and he was not going to cook for anyone. These general terms proved acceptable to the workers. They toiled hard at it from the first day. By the fifth day, they had dug a very deep well. But they were shocked that they were no closer to water. So they went back to Mr Adetola and told him:

'The water is very far away.'

'Is it?' asked Mr Adetola.

'Yes. One thousand naira too small. The water too far.'

'So if you had found water nearer the surface you would have charged me less money?'

'Is our luck,' the workers chanted.

'And whose luck is it now that, as you say, the water too far?'

The workers laughed. Their leader piped up.

'Oga must put more money. Otherwise we no go work again.'

'How much do you want?' Mr Adetola knew that to be a ploy which never failed. It embarrassed the workers. They did not want to appear either foolish or greedy.

The workers withdrew for a tête-a-tête. When they returned, their leader was smiling. He said they wanted two thousand naira.

'Right, you have it. But you must get to the water before I pay you.'

The workers said they wanted some money to buy food. My uncle obliged them. Two hundred and fifty naira he paid. And there were smiles all round. They all parted on the best of terms – my uncle to pursue his daily labours, the labourers to continue digging their well.

They toiled away for two more days. And still there was no sign of water. Then they left, unceremoniously. They did not tell my uncle. And we did not ever see them again.

'This well will drive me mad,' said my uncle to his wife when it became obvious that the labourers had abandoned their task.

'I hope not,' his wife replied.

'I don't see how not. First, Adisa the contractor disappears with one thousand naira. Then I choose to do it by direct labour. Now the labourers have abandoned the job.'

'Fair enough. You have spent one thousand two hundred and fifty naira. Maybe you will find some workers who will get to the water-level for another one thousand two hundred and fifty naira. The well is deep enough already. Water should not be far away.'

This assuaged my uncle very much. I believe he went to bed a very happy man. Because he woke up early the next morning and hired two labourers, bought them tools and urged them to dig away. He offered to pay them thirty naira per day. At the mention of this princely sum, the labourers jumped into the well with alacrity and worked their hearts out. My uncle said the two men were Wagadugans – tall, swarthy, black men from a far-away land where, unlike Lagos, they liked to work.

But even then, he decided not to take any chances. He stayed at the well-head, supervising the Wagadugans and making sure that work went on every minute of the day. Close supervision paid off. At the end of fourteen days, to our delight and the chagrin of the workers, we struck water. At less than two thousand naira.

A pump at the bottom of the well, some electrical connections, and we had water in our home. Thus did Mr Adetola become the first man to have pipe-borne water in his house. That he was the first man to do this was not controvertible. He set an example which was to be followed by every householder on Adetola Street. Electricity was installed later.

Already, several men and women had begun to build houses on the Street. There was great activity all around. From morning till night, the vehicles rolled in, bearing sand, cement blocks, concrete mixers and other building material. The houses went up quickly.

My uncle described the pace of events in Lagos as giddy. He said this was because there was oil in the swamps of the Delta. I did not quite understand how the presence of oil in the swamps enabled houses to spring up fast on Adetola Street. But whether I understood or not, the houses went up. Some of them were huge, many-storied buildings; others were mere huts hastily put together with timber, cardboard paper or burnt bricks. Some were covered with the most modern building material; others were hastily laid over with rusty corrugated iron sheets picked from the rubbish dump or stolen from some building site.

It was not only on Adetola Street that activity was moving apace. All over Lagos, according to my uncle, there was feverish activity. I often overheard him tell my aunt that business was good. I did not understand what he meant. But when he said that beautiful new cars were coming into Lagos on ships, and the shops were full of many wonderful goods from across the seas, I understood him better. He said that if care was not taken, Lagosians would build houses on every available piece of land, because everyone was anxious to build a house. When I looked at our Street carefully, I saw what he meant. Because almost all the space on Adetola Street, except the road itself, had been built on. The roofs of the houses touched each other and struggled for space. We could see and hear what was happening in our neighbours' houses. Houses, houses, houses. Soon, Adetola Street was almost completely built up. It had over four hundred houses.

That was not all. There were two or three sectarian churches and a mosque. "Houses of Prayer" sprang up and died like the wind. But perhaps the most enduring monument on the Street was the market.

Everyone called it Adetola Market – another feather in the cap of my uncle. It contained everything on earth.

It sat on one of the open lots between the houses. Traders merely erected shacks on the lot; as more traders settled in, the shacks spilled over the road, like a stream overflowing its banks.

Perhaps the most popular section of the market was where *gari* was sold – *gari* being our staple food. Here you would find beautifully arranged rows of large, colourful enamel basins piled high with varieties of *gari*, rice and other cereals, each in a shade of yellow or cream.

Next to it was the fish section with croaker, mullet, red snapper, sole and baracuda, all with shiny eyes and gleaming scales. And there were crabs, lobsters, oysters, and prawns. Dried fish too, smoked on charcoal fires, whose aroma competed with that of Scandinavian stockfish, a particular delicacy.

The meat section had whole sheep's heads, pickled cows' hides and heaps of trotters. There were live goats too, bemused goats, staring foolishly into space, unable or perhaps unwilling to bleat. Sheep's head was a favourite with beer drinkers of whom the Street had more than its fair supply.

Of cloth, there was a long line with every type displayed in a blaze of colours. There were both the traditional and imported prints; men's suiting materials, including woollen and heavy damask; baby wear, underwear, a vast array of smuggled Italian shoes, Spanish handbags, dresses from Paris and London, shirts and trousers from Hong Kong. As well as colourful trading beads and other jewellery.

Perhaps the most important section was that where charms, traditional herbs and remedies were sold by a Holy Man who chanted spiritual ditties throughout the day. He was a very popular man and did, as might be expected, brisk business. Near to him was a bottle and tin shop where second-hand bottles and tins along with old newspapers were sold. Everything had its use on Adetola Street.

Close to the road and taking up quite some space were fruits and vegetables, including pineapples, mangoes, bananas, coconuts, grapefruit, pawpaw, tomatoes, potatoes and onions, white cabbage, green beans, anchovies, okro, red hot pepper, fresh green peppers and cucumber.

Adetola Market was colourful; full of bustle, vast numbers of people, noise and dirt, with drains, deep and murky, ready to swallow the unwary.

Those who did not want to shop there could do so conveniently from the tribe of hawkers who serenaded passers-by or motorists caught in the usual traffic jam with jingles advertising various wares. Women sold snacks from basins and baskets on their heads, small boys dispensed drinks from cool boxes; smuggled apples, bread and groundnuts in small cellophane bags, ironing boards, birth certificates, watches, spanners, umbrellas, chiming door-bells, car blinds, car aerials, keyrings, tea sets, bathroom scales, saucepans, chest expanders, coat hangers, cutlery, telephones, pirated Parker pens, tumblers, flasks, razor blades, wheel covers for Mercedes-Benz cars, telephone locks, plugs, crucifixes, breakdown triangles for cars, alarm safes, calculators, biscuits, cucumbers, carpet sweepers, waste-paper baskets, fancy bottle-openers, onions, dish cloths, model cars, *Time* and *Newsweek* magazines, newspapers, margarine, Vick's cough drops, egg rolls, bathroom cabinets, hub caps, carving knives, handbags, fans, radios, pirated video-tapes, blank video-tapes, air freshners and mirrors were the staple of this travelling market which extended the entire length of the Street, every minute of the day and a fraction of the night as well.

If you could not find all you wanted in either the immovable market or the moving market, all landlords obliged you: they had all converted their garages into shops. You had the feeling that the Street was truly a market. This accorded well with traditional wisdom which states that "all the world is a market place". You came, you bought or sold, and you went away. Our world was one huge haggle.

Adelota Street was one of the longest streets I have ever seen. My uncle confirmed that it was the longest Street in Lagos. He said so with pride. As my aunt said, when the longest street in any town is named after you, you have to be proud because it means that you are a very important person.

I guessed it must have been very important to be a very important person on Adetola Street. Because the Street was full of people. People! They lived in the houses which were completed; they lived in the houses which were under construction; they squatted on the plots of land on which houses were yet to be built; they thronged the roads, they filled the Street with chatter and noise. They slept in the marketplace at night. People. My uncle said they came in search of money, in the wake of the riches which had been brought into Lagos by oil money.

People! They came from several countries. From Ghana, from Burkina Faso, from Sierra Leone, from Cameroun, Chad, Benin Republic. Black people. My uncle called them our brothers and sisters. They all poured into Adetola Street.

But we did not only have black people. There were also white people from Europe and America, brown people from Japan, Hong Kong and Taiwan. They all came, my uncle said again and again, in search of money. Money! There was a lot of money in our Street, according to my uncle. And money had a way of attracting people. People and money therefore became important to Adetola Street. In a comradely sort of way. I was to know more about that in the years ahead.

Adetola Street was indeed a very busy Street. It had to be, since every single activity on it was aimed at the possession of money, quick money. Speed was essential to everything. And impatience. All morning and all night, lorries, trucks, buses and cars drove noisily past, honking loudly all the time. Going where I knew not.

The taxis and buses were painted a loud yellow and each bore an inscription, a motto often painstakingly painted by hand on the body and front. The motto represented either the aspiration, hope or philosophy of the owner of the vehicle. Or of the driver of the vehicle. And as both ownership and driver changed fairly rapidly, the mottos changed too. One of the most outstanding ones was *No Condition is Permanent*. Also popular was *Salutation Is Not Love*. This was an injunction to everyone on the Street to remain suspicious of the next. *Live and Let Live* was exhortation in the same world. There was enough for all to share, and people did not need to run over one another in the search for the good things of life – primarily money. *It is good to be good* was as good as its word. It showed that there were people on the Street who knew what was what and it was as fair warning to hoodlums and thugs as *ESIN MI RASCALITY*, a clear exhortation in the same mould in Yoruba and ancient English. *Young Shall Grow* was a reminder that newcomers, not necessarily the young, had a real chance of growing as rich as any. The last word was left out, but wealth was certainly meant, since no one wanted to grow old. *Remember Six Feet* was a threat, a sure threat that anyone who stood in the way of the bus would certainly go to the grave. Its driver kept a hand on the horn all of the time.

But the motto which epitomized everything Adetola Street stood for was proudly inscribed on the most rickety of the buses which plied the Street and beyond. *PSALM 31* was inscribed between two painted crosses across the face, on both sides, and at the back of the rickety bus. The inscription became the bus.

Psalm 31. "Rescue me speedily!" The bus drove fast. "Take me out of the net which is hidden for me". The roads which the bus plied were full of potholes and crevices ready to swallow bus and passengers. "Thou hast seen my affliction". There was no doubt about that. The bus had been battered several times; it bore many signs of repeated and incompetent panel-beatings. "Taken heed of my adversities". Yes, they too were many and included the absence of spare parts. "Hast not delivered me into the hand of the enemy". No. The Vehicle Inspection Officer had refused to condemn it to the garbage heap where it truly belonged. "My strength fails because of my misery, and my bones waste away". You could hear the squeak of the parts, the splutter of the exhaust and the groan of the engine, from miles away. "I am the scorn of all my adversaries, a horror to my neighbours, an object of dread to my acquaintances; those who see me in the street flee from me". By what perspicacity were you named, oh bus! No wonder you haven't paid the hire-purchase firm. "I have become like a broken vessel". Understatement. You are a broken vessel. Utterly broken. "Yea, I hear the whispering of many – terror on every side! – as they scheme together against me, as they plot to take my life". Surely, you are due to be repossessed. And who could blame the hire-purchase man? Surely the Vehicle Inspection Officer must have a limit beyond which even his greed will not go? You will certainly end up in the mechanic's shed where you will be cannibalized. For you are a disgrace and do not deserve to live! But for the moment, *Psalm 31* remained on our Street; it and its owners were grateful for the fact. "Blessed be the LORD, for he has wondrously shown his steadfast love to me when I was beset as in a besieged city. I had said in my alarm, 'I am driven far from thy sight'. But thou didst hear my supplications, when I cried to thee for help". Amen.

Psalm 31 continued its dangerous existence. As did many others of its ilk. We relied on it for our movement along the Street and to other parts of the city. It connected Adetola Street to the outside world; its very presence on the Street was a unifying factor of all our endeavours.

It was not only the buses and taxis which bore slogans. The tradesmen on the Street also had colourful messages. Messages written on signboards which had a life all their own. They rose and fell with the brittleness of soldiers in a ferocious war. They assumed all shapes and sizes. They told tales of the fond hopes and aspirations of the men and women who owned them. And they stood on the Street in the disorderly style which was our hallmark.

Taken together, what they said in so many dissonant tones was that Adetola Street and the men and women who inhabited her were on a long journey towards the achievement of money and that each was prepared to offer the next an invaluable service that might impede or conduce to the final destination. There was, for instance, a noted herbalist who styled himself "N. Dr Ndu" whose signboard, placed at three different points on the Street, proclaimed that he was a great healer of diseases such as gonorrhea, madness, infertility, boils and other unseen afflictions. As new diseases were discovered by the inhabitants of the Street, the list on the notice board increased. Each new disease was written in a different colour and in different characters, so that in time, the herbalist's advertisement board became a tourist attraction.

Perhaps the most colourful of the three signboards was that which stood on two legs right opposite our house. It read as follows, in detail, the only form in which it can best be appreciated:

> N. Dr Ndu Herbal Centre
> Reg. In Nigeria No. 000004234561
> Gonorrhea Killer
> Why die In Silence?
> Call now for all types of DISEASES
> SUCH as GONO, DIARRHEA, JAUNDICE, STOMACH TROUBLES, WAIST PAIN AND PrEGNaT WOMAN Tonk E.T.C.
> Also CONSULT YOUR VIRGIN PINS AND CHARMS
> LIKE BUSINESS and PROMOTION CHARM
> AND LOVE CHAS
> SEEING is BELIVING.
> NEW GONO = 4 DAYS GRANTEE
> CHRONIC GONO = 8 DAYS GRANTEE
> ACUTE GONO = 12 DAYS GRANTEE.

The last three items were fully illustrated by painted pictorial obscenities.

Even to the uninitiated, the signboard was fairly eloquent of the marvellous powers of this mysterious man. The first part of the signboard, that is. As a virgin, I did wonder over and over again what were virgin pins and charms. I could not fathom the mystery, try as much as I would. Promotion charms were fairly old hat. They aided students in secondary schools to pass their end-of-year examinations, and assisted young clerks in earning promotion in offices. They were most popular. You did not have to work. Progress came by magical charms and incantations. This was central to the ethos of the Street.

As for love charms, there were a lot of amorous young men who relied on them to hypnotize their fancied young women and entice them to trysts in hidden corners. It may be suspected that young women needed virgin pins as protection against such love charms. On the other hand, a young woman might also need love charms to attract a desired beau or make a sugar-daddy financially generous. Hypnotism, as we shall soon see, was a necessary part of our life on Adetola Street. As was the ability to support both sides of any argument and profit from both.

As indeed was the ubiquitous disease, gonorrhea, which bestrode the Street like a colossus and operated in three dread stages. Native Doctor Ndu undertook to cure it in a maximum of twelve days. Even in its most acute form, he guaranteed (or granteed) to get rid of it in no more than twelve days. Lower forms took fewer days – four days less in each case. It was all quite mathematical if not scientific.

And be it noted that Native Doctor Ndu had no identifiable address. This added to his Mystery Man status and ensured that only those who needed him could find him. Obviously, no law-keeper was allowed to nose around for him. None dared. None ever did.

In keeping with the traditions of Adetola Street, there was a counter to N. Dr Ndu, a competitor. Another anonymous doctor represented as usual by a signboard, loud in its claims and insistent as to its owner's purpose. It said:

> N. Dr who cures Diseases with Herbs & Roots
> Is Now In Town to Help with Your Problems
> Such as Dying, Weakness of Penis, Dysentary, Gonorrhea.

Wherever he was hiding on our Street, his presence was certain insurance to life, good health and virility. Any man who could banish death had to be in high demand. He was.

Right at the beginning of the Street was a modern petrol-filling station complete with neon lights and set out in an orderly manner quite out of keeping with the rest of the Street. The owner of the station kept a signboard in a prominent part of the station. It read:

> Why Pushing the Car?
> Ha! Batterey.
> Stopping here to charging
> Yours batterey
> And Vulganizing Tyres

Next to the petrol-filling station was a man whose signboard proclaimed him to be an "Iron Bender and Re-wire". That signboard puzzled me no end. I often watched the man at work. It soon became obvious to me, from what he did and from what my uncle said, that he was both an electrician and a blacksmith. Iron Bender and Re-wire.

It was by the nature of our Street that, in addition to N. Dr Ndu's herbalist home, there was a modern clinic whose resident physician had trained in Harvard University. My uncle said that it was the responsibility of the Harvard-trained physician to take over the patients whom N. Dr Ndu could not cure. The physician was a sort of doctor of last resort in whose consultancy patients who had no hope went to die. N. Dr Ndu's cure was of course far cheaper than the Harvardman's attention. And the people of the Street sought the cheaper variety of medical cure first. This caused more death and distress on the Street than was expected, my uncle said. But it was in the interest of the Street that this fact be not obvious to the people.

Beside the Zuma Pharmacy, an orderly, well-lit drug store, was the more popular Sanctus Patent Medicine Store where all sorts of medicament could be bought. My uncle always sent me to the Zuma Pharmacy, forbidding my ever buying anything at Sanctus Patent Medicine Store where, my uncle said, the drugs were all out-of-date and useless. If this was the case, I wondered why so many people in the Street flocked to Sanctus. The owner of Sanctus Stores was a phenomenal man. He was said to be a pharmacist, a nurse and a doctor all rolled into one. He administered injections to all patients and everyone agreed that he was a better physician than the owner of Zuma Pharmacy who only sold injections if they were prescribed by a qualified doctor. All Adetola Street agreed that the pharmacist of Zuma Pharmacy was in partnership with qualified doctors, their joint aim being to make as much money as possible from the inhabitants of the Street. He was not therefore a popular man.

A very popular establishment on our Street was Quickpenny Spares Parts Stores. The name of this establishment proved something of a tongue-twister and so everyone referred to it as Quickpenny and the owner of the establishment became known by that name. Quickpenny. He conjured vistas of huge sums of money, a mountain of coins laid quickly aside, making him a very rich man in record time. He was said to have the parts to every brand of lorry, truck, bus, taxi and car. His notice board proclaimed him to be, apart from a merchant of motor spares, a doctor of vehicles. Everyone complained of the high cost of his merchandise and services. Yet everyone went to him for help. For the Street being full of potholes was a veritable death trap to all vehicles, damaging or destroying exhaust pipes, shock absorbers, tyres and carburettors as soon as they were fixed. Some naughty drivers said over a beer that many of the parts sold by Quickpenny were not original. They were either copies made in Hong Kong and Taiwan, or they were "second-new", which meant that they had been cannibalized from broken-down vehicles and were being sold as new. It helped explain why Quickpenny was a very rich man. All this was rumour, of course. No one could swear for the truth because no one knew it.

Next door was Mama Badejo's *buka*, a shack erected by the roadside, beside which Mama Badejo, a large woman of extraordinary proportions, fried plantains and *akara* in a huge pot on a flaming charcoal fire. Most people depended on her to fill their stomachs. Tired, hungry men found solace in her famous *buka* – a shack with cafeterian pretensions. Many patrons even referred to it as a *bukateria*.

Most activities on the Street centred on an establishment by the name of Dandy's Bar where everyone went to have a drink and a chat. Dandy's Bar was very popular with the men. A run-down, seedy establishment in a single room in one of the houses on the Street, it was dimly-lit, unswept, full of cockroaches, lizards and mice. Cobwebs hung freely in the four corners of the room. Several signs hung proudly on the walls of the Bar. "Break and Pay", "No Credit Today, Come Tomorrow", "In Case of Nuclear or other Fall Out, Keep Cool, Pay your Bill and Run". A sign indicated the toilets beyond. Dandy was more often found in the toilet than in the Bar proper. This fact was attributed to his hard drinking. The Bar itself contained three or four tables with hard, wobbly chairs ranged round each table. High stools stood beside the counter. Near to the wall was an open, wooden cupboard made out in shelves.

It was a simple establishment, but it served the Street well. I stopped at Dandy's from time to time to buy a bottle or two of cold stout for my uncle. That was how I came to know the barkeeper and proprietor of the Bar. Everyone called him Dandy, presumably because his Bar was named Dandy's Bar.

He was a jet-black, portly man who was careful about his personal appearance. Well-built and fairly-well-kept, he wore a bowler hat perpetually and always spotted a clean pink shirt and well-pressed trousers with outstanding creases. He wore an engaging and ready smile and walked with a shuffle. The rumours about Dandy on the Street were many. I learnt a few of them from my uncle who knew most, if not all, of the rumours of the Street.

No one knew where Dandy came from. Some said he was an Ijaw man from the Delta in the east of the country, because all his jays became zees; others said he was from Fernando Po. Yet there were some who swore that he was a Saro man, from Sierra Leone, that is; that he had worked in the merchant navy, had jumped ship and set up shop in Lagos. He was often drunk, a fact that was attributed to his past life as a sailor, and he had a fund of seemingly inexhaustible anecdotes, as all travellers tend to have.

No one knows exactly how he had managed to keep the Bar alive. But it was commonly said that he wanted to leave the Bar for a better paying business. This was in keeping with the ethos of Adetola Street where everyone was in a perpetual search for greener pastures. However, since he had not found these pastures, Dandy continued to tend the Bar. And of his methods, more will be seen later.

Dandy was said to be a bad businessman, because he drank more alcohol than he sold. But because he gave away drinks on credit, even to strangers, he was a very popular man. His generosity attracted a strange assortment of people to the Bar.

Perhaps the most regular customer of Dandy's Bar was Josco, who later became Dandy's best friend, if friendship could be used to describe their fitful relationship. A small, wiry man with shifty eyes, he wore a black cap always and walked with short, quick steps. He drank a lot and that, possibly, was his deep attraction to Dandy. He did not live on the Street. Rumour had it that he lived in a tin shack under the newly-completed Eko Bridge. It was commonly held that he had a criminal past and was on the run from the Police. He was said to be very familiar with many shady characters in the Lagos underworld. Most of the contraband goods which were freely sold at Dandy's Bar were said to be easily traceable to him; he was both procurer and vendor. He lived on earnings from this illegal trade. He was said to be as anxious as any to earn quick money and had no qualms what he did and whom he used to achieve that high aim. Which made everyone wary of him, behind his back.

But perhaps the most interesting man on the Street was Basi. He was quite a character. A tall, lanky, debonair man who walked as though ants were biting his toes, he was known to be worldly-wise and cunning in the extreme. He was a favourite of all the children on the Street. He wore a blue cap perpetually. On the face of the cap was emblazoned the name MR. B. So all the children called him Mr B. He sometimes wore a red singlet on whose front was emblazoned cryptically the slogan "To be a Millionaire". But when he turned his back, the message was completed by the words "Think Like a Millionaire". This motto gave him added status on the Street because everyone presumed that the singlet was a prize given him when he made his first million. He, for his part, happily fuelled the speculation which surrounded him by frequently asserting either that he was a millionaire, or a millionaire-on-the-make or both, as occasion demanded. Which made some people believe that he was either confused or mad or that he lived in a perpetual dream.

Not that any of these mattered to Basi. What people said or thought of him had no effect whatsoever on him. He was a man in search of big, quick money. His landlady could testify to that. She knew him well enough. She was none other than Madam, the proud owner of No. 7.

When my uncle heard that Madam had secured for herself a millionaire tenant, all he said was, 'That woman! That woman!'

The relationship between Basi and Madam had reached folkloric proportions. People on the Street said all sorts of things about landlady and tenant. As for instance, that he had refused to pay his rent ever since he got into her property. As that she had refused to throw him out because she thought he was a millionaire who was only feigning poverty. As the fact that she hoped one day to marry him and have access to his many millions of money. On the other hand, it was widely said that Basi had secret designs on Madam's wealth. It was held that he would not mind marrying her, so as to have access to her wealth and, more especially, her home.

Yes, her home is the famous No. 7, rumoured to be the first building on the Street, although that claim has been dented by the fact that the foundation of my uncle's house was laid before she laid the foundation of her house. All the same, Madam's property shows all the signs of old age. The corrugated iron sheets used in roofing it have all gone rusty. The walls have not been painted since anyone can remember, and some have said that the house is either sinking gradually or that the walls show signs of tottering. But all that is of no consequence. The most important thing is that Madam is safely installed in the top flat of the building. Hers is the only flat, with three bedrooms, a lounge-cum-dining room, a kitchen and conveniences. When Madam built the house, it was termed ultra-modern. It remains so now, even though it has made no room for the latter-day fad of having a servant's block at the rear of the main building. Accordingly, Madam lives alone in her flat, because there is absolutely no question of her sharing any of her conveniences with a servant or a close relation, or any but a very select band of friends, mainly members of the American Dollar Club.

Madam's lounge, which is the only part of the flat anyone has ever seen intimately, is a wonder of jarring, loud colours, from the green of the settee to the dark brown and blue of the carpet on the floor, the pink of the curtains and mauve nets of the window. The dining section has a fridge, a cupboard for the storage of wine, cutlery and crockery. On the wall hangs a picture of the risen Christ, and next to it, a picture of Madam herself in full colour. There are two other famous possessions in Madam's lounge: a framed certificate of membership of the famed American Dollar Club with its famous motto "Cash Is Power". Only the rich and powerful women in our part of Lagos are allowed to belong to the Club. If you do not live around Adetola Street, do not be surprised if you never heard of the society. It exists to assist its members make big money quickly; to offer its members a forum for the display of quick wealth to other members of the society through loud parties and meetings at which food is gorged, drinks are quaffed and gossip generated and spread. The Amerdolians, as they style themselves, dress expensively in smuggled jewellery, fabric and shoes. The more expensive the smuggled items come, the better for the Amerdolians who are a familiar sight in government offices which they traverse constantly as they wheel and deal for "contracts" – contracts for the supply of a variety of items, ranging from office pins to helicopter spare parts; contracts which are paid for before they are completed; contracts which are never completed, nor are meant to be completed; contracts inflated in value to satisfy the greed of winner and awarder. The other prized possession in the lounge is a mirror, once again traceable to the American Dollar Club. It is a condition of membership of the Club that all Amerdolians take a final look at their make-up and dress before they step out of their houses. Amerdolians are independent and proud. They are mostly unmarried, but if married, they play the dominant role in the family, shunting their poor husbands to one side. If such hapless men complain, the Amerdolians shut them up by giving them a supply of "abundant cash". If Amerdolians have children, they send them to their mothers and aunts back in the village or leave them with illiterate, poorly-paid nannies in the back house, for children are an impediment in the pursuit of "abundant cash".

Madam is a true Amerdolian. Much is not known of her in the Street. Everyone agrees though that she is a "thick Madam", which means that she will not accept nonsense from any quarters whatsoever. She is also said to be a "thick businesswoman", although she employs no one. She is said to have "abundant cash", proof of which lies in the way she dresses, the cars she owns, and the numerous other property she owns in several parts of Lagos. As is usual on Adetola Street, no one knows exactly where she comes from. Some say she is an Itsekiri from the coastal middle of the country where the women are very liberated and beautiful; others say she is an Igbo, from Asaba; some say she is a Saro woman whose parents settled in Port Harcourt many generations back. Madam herself is not telling, if indeed she knows. She prefers to be known as a Lagosian so that she can profit by the numerous advantages which native Lagosians have in Lagos.

Madam is a beautiful woman. Her nose is different; it is not flat like other noses; there are rings, natural rings around her finely-shaped neck; she has full, bra-bursting breasts which belie her age, and she is of that full, rounded shape which is the pride of a beautiful woman in her prime. Her smile displays a full set of ivory teeth, looming in graceful order from black gums over full, sensuous lips. These days, lips have become important to our women, and they are often painted. Madam never paints hers. She knows exactly what is right, in dress as in business.

That is why, although she built her house long ago, she had the wisdom of making the ground floor a warehouse or garage or both. This ensured that whatever she had to supply the government was properly stored and accounted for to make delivery easy. She had the wisdom too to leave room for a tenant, because if business was bad, the tenant could alleviate matters by paying rent.

It is a single room, the one she let to Basi, exactly when, nobody can say. She alleges that Basi has not paid her rent for ten years, which would presume that he has been in tenancy for that length of time. Basi himself hotly disputes Madam's count of the years. And he at least ought to know exactly how many years he has lived in the "Palace". But on Adetola Street, time is not very important and people are wont to exaggerate numbers, as Basi himself has exaggerated his bedsit to the status of "Palace".

That, indeed, is what Basi styles his tenancy below Madam's upstairs flat. It is like Basi to see his residence in hyperbolic terms. Or maybe not. Because for all the Street knows, he may have a palace under the screed floor of the room. Anyway, it is known that the "Palace" contains but a narrow iron bed, with a mattress and a pillow, a clothes rack, two lounge chairs, a centre table and, in one corner, a wooden food cupboard on which is perched an ancient kerosene stove. On the walls hang cuttings from old calendars, one showing footballers, the other dancing girls. The ceiling of the room is false; no one can understand why Madam judged it necessary to make a false ceiling; some have said that it is what makes the house "ultra-modern". Anyway, it now holds a great number of rats who gambol there at night, having spent the day feasting in the markets or in the numerous rubbish heaps which are the pride of the Street. Basi objects to their presence in his "Palace", but there is nothing he can do about them. Nor do they alter, for him or for anyone, the status of the room as "Palace".

This claim, added to his motto "To be a millionaire, think like a millionaire", put a feather in the Street's cap, if envious men will confess it. Many a Lagosian, hearing of Basi's fame, has come to the Street in search of his "Palace". And it was in the nature of the times for such an inquirer not to disabuse others, but to re-inforce the belief. Thus did Basi's fame spread through the Street, throughout Lagos until it spilled into the wider world, like the waters of a flood. It became the subject of poems, stories, plays and even of television comedy.

One other more than visible inhabitant of the Street was Segilola. Everyone who knew her called her Segi. She was a young woman of twenty-five or twenty-six, and at her age quite knowledgeable of the affairs of the world. She was a very delightful person, elegant of dress, soft-spoken and very comely. She had wide, beautiful eyes which won her the sobriquet "the lady with the beautiful eyes", or "the lady of the lovely eyeballs". She knew the gossip of Adetola Street to her finger-tips and often shared them with me. It helped that we were of the same age – there being but seven or eight years between us. She could chat with me as with no one else and share confidences with me. I learnt a lot from her.

Segi had ambition to go to University, but was not in a hurry to get there. There was money and excitement on Adetola Street and she preferred these to what learning there was in a University. In this I differed with her. I wanted badly to go to University and looked forward to the day when I would gain admission into one. My uncle was determined that I should leave the Street as soon as possible before, as he put it, I got "contaminated". Segi's example, he often told me, was a bad one. He could not understand, he said, how a young woman could dress so well and so expensively when she had no visible means of livelihood. Segi knew many of the most powerful men in Lagos and luxuriated in the fact. She travelled abroad quite often, to do what, she would never say. And each time she travelled, she returned with tales of excitement, portmanteaus of clothes, perfumes and jewellery and a desire to travel even further.

These eminent men and women of Adetola Street would have lived independently of each other, as most people on the Street did, but for certain fortuitous events.

It all began with a young man who had existed on the Street for quite some time, but of whom we scarcely took notice. It was my aunt who drew my attention to him.

As the Street developed more and more potholes, the danger grew that someone might be buried in a pothole one day. As usual, this was nobody's concern. The road had been built and had reason to take care of itself. Being unable to do so, it deteriorated quite fast, the more so during the rainy season. Matters would have grown worse if an intrepid, young man had not decided to put a halt to them, and to benefit by so doing.

So it happened that one day, residents of the Street found a bare-bodied, handsome, young fellow, spade in hand, standing by a mound of broken bricks placed in the middle of the road at the beginning of the Street. On top of the mound was the inevitable signboard, painted white, with characters lovingly written in red. It read as follows:

ONE MAN CONTRACTOR
PLEASE HELP ME
SIR, MA.

This was an appeal to the heart of all men and women of goodwill who passed by to admire and reward the charitable contractor who, stung by the irresponsibility of government in neglecting to repair the road, had awarded himself the repair contract. This meant that he had to find the funds to execute the contract. And he did so by the clever ruse which began with collecting the broken bricks from one of the many building sites nearby. It was an action entirely in keeping with the ethos of the Street, as my uncle said. And it touched the hearts of the residents.

Many passers-by, seeing the bare-bodied young man stoop to shovel some bricks into a pothole, willingly parted with their money. The young man naturally paid more attention to the passers-by than to the work he had chosen for himself. When a lady in a car stretched out a bejewelled hand and gave him a five naira note, he took it with deep gratitude and childish glee, piping out a flattering 'Madam de Director' in an excited voice, followed by a wild laugh.

It often transpired that having been so "helped", the intrepid contractor would retire to Mama Badejo's *buka*, have a meal and that would be enough work for the day.

The next day, he might move his bricks and signboard to a different part of the Street and resume his activities. It would normally escape the attention of most that he had not filled any pothole, but might in fact have worsened the condition of the road by his unsolicited intervention. For the presence of bricks in the middle of the road forced all vehicles to skirt the obstruction and so dig into the soft verges near the open drains. He slowed the traffic too, this young contractor. And although this might have set the drivers cursing, it pleased the street traders for whom each traffic-jam was a boon, as it normally increased sales.

The one-man-contractor had gone on working for some time before he caught Basi's attention. Basi wasted no time in befriending him. He found out everything about him at their first meeting. The young man had been in Lagos for about six months. He had come to town in search of a job, a search that had proved as fruitless as it had been difficult and tiring. He had kept searching, the while he slept in the open air, in a tin shack under the Bridge or wherever night caught up with him. He was at the point of despair when he found out about Adetola Street and hit upon the one-man-contractor idea. It had saved him from going without meals for days on end, though it had not been able to assuage his great hunger.

Basi, clever as ever, knew he had in the young man, whose name was Alali, a hidden asset. Here was a man whom he could use, a man whose services would prove invaluable, a companion, an ally and a friend. He wasted no time in inviting him to the "Palace".

Alali found in the "Palace" a home and in Basi, a mentor of immense value. And so began a close relationship which was to last a long time, and bloom in adversity, as, in keeping with the ethos of Adetola Street, Basi continued his search for the elusive, illusive millions.

* * *

Such indeed was our Street, a place so difficult to describe in words that I would say of it with Native Doctor Ndu, "Seeing is Beliving", which again would depend on what construction one chooses to put on the last word. All of which goes to show that nothing was really predictable on our Street, reality being seen through the reflection in the quagmire of the gutters. The Street bred strange events, strange habits, strange people, as my uncle said. Of the events, I was to see much in time.

The Transistor Radio

The gift to Segilola of a transistor radio by an admirer was at the centre of the events which united the men and women who were to become the best known actors on the stage of Adetola Street.

It was late evening, and Segi was, as usual, on her way to the main shopping area of Broad Street and did not want the inconvenience of a transistor radio on her person. She stopped at Dandy's Bar and handed it over to Dandy who was, as usual, slightly drunk. The Bar held no customers at the time and Dandy was busy serving himself. He was happy to see Segi when she rushed in through the door.

'Segi, the lady with the lovely eyeballs,' beamed Dandy.

'Dandy, Dandy,' called Segi. 'The Bar's empty today.'

'So I see,' replied he. 'Business is bad.'

'Could you please take care of this for me?' said Segi as she placed the brand new radio on the bar.

'Sure,' replied Dandy. 'It's a beautiful set,' said he, admiring it.

'It's a gift from a valued friend. I don't have the time to go and keep it at home, and I'm going to Broad Street. Please take care of it for me. I'll soon be back. Don't lend it, don't sell it, don't pawn it. I hope you don't mind.'

'No,' answered Dandy. Won't lend it, won't sell it, won't pawn it.'

Segi dashed out of the Bar, caught *Psalm 31* and was soon out of sight. Dandy stared after her for some time, shook his head and returned to his bottle – a miniature bottle of brandy, his favourite drink. He carried the bottle around at all times, sipping the drink as his thirst demanded.

The radio proved quite tempting and Dandy could not resist tuning it. Music oozed forth and Dandy began to dance, rolling his wide waist to the beat of the music. He was at it when Josco stepped into the Bar.

'Dandy, Dandy, there's music in the Bar today,' said he.

'Yeah,' Dandy answered proudly. 'Segi left her radio with me for safe-keeping. I decided to enzoy it a bit before she comes back for it.'

'Good,' replied Josco, and he ordered a beer. Dandy obliged him. The radio blared forth a local hit tune. Josco rocked from side to side to the beat of the music. He took a long draught of beer from the bottle. Dandy took a swig of brandy from his ubiquitous bottle.

'Dandy, I think we can make some money from the radio,' said Josco.

'No way. I'm not going to sell the radio. I promised Segi.'

'I'm not asking you to sell the radio, man,' said Josco.

'Won't pawn it either,' replied Dandy. 'Won't lend it, won't sell it, won't pawn it, I promised Segi.'

'Who's she?'

'The lady with the lovely eyeballs. Lives down the Street. Pretty girl. Lucky too. An admirer, the Police boss, gave her the radio. She's gone to Lagos Island. Will return soon for it.'

'How long is she away for?'

'Don't know. I expect she'll be back before midnight.'

'Good. We have six to seven hours before she returns. We could earn hundreds of naira before then.'

At the mention of that considerable sum of money, Dandy's eye almost popped out. 'How?' asked he with interest.

'You'll take the radio to any house on the Street. Pretend to be promoting Saros Lager Beer. Offer the radio to anyone who has an empty bottle of beer at home.'

'And if they have the bottle, I'll give them the radio?'

'Yes.'

'Impossible!'

'Hold on, man. Once you've given out the radio, I'll go to the same house and demand a licence.'

'Why?'

'All radios should be licensed. Government regulations. But no one obeys regulations in Lagos. Sure they won't have a licence. And I'll demand payment in lieu of prosecution.'

'But how do we get back the radio?' Dandy asked.

'I'll ask for a receipt of purchase. Which they will also not have. So, I'll take away the radio. They will have nothing to lose except what they pay for not having a licence. We'll make quick money, I tell you. A visit to several houses and we'll be rolling in money. Good money.'

It appeared practicable and sensible. Dandy decided to give it a try. He went to the room behind the Bar and retrieved a tie and a jacket. Then picking up the radio, went towards the door.

'Where d'you go to first?' asked Josco.

'No. 7 Adetola Street. There's a lady there. Madam the Madam's her name. Rich woman. Zentle lady. Sure she'll have an empty bottle of Saros beer at home. Always buys beer by the carton. See you later, Zosco.'

Dandy touched his bowler hat, adjusted his tie and stepped out of the Bar into the Street.

'Good luck!' shouted Josco after him.

But Dandy had gone beyond earshot. He bent his steps assiduously towards No. 7. Night had fallen, but the Street still bustled with honking cars and buses, and men and women returning from the market. *Psalm 31* spluttered away as she toiled down the Street, negotiating the potholes clumsily.

At about the same time, Alali was on his way to the "Palace", Basi's hired room at No. 7 Adetola Street. He had been squatting there at Basi's invitation for well on a month. Madam the Madam, the landlady, was unaware of the fact. Basi had used every possible ruse to keep Alali away from her.

Alali had been tending his mound of bricks on the Street that morning. Receiving no response to his pleas for help, he had gone on to Ikeja, the industrial heart of the city, in search of a job. As usual, he was not successful. He returned to Adetola Street in drenching rain, quite disconsolate. He had to trek all the way, saving the only naira note he had in his pocket for another day.

He arrived at the "Palace" about eight o'clock. Basi was in bed, as usual, his feet up. When he heard footsteps at the door, he thought it was Madam come to demand her rent. He pretended to be asleep. Because, contrary to what was thought on the Street, Madam was always breathing down Basi's neck, demanding accumulated rents which Basi had been unable to pay over the years. These demand sessions were always a terror to Basi and he abhorred and dreaded them with every fibre in his soul.

Alali opened the door and walked into the room. He was very hungry, and thinking Basi to be asleep, crept carefully towards the food cupboard. He was about to remove the lid of the pot on the stove when Basi, who had been watching him from the corner of his eye, said in a loud voice, 'Drop that pot!'

Startled, Alali let go of the pot which clattered to the floor.

'I'm sorry, Mr B,' said Alali apologetically.

'I've warned you time and again, to keep off my pots,' said Basi. 'You have always to obtain my permission before you touch my property,' he concluded.

'I thought you were asleep,' Alali said.

The Transistor Radio

'So you proceeded to steal. Thief!'

'I'm no thief. Besides, the pot's empty.'

'There's logic for you,' said Basi, getting up from his bed. He took the remains of a cigarette and lit it. He smoked whenever he was able to cadge a smoke from a friend. 'You have to respect my property,' he said, puffing out smoke.

'I'm starving, Mr B,' said Alali.

'Go to bed, man. Sleep. You'll feel better.'

'I can't sleep on an empty stomach. I haven't eaten all day. Give me something. A few grains of *gari*. Some groundnuts. Anything to stay the wolf that's tearing my insides,' pleaded Alali.

'I say there's nothing in the house. You can search, if you like.'

Alali rummaged through the food cupboard. He found nothing to eat. 'I'm sick of it all. Sick! Sick! Sick! Pity is, each time I make up my mind to quit, my courage fails me.'

'Stop complaining, Al. What have you to complain about, anyway?'

Alali catalogued all the tribulations he had suffered in his six-month sojourn in Lagos.

Basi laughed. 'Big deal,' says he. 'Have you slept under Eko Bridge? Or in the rubbish dump at Isolo where men who have lost their sense of smell live and scavenge right in the dump, waiting for the lorries bearing the waste of rich and poor alike? Have you been thrown out by a landlady for non-payment of rent? Have you taken refuge in the back of a truck and woken up to find yourself one hundred kilometres away without money for the return journey?'

'No,' said Alali. 'Have you?'

'Yes, Al. I and the streets of Lagos are friends. I know their names, they recognize my very footsteps. Ten years, no job. I roughed it, man. Then one day, I got a job. Next day, I was fired.'

'What for?'

'For getting the job. My fault, I suppose.'

'How d'you mean?' asked Alali.

'Looking for work at all. No one works here. They all get millions for doing nothing. Millions.'

'Millions!' echoed Alali.

'But I'm not complaining. I've joined them. I'm not carrying bricks. Oh no. None of that one-man-contractor thing in the sun. No, sir!'

Alali laughed, roared and cursed by turns. He yelled so loud, Basi had to warn him to be careful or the landlady would come after them. But there was no stopping Alali. He went on and on. 'I'll hang myself one of these days,' he said.

'Excellent,' said Basi. 'But don't do it here. Go to Eko Bridge, stand on the railings and throw yourself into the waters below the Bridge. But do it in broad daylight.'

'Why?' asked Alali.

'So someone sees you. Rescues you. It's happened before.'

'Really? Tell me what happened.'

'I will. But light the stove first.'

Alali jumped up. 'So there's food after all,' he said.

'Not much. Only a tea bag.' Basi threw it to him.

Alali was already by the stove. He struck a match and the flame flared dangerously. The kerosene was adulterated. Alali battled his way through to safety and put the water on the boil. He returned to where Basi was seated on the chair.

'Now, about the man who jumped from the Bridge,' he said, rubbing his palms together.

'He made it big in the end,' said Basi, puffing another cloud of smoke from his cigarette.

'No!' shouted Alali excitedly.

'Yes. He was rescued by the Police, someone offered him a job. Today he owns cars, houses, four wives, and is even a Minister.'

'I'll go to the Bridge right away,' Alali said.

'Go on,' encouraged Basi. 'But let me have my tea first.'

The kettle was already singing on the fire. Alali made the tea. There was no sugar. Basi drank and spluttered. Alali gulped it all down and squeezed the tea bag into his mouth, savouring the bitter taste.

They had not finished drinking when there came a knock at the door. Basi divined it was Madam the Madam, his landlady, come to demand her rent. She was for ever at Basi's neck over the rent, making her demands wildly and vociferously at any moment when she chanced to find Basi at home. Basi did all in his power to hide away from her lest the sight of him should stir those hormones which drove her to her high horse.

As soon as Basi heard her steps on the stairs, he dived under the bed and asked Alali to lie down and feign illness. Alali lay down, moaning, 'My stomach! My stomach!'

Madam erupted into the room, brandishing an empty bottle of Saros beer, her eyes flaming with anger and a set determination in her face. Madam spoke different Englishes according to her mood. Sometimes she spoke standard English, at other times pidgin English, and she had an English reserved for the most vicious moments – rotten English which was a mixture of all types of English, her mother-tongue which she hardly ever spoke, and the predominant Yoruba of Adetola Street.

As soon as she entered the room, she headed straight for the bed on

The Transistor Radio

which Alali was writhing in apparent pain.

'Get up, *wayo* man, get up,' Madam said, bearing down on the form in the bed.

'I'm dying. Save me! Help me!' moaned Alali.

'*Wuruwuru wayo* tief, get up, I say!' Madam hissed. 'You're not ill.'

'Help! Help!' Alali moaned on, facing the wall.

Madam loomed over him. 'If you no answer me now now I go broke your head-oh,' she said, brandishing the empty bottle dangerously. As Alali still refused to answer her, she dragged him by the hair. It was only then she found out that she had not been speaking to Basi.

'Look my trouble – oh. Wey Basi? Who you be? Wetin you dey do here for Basi house when Basi no dey?' she asked.

'Who said Basi was absent? . . . I mean . . .' But the cat was already out of the bag.

'Is that so? Una de make cunny, ehn? Basi! Basi!'

Basi emerged from under the bed.

'Don't be angry, Madam. Please!' he pleaded.

'Foolish man. Why I no go vex? Rent you no wan pay. And every time you wan play me *wayo*. Which time you go pay the rent wey you owe?'

'Please, Madam,' pleaded Basi.

'Don't please me no please, Basi. If you can't pay your rent, check out of my house. Go live under Eko Bridge. Nonsense man.'

'Pardon, Madam. He'll pay you soon,' interposed Alali.

This drove Madam wild. She questioned Basi as to Alali's presence on the premises. She asked a hundred questions in a torrent, threatened Basi with the empty bottle, dropped the bottle, cursed, clapped her hands, invoked the gods against Basi and his new-found friend.

'Patience, Madam, please. I'll pay everything I owe. I have a deal coming through. I'm going to earn a million naira. Millions! I'll buy houses, go on a world cruise, take you with me . . .'

Madam had heard that ever so often. 'You too dream, Basi,' she said. 'You no be better man.'

'Oh, Madam!'

But Madam had made her point or so she thought. She swept out of the room with a final warning: 'If you no pay all my rent by month ending, I go show you pepper, you hear?'

Basi breathed a sigh of relief. He was happy that she had left without implementing her threat to destroy him with her bottle. In her anger, she had even left the bottle behind.

She walked angrily upstairs and slammed the door. Close on her heels came Dandy. 'Anyone in! Anyone in! Mr Saros calling!' he chanted. 'Your chance to win one of many prizes!'

Madam opened the door and Dandy walked into her lounge.

'Transistor radio! Transistor radio! All yours if you have an empty bottle of Saros beer in your house this moment.' He placed the radio on her centre table and struck a pose.

Madam took a look at the transistor radio. She loved it. Her mind darted back to the empty beer bottle she had just left downstairs. She offered to go and fetch it for the beer promoter.

'Sorry, Madam, you lost your chance,' said Dandy, and he touched his bowler hat respectfully, took the radio and walked out of the room. He went downstairs and knocked at Basi's door.

Basi and Alali had been discussing Madam's threats and the bottle she had left behind. Alali had thought there was beer in the bottle.

'She's a clever woman. She won't leave a full bottle of beer behind. I bet she returns for the empty bottle soon. She's a wily one. You have to deal with her diplomatically.'

'She can be vicious,' Alali said.

'Oh yes. You haven't seen her at her worst. You need brains to deal with her. As indeed you have to be clever and smart if you have to live in Lagos. You need brains to bargain in the market; brains to avoid the policeman on the prowl for bribes; brains to earn the millions.'

'So you think I can earn the millions?' asked Alali.

'Sure, man. Why not? Anything goes here. You'll be stinking rich. You'll own half the houses in Lagos. Your cars will fill the roads, your planes the airports and your yachts the high seas. Oh, you'll be so rich, there won't be enough banks to hold your money.'

'Really?'

'So long as you're with me. Because the millions are mine. Together we'll swim in golden pools, ride a private plane, sleep on wide, soft beds. Al, the millions will come rolling into this Palace.'

As he spoke a rat came running from the food cupboard towards him. He jumped up. The rat took fright and ran outside through the space between the door and the floor. 'The Palace is full of rats,' thought Alali. He did not have time to ponder this further as, at that time, Dandy came knocking at the door.

For a moment, Basi thought it was Madam who had returned either to demand her rent or her empty bottle. In either case, Basi did not wish to see her. He darted to the door and attempted to bolt it. Too late. Dandy had already entered the room.

In a matter of minutes, the radio and empty bottle of Saros beer had changed hands and Dandy was on his way back to the Bar, his mission accomplished.

Basi and Alali could not believe their luck. Anywhere else, the entire

The Transistor Radio

proceedings would have seemed strange. But those familiar with the ways of Adetola Street and of Lagos, where daily events were stranger than fiction, would have no difficulty accepting this event for what it was: reality.

Alali did not even have time to think about what had happened. He was for selling the radio immediately so they would buy dinner. Basi wanted to have some fun first of all. He decided to turn on the radio.

Alali loved to dance and he indulged himself to whoops of delight from Basi. Alali danced, tuned the radio to its loudest and danced on. Basi got alarmed at the loudness of the music.

'Not so loud, Al, not so loud! Madam will hear it!'

'What's the use of a radio if you don't let the neighbours know you own one?'

'Don't be silly, Al. Madam will . . . God, I think she's coming! Turn off the radio, Al. Hide it. Take cover!'

Alali succeeded in shoving the radio beneath the bed, but before they could hide out of sight, Madam had burst into the room. An embarrassed silence followed.

Madam broke the silence. 'Where's my empty bottle?' she asked gruffly, staring from Basi to Alali.

'Bottle?' asked Basi, feigning ignorance of the bottle.

'Yes, bottle. An empty bottle of Saros beer.'

'You left no bottle here,' Basi lied.

'Liar. You no remember de bottle wey I wan use broke your head jus now?'

'No, Madam. I don't recollect you having a bottle when you came in here. Do you, Al?'

'Nope,' replied Alali, and they exchanged looks.

'Shurrup!' Madam snapped at Alali. And then turning to Basi, she said, 'You no wan pay my rent. And you come tief my bottle too.'

'What's so special about the bottle, Madam?' Basi asked.

'Whosai you keep am?' she asked.

'Truly, you didn't leave it here. Al, did she?'

'Nope.'

This incensed Madam further. She appeared to have developed a strong antipathy to Alali. 'Shurrup, you bottle tief!' she said from between her teeth.

'Madam, hold it. Is a bottle the best thing in the world to steal?'

Madam flew into a rage. She beat her breast. 'Insult, insult. Basi, you bring your friend here to insult me, not so? Make I warn you. If you no pay my rent by tomorrow, I go punish you. You and your friend. I show you pepper. Believe me yours sincerely.'

Basi went on his knees. 'Madam, please! The rent has nothing to do with the missing bottle. Please!'

But Madam was not listening anymore. She stood by the door, and with one hand on the door-knob, let forth a volley of insults. She fired a parting shot. 'Teeves. Rent teeves. Bottle teeves. Armed robbers!' And stumped out of the room.

Basi breathed more easily. 'Good thing she didn't see the radio. She might have seized it.'

'Let's go and sell the radio,' suggested Alali.

Basi did not want to go out that night to look for someone willing to buy the radio, although Adetola Street being Adetola Street, there would have been no shortage of buyers, even at that time of night. 'We didn't steal the radio,' he said. 'We don't have to sell it in a hurry. We won't get a good price.'

'I'm hungry,' Alali said. 'I'm off to find a buyer.' And he made for the door.

'No, you don't,' said Basi, standing in his way.

'Let me go. The radio's mine.'

'It's mine.'

'Mine.'

'Stand off,' said Basi.

'Is that a part of your Lagos smartness?' Alali shouted.

'Stop shouting. Madam will return.'

There was a knock at the door and Basi dived under the bed. Alali stood behind the door, ready to make a hurried exit as soon as the door opened.

When the door opened, it was not Madam it let in, but Josco. Josco, dressed as a licensing officer from the Post and Telegraphs Department. Dandy had informed him where the transistor radio was to be found and warned him to ensure that he returned with it. He had pulled Josco by the ear, just to satisfy himself that Josco heard him right. Josco had said there was nothing to fear.

Now as he entered Basi's vaunted Palace, he looked round quickly and saw the radio.

'Anyone with a radio here?' he asked perfunctorily.

'Yes, it's for sale,' Alali replied quickly.

Basi came out of hiding.

'I didn't come to buy your radio, fellow,' Josco said.

'Out then, out, I say!' Alali motioned to him to get out of the room.

Josco introduced himself as a licensing officer attached to the Posts and Telegraphs Department.

'Did the landlady send you here?' Basi asked.

'No,' replied the "officer". 'Can I see your radio?' he asked.
Alali held up the radio. Josco inspected it carefully.
'A good, new radio. Got a licence for it?'
'What a stupid question!' Alali said.
'This is official, mark you. Anything you say will be put against you. So be careful.'
'Pish!' spat Alali.
'Good. Now, I'll put the question again. Have you got a radio licence?'
'A licence for a radio! Are you mad?'
'I'll take note of that,' said the officer. He wrote in his book "Are you mad" and repeated the words aloud.
'Is a radio a gun, a bicycle or a car?'
'Every radio must have a licence,' said the "officer".
'Who said so?'
'Regulations. Government regulations.'
'Regulations,' repeated Basi, nonplussed.
'Yes. Government re-gu-la-tions. You need a licence. Five naira or two hundred naira in court. Are you ready to buy the licence?'
Alali was decidedly confused. He had never owned a radio all his life. He did not know that a radio needed a licence. He did not have money for a meal and certainly not for a licence for a radio which he did not need. He told the "licensing officer" so.
'In that case, I'll have to arrest you,' the "officer" said.
Alali pleaded with him. He explained to him how he had been leading a hand-to-mouth existence in Lagos. How he had not eaten the whole of that day. 'Frankly, I have no money,' he concluded.
'And yet you own a radio. A likely story indeed,' said the "officer" in his most officious tone.
'But someone gave it . . . I mean . . . I won it . . .'
'You can tell them that at the charge office when we get there.'
Alali was not about to give up. 'I'm jobless,' he pleaded, 'and have been ever since I stepped into Lagos.'
'What's this rigmarole got to do with the purchase of a licence?' asked the "officer".
'Do you want me to sell the radio to buy a licence?' Alali asked.
'Suit yourself,' said the "officer". And then mellowing his voice in the manner of an Adetola Street official, he said, 'Do something, man. Say something. Speak up!'
'But he has been speaking to you,' interposed Basi who had been watching the proceedings in a curiously detached manner.
'Yes, he has been speaking to me. But doesn't he know I'm an official? He has to speak to me officially.' He turned to Alali and fixed him with an

official gaze. 'Don't you understand? Don't you know? Say something. Anything. Do what you ought to do.'

Alali scratched his head.

'Blockhead!' shouted the "officer". And he cupped his right hand behind him.

'Oh, I understand,' said Alali, breaking into a smile.

'Now do something,' said the "officer".

'One naira,' offered Alali.

'Don't speak so loud,' cautioned the "officer". 'Walls have ears. Two,' he whispered.

'Two naira? I might as well buy the licence right away.'

'Suit yourself.'

Alali moved over to where Basi stood beside the food cupboard.

'Lend me a naira,' he said to Basi.

'Haven't got a kobo anywhere in the world,' Basi said.

'What shall we do?'

'What d'you mean "we"?' asked Basi. 'The radio is yours, isn't it. Save it if you can!'

'I don't have two naira.'

The "officer" was getting impatient. He motioned to Alali with his finger, and when Alali drew close to him, said, 'Mister, one naira. Quick! Time is precious.'

Alali dug into his pocket for the solitary note he had been saving for any emergency.

'Quick,' said the "officer". 'Time is running out.'

Money changed hands. The "officer" smiled happily.

'Good man. Thank you. And now I'll have to take away this,' he said, grabbing the radio.

'Why?' asked Alali, alarmed.

'Because you stole it. Or d'you have a receipt of purchase? It's a brand new radio. When did you buy it? Where?'

'I . . . I . . .' stammered Alali.

'See? Stolen property. I'll keep the radio to keep you out of jail. We're friends. See? Goodbye.' And he made to go.

Suddenly, a loud, officious voice rang out. 'In the name of the law!' It was Basi in an assumed voice.

'What d'you mean?' asked the "officer" in a voice that trembled slightly. He put back the radio on the chair in the room.

'I arrest you in the name of the law!' shouted Basi.

'Why?' asked the "officer". Then pointing to Alali, he said, 'Arrest him! He stole the radio, not me.'

'I warn you, anything you say or do will count against you,' said Basi in the stentorian tone of a police officer.

The "licensing officer" was already wet about the ears. He wished he had been miles away from where he stood at that moment.

'I say, who are you?' he asked again.

'Sergeant Basi of the C.I.D. Working under cover.'

Even Alali was taken aback by this manifestly false claim. He almost let forth a guffaw. Only the "licensing officer's" muttering of the word "Impossible" stopped his guffaw.

Basi had moved in towards the "officer" for the kill. He bored into him as with a drill. 'Don't argue; you'll only worsen your plight. You have taken a bribe and tried to steal a radio. Your name, sir?'

But the "licensing officer" was not waiting to answer any more questions. He turned on his heels and attempted to leave the room. However, Alali was there on him like lightning, effectively stopping him from making his escape. Alali lifted him up. The small, wiry man hung in the air, swinging his arms and feet wildly.

'Hold on,' said Basi encouragingly. 'Watch him carefully, Al, while I get pen and paper.'

The "officer" stopped struggling and watched Basi deliberately obtain pen and paper from his jacket on the clothes line. He returned to face his victim squarely, towering over him.

'Now then,' says Basi, pen and pencil in hand, his head cocked to one side. 'Your name?'

'I beg, sir,' replies the "officer".

'Occupation?'

'I beg, sir.'

By this time, he has become incapable of saying the words coherently, and what escapes his lips is best described by the sound of "abegsah", said in a faint, whining voice.

'Pardon?' asks Basi.

'Abegsah.'

'Speak up! How old are you?'

'Abegsah.'

'Address?'

'Abegsah.'

Basi has been taking notes furiously. Now he holds the notes conspicuously and reads out in a manner designed to strike terror through the entrails of the fake officer:

'Name: abegsah. Occupation: abegsah. Age: abegsah. Address: abegsah. Very good. Now, Mr. Abegsah of Abegsah Street, I beg to inform you that I'll have to take you to the Police Station.'

'Master, please!' whines the fake officer.

'Come on! Will you?' orders Basi gruffly.

'Mercy! Chief, mercy!' the little man whimpers.

'Impostor, you deserve no mercy!' This firmly, without a trace of compassion.

Alali watches Basi's masterly performance with the adulation of a pupil for his teacher.

The fake officer begins to grovel. 'Forgive me, sir,' he sobs. 'You see, my mother-in-law and her entire family came to my place yesterday. I have no money. What could I do? You know how difficult the times are. We must live, somehow. Forgive me, sir. God will bless you, sir.' By the time the speech is over, the fake officer is lying at Basi's feet, wracked by fear and snivelling piteously.

Basi's next words are sweet music in his ears.

'All right, all right. In view of your plight, I will not arrest you. You must issue the gentleman with a licence.'

The "licensing officer" is relieved at his reprieve but is shocked by the demand on him. 'The licence will cost me five naira, sir.'

'So what?' asks Basi. 'Would you rather go to jail?'

'No, sir. Oh no.' It is obvious that the gentleman has an absolute antipathy to going to jail.

'Ah, very well then. Make out the licence. Go on! Will you?'

The man's hands tremble like a leaf in the wind as he pulls out paper and pen, the same as he was brandishing below Alali's nose a while before. He whines as he writes: 'The times are hard, very hard. A small pay packet. And a big family to care for. What can a man do?' The writing over, he hands over the licence, with a 'Here, sir, the licence.' There remains a shifty look in his eyes, as if he is not exactly sure that what he is doing is proper.

Basi takes the licence and orders the man to give Alali his one naira note. The man rifles through his many pockets – trouser pockets, shirt pockets, even the pockets in his underpants. He finally extricates a crumpled note and hands it over to Alali. Alali glares at him and snatches the currency note from the man.

With gratitude in his heart and eyes, the man slinks out of the room.

Alali was delighted. He said, 'Thanks, Sergeant. That was real smart, Mr B.'

Basi felt flattered. 'When you're on Adetola Street, you have to be smart. Too many fakes in town.'

'Yes,' Alali agreed. But he was not listening. He was examining his licence closely.

'Anyway, we've got a licence free of charge,' Basi exulted.

'A licence free of charge? Huh! Look at this. It's fake.'
'Fake?'
'Precisely.' Alali thrust the licence into Basi's hands. The latter looked at it and burst into laughter.
'He was a fake licensing officer!'
'And you a fake Police Sergeant!'
'Holy Moses!' roared Basi. 'I thought I was smart. He was even smarter. Ha! ha! ha! I'm damned!'

He stopped when he observed that Alali was not enjoying the fun with him.

'Come on, Al. You're not laughing. Don't mourn the loss of the licence. You still have the radio and your naira note,' he consoled.

'He returned a fake naira note in place of my genuine note.' Alali handed him the counterfeit note.

Basi remained speechless for a minute. When he found his voice, all he could say was, 'Holy Moses, no! Lagos! Lagos!' And he shook his head mournfully, managing a chuckle just the same.

A Company is Formed

Later that same night, Segi returned from Lagos Island and went to the Bar to collect her radio from Dandy.

Dandy sat disconsolately at the Bar, drinking brandy from his usual miniature bottle. He had had more than was good for him, and found solace in the empty bottle of Saros beer he had exchanged for Segi's radio at No. 7 Adetola Street. He hugged the bottle.

On his return from his adventure, he had warned Josco to ensure that he played his part successfully and retrieved Segi's radio. Josco had left with the sweet smell of success oozing from his assurances. And now Dandy had been waiting an inordinately long time for his return. He seemed to have been away for ages. Dandy had passed the time drinking and dancing all alone at the Bar.

When Segi breezed into the Bar, Dandy knew there was going to be trouble.

'Dandy, Dandy!' Segi greeted him cheerfully.
'Segi, the lady with the beautiful eyes!'
'What's that you're fondling?'

'Empty bottle of Saros beer. Mazic bottle. Mazic!' And he smiled, showing a black tooth in the bottom row.

Drunk as usual, thought Segi. 'Where's my radio?' she asked.

'Radio? What radio?'

'The radio I asked you to keep for me. Remember I told you . . .'

'Don't lend it, don't sell it, don't pawn it . . . I remember,' said Dandy.

'So where is it?'

'I esanzed it!' That was his way of saying "exchanged".

'Esanzed my radio, as you put it? What for?'

'Empty mazic bottle,' Dandy said, and held up the bottle with a smile.

'You're even more drunk than I thought,' Segi said disdainfully.

'Oh no. Radio went for a walk,' Dandy replied.

'Wake up, Dandy. What d'you mean? Radios don't walk.'

'Oh no. Radios don't walk. I sent it to your house. Couldn't keep it here. Too many thieves. Went for a walk.'

Segi was mad at him. 'I don't understand your incoherent drivel,' she said. 'If that radio is not at my place when I get there, you'll drink a sea of brandy, Dandy.' And she left the Bar.

'Any day, Segi,' said Dandy, oblivious of the fact that Segi had left the Bar. 'Give Dandy brandy any day. Yeah!' And he took a swig from the miniature bottle.

He was at it when Josco entered the Bar. 'Dandy! Dandy!' he called.

'Boy Zosco! Where's the radio?' Dandy asked.

'The radio?'

'Sure, the radio.'

'I lost the radio, Dandy.'

'Lost the radio? Segi's radio?'

'The man took it from me.'

'Who?' asked Dandy.

'The Police Sergeant.'

'Hell, I should have known that!'

'You shouldn't have given the radio to a Police Sergeant. I don't like the Police. Got scared, Dandy, I did,' Josco said.

'Hell, I should have known that!' said Dandy, and drank from his bottle. 'I'm finished. Segi will kill me,' he said, and drank again. Josco presented an empty glass. He needed a drink, a bit of alcohol to steady his frayed nerves. The escapade at Sergeant Basi's had left him quite enervated if not thirsty. Dandy refused to serve him.

'Segi will punish me well this time.'

'Has she been here yet?'

'Yes.'

'What did you tell her?'

'I told her the radio went for a walk.'

'For a walk, Dandy? That was clever. Very clever.' And he chuckled.

'Shut up, Zosco,' Dandy replied hotly. 'It wasn't clever of you to lose the radio. And now I'm landed with a useless empty bottle. What do I tell Segi?'

'Tell her exactly what happened. Be honest.'

'Honest! Who's talking of honesty? Was it honest to bait people with a radio and then turn round to demand licences?'

'I got a naira, Dandy,' Josco said, changing the conversation. He took the note from his pocket and shoved it under Dandy's nose. 'Exchanged it for an ugly one I got under the Bridge.'

Dandy snatched the money from him. 'Stupid, Boy Zosco, stupid. The radio cost over two hundred naira. You lost a brand new radio and you get a naira in return. Big deal!'

'The radio's not lost, Dandy.'

'How not?'

'We know where it is, so how can it be lost?'

'It's not in Segi's keeping. That's what.'

'We can always get it back.'

'How?'

'When Segi comes, send her to the Sergeant at No. 7. Sure she'll get back her radio.'

'Hell, I should have known that!' Dandy yelled.

'Tell Segi the man stole it from your Bar and you followed him to his house. Leave the rest to Segi. She's a woman. She'll know what to do.'

This seemed quite sensible to Dandy. But he knew he could not face Segi if she returned that night. He locked up the Bar. When Josco demanded his naira, Dandy refused to return it. Josco had to walk back to his tin shack under Eko Bridge.

When Segi returned to the Bar to inform Dandy she had not found her radio at home, the Bar was locked shut. She went away quite disconsolate.

The transistor radio was all that night a source of worry for Alali and Basi on the one hand, and Segi and Dandy on the other.

At mid-morning the next day, Segi was at Dandy's Bar. She was in a state. 'Dandy, my radio's not at home.'

'Who said it was?' asked Dandy from behind the counter.

'You did,' Segi replied.

'I said the radio went for a walk.'

'Radios don't have legs, do they?'

'Hell, I should have known that!'

The buffoon is making a jest of me, thought Segi. I'll have to be really firm with him or he'll spend the rest of the day clowning. I suppose he doesn't have enough to occupy him. Segi threatened to report Dandy to the Police.

'Oh no, Segi. Please,' Dandy pleaded.

'I'm serious. I want my radio this minute. Will you give it to me?'

'It was stolen from the Bar.'

'Stolen?'

'Yes.'

'How d'you know?'

'Zosco told me. He says a guy brought him a brand new transistor radio to sell. The asking price was so ridiculous, he became suspicious.'

'So Josco's got the radio.'

'No. Says he refused to accept it. Zosco doesn't sell stolen property.'

'That's not true. Is Josco your friend?'

'Sure.'

'Then he must sell stolen property. Smuggled goods. The lot. To you.'

'Well, he refused to sell your radio.'

'Why?'

'Didn't like the look of the radio. Zosco has a nose for trouble.'

'Did he say where the thief lives?'

'Yes. No. 7 on the Street.'

'Any description of him?'

'Yes. Tall man wearing a cap. Walks with a stoop in little zumps as if ants were biting his feet.'

'Good. I'll go look for him. And when I get him, I'll throw him into jail. But if I don't get my radio, Dandy, you'll be in the soup.'

And giving him an angry, black look, Segi left the Bar.

'Wasn't my fault, Segi,' Dandy shouted after her.

'Stop whining, you drunken oaf,' Segi shouted back, and walked into the Street.

Adetola Street was already bustling with great activity. Mama Badejo was hard at work in front of her *buka*. The acrid smell of hot palm oil hit Segi in the nose. Some hawkers pressed their wares on her. Passing buses and cars raised a cloud of dust. Segi felt uncomfortable in the hot, humid day.

Hot, humid or otherwise, Basi and Alali were not in a position to know. They were still asleep in Basi's vaunted Palace, far from the hot eye of the day. It was Basi who stirred first, and he immediately woke Alali up.

Alali was still smarting under the loss of his only naira and gave vent to his feelings as soon as his eyes were open.

'You can't complain, Al,' Basi said. 'We still have the radio.'

'I don't trust that deal, Mr. B. I've told you once before. And I tell you

again, there's a catch in it some place.'
'You're inexperienced, that's what.'
'Suppose someone's trying to plant something on you?'
'Why would they want to do so? Who would want to do it?'
'Madam, for instance? She wants to throw you out of this room . . .'
'For room, say Palace,' Basi corrected him.
'She wants to throw you out because you haven't paid her rent. She doesn't want to go through the courts. What better than to send you to jail for a criminal offence?'
'Madam won't do that to me.'
'Why not?' Alali asked.
'Somewhere in her soul, Madam has a soft spot for me.'
'So you think.'
'I know it.'
'Then why does she constantly come here to harass you for her rent?'
'She's always looking for a reason to come to the Palace to see me. The rent is a convenient excuse.'
'You're too sure of yourself, Mr B.'
'I know what I'm talking about,' Basi replied, as he returned to his morning ablutions. Alali rolled up the mat on which he had been sleeping and washed his face in the bucket of water next to the food cupboard.
'You ready, Alali?' Basi asked.
'What for?'
'I think we should go and sell that radio. I need a gin before breakfast.'
'Now you're talking. We should have sold the radio last night before that buffoon of a licensing officer came around.'
'Where can we sell it?' Basi asked.
'Anywhere. On the Street here or under Eko Bridge among the tin shacks. On top of the Bridge during any of the usual traffic jams. It's no problem selling a radio.'
'Yeah. But I couldn't sell it myself. A bit compromising, don't you think?'
'Oh yes. We have to find someone to do it. Millionaires don't go selling radios on the Bridge, do they?'
'No.'
Basi thought for sometime what to do. Then he motioned to Alali to get ready.
'Found an answer?' Alali asked.
'Yeah. I'm equal to all problems. The only problem that has defied me so far is Madam's rent. But I should solve that soon.'
'And the problem of your first million?'
'That's no problem at all,' Basi boasted. Then for good measure he

added, 'To be a millionaire, think like a millionaire!'

Alali cheered him. He stooped to collect the radio when the door opened and an absolutely entrancing young woman came in. She greeted them and confidently introduced herself. 'I'm Segi,' she said.

Basi rose to the occasion. 'I'm Basi, my friends call me Mr. B.'

Alali pushed the radio under Basi's bed. He quickly introduced himself to the girl. 'I'm Alali. My friends call me Al.'

Alali and Basi joked away at the young woman's expense. But she was not smiling. Basi finally invited her to one of the two chairs in the room, and sat opposite her. Alali sat on the bed, next to Basi.

'To what do I owe the pleasure of your visit?' asked Basi.

'Someone's stolen my radio,' Segi said.

'Goodness gracious!' roared Basi. 'What won't happen in this Godforsaken city of sin? . . . So you were not at home when the robbers came. And they had a field day up at your place, eh? Drank your beer, ate your biscuits, emptied the pot of soup? Ah, I know what these guys normally do. Am I right?'

'Not exactly.'

'They were frightened away by a neighbour and took away the only handy item at home.'

'No.'

'You've lost your radio, anyway,' Alali said.

'Yes. A gift from the Police boss, a friend of mine.'

Alali and Basi exchanged looks.

'I have a sentimental attachment to the radio.'

'I'm sure you do. You should,' agreed Basi.

Alali took Basi aside. 'Does that ring a bell, Mr B?'

'What?' Basi asked.

'I told you there's more to that radio than meets the eye. We get it in exchange for a worthless empty bottle; a bogus licensing officer tries to cheat us out of it. Now an absolutely ravishing girl comes to lay claim to it, saying it was given her by a Police boss. Before you know a thing, the Police boss himself will be here and we'll be in jail.'

Basi thought for some time about what Alali had said. 'I get the argument. What d'you suggest we do?'

'Hand over the radio to her.'

'And confirm that we stole it? No way!'

'Tell her exactly what happened.'

'No. How did she find her way here? I must get to the bottom of the story. Besides, I won't let this luscious, well-connected girl out of my safe-keeping. She's a fruit that must be plucked.'

'She's a danger, Mr B.'

A Company is Formed

'I love danger,' said Basi, as he turned to Segi and said in his sweetest voice, 'Hi, lady, I think I've seen your radio somewhere.'

'I thought so,' said Segi knowingly. Her eyes shone with delight.

Basi drew the radio from under the bed and showed it to her.

'Oh, you're wonderful!' gasped Segi.

'Your name's Segi, you say? asked Basi.

'Yes.'

'Now, Segi, stop playing games with me. You did not just wander into my Palace in search of your radio.'

'No.'

'Someone told you about me.'

'Certainly.'

'What did he say about me and how I came by the radio?'

'Not much. He said you stole the radio.'

'Stole the radio?' yelled Basi. 'I, Mr B, a millionaire-on-the-make steal a radio? You and your friends won't get away with this. I say, you won't get away with it.' And he hit the centre table with the palm of his hand.

'Easy, Mr B. Madam will hear you,' Alali pleaded.

'Madam or no Madam, Segi has to produce her informants.'

Segi got up. She appeared to have been waiting for Basi's request. Without another word, she withdrew from the room.

Basi's shout had drawn the attention of Madam. She entered the room as Segi swaggered off. She cast a critical look at the retreating figure of the young woman and then turned to Basi. There was venom in the tone of her voice when she spoke.

'Basi, so I no go sleep for my house again because you and your friend dey enjoy with woman, ehn?'

'Madam, I'm in no mood for a joke,' Basi said.

'Who dey joke with you?' asked Madam. 'You no wan pay your rent, but you get money to give beautiful gals. Foolish man. *Shebi*, I hear you dey boast for de girl say you be millionaire?'

'Madam, I wasn't bragging. I'm a millionaire. To be a millionaire...'

'Think like a millionaire!' cheered Alali.

'Nonsense millionaire... Millionaire wey dey tief bottle, common empty bottle. Make I tell you, you must return dat my bottle. You hear?'

'How much does that bottle mean to you?' asked Basi.

'No worry. Who no know go know. Now wey you don dey bring fine fine gals to dis my house...'

'Madam, 'e dey me like say you dey jealous small,' teased Alali.

'Jealous. Me? For what? Wetin man like Basi wey no fit pay him rent, dey tief bottle, fit give woman? Not to talk of woman like me? 'E fit dey deceive young gals. Not me. I wan my bottle. Das all.' And she sighed.

'Madam, you'll get back your bottle. I know why you want it,' Basi said.

'Why?' asked Madam.

'Because you hope to exchange it for a transistor radio.'

'Na who tell you?'

'Ah, Madam, you are a Lagos landlady, but there are a few things you don't know about this city.'

'Tell me something!' said Madam.

'Well, I can tell you this. You're lucky you didn't have that bottle when the con-man called last night. You would have been duped of your enormous riches.'

'Tell me something!' said Madam, placing her palms on her chest.

Basi moved in for the kill with a glint in his eye. He had been waiting for the invitation for a long time.

'Madam, you have to thank me. Go upstairs, get me a bottle of gin. I'll tell you the full story after I've had a drink. I'll charge you a fee for saving you, of course. And I know when you know the facts, you'll pay happily. I'll be charging you only one million naira.'

'It's a matter of cash!' said Madam, as she turned to leave the room.

Basi and Alali watched her go with immense satisfaction. When she was out of earshot, Alali turned to Basi and offered his congratulations.

'Mr B!' said he in admiration.

'That's me!' Basi replied.

'To be a millionaire . . .'

'Think like a millionaire!'

This euphoric mood at the "Palace" contrasted strongly with what was going on at Dandy's Bar at about the same moment in time. Josco was at the Bar as usual, seeking refuge from the daily Police raids on the men who lived in the tin town under Eko Bridge. Dandy informed him that Segi had come asking for her radio and that he had sent her to Basi's.

'D'you think she'll get back the radio?'

'Yeah. Otherwise you'll be in zail once again,' Dandy said.

'She must get the radio.'

'I didn't get it,' Segi said, breezing into the Bar.

'Why not?' asked Dandy.

'Basi insists on seeing both of you before he'll give it back to me.'

'Sergeant Basi of the Criminal Investigation Department?' asked Josco. 'Dandy, we're lost.'

Josco was so frightened, he could barely stand on his feet. Argue as much as she would, Josco refused to believe that Basi was anything else but a keeper of the law. And when Segi insisted that they all go to see Basi so she could recover her radio, Josco pleaded being extremely busy.

A Company is Formed

'Oh no, you're not,' Dandy told him. 'Segi's given orders and we'll obey. You know her connections with the Police bosses. Not zust the serzeants.'

That ended the argument effectively. Josco agreed to go to Basi's. Dandy put the empty bottle of Saros beer in his trouser pocket and asked Josco to lead the way. Josco said he'd rather walk behind Dandy. Dandy said he was not going to allow that. It was possible for Josco to disappear into thin air or into the crowd at the Adetola Market or among the hawkers. In the end, Josco had to be closely guarded to Basi's "Palace".

Segi appeared to be enjoying herself. She had enjoyed her meeting with Basi. She admired his looks, the smoothness of his speech, his clothes and even the fact that he wore his name on his cap. She had heard about him, but had not met him in person. And now she looked forward to the confrontation between Josco and Basi. It promised to yield enough laughter for another month or so.

There was enough laughter at Basi's "Palace" where Basi was already savouring the pleasures of the fee he expected to earn from Madam for saving her from the con-man with the transistor radio. He knew he was going to recover Madam's empty bottle and he expected Madam to keep her promise to give him a bottle of gin so he could tell her the full story of the con-man, quite apart from the promised million.

It was natural with Basi for the millions to trip off his tongue. He, like many of the people on the Adetola Street, was not particularly numerate and had no definite conception of what a million of anything was. He cherished the notion that a million of any money could get the best things of life. And that was enough for him.

'You're sure Madam will pay us the million naira?' asked Alali.

'Sure!' Basi replied.

'Fantastic! To be a millionaire . . .'

'Think like a millionaire!'

Josco, Dandy and Segi who were at the door were not thinking like millionaires. Josco was hoping that the Sergeant would not be there when they arrived; Dandy did not quite know what to expect; and Segi's only desire was to recover her radio.

At the sight of them, Basi who was in an exuberant mood, welcomed them extravagantly.

'Welcome, Segi,' he said. 'How beautiful you do look. And those eyes! Like fireflies in the depths of the forest. Ah, and that's Mr Saros and our friend the licensing officer. Welcome, everybody.'

'Mr Saros? Licensing officer?' asked Segi. 'He is Dandy, the owner of Dandy's Bar down the Street, and the other is his friend, Josco.'

'Dandy and Josco. I see,' said Basi. 'We know them well, don't we, Al?'

Basi and Company

'Oh yes,' agreed Alali. And pointing to Dandy, he said, 'He is Mr Saros, employed by the breweries to promote the drinking of Saros beer. The other gentleman is a licensing officer, attached to the Department of Posts and Telegraphs, his duty, to ensure that all owners of radios possess radio licences.'

'Is it not so, gentlemen?' asked Basi pointedly.

'Sergeant Basi, please sir,' begged Josco.

'Oh no, sir. You had your fun last night. You must allow us to have ours now.'

'Spare us, sir. Please spare us,' pleaded Dandy.

'We know their type, don't we, Al?' asked Basi.

'Certainly,' replied Alali.

Turning to Dandy, Basi invited him to say how he had come by the transistor radio. Dandy hemmed and hawed for some time. Finally, he narrated how Segi had given him the radio to keep for a while.

'And you gave it to me?' Basi asked.

'No.'

'Tell Segi how I came by it.'

Dandy coughed, touched his hat, rubbed his chin and drew down Basi's anger on himself.

'Speak up, man. Stop fidgeting,' Basi ordered.

'Well, ehm, you know the way things are, Segi. Zosco and I decided . . .'

'We didn't decide. You came to me with the radio . . .'

'You saw me with the radio and suzzested that . . .'

'I suggested nothing. You said we should try to earn some money with the radio before you'd return it to Segi.'

'Liar!' shouted Dandy.

'I'm not lying,' said Josco.

'You are,' said Dandy.

'I'm not!' said Josco.

'Quiet, gentlemen,' Basi hushed them. 'Just tell us how you were going to earn the money.'

'Simple. I'd pretend to be doing a promotion for the breweries. Whoever had a bottle of Saros beer at home would win the radio. Shortly after, Zosco would appear and demand a radio licence from the winner. Whoever did not have a licence would forfeit the radio and pay good money to avoid prosecution.'

'Ingenious, wouldn't you say?' Basi retorted.

'Perfect,' replied Alali.

'Absolutely thorough,' agreed Segi.

'And who planned all this?' asked Basi.

'Zosco's idea,' Dandy replied. And he turned a cruel look on Josco who had his eyes fixed on the floor.

'Al, the man's an original, is Josco,' Basi said. 'And did you guys earn a lot of money last night?'

'A little,' Josco lied, still looking at the floor.

'Including the naira you took from Al here in exchange for your counterfeit note?'

'Yes, sir,' replied Josco.

'I see,' said Basi. 'Well, will you return the money to me immediately?'

Josco motioned to Dandy to give the naira note to Basi. He did so.

'Thank you.' said Basi, receiving the money. 'And where's the empty beer bottle you took from me?'

'Here, sir,' said Dandy, retrieving it from his bulging pocket.

Segi watched the proceedings with quiet amusement, a gentle smile playing round the corners of her lips. She found Dandy's discomfiture quite entertaining. But Basi's masterly performance was even more engaging.

Basi thanked Dandy, then took the radio and handed it back to Segi, with a 'Now you know the type of friends you keep!'

'Thank you, Mr B,' said Segi gratefully.

Josco expected the worst. Dandy too. But that would not have been in keeping with Basi's character, who was always quick to see several opportunities in a single event. His next words came as an utter surprise to everyone, including Alali. For he did not demand money for his services as he would normally have done. He paced the room for a while, then said:

'Well, lady and gentlemen, I think we all ought to celebrate. As you know, or ought to know, I'm on my way to making my first million. And when you're on that sort of journey, you don't go around making enemies. You all have talents in your various ways. I'm sure we can be useful to one another.'

'Certainly,' said Josco and Dandy together.

Basi was delighted; he had established his supremacy over them. 'So let's be friends,' he said. 'Let's celebrate. Al, the glasses please.'

Alali went to the food cupboard. There was but one glass; he returned with it, gave it to Basi and whispered to him that there were no drinks.

'Holy Moses! No drinks!' said Basi, without embarrassment.

At that appropriate moment, Madam barged into the room, a bottle of gin in her hand.

'The bottle of gin I promised you, Basi,' she said. 'If you've found my empty bottle of Saros beer.'

'Fantastic!' said Basi. 'Madam the Madam!' he flattered her.

'It's a matter of cash!' she replied.

Basi gave her the bottle of Saros beer and got the bottle of gin in return. He did not bother to tell her all that had happened. He only said, 'The empty bottle is fair exchange for the bottle of gin, Madam. Fair exchange is no robbery.' He opened the bottle of gin, then turning to the rest of the company, said, 'Lady and gentlemen, let's drink to Madam's health.'

He poured himself some gin in the only glass, raised it to his lips, drained it, smacked his lips and winked to the Company. Everyone looked at him in stunned astonishment.

Thus was the company formed. No oaths were sworn to, no papers were signed. It was an unwritten agreement in the fashion of Adetola Street. Everyone was allowed to interpret it in their own way, according to their perception of reality. There were bound to be problems.

A Shipload of Rice

There were problems from the very beginning. Because money was being made quickly on Adetola Street, and Basi was not the only one who wanted to make his pile using others. As my uncle said, the love of money is the root of all evil. When big money is in contention, people can be expected not to keep faith in a big way.

It was ironic that Basi was to be one of the first victims of the group he had put together hastily.

It all started with Madam who was said to have been very incensed by Basi's suspected dalliance with Segi and the brag she had overheard him make to her that he was a millionaire-on-the-make. Her patience with him ran out like the sand in an hour glass at the top of the hour and she got her lawyer to send him a quit notice.

The notice was slipped under Basi's door in his absence on one of his numerous "business" trips to central Lagos. When Basi slipped back into the "Palace" with Alali that afternoon, there were envelopes waiting for him. He tore the first letter open and read it. His face fell immediately when he realized it was a quit notice from Madam's lawyer.

'Believe me, Al, Madam's getting more vicious these days,' he said, throwing Alali the letter he had been reading.

Alali dropped the other envelopes and read the letter.

'It's a quit notice!' he shouted.
'From Madam's lawyer. She's serious this time.'
'Nope. She's in love with you,' teased Alali, remembering that Basi had said as much on a previous occasion. 'Marry her.'
'Forget it,' Basi replied. 'I won't marry that hag.'
'I bet she comes downstairs soon . . .'
'To harass me,' Basi interposed.
Alali refused to be overawed. 'To see if you'll propose to her,' he said.
'Not even if she pays me to do so!' Basi said with great determination.
'So what do we do about the quit notice?'

Basi sat back on his bed, distressed. He did not mind Madam badgering him for the rent. He could always deal with that. But the introduction of a lawyer into the affair was more than he had bargained for. He dreaded to deal with an Adetola Street lawyer. He was shrewd enough to know that. He held his chin in his hands.

Alali who had been opening the other envelopes, gave him worse news.
'Here's the electricity bill,' he said.
'Oh no!' shouted Basi incredulously.
'Twenty five naira for last month. One hundred outstanding previously. Total, one hundred and twenty five.'
'Holy Moses!' exclaimed Basi. He did not ever expect an electricity bill. The Power Authority men did not bother to read meters, and could not be bothered to send bills to consumers. The arrival of the bill along with a quit notice made Basi very suspicious. He could see the hand behind the bill.

'The doctor's also sent a bill.'
'For how much?'
'Forty naira. You consulted him?'
'Yes. A single consultation. And what was it he gave me? A few tablets of paracetamol,' groaned Basi.
'Paracetamol!' echoed Alali.
'I won't pay. I won't! I'm not ill. The hard times have given me a headache, that's all. If I found some way of earning some real money to offset outstanding debts, my headache would go.' And he gritted his teeth.

Alali went close to him and felt his temple. He said Basi's temple was throbbing and was sure his blood pressure was going up. Basi said he wasn't going to give up.

'Don't,' urged Alali. 'The tax people were here too. They left a tax return.'

Basi was truly alarmed, and the conspiracy theory he had formulated in his mind took root. 'They found their way to my Palace?'

'Apparently. They're mean!' Alali replied.

'Absolutely mean! I don't mind paying my tax. But I won't be harassed into doing so.'

'How d'you pay tax when you're jobless?' Alali wondered.

'Why pay tax at all, anyway? The roads are full of potholes, schools have no books, hospitals no medicines. And there's no food to eat.' Basi gritted his teeth once again. Then he yawned hungrily.

'Talking about food. Know the fat woman in the *buka* down the Street?' asked Alali.

'Mama Badejo?'

'Yes. I offered her one naira for a plate of rice yesterday.'

'You had the money?' asked Basi.

'She laughed to my face. "One plate of rice na two naira," she said.'

'Holy Moses!' exclaimed Basi.

'I said I didn't want to buy her *buka*. And I'd pay cash. She went wild. Called me a thief and a layabout, and drove me away.'

'Things couldn't be worse,' Basi sighed, the troubles of the world written boldly on his face.

'By the way, I understand a new shipload of rice is expected to dock at the wharf any day now. American long-grain. Parboiled.'

'I don't need a shipload of rice,' Basi said gruffly. 'I want something to eat now. Shipload of American long-grain parboiled rice indeed!' He spat the words from between his teeth.

'I hear each bag is being offered at twenty-five naira,' Alali persisted.

'Impossible!' said Basi.

'That's what it costs ex-wharf. In Adetola Market, it's going for two hundred and seventy-five.'

'Holy Moses!'

'By the time Mama Badejo cooks and sells it to us, it goes for a thousand naira.'

Something immediately clicked in Basi's brain. 'Holy Moses! People are making it big on rice!'

'Since government classified it an essential commodity, it's become a luxury,' Alali observed accurately.

Basi ignored the truth of the statement. What mattered to him was the fact that there were millions to be made on rice. Alali said he had never thought of rice as something to make millions from. He had always seen it as Mama Badejo's portion with a dash of stew and two pieces of meat.

Basi went into instant calculations. When confronted with such problems, he always did quick calculations. 'If we buy a bag at twenty-five and sell at two hundred and seventy-five, we make two hundred and fifty the bag. One thousand bags earn us a quarter of a million. Four thousand bags earn us a million!'

Alali was suitably impressed. 'To be a millionaire . . .' he said.

'Think like a millionaire!' Basi exulted.

His headache eased, his flagged spirit recovered, and the eternal optimist in him found fire. He drummed excitedly on his bed.

'How do we get the money for one bag, one hundred bags, one thousand bags or four thousand bags?' Alali asked needlessly.

Basi was not listening. He was calculating in his head.

'How many bags of rice are there on the ship?'

'Two hundred thousand bags,' replied Alali.

'Well, we have the answer!' Basi was radiant. 'At five naira the bag, we make a million. And we need never touch or see a bag of rice.'

'How?'

'We'll just earn a commission. As commission agents. Simple.'

'But how do we corner the entire shipload?'

This was not a problem where Basi was concerned. He knew exactly what to do. He understood such matters only too well. Years of hustling in Lagos had taught him a lot.

'You know who owns the shipload of rice?'

'A Lebanese merchant,' Alali replied.

'Look for him. When you find him, say we want to buy the entire shipload.'

Alali was shocked. 'Buy? The shipload? Suppose he asks for money?'

'Tell him to sell us the shipload in principle. And we'll send him the money . . .'

'In principle?'

'We'll send him the money. Tell him I said so.'

It was as though once he had spoken, everyone was bound to accept and act on the basis of his name. So confident was he, so self-assured, that Alali did not argue anymore. Leafing through the various letters he had before him, Basi poured forth his scorn for such trash. 'Bills, bills, bills! Quit notices! Pah!'

Alali was infected by his disdain. 'Once we conclude this deal, we'll pay off Madam,' he said. 'Shut her up. Make nonsense of her quit notice.' And he laughed.

'No, Al. We'll buy her and her house. Teach her to send me a quit notice. Millionaire-on-the-make!'

'Mr B!' cheered Alali.

'That's me!' exclaimed Basi, thumping his chest.

And he hurried Alali off in search of the Lebanese merchant.

Josco it was who was busy spreading news of the imminent arrival of the shipload of rice. The arrival of the ship bearing rice, that is. This was not unusual. The whole of Lagos was in a state of euphoria over rice. My uncle said it was a plot to enrich a few people and take the nation's oil money away to America. He banned the eating of rice at home, saying that rice had no more food value than cassava or yam, of which there was plentiful supply.

He said rice should be eaten once a year, as was the case before oil money opened the eyes of Lagosians to the madness of importing it from America. I am sure my uncle was right. But no one was listening to him. All ears were waiting for news of the arrival of imported rice from which everyone expected to make a killing. From exporter, through importer, clearing agents, middlemen of the first order, middlemen of the second order, middlemen of the third order, middlemen of the fourth order, wholesale dealers, retailers, hoteliers and *bukaliers*, everyone was in on the game.

Thus when Josco passed word round on Adetola Street, about the new shipload of rice, no one was surprised. Josco had access to all such information. He retailed the information for a fee from those who could afford it, for a drink from his associate Dandy, or for free to the likes of Alali from whom he expected other forms of payment. He had tipped off Segi earlier in the day, saying that the owner of the consignment had made him an offer.

'I can introduce you to him for a fee,' he had concluded.

'How much?' Segi had asked.

'Twenty naira only.'

Segi had paid. And when she had asked when she could meet the importer, Josco had said matter-of-factly:

'Tonight. Maybe I'll fetch you the documents. Save you the trouble.'

This had pleased Segi beyond description. She had gone off immediately to tell her friend whom she called "The Alhaji". The mention of the title on Adetola Street conjured, not a man of Allah's ways, but a rich businessman who happened to belong to the Muslim faith. He was a man whose fingers dripped with gold and diamonds, whose signature or squiggle was worth millions. Segi had gone for him, knowing that once he heard of the rice, he would buy the entire shipload and pay her a finder's fee.

In due time, Dandy heard of the import. From Josco. Josco had gone to the Bar to cadge a drink from Dandy, as usual. Speaking about the rice, he promised to put Dandy in the picture in return for a drink.

Dandy obliged him. 'Click away, photographer,' Dandy said.

Josco drained the glass. 'I met a Lebanese at the hotel yesterday. Told me he's sold a shipload of rice to someone at No. 7 Adetola Street.'

'Hell, I should have known that!' exclaimed Dandy.

A Shipload of Rice

'Someone around here's about to hit it real big!' said Josco, with a glint in his eye.

Dandy did not waste a further minute. He concluded that Madam was the lucky inheritor of the rice deal. And swearing not to be left out as usual, set off for Madam's. 'She must give me a piece of the action! She must give me a piece of the action! A piece of the action! The action! The action!' he said as he threaded his way through buses, hawkers, potholes and open sewers to No. 7 Adetola Street.

Madam was at a lunch of rice and stew when Dandy knocked at the door. She had piled the plate high with rice and dug into it with a spoon in luxurious abandon. In reply to the knock on her door, she said, 'Come in if you are handsome and rich!' through a mouthful of rice. Dandy stepped into the room with a 'Madam the Madam!'.

'It's a matter of cash!' Madam replied, through the rice.

'I hear you are swimming in the commodity these days,' Dandy said, referring to "cash", not rice. And he sat opposite her at table.

'Everything's tough, Dandy,' Madam replied, and shovelled rice into her mouth.

'When the going gets tough, the tough get going,' said Dandy. Madam munched on majestically.

'Things no just tough; they rough,' she said. 'Tenants no gree pay rent, judges dey take bribes, as for the police, . . . ha!'

'You can't complain, Madam. These people were always your friends.'

'No be matter of friendship. You must pay first before.' And she shovelled up more rice.

'Now you've got the shipload of rice, you'll be able to pay them all off.'

'Rice? What rice?'

'I'm told a shipload has been made over to someone at No. 7 Adetola Street. I thought it would be you.'

'No. 'E fit be Basi. I sure say na Basi.'

'Hell, I should have known that! He's the only one who'd do such a fast deal,' said Dandy.

'E no get common kobo to buy something. 'E go come to me. Never mind. It's a matter of cash!' said Madam. And she drank wine.

'I want a piece of the action, Madam. You must give me a piece of the action, no matter how tiny. Please! Remember that I introduced you to the deal. Please!'

Madam assured him that she would remember the fact. And they parted on the best of terms. Dandy returned to the Bar, a reasonably happy man, and had a celebratory brandy. He reckoned that a tiny bit of the action would earn him something close to a million naira. And he was pleased.

As pleased as Alali who returned to the "Palace" with a letter signed by a certain Managing Director of *Assam International Limited* authorising "the bearer" to sell the entire rice on board the *M.V. Engelbert*. And stipulating that the sales would not be regarded as completed until funds had been paid to the undersigned Managing Director.

'So he didn't ask for money or a bank guarantee?' asked Basi.

'Nope.'

'Holy Moses! I don't believe it. The man's a bonanza. Unreal!'

'Have some faith in humanity, Mr B,' urged Alali.

Basi demanded to see the letter. He read it and read it again, nodded in satisfaction and declared it to be a good letter.

'Gives us full control over the commodity. Makes us millionaires right away. We've joined the big league, Al. We're tycoons!' And he danced round the room.

'I should sell the rice before counting the profit,' cautioned Alali.

'Have some faith in humanity, Al. What could go wrong? The rice is on the high seas. We have the letter of offer and the whole country – every man, woman and child in it – is waiting hungrily to devour the shipload at no matter what cost. I say we're made. To be a millionaire...'

'Think like a millionaire!' Al joined in the happy jig.

Basi suggested that they go selling the rice immediately.

'That's not how it's done. First, we issue ATCs – Authority To Collect – to prospective buyers for a small deposit against the total quantity required. The receiver in turn issues his own ATCs to other smaller buyers against equally small deposits. In this way, the whole shipload gets committed in full even before the ship arrives', Alali said.

'Fantastic! It's all a matter of ATCs. Paperwork.'

'Yes. And if we get one big buyer who can take the entire shipload, our work is done.'

'Good. I'll go see Madam right away. I bet she and the loaded Madams of the American Dollar Club will snap up the deal.'

In this, Basi was, as usual, correct. The Amerdolians – short for members of the American Dollar Club – had a nose for deals of this variety and Madam was an Amerdolian of the deepest hue.

When Basi knocked at her door that afternoon, Madam had just finished her lunch and was relaxing in a settee, coolly picking her teeth, as though she did not have a care in the world. She invited the caller in with her customary "Come in if you're handsome and rich!". She always emphasized "and" to show that it was essential for the caller to satisfy both conditions as stipulated.

On Basi's entry, she said laconically, 'Ah, Basi, you got my quit notice. And you've come to pay your rent.'

A Shipload of Rice

Basi sat down and said, 'Madam, there are things more important than rent collection.'

'Like wetin?' Madam challenged him.

'Earning a million, millions for one,' Basi replied.

'I don tire for your million, million. No be million I want. I just wan few naira to take repair my house.' She picked her teeth.

'You shall have them, and more,' Basi said proudly, adding, 'I've brought you a deal worth millions.'

'Na de shipload of rice?'

'How did you know?' Basi asked in surprise.

'I get big ears and I keep dem close to the ground.'

'Well then, are you buying?'

'The whole shipload.'

Basi gasped. Was he delighted! 'It will cost you six million,' he said.

'It's a matter of cash!' replied she, picking her teeth.

'Madam the Madam!' cheered Basi.

'It's a matter of cash!'

Basi excitedly demanded a deposit. Madam said she would pay when the ship arrived. Basi said she had to pay before the arrival of the ship. Madam demanded to see relevant documents. Basi showed her the letter.

'The entire shipload is mine. See? Once you pay me the deposit, I give you the Authority To Collect. ATC. From that moment onwards the shipload is yours.'

'And then?' asked Madam.

'When the ship arrives, you pay directly to the importer of the rice the sum of five million naira and the rest, less your initial deposit, to me.'

'Good,' said Madam.

'Madam, I'm jealous of all that money you are going to make,' teased Basi.

'It's a matter of cash!' she replied, and added, 'You will make plenty money too, Basi.'

'A cool million, Madam. To be a millionaire . . .'

'Think like a millionaire! as you used to say,' replied Madam.

Basi fell to negotiating the matter of the initial deposit. They finally settled on one thousand naira, which Madam paid on the clear understanding that Basi would not spend any of it before the arrival of the ship.

'If you spend de money and de ship no come, God don punish you. I think you understand?'

'Understood, Madam. I assure you this deal is foolproof.'

'We shall see,' said Madam.

Handing over the documents, Basi said, 'From this moment, the shipload of rice is yours.'

'It's a matter of cash!' said Madam. She smiled blissfully as Basi took leave of her.

As soon as Basi was gone, she dressed up and went to meet her colleagues of the American Dollar Club. Committing the shipload of rice was no problem at all. Everyone she met wanted to buy the entire shipload. Such were the times, and such the people they bred. She returned to Adetola Street quite elated and satisfied with both herself and her worthy tenant.

Basi was similarly satisfied with himself. He reported his success to Alali on his return to the "Palace".

Said he, 'Al, Madam has taken up the entire shipload. She deposited point oh oh one million naira.'

'We can have something to eat,' Alali said.

'In the best restaurant in town.'

'And when the ship docks?'

'Well then, that's another story.'

They made ready to go to lunch. Basi sang lustily the song he always sang when he was in good heart:

> Oh what a wonderful morning
> Oh what a wonderful day
> I've got a millionaire's feeling
> Everything's going my way.

They met Dandy on the way. He asked after the shipload of rice, only to learn that it was all gone.

'Really?' asked Dandy. 'Does that mean I won't find even a thousand bags to sell?'

'I'm afraid it's so,' replied Basi.

'Who's cornered the stuff?'

'Madam.'

'Hell, I should have known that! I'll have to ask her for a small quantity.'

'Please, do,' Alali encouraged him.

'Where are you guys off to?'

'To lunch,' Basi replied.

'Where?'

'Some nice place. Quiet and nice,' Alali answered.

'As befits guys who zust sold a shipload of rice?'

'You said it, Dandy. To be a millionaire . . .'

'Think like a millionaire!' replied Alali and Dandy in unison.

They parted ways, Dandy to see Madam, Alali and Basi to the most expensive restaurant in town. There they gorged themselves on caviar –

yes, it was available – wine, also imported, Evian water, duly imported, and imported apples. It was a cardinal principle on Adetola Street that imported things were the best.

Dandy did not have much joy with Madam. When he asked her for fifty tons, she told him the entire shipment was committed. Sold out! To the members of the American Dollar Club. 'I'm sorry,' she concluded.

'Madam, squeeze me fifty tons. After all, I put you on to Basi.'

'I know, Dandy. But I no fit disgrace my friends. Sorry-oh.'

Dandy begged, pleaded and cajoled. Madam remained adamant and obstinate. So Dandy turned nasty and abusive, accusing her of being greedy and selfish. At which Madam drew on her abundant reserve of invective: 'Nonsense man, beast of no nation, *mumu*, *akamu* man, salt-water idiot, bomboy, armed robber, transfer desk, smuggler, pancake!'

'Get out!' yelled Dandy.

'Get out!' replied Madam in even louder tone.

Get out, Dandy did. After all, the house was not his. He did promise to have the last laugh. At which Madam laughed boisterously. 'Last laugh,' she said. 'Stay there, last bus go leave you go. Foolish man.'

A week passed. And then a second week. Dandy sat in his Bar licking his wounds. He had no wish to see either Madam or Basi. Josco did not show up at the Bar either. Nor did Segi. It was as though the shipload of rice had come to split them.

For their part, Basi and Alali maintained a close watch on the port for the *M.V. Engelbert*. Madam too, although she relied heavily on information from Basi and Alali.

Basi knowing Madam for what she was, kept strictly out of her way. He knew that given her fiery temper, there was nothing stopping her from demanding to be shown her money whenever she felt like doing so. And he had been spending it, contrary to her clear orders. He prayed all the safe winds to guide the *M.V. Engelbert* safely to the docks of Lagos.

In the third week, something happened. Segi stopped by at Dandy's and Dandy seized the opportunity to regale her with stories of Madam's perfidy. 'I introduced her to the rice and she won't let me have a piece of the action,' he moaned. 'She's mean. Very mean.'

'Not to worry, Dandy,' said Segi. 'You can buy rice if you want to.'

'How?' Dandy asked.

'I've been offered a shipload of rice too. I only just got the letter of offer.' And she showed it to him. There is good profit to be made on it.

'Most interesting!' said Dandy.

'What is?'

'Your letter. Can I keep it?'

'Sure! You have to help me sell the rice. Alhaji's out of town. I need a commission of five naira the bag. You're free to earn what you please on top of that.'

'You want to earn a million naira, Segi?'

'Sure!'

'Millions are not made so easily.'

'Elsewhere, no. But in Lagos, anything can happen. Everything happens. Ciao, Dandy!'

So saying, she wriggled and wiggled out of the room. "Ciao" was a way of showing everyone on the Street that she was a "been-to". One of those women who travelled abroad frequently in search of whatever. In the old days, they went in search of education and returned with what was popularly known as "the golden fleece". They were argonauts. In the new dispensation, they remained argonauts, but education was not their search. They returned with gold, trinkets, money. They were lawbreakers, smugglers. I had an impression Segi would gladly not have joined the racket – but she did, to oblige friends once in a while. More for fun than for profit. Because deep in her heart, she did not really care very much for money. But who could live on Adetola Street and not be touched by the prevailing ethos of the Street?

Armed with the letter Segi had given him, Dandy went to see Madam "to compare notes", as he put it. Madam didn't bear a grudge for long, and had forgotten her quarrel with Dandy. When the latter asked her for the documents of the shipload of rice, she gave them to him willingly.

Dandy compared both letters and declared them identical.

'Wetin that one mean?' asked Madam.

'Either there is no rice at all or the rice is being sold to several people on the same terms.'

'Tell me something!' Madam said, in wonderment.

'You didn't pay money to Basi, did you?'

'I paid. A thousand naira.'

Dandy laughed. A mocking, broad laugh. 'You better keep an eye on Basi, rice merchant,' he said, with just the stinging hint of sarcasm that was meant to, and did, drive so many pins through Madam's lovely heart.

She went after Basi, with murder in her heart. The fears which assailed her had been with Basi for two weeks and more. That day, he asked Alali for the umpteenth time if there was news of the ship.

'Nope,' Alali replied.

'Is there a shipload of rice on the high seas?'

'There is, I believe.'

'You believe. But you told me for certain there's a ship. The *M.V. Engelbert*. And the Lebanese merchant confirmed it.'

A Shipload of Rice

Alali's eyes fluttered for some moments. He remained silent for a while, then said that the Lebanese had re-confirmed the facts that same day.

'Well,' said Basi, 'Madam's in a state, I'm sure. She asked me yesterday for the rotation number of the ship. Has the ship been rotated?'

'I don't know. Haven't checked. I don't even know what is a rotation number.'

'You better go to the Ports Authority to find out before Madam strikes me dead.'

He had hardly finished speaking when Madam barged into the room. Basi hid under the bed in a flash of lightning. Madam asked Alali after him.

'He's gone to the wharf to see if the ship has arrived,' he lied.

'Are you sure?'

'Yes. Why?'

'Because de man dey scarce like naira nowadays. Each time I ask for am, I go hear say 'e don go wharf or to the Lebanese man. Na wetin?'

'That shipload of rice is giving him quite a headache.'

'Make 'e no be say 'e don spend de money I bin give am-oh.'

'I wouldn't know, Madam.'

'Because if 'e spend even one kobo of my money and I no get de rice, I go show am pepper. I think you understand?'

'It will be okay, Madam. There is no need to fear.'

Madam was not very convinced. She lifted the fold of her cloth, adjusted the tuck and glaring at Alali, departed. Basi emerged from hiding. There was worry in his eyes.

In another week, the only happy man in the group was Dandy. When Segi called on him at the Bar to find out if he had sold the shipload of rice, he calmly told her that there was no shipload of rice.

'No rice?' asked Segi, surprised.

'None. I'm so happy! You know, I asked Madam to give me a piece of the action. She refused. Said she'd sold everything to the members of the American Dollar Club. And she had paid Basi one thousand naira as a deposit on the finder's fee.'

'Really?'

'Basi and Alali went to town with Madam's money. They ate caviar, drank wine and slept for three days. And now, four weeks later, there's no ship.'

'Madam won't like that,' Segi said.

Dandy laughed. 'When she knows what's what, there'll be quite a to do.'

Suddenly, the truth hit Segi between the eyes. 'We've been tricked,' she said.

'Sure you have,' Dandy exulted, and he took a swig of satisfaction from his miniature bottle.

Basi came into the Bar for a drink.

'Good Mr B!' hailed Dandy.

'That's me!' replied Basi. 'Segi, the lady with the beautiful eyes,' he greeted Segi.

'How's life, Basi?'

'Everything's okay. Perfect.'

'Any news of the ship?' Dandy asked, barely concealing his impish delight.

'No.'

'I thought so.'

'What d'you mean?'

'I don't believe there's a shipload of rice at all.'

'Why not?'

'Because this document which fell into my hand some time ago looks like the one you gave to Madam.' He gave Basi the letter of offer he had taken from Segi. He watched Basi's reaction to the letter with keen interest. Basi read and re-read the letter.

'Are they the same, Mr B?' Segi asked.

Basi examined and re-examined the letter. Slowly, he said, 'Yes, they're identical.'

'Looks like someone's pulling a fast one on you,' sneered Dandy.

Basi did not wait any longer. 'I smell a rat, I smell a rat!' he moaned, and ran out of the Bar.

What happened is well-known and has been chronicled several times. Although several ships laden with rice arrived in Lagos port, the *M.V. Engelbert* was not one of them. The man who was supposed to own the rice was not a Lebanese at all, but an Indian representing an American big-wig. Although several middlemen of the first, second, third and fourth order received rice, passed it on to others and earned a sweet commission, Basi, and by consequence Madam, was not one of them. Some members of the American Dollar Club had not relied solely on Madam's offer and they made a killing through other sources. Basi found out late in the day that Alali's informant was Josco who had forged the documents and passed them all over Adetola Street, earning quite some money in the process.

When the people on the Street found out what had happened, they merely shrugged. Even those who had lost money to their friends or directly to Josco merely shrugged. Although Josco went underground for a while, he soon reappeared on the Street. No one questioned him. And he went about as usual.

The only person who was not amused was Madam. She demanded a return of the deposit she had given to Basi. And when she found that Basi had spent a part of the money, she kept her promise to "show him pepper". Against Basi's protestations and pleas for mercy, she removed his pillow and mattress, vowing not to return them until Basi had refunded her money in full.

Hot stuff!

The Mattress

Basi had to sleep that night without his mattress and pillow. He insisted on sleeping on the bare springs of his mattress because, according to him, a millionaire should sleep only on a bed. Not for him, Alali's usual place on the floor.

He woke up with a blistering headache and deep marks on his back. He stretched painfully and groaned aloud.

'Believe me, Al,' says he, 'Madam has reached the limit this time.'

'She's mean,' Al replies.

'Mean and arrogant. Fancy her treating a millionaire-on-the-make this shabbily.'

'What's she going to use the mattress and pillow for?' asks Alali.

'That's what I should like to know . . . Ach! my sides ache. And Al, you've been sleeping comfortably on the floor!'

Basi is envious, but Alali won't be drawn.

'Mr B, leave me alone,' he says. 'I'm not your problem. I didn't take your pillow and mattress. Madam did. She's your problem.'

'A problem which I must solve soon,' Basi vows.

'The question remains, how?'

'Not to worry, Al. A man who can earn millions must know how to recover his property from a mean, cantankerous, ageing landlady,' Basi replies.

The words have hardly died on his lips when Madam comes into the "Palace".

'Ageing landlady,' says she. 'Abi na me you dey abuse so?'

'No, Madam,' Basi says.

Madam is not interested in whatever answer Basi proffers. She has come to savour her victory over him, to drive the nail into his coffin, to rub salt into his wound.

She had dressed up gorgeously for the task. It was necessary to impress upon Basi the fact that she had slept soundly the previous night on a bed of roses. She stands by the door, while her tongue darts before her like the forked tongue of a viper.

'So, millionaire Basi, how d'you feel sleeping without no pillow and no mattress?'

'It's no joke, Madam,' Basi answers truthfully.

'I'm sure. Yes. I sure say you enjoy yourself well well last night.'

'I sure did,' Basi answers without lifting up his face. There is murder in his heart. He is doing his best to control himself.

'And you go enjoy again this night.'

'You won't return the pillow and mattress tonight?'

'At all, at all. Not today, not tomorrow, never never. Make Basi know wetin *wuruwuru* mean.'

'Madam, I did not . . .'

'Rent 'e no go pay, and when I come give am money for business, 'e just go blow de money for chop and woman.'

'It wasn't my fault, Madam,' Basi reiterates.

'I know say you no go 'gree, Basi. Your *wayo* don too much. Your *shakara* full my belly; your *jibiti* full de house, your *biribiri* my mouth no fit talk 'am. God don punish you, foolish man! Sleep well for dat your bed, you hear? And dream about your mattress and pillow.'

She laughs sarcastically and swaggers out of the room.

Basi can hardly hold himself. 'You hear her?' he asks. ' "Your *wayo* don too much. Your *shakara* full my belly; your *jibiti* full de house". Who is the queen of *wayo*? Is it not Madam? Who's the mother of *shakara*? In whose house has *jibiti* found a happy home? Who is *wuruwuru's* best ally on this Street? And how she gloats! Adding insult to injury!'

'It's mean,' Alali says.

'I'll deal with her yet. And as for getting back that mattress and pillow, I assure you, I will,' Basi asserts.

'Hey, man, sure you can buy another mattress and pillow.'

This angers Basi. He walks up to Alali and pulls him by the ear, hissing loudly, 'Costs money, fool!'

'Okay, boss, okay. My fault,' Alali apologises, having got the message.

'That's better, Al. And you better think how I'm going to recover my things from Madam.'

Alali thinks about that for some time. He gets his clothes from the clothes rack, dresses up and tells Basi he'll go to seek the assistance of

Dandy and Segi. He believes, he says, that between the three of them, they will be able to solve the problem. This pleases Basi.

'Great lad!' he shouts. 'To be a millionaire . . .'

'Think like a millionaire!' Alali answers as he goes out to Dandy's Bar.

Dandy is busy cleaning his Bar when Alali arrives. He does not usually clean the Bar, but for some unexplained reason, he is doing so on this occasion. He has not forgotten that Madam has confiscated Basi's pillow and mattress, an action which has given him considerable joy.

'How did Mr B spend last night?' he asks Alali.

'On springs. He didn't sleep a wink,' Alali replies.

'A millionaire sleeping on springs. Ha! ha! No mattress, no pillow. Madam's "shown him pepper" this time.'

It is obvious that Dandy is enjoying Basi's discomfiture. But Alali ignores that. He knows what he wants from Dandy. So he tells Dandy that Basi wants his mattress and pillow back. Dandy suggests that as a millionaire, Basi could walk into any shop on Adetola Street and purchase a new mattress.

'Course he could,' Alali asserts, 'He doesn't want to.'

'Why not?'

'He has a sentimental attachment to the old ones.'

This amuses Dandy and he laughs heartily. 'A sentimental attachment! And if Madam chooses to burn the mattress, she'll burn Basi's sentiments too?'

This bit of information shocks Alali. He has not thought that Madam might do such a thing. He plies Dandy with questions related to Madam's full intentions about the mattress.

'D'you think she'll burn the mattress?' he asks.

'Why not?' Dandy replies. 'I've heard Madam say as much, and she always means business. She's a businesswoman.'

'Good heavens!' exclaims Alali, visibly shaken.

'What's the matter?' asks Dandy, in surprise. He has seen the effect of his words on Alali. But Alali quickly recovers his poise and with urgency in his voice suggests that everything has to be done not only to stop Madam from burning the mattress, but also to make her return it to Basi.

'I will tell her so when next I see her,' Dandy mocks.

Alali does not appreciate the mockery in Dandy's statement and thanking Dandy for being so solicitous on Basi's behalf, goes away in search of Segi.

No sooner is his back turned than Dandy sits back and roars with laughter, his fat torso shaking tremendously. He does not even notice when Josco comes into the Bar. Josco's voice saying 'Let's share in the fun' makes Dandy aware of that worthy's presence in the Bar. He is happy to share his relish with another.

'Mr B's been sleeping on the bare springs of his bed.'

'Yeah?' asks Josco, as if he has not heard the story before.

'And he's sent Alali to ask me to plead with Madam on his behalf,' Dandy adds, still laughing. The tears have started to run down his cheeks.

'Why doesn't he go and buy a new mattress and pillow from the shops?' asks Josco.

'Zust the question I asked Alali,' Dandy says, wiping the tears with his handkerchief. 'That one says Mr B has a sentimental attachment to the old ones. Which makes me quite suspicious.'

'It is suspicious,' Josco asserts forcefully.

This sets Dandy thinking. Several ideas run through his besotted mind. But he can connect nothing with nothing. He gives up after a while and says to Josco:

'It's suspicious. Very suspicious. What's particular in that mattress? That pillow?'

'Why should a millionaire-on-the-make sleep on the bare springs of his bed? That's unlike Basi,' Josco says.

'I tell you what. There's more in all this than meets the eye,' Dandy states. 'We'll have to find out,' he resolves.

He stops his half-hearted attempt at cleaning the Bar, offers Josco a drink and takes a swig himself. He refuses to say another word. Because wild thoughts as to what Basi might have hidden in the mattress race through his mind. He thinks of the section of Adetola Market where charms, traditional herbs and remedies are sold by the chanting Holy Man. He thinks of Native Doctor Ndu and his claim to supply "business and promotion charms". He tries to recollect if he has ever seen or heard Basi in conversation with the Holy Man. He is not sure. And uncertainty breeds fear in him. A wild, gripping terror of the unknown, which he does not divulge to Josco or anyone else.

He is afraid because at the back of his mind lies his perception of Basi as a magician. Which is why he has believed, in spite of all available evidence to the contrary, that Basi is a millionaire.

He is so unusually taciturn that Josco finds him rather boring. So after another drink, Josco takes leave of him.

Alali has not been able to find Segi. He has been to her flat down the Street, but as usual, Segi is absent. He returns to the "Palace" to find Basi absent and rummages in the cupboard for food. There is a bit of *gari* which he munches gladly, wondering where both Basi and Segi have gone to. He does not have long to wonder, for Segi comes into the "Palace" to ask after Basi. Looking around the "Palace", she notices that the bed has no mattress and pillow.

The Mattress

'Madam's still keeping Basi's mattress and pillow?'
'Yes. And Basi's been sleeping on the bare springs.'
Segi knew as much. The news was already all over the Street.
'Bare springs! I'd have thought the floor would be more comfortable,' Segi says.
'Oh no. Mr B can never sleep on the floor. He's a millionaire.'
'How long is he going to sleep on springs?'
'For as long as it takes him to recover his property from Madam.'
'Why doesn't he buy a new mattress and pillow?'
'He has a sentimental attachment to the old ones.'
'Nonsense!'
'And Madam knows it.'
'You think so?'
'I'm positively sure,' Alali asserts. 'In fact I've heard her say she's sure Basi has medicine for love in the pillow.'
'Medicine for love!' Segi echoes. She is not unfamiliar with the idea, and from their very first meeting, she has had certain feelings of love for Basi whose suavity and handsomeness she has admired.
'Madam thinks if she keeps the pillow long enough, Basi will fall in love with her, propose to her, marry her and she'll then have access to his many millions,' Alali says.
Alali knows the story has been circulating on the Street, and that his words are bound to have some effect on Segi. For Alali, the one-man-contractor, is no fool. He knows some of the tricks in the rule book, and he is correct. Segi gets incensed.
'The old hag!' she says. 'She musn't be allowed to get away with this one.'
'That's what everyone says,' Alali says to her, adding for good measure, 'I believe she suspects what we all know: that Basi has a soft spot for you.'
This pleases Segi and she rolls her beautiful eyes a full three hundred and sixty degrees, saying coyly, 'Really?'
'Definitely,' says Alali. 'It's not Basi she's after. She's after you. Look out, Segi, look out!'
Segi does not require further prompting. She has made up her mind that she will help recover Basi's mattress. She only has to think the best way of doing so. She plans a quiet strategy.
The days pass. The impasse lingers on. Madam is not thinking of returning Basi's property. Publicly, Basi puts up an I-don't-care attitude. But every night is a nightmare. As dusk falls, his anger with Madam increases, his discomfort mounts. But he is impotent because he owes Madam money, and is in no position to repay. Moreover, he

knows that Madam, tough as a cookie, will not relent. However, he remains optimistic. Basi lives on hope. And truly, without hope, what would anyone be doing remaining alive on Adetola Street? So my uncle has always said. Basi's hopes were to be duly rewarded.

Several weeks after the loss of his mattress, he goes to Dandy's Bar for a drink and meets Josco. The affair of the shipload of rice has become history. Basi hardly remembers it. There is the pressing matter of his mattress and pillow, so he does not bother about Josco's part in the rice fiasco.

Josco himself does not give Basi the opportunity to think of rice. At the sight of Basi, he raises the spectre of Madam.

'Mr B, I hear Madam is determined to humiliate you,' he says.

'She can't,' Basi boasts.

'You have a sentimental attachment to the old mattress and pillow?'

'Oh yes. I won't replace them. And I will get them from Madam. They mean a lot to me.'

'Just how much?' Josco pries him.

'No one can quantify it. In monetary terms, I should think they're worth several bars of gold.'

'Several bars of gold . . . In the mattress?'

'And the pillow.'

'Jesus!' exclaims Josco.

'And if she doesn't give them back to me, there'll be real trouble soon on the Street. I have been very patient with her. But she must beware the anger of a patient man.' He waits for a few moments for the message to sink in and then adds, 'Real trouble!' with a menacing flick of his thumb. And he steps resolutely out of the Bar.

Basi's words have a devastating effect on Josco. He keeps repeating what he has heard: 'Several bars of gold! Several bars of gold!'

Dandy, who has not heard the conversation between Josco and Basi because he was in the gents, returns to the Bar and overhears Josco.

'What bars of gold?' asks he of Josco, his eyes lighting up.

'Basi just left,' Josco says. 'Says he has several bars of gold in the mattress Madam seized.'

'Hell, I should have known that!' Dandy says. 'That's what Alali meant by saying that Basi has a sentimental attachment to the mattress and pillow.'

'You know Mr B has no bank account.'

'So he hides his millions in his mattress.'

'That way, no one can ever know exactly how rich he is. Most rich people in Lagos do it. Especially if they've stolen the money from government.'

The Mattress

'Hell, I should have known that!' howls Dandy yet again. And he quickly adds, 'Mr B must not recover that mattress.'

'Madam won't give it back to him, don't worry.'

'And Madam must not be allowed to keep it either.'

'No?'

'Of course not. She's not to know that there are gold bars in it. Otherwise, she'll not give it to me.'

'Do you want it?' Josco asks unnecessarily.

'Sure!' replies Dandy. 'I could do with those gold bars. I own Dandy's Bar. A few more gold bars and I'll be Leader of the Bar.'

When Dandy is under the influence of alcohol, which is every waking minute, no one can predict his predilections. Even Josco never tries to. All he wants from him is free drinks and he is always ready to flatter Dandy to achieve his purposes.

'Good show! Jolly good show!' Josco shouts, lifting his arms above his head. 'Let's have a drink, Dandy.'

'I must get that mattress from Madam,' Dandy swears as he pours Josco a drink.

From that moment, events move with great rapidity. Because Madam now has ranged against her all the forces of the Street. But she holds the ace, the trump card. And her opponents know it. There are discussions and meetings. And strategies are outlined, in the fashion of Adetola Street.

One afternoon, Madam is having her siesta after a happy meal when Segi calls on her. She wakes up at Segi's entry and welcomes her.

'Basi's been sleeping these many weeks on the bare springs of his bed,' Segi says, as though Madam did not know.

'Serves the love-sick debtor right,' Madam replies.

'He's love-sick, is he?'

'De *wayo* man. Rent 'e no wan pay. Plus 'e come dey give my money to him girl-friends.'

'So what are you going to do with his pillow and mattress?'

'I no go give dem to 'am, *lai-lai*,' Madam asserts.

'What do you really want from him?'

'Me? Want sometin from Basi? God no gree bad tin. Wetin Basi get to give me?' And she sighs, screwing up her face in disgust. 'I tell you wetin I want. Make 'e commot for my house.'

'Suppose he pays what he owes, will you return his property?'

'At all.'

'Suppose I pay his debts, will you give me back the pillow, for instance?'

'At all, at all,' Madam replies. 'But Segi, which one be your own?'

'I'm only trying to help,' Segi says.

'Trying to help. Na so? Awright, if you want help am, tell am make 'e commot for my house.'

'And then you will let me have the pillow?'

'Yes.'

Segi has heard enough. She decides to go to Dandy to relate the latest development. But Dandy is not in the Bar, he is on his way to Madam's. He gets there soon after Segi has left.

'Come in if you're handsome and rich!' Madam answers as soon as Dandy knocks on her door. She is drinking a beer.

'Madam, I have hot news,' Dandy says as soon as he enters.

'Tell me something!' Madam replies.

'Do you know that Basi is planning to burn your house?'

'Na lie,' Madam says nonchalantly, and drinks her beer.

'He's so mad at the seizure of his mattress and pillow, he's sworn to destroy this place.'

'Impo,' says Madam with a chuckle. Short for "impossible".

'Why?' asks Dandy.

'Whosai 'e go live? 'E no fit burn de only place wey 'e don live inside without no rent since ten years now.'

'Is it so?' asks Dandy.

'Na so,' replies Madam, drinking with gusto.

'Madam, that mattress will cause you a lot of trouble.'

'By how?' asks Madam.

'Well, you can't even store it comfortably. Takes too much space. Smells bad.'

'Na who tell you?'

'Bad news travels fast.'

'Go siddon.' Madam empties the glass and pours herself some more beer from the bottle.

'It's full of cockroaches and bedbugs.' Dandy is fishing.

'Na lie.' Madam does not take the bait.

'So what does it contain?'

'Wetin dey dey inside mattress?'

'You haven't seen any strange thing in Basi's mattress?'

'At all, at all.'

Dandy is relieved. Madam doesn't know the truth. He is excited too.

'So if Basi pays his debts you will return the mattress to him?'

'God forbid! I go gi'am him mattress if 'e commot for my house.'

'Wonderful!' says Dandy.

'Na which one be your own for de mattress sef?' Madam asks.

'I want to punish Basi. Torture him. I want him to sleep on bare springs the rest of his life. He and his many millions!'

'If you fit make am commot for my house, I go give you de mattress.'

This pleases Dandy, and he leaves Madam's lounge. He runs down the stairs to Basi's vaunted Palace. Basi is alone at home and Dandy does not waste time exchanging pleasantries.

'I'm sorry to see Madam treat you so bad,' he says.

'She's a mean, arrogant, cantankerous woman. And I'll deal with her in my own time,' Basi affirms.

'I hear she won't give you back your mattress till you quit the premises.' Dandy is most solicitous, duly inflecting the right pronouns to reflect perfidy and pity respectively.

'I know she means to keep the mattress forever.'

'Does that mean you won't ever quit the premises?'

'I don't mind quitting, but I won't do it under duress.'

'You confirm you'll quit the premises?'

'Under the right conditions, yes,' Basi says.

'Such as the full payments of outstanding amounts to Madam?'

'No, not that.'

'What else?'

This torrent of questions arouses Basi's suspicions. It was in the tradition of Adetola Street that undue interest in your personal affairs should make you wary. Because personal interest, personal profit had to be your prime motive, a motive which made you cultivate the failure of your friends and associates. So that everyone stood still, like the green, algeous waters in the gutters, and society as a whole did not progress. Thus, as Dandy plies him with questions, Basi decides to look into his bag of tricks and pull out one or two of his best.

'What's your interest in all this?' he asks.

'I care for you, Mr B. I hate to see you sleeping on those bare springs. I hate to see Madam torturing you. It is in the interest of everyone on this Street that you are freed of her wicked designs.'

'You are a good friend, man,' replies Basi, eyeing him closely.

'So you should quit these premises,' Dandy stresses.

'I will, under the right conditions.'

'Good Mr B!' says Dandy, offering Basi a hand of friendship.

'That's me!' replies Basi, taking Dandy's proffered hand.

They shake hands and part. Basi is confused, somewhat. For he regards Dandy as something of a duffer, and incapable of any tricks whatsoever. Moreover, he does not expect Dandy to assist him in his difficulties. However, Basi has left Dandy dangling and that is satisfactory to some extent.

Days elapse. Nothing happens. Dandy and Segi have been anxious to see each other but have not been able to do so. The meeting finally takes place in Dandy's Bar. First, they compare notes.

'Madam's determined not to return Mr B's mattress,' says Dandy.

'She wants Basi to quit her premises.'

'So you've confirmed that too?'

'Yes. The news is all over the Street. How can Basi bear such humiliation?' Segi asks.

'You don't know that man. He has a skin thick as a crocodile's.'

'He's tall, handsome and rich. I wish he were not under the spell of that wicked woman.'

'Do you really think he's under her spell?'

'Think? I'm sure of it. That's why he's refused to quit her premises. I'm sure she thinks if she keeps her pillow long enough, he'll propose to her.'

'Basi will never propose to Madam. He has a very low opinion of her.'

'Then he should leave her premises,' Segi says.

'He told me he doesn't mind leaving, provided the conditions are right. But what are the right conditions?' It is obvious that Dandy is in torment.

Segi has experience in the matter. It is not in vain that she is a "been-to". She is aware that a landlady or landlord who wants a tenant to quit, can offer the tenant either new accommodation or pay the tenant money to quit. She passes the idea to Dandy.

'Hell, I should have known that!' Dandy exclaims.

Segi knows that Madam will never pay Basi off and so she offers to do so. The only question is how much will satisfy a man as greedy as Basi. He might demand an impossible sum.

Dandy is sure that he will not because he is stone-broke, his bank having been taken away. This surprises Segi.

'What bank?' she asks.

'Where he keeps his wealth. It's not available to him right now,' Dandy chuckles with satisfaction.

'Seems the right time to make him an offer he can't refuse.'

Which is what they do jointly. Apparently, their offer is not unexpected by Basi who, ever since his discussion with Dandy and following certain independent inquiries, has concluded that he will soon get a mattress. And as usual, he goes about bragging. 'After I've put back a mattress on my bed, Madam will see red,' he tells all his acquaintances. His stock grows on the Street.

Consequently, when Dandy and Segi make him an offer he cannot refuse, he does not refuse it. In accordance with the ethos of Adetola Street, he offers them a million thanks for their kind attention, receives their money happily, and informs them he will leave the premises immediately. He is pleased, he says, for the opportunity to have his own back on Madam.

Segi and Dandy are delighted by the turn of events and decide to go upstairs to inform Madam about their signal success. As soon as they leave, Basi invites Alali to work.

'Come on, Al,' he says. 'We must get busy immediately.'

'Where do we move to?' Alali asks.

'Ask me no questions, and I'll tell you no fibs. Come on before the shops close.'

They stand by the road for a while before *Psalm 31* draws up. Basi and Alali take a ride in her down the Street to Adetola Market, to the bedding section. Basi selects a beautiful mattress with a red design and he and Alali lug it down to No. 7 Adetola, where Dandy and Segi are very busy with Madam.

'We finally made it, Madam,' Dandy announces triumphantly.

'And not without a struggle, careful planning and a lot of money.'

'Mr B has finally agreed to quit your premises,' says Dandy.

'Impo,' says Madam.

'He's going to leave immediately.'

'Whosai 'e dey go?'

'Where the landlady will not seize his mattress,' Dandy says.

'And his pillow,' Segi adds.

'Impo,' replies Madam.

'What do you mean by impossible?' asks Segi.

'Basi no fit commot for my house. Since ten years now I don try to commot am and 'e no gree. I beg am, I beat am, I give am assault, I pour am hot water, pour am cold water; I even try to broke him head with beer bottle. Still 'e no gree commot. Wetin go make am go now?'

They watch Madam closely. Dandy is the first to speak.

'Madam, are you trying to break the agreement I had with you?'

'Or the promise you made me?' asks Segi.

'Which agreement? Which promise?' Thus Madam, unable to believe Basi is about to quit her premises.

'You said as soon as Basi left the premises you'd give me his mattress.'

'And me his pillow.'

'His mattress. His pillow. De man no wan de both sef. Since I take dem 'e no come one day come ask for dem! E no wan dem. Which kain man be dis?'

'He's a proud, handsome, young millionaire. He doesn't deserve to sleep on a bed without a mattress.' Segi speaking.

This stings Madam to the quick. 'Proud, handsome, young millionaire,' she mocks. 'Which time you learn dat one?'

'You have to keep your promise, Madam,' Dandy says.

'Awright. I go do wetin I talk. No trouble. But make I tell you sometin. I no believe say Basi go leave my house. He too clever to do such kain tin. Basi too clever. Foolish man.'

But Madam is in for a little surprise. From the room below comes the sound of moving furniture. Sweet music to Segi's jealous ears.

'Listen carefully,' she taunts Madam. 'Don't you hear movements downstairs? Mr B is already packing. He'll soon leave your rat-infested premises.'

'Impo! Imposi!' says Madam. 'Impossible!'

Without another word, she re-does the tuck of her loin cloth, throws a headtie round her head, slips on her rubber slippers and goes downstairs to see things for herself. Could her wish have come true? Dandy and Segi rush after her excitedly.

In Basi's vaunted Palace, there is tremendous excitement, whoops of delight. Josco has joined Alali and Basi to celebrate the arrival of the new mattress and pillow.

'It's a beautiful mattress,' Basi says, throwing himself on it and kicking his legs in the air like a child.

'The pillow too,' adds Josco, pawing it.

'Madam will faint when next she comes here,' Alali chuckles.

'I promised she'd see red, didn't I? I'll teach her to trifle with a millionaire-on-the-make!'

And turning to Josco, he thanks him for making Dandy believe there were gold bars in the mattress. Josco is shocked. He too had thought there were gold bars in the old mattress. He questions Basi insistently as to what the mattress truly contains.

'It's full of bedbugs and roaches with teeth strong enough to eat up all the gold bars in the world,' the old tortoise says.

'I'm finished,' moans Josco. 'Finished. Dandy's going to ban me from his Bar for ever. What shall I do?'

Neither Basi nor Alali is in a mood to commiserate with him. His moan falls on stone-deaf ears. Basi is coolly relaxing in his bed and Alali is pacing the room proudly.

When Madam, Dandy and Segi rush into the room, they are surprised at what they see.

'Basi!' Madam blurts out. 'Wetin you mean? You no dey commot for my house according by the quit notice?'

'Quit? Why on earth would I quit these lovely premises, my Palace?'

'But Dandy and Segi talk say dem pay you to commot for de house.'

'Pay me to quit? What a preposterous idea! Basi is no quitter. 'I've been here so long, I'm almost the landlord. Not so, Al?' Basi asks.

Alali agrees. 'Sure, man, sure,' he exults.

Dandy protests. 'But you took money from us . . .'

Basi cuts him short, on the instant.

'Took money from you? Don't insult me. You offered me money for the old mattress which as you well know (and here he winks mischievously) has gold bars hidden in it. And the pillow with its love potions. You and Segi are welcome to them, gold digger and lovelorn lady. See that you get them from Madam. For me, there's this lovely new mattress and an even softer pillow. A million thanks for your kindness.'

He lies back in his bed, an impish smile on his lips, his eyes alight. Madam is very distressed. She sighs, eyes him roundly and walks sedately out of the room.

Dandy is mad with Basi. He pours a heap of invective on him.

'Double-crosser! Rascal! Crook! Devil!' He leaves the room when he runs out of appropriate epithets. Segi and Josco follow him.

Basi and Alali laugh and shake hands with each other.

The Vendor of Titles

The incident of the mattress was only diversionary. However, it did a lot to increase Basi's stock on the Street, as it became popular belief that he kept his millions in gold bars in his mattress.

Even when Dandy let it be known that Basi himself had confessed that his mattress contained only bugs and roaches, no one believed him. 'Dandy thinks we're all fools,' some said; others said it was a question of sour grapes for Dandy. There were quite a number who stated categorically that the mattress was full and there was need to start filling a second one. The fact that the old mattress was in Madam's keeping was explained away as a part of the old game both Madam and Basi had been playing for over a decade. After all, it was argued, had Madam handed over the mattress and pillow to anyone else? She had them safely ensconced somewhere in her house – for obvious reasons.

Dandy and Segi were the losers, and no tears were shed for them. They deserved what they got, it was generally agreed.

Men of Basi's ilk were deeply respected on the Street and beyond. Being very clever and very rich, they did whatever they wanted to do, in total disregard of the law. Nobody asked how they made the money which everyone knew they had buried in their gardens, or stashed away in the ceilings of their houses or cemented into the walls of their kitchens or, as in the case of Basi, hidden in their mattresses. This was comforting thought to Basi.

With the mattress back on his bed and his nightly comfort assured, he had time to mull over the shipload of rice which, it was said, he had lost by a hair's breadth. Not in any resentful manner. No. What interested him was who had secured the shipload and earned the easy millions. He knew that the proud owners of the new millions would be looking for ways of spending them and of telling the rest of the Street that they had money in their pockets.

Evidence of the owners of the new money was about sooner than anyone had expected.

It came in brand new cars of all shapes and sizes from different corners of the globe; in television sets, stereo sets, video-cassette recorders, outsize refrigerators, cameras and elegant furniture. These quickly replaced similar items which were dumped in big rubbish heaps in the middle of the Street once they showed the slightest sign of wear and tear. It was a cardinal policy of the Street that you did not repair anything; you replaced it.

It came too in the full-page advertisements which drove the news, feature articles and all such irritating tit bits to the most obscure pages of the national newspapers. Basi spotted these advertisements fast and devised the means to cash in on the fad and so make the millions he had vowed to make since his arrival on the Street.

He outlined his plans one evening to Alali who, having spent most of the day at the ports in search of work, returned home tired and hungry, as usual.

'We're going to roll in the millions soon,' Basi told him.

'I want some food, Mr B. I don't want to roll in the millions.'

'Right. I'll feed you. Just to fortify you before you die of excitement.'

'So there's food for once in the Palace?'

'Not much. A few grains of *gari* as usual. A cube or two of sugar. But that will do for now. The millions will soon roll in and we'll have caviar and wine everyday.'

Basi placed the *gari* and sugar on the table. Alali fetched a cup of water and a spoon, mixed, and gulped the paste down at lightning speed.

'I feel better already,' Alali announced.

'Splendid!' said Basi. 'Ever heard of the idle rich?'

'Yeah. They who have so much money, they need never work.'

'Right. Know who they are?'

Alali hesitated. Basi quickly answered the question he had posed.

'Kings and queens, princes and princesses, chiefs.'

'Don't say you want to be a chief now, Mr B.'

'Oh no. Not me. But I know who want to be!'

'Dandy?' asked Alali.

'Not that lazy fool... The men and women who corner the shiploads of rice and cement and what have you, and make the millions doing nothing. Take a newspaper any day and you have it all there in centre-spreads. Congratulations to chiefs, installation ceremonies of new chiefs of nondescript villages, all such crap.'

'All citizens can't be chiefs. Whom are they going to rule?' asked Alali.

'A question I used to ask myself. But now I've stopped asking. I scan the newspapers carefully. And now, my nose tells me there are millions to be made from the chieftaincy institution.'

Basi threw Alali a copy of the day's newspaper. The latter flipped over the pages and saw men in all sorts of costumes proclaiming themselves to have been installed "chief" by some other chief bearing strange names. He chuckled as he read some of the captions.

'Ugly costumes,' he said.

'What does an accountant or professor in Lagos want with the chieftaincy title of a village to which he never goes?'

'Right,' replied Alali.

'I have the answer. These are rich fools going on ego trips. And we're going to help them on their voyage, Al.'

He stopped speaking, took a cigarette from its pack, struck a match and started smoking. When he started speaking again, his voice was full of excitement.

'Suppose one million men and women buy a title at one naira each? A million naira. Multiply that by ten. A title at ten naira each. Ten million. See what I mean? Everywhere you turn in this land, there are millions to be made!' He stopped and flicked the ash from his cigarette.

'They want to be chiefs, but will they pay for the title?' asked Alali.

'Of course they pay. To some chieftain in the provinces who's strapped for cash. And they buy the space in the newspapers too to advertise their foolishness. They're rich. They pay. They will pay.'

'Will they buy from you?'

'They will buy from anyone. These purchasers of titles don't think. A title is a title. Satisfies the buyer's ego. I have to start selling titles, man. To be a millionaire...'

'Think like a millionaire!' said Alali. 'Where do we start?'

'Right here in our backyard. We'll sell the first title to Madam.'

'Madam? Why Madam?'

'She's a good candidate. If she swallows the bait, you can be sure all others on the Street and beyond will do the same. And it never hurts to start with her. If we fail, we don't have much to lose.'

Alali liked the idea. He wondered when they might be able to start.

'When next she comes here on the routine demand of her rent.'

They did not have long to wait, for Madam was upon them already. She was dressed up most resplendently in her usual high headtie, heavy loin-cloth, red shoes and matching handbag. Madam did dress well. And she looked entrancing.

'Talk of the devil,' said Alali hastily, clearing the plates in which he had eaten.

'Na who you dey call devil?' Madam asked.

Basi knew he had to go after her immediately. It was always dangerous to give Madam the opportunity to speak first.

'Madam, do you look gorgeous! What's up?' Basi asked.

Madam always loved Basi's noticing of her dress. She dressed carefully, whatever else she did not do, spending enormous sums of money on imported fabrics and jewellery. Her beautiful face lit up at Basi's words.

'De members of American Dollar Club dey make meeting today.'

'Is that so?' asked Basi.

'Oh yes. One we member dey make chieftaincy.'

'Al, do you hear that?' asked Basi, motioning to Alali to speak to Madam.

'What?' demanded Madam.

'Basi was saying before you came in that our landlady is the only woman of substance, of real substance on this Street, indeed in Lagos, who's still answering "Madam".'

'Wetin de oders dey answer?' asked Madam.

'They are all Chief Missus. Isn't it so, Mr B?'

'Sure!' Basi quickly answered. 'Madam, anyone who is anyone in Lagos is a chief. Chief Doctor So-and-So. Chief Missus This-and-That. Chief Doctor Missus Up-and-Down. Titles. They wear them like trinkets. As toys in the hands of children. And I ask myself, why isn't my own landlady a chief?'

'If I am chief, 'e go help you?'

'No. But it would help you.'

'By how?' asked Madam.

'Well, you'd be more important in the eyes of all who know you, including the Amerdolians. And of the rest of the world, including your tenants.'

'You go pay all de rents you owe if I be chief?'

'It could make others pay up.'

The Vendor of Titles

'How about yourself?'

'Madam, we are talking about you. What's a few naira rent compared with the possibility of your earning millions?'

'Millions?' asked Madam, her eyes widening. She immediately sat down on one of the chairs, opposite Basi's bed.

'Yes. From contracts, bank loans, import licences, dealerships for beer, cement, rice, et cetera, et cetera.'

'Tell me something!' said Madam eagerly.

'You could even become a Minister,' Basi said, improving the flavour.

'Tell me something!'

Alali added the seasoning. 'Oh yes. I know many people who'd be nobodies if they hadn't taken chieftaincy titles.'

Basi came on again. 'And as a woman, you'll be doubly powerful when you are a chief.'

'True?' asked Madam, wide-eyed.

'Oh yes. You will be doubly powerful. Landlady, chief,' said Basi.

'Tell me something!'

'And you can become a chief right away.'

'Chief of where, Basi?'

'Chief of Adetola Street, of course.' Basi stood up and looked through the window on to the Street. 'You will be the Ade of Adetola,' he said, staring at Madam as if the Street had authorized him to offer her the title.

'And everybody in this Street go come under my power?'

'Sure! We'll all be your subjects,' confirmed Alali.

Madam stood up. She said excitedly, 'You must make me chief as soon as possible.'

'Give me the go-ahead,' Basi said, 'and it will be done.'

'Go ahead!' said Madam, turning to go.

'It's not that easy, mind. There are a few little formalities,' Basi said, moving towards her.

'Wetin be formality? Go ahead, das all.'

'The cost of the title, Madam. Titles cost money.'

'How much?'

'Not much. A small advance will help me prepare for it.'

'How much?' Madam demanded impatiently.

'Say two hundred naira.'

'It's a matter of cash!' said Madam, waving her hand carelessly through the air.

'And that's only an advance. To help me buy the regalia.'

'It's a matter of cash!' said Madam proudly.

'A good investment, Madam,' said Alali.

'You will be happy that you invested in the chieftaincy, Madam. You will be powerful. You will be richer,' added Basi.

'It's a matter of cash!' Madam boasted. She dipped her hand into her handbag and carelessly dropped a wad of notes into Basi's extended palm.

As Basi felt the money in his hands, he said flatteringly:

'Madam the Madam!'

'It's a matter of cash!' Madam replied.

'Proud Amerdolian!'

'It's a matter of cash!'

'The Ade of Adetola!' yelled Basi.

'It's a matter of cash!' said Madam as she left the room, in proud, measured steps worthy of a chief.

The news was all over the Street in a matter of days. And it was received by all and sundry as a matter of course. It did not matter to most people that the title was to be conferred by Basi. No one questioned Basi's right to confer the title. In fact it began to be said that government had given Basi a licence which authorized him to sell the titles. Inquiries began to pour into Basi's "Palace"—discreet inquiries made through friends.

My uncle, of course, did not believe in it all. He attributed it to the prevalent foolishness of the Street which made people believe and do things which, according to him, were stranger than fiction. He dismissed Madam's impending honour with a wave of the hand. He did not see what effect a bogus chieftaincy title, bought by Madam from a con-man would have on anyone. But he was alone on his side of the fence. At least so we thought, until opposition appeared from certain not-so-unexpected quarters.

Since the affair of the mattress, a certain chumminess had developed between Segi and Dandy; as unreal a friendship as might be expected only on Adetola Street. This chumminess was aimed at the destruction of Basi and Madam; thus the chieftaincy title affair which ranged both of them on one side was something of a God-send to Segi and Dandy who immediately saw their opportunity and seized it.

Although Dandy had had some inkling of the affair, he had dismissed it as casually as my uncle had done. It was Segi's presentation which put the proper construction on it. Segi stopped at the Bar one night and asked Dandy if he had heard what was happening. Segi was something of a gossip, and was of interest for that reason.

'The whole of Adetola Street is flooded,' Segi said, as she took her place at the Bar and ordered a drink for herself.

'Oh yes. It's been a terrible flood. Almost ruined the Bar.'

'This is worse than the flood,' said Segi. 'It's an absolute disaster.'

The Vendor of Titles

'Good Heavens! I hope it's not an earthquake?'
'I'm talking of Madam's chieftaincy title.'
'Oh that. It's not important.'
'So you think. But you wait till you know who's behind it.'
'Who can be behind it?'
'Basi, for instance?'
'Hell, I should have known that!' said Dandy, alarmed.
'But that's not my worry.'
'It is my worry,' said Dandy. 'I don't mind Madam taking a chieftaincy title.'
'I do,' said Segi.
'Why?'
'Because she will be too powerful for the women. Too arrogant. I can't stand it.'
'I don't mind that. But Basi behind her is another matter. He won't be doing it for charity, and he won't stop with Madam. Soon he'll be selling titles to the whole country. And he'll grow rich. Too rich for us all. I won't have it.'
'D'you think people will want to buy Basi's titles?'
'You don't know the people of this Street. Vain, useless men and women. Brainless too. They won't do what others are doing. Surzeons overseas are thinking of heart transplants; our own surzeons are transplanting chieftaincy titles. Making Basi and people like him rich overnight. Once Madam is a chief, all the members of the American Dollar Club who are not yet chiefs will go to Basi to purchase titles. How I hate that man and his many schemes!'

So because Dandy did not want Basi to get rich selling titles, and Segi did not want Madam to buy a title for whatever it was worth, a pact was made. By the terms of the pact, Dandy was to dissuade Madam from purchasing Basi's title, and Segi was to dissuade Basi from selling Madam a title. A tall order if there was one.

If anyone was in doubt as to the magnitude of the task ahead, Josco's business visit to the Bar the following day put paid to such doubts.

'Dandy, Dandy!' Josco called cheerfully as he entered the Bar.
'Boy Zosco!' replied Dandy equally cheerfully. 'How's life?'
'Life goes on, man. Care to be a chief?'
'Are you selling chieftaincy titles too?' asked Dandy.
'Yeah, man. Lots of money in it. Mr B's paying me hefty commissions!'
'Hell, I should have known that!' moaned Dandy. 'He'll be very rich soon!'
'Cool!' exulted Josco.
'He'll make millions!' said Dandy, biting his fingers.

'Sure! Lagosians love titles. Chieftaincy titles, honorary doctorates, certificates, beads, toys. Man, they'll do anything for a title from anywhere. Even from a dustbin. You should see how they come after me. All they want to see is that someone has bought a title from Basi, and they'll follow suit. We'll be very rich, Mr B and I.'

'Hell, I should have known that!'

'So, will you buy a chieftaincy from us?'

'I'm not that foolish, Zosco,' said Dandy.

'Come on, man. It need not be a chieftaincy. We can sell you any other title. Leader of the Bar, Doctor of Beer, Architect of Alcohol, anything.'

'Mr B has no right to sell titles to anyone.'

'Who said?' asked Josco.

'I'm saying,' Dandy replied.

Josco looked him over coolly and then sternly handed over a warning whose import could not be mistaken.

'Man, don't stand in Mr B's way. He's going to earn the millions this time. He'll crush all obstacles in his way. Got it?'

'We'll see, Zosco,' replied Dandy.

'Don't say I didn't warn you!' A parting shot from Josco.

'Get out! Vermin of Eko Breeze.'

Dandy began to see what forces were ranged against him and Segi. He began to see that he would have to work very hard to win, having lost on the matter of the mattress. Beaten hands down. He did not expect to lose this time round, or he might be on his way out of the Street. He fortified himself for the contest with great quantities of brandy.

Preparations proceeded apace for the much-expected installation of Madam as the Ade of Adetola. Basi went into Adetola Market and bought certain bits and pieces which he referred to as "the regalia". They included a feather, some chalk, a few beads made of glass and a small tortoise. He made sure that he did not spend a lot of money on these. Thus were he and Alali able to have decent meals for some days.

Madam, for her part, went shopping for the best clothes. Elegant shoes from Paris, coral beads from Italy, damasks from Austria. She shopped with great joy and excitement, inviting one of her closest friends in the American Dollar Club to help her as she made her choice. The day had not yet been fixed – she was going to leave that as a final surprise – nor had she formally notified her colleagues, the Amerdolians. However, she had a time-scale for the investiture – it had to happen before the end of the financial year when a whopping supply contract running into millions was going to be hurriedly awarded to a contractor. Being titled, she had been told by her sponsors, would swing the deal in her favour. She had known as much, even when Basi was making the initial proposals to her. But she was not telling. Crafty she-devil.

At the time Dandy went to see Madam, her arrangements had gone quite far. On the day, she was busy examining the many clothes she had bought, from which one was to be chosen.

'Come in if you're handsome and rich!' she piped out when Dandy knocked at her door. When Dandy entered, she teased, 'What brings you here, Dandy? Don't say you've come for Basi's mattress!'

'Madam, there's bad news,' Dandy replied.

'Bad news? By how?'

'I hear you want to take a chieftaincy title.'

'Dat na bad news?'

'I didn't say so,' replied Dandy. His eyes caught the array of dresses before Madam and he fell to admiring them, oohing and aahing as he felt them in his hands.

'Wetin you mean by bad news, Dandy?' Madam asked him.

'The chieftaincy title, Madam.'

'By how?'

'I think Basi has been deceiving you.'

' 'E don sell my title to anoder woman?'

'No.'

' 'E don sell my title to anoder man?'

'No.'

' 'E chop my money?'

'I don't think so.'

' 'E no wan make me chief again?'

'No.'

'Wetin happen now?'

'Simple, Madam. Basi has no right to sell you a title. For one, he is not a chief. How can he make another person a chief? His title is bogus.'

'Bogus? Wetin you mean bogus? Suppose sef 'e bogus, no be chief still? Bogus chieftaincy, no better pass nuttin?'

'Who recognizes a bogus chieftaincy?'

'Myself.'

'Government doesn't.'

'Dat na government own trouble. Dem go say make I no put "chief" in front of my name? Make I no answer Chief Madam?'

'No.'

'Dere you are!' said Madam triumphantly.

'But you know Basi is doing all this to earn money.'

'So? Dem talk say make Basi no earn money?'

'What about all that rent he owes you?'

' 'E go pay am now wey 'e don begin get money.'

'So why doesn't he use the rent against the cost of the title?'

'Which one concern you inside? De rent na my own. De chieftaincy na my own. Which one be your own inside?'

'Madam, I think you're going to cause trouble on this Street. Before you know a thing, Basi will be selling the same title to all the women on the Street. Zust to create confusion.'

Madam got angry. She stood up. 'Until den,' she said.

'Madam, I see you are determined to get the title.'

'Like iron.' There was iron in her voice.

'I've warned you against Basi.'

'I don hear. Thank you. As far I am the number one woman to be Ade of Adetola, I no mind at all.'

'And if Basi sells the title to others before you?'

'Lef dat one for me. Na me and him.'

'Alright, Madam. But don't say . . .'

Madam did not let him finish. Giving him the short end of the stick, she shooed him out of her lounge and returned to her preparations.

As Dandy passed by Basi's "Palace", he heard Segi's voice. Segi was coincidentally at work on Basi at that same time. She had met Basi admiring the bric-a-brac he had bought for Madam's investiture.

'Basi, what are you up to now?' she had asked as soon as she entered.

'What d'you mean what am I up to now? I'm a busy man,' Basi replied.

'Busy doing what?'

'Laying out plans for making big money. The millions. Segi, the future is bright.'

'So I hear.'

'You better believe it.' He went to take a few more beads from the food cupboard. 'You better believe it,' he repeated, as he returned to his seat on the bed.

'I understand you now sell titles,' Segi said.

'What can I do, my sister? I have to serve society in my humble way.'

'And the best way to serve society is to inflict vermin on her?'

'What d'you mean?'

'What's the point in making Madam a chief?'

'She deserves to be one.'

'Show me how.'

'She's rich, she's a landlady – my landlady – she's an influential member of the American Dollar Club, I owe her money, she's looking for fame . . .'

'Is that all?' Segi asked.

'She's virtually on her knees, crawling in the dust at my feet for the title, and now I've not heard much of the rent I'm owing her.'

'And you think I'm going to be impressed by that story?'

'I don't have to impress you,' replied Basi, looking at Segi with quiet amusement.

'Oh yes, you do,' answered Segi, with as much menace in her tone as she could muster.

'Pray, why?'

'Because, you loud-mouth, you know and I know that you have no right whatsoever to be selling chieftaincy titles. And you know and I know that all I need do is inform the Police and this hovel of yours will dissolve with you into jail.' Segi spoke spiritedly.

The effect of her words on Basi was electric. He received a real shock. He did not like the sound of Segi's voice; he hated the import of her words. He could not bear the thought that all his recent endeavours might have been in vain. He had spent Madam's money, and did not want her to come seizing his mattress and pillow or whatever caught her fancy, once again. His instincts told him to come to some accommodation with Segi. She had wide contacts, and could, if she so desired, be a source of embarrassment. Josco had been doing some brisk business marketing the titles. He had to earn the millions. Segi must not be allowed to spoil things for him.

The mattress affair came flooding back to Basi's fertile mind. Segi cared for him in a special way, he knew; he would have to exploit that feeling to the fullest advantage. He moved up to Segi, and passed his arm round her.

'Segi, don't speak like that, please. You know I've always loved you,' he said in a soft, lilting voice.

'Loved me! Love indeed! And when you strike upon a beautiful, new idea you pass it on to someone else. Love! Ha!'

'Oh, Segi, don't be hard.'

'I'll be as hard as stone. You've wounded me mortally.'

'Let me make amends, please,' Basi pleaded.

Segi considered that for a moment, threw her head away coquettishly, placed her right hand on her elegant hips, rolled her eyes captivatingly and said to the ceiling, 'I demand that you do not make Madam a chief.'

Basi would not hear of it. 'I need the money, Segi. My first million. Once Madam is a chief, all the members of the American Dollar Club will follow suit and I shall be a millionaire. The money will flow. I shall be rich.' He waited a while to see the effect of his words on Segi and then added, 'Exactly what is your objection to Madam's chieftaincy?'

'How will the rest of womankind survive with Madam as a chief? She already throws her weight about enough. And she's not yet titled. The title will ruin us. No, Basi, we won't allow it.'

Basi did not bother to ask who "we" referred to. Women could be really vicious when they meant to be. Segi was not to be underrated, there was nothing stopping her from using her enormous powers of allurement to ruin his plans. He thought fast. The answer came in a flash.

'Segi, I've got an idea,' he said solemnly. I'll make you a Princess.'

'You have a Princess-ship for sale too?'

'I can't sell that. I'm giving it to you as of right.'

'You're trying to bribe me, Basi!'

'No. I love you, Segi. You should be a Princess,' Basi concluded, with a mischievous smile playing on his lips.

She was moved. A faint smile played round her lips. She said she would think about the offer. And they parted on as friendly a basis as may have been expected.

Basi felt sure that Segi would accept his offer. And on this assumption, preparations for Madam's Big Day proceeded apace. Everyone on the Street knew about Madam's approaching elevation, but they paid scant attention. Most knew that Madam was only looking for leverage for extracting certain advantages from government. It was entirely her business. After all, it was a question of the survival of the fittest.

The only exceptions to this general attitude remained Dandy and Segi. Segi's reasons had been clearly stated in her meeting with Basi. Dandy's objections were based primarily on the fact that he had not been offered "a piece of the action", quite apart from the fact that Basi would get very rich. That situation had still not changed. And the rule on the Street was that you were either a part of a scheme or you frustrated it.

Madam's resolve to obtain the chieftaincy title had upset Dandy, although she had unwittingly created a loophole for him to exploit. When Segi finally informed him that Basi had offered to make her a Princess, he saw his opportunity. He urged Segi to accept Basi's offer.

'I won't join Basi's tomfoolery,' she said.

Dandy gave her reasons why she should accept it. It had to do with stopping Madam from obtaining a pre-eminent position among the women of the Street. Dandy felt sure that if someone else had pride of place, Madam's vanity would be tickled and who knew what would happen once Madam was upset?

The day before Madam's investiture was due to be held, Segi went to see Basi to inform him that she was ready to accept the title of Princess. 'Great girl!' said Basi. Ranged before him were the bric-a-brac he had purchased for Madam's show. Beads for her neck, her wrists, her waist. A ragged crown for her head. Feathers for the crown.

Basi adorned Segi with them and stood back to assess the effect of them. Satisfied with her looks, he put some chalk round her eyes. 'All we

The Vendor of Titles

need now is a photographer and some witnesses and you become for all time, Princess Segilola, the lady with the beautiful eyes!'

Dandy walked in at that very moment and feigned surprise at seeing Segi in costume.

'Hey, what d'you know! Segi, you're all done up in lurid attire!' he said, and walked around her in feigned admiration.

'She's now a Princess,' Basi said proudly.

'You've sold her a title too?'

'She truly deserves to be a Princess.'

'And you a multi-millionaire.'

'To be a millionaire, think like a millionaire!' Basi replied, adding, 'Please do us a favour. Go and fetch Josco and Alali; ask them to get the photographer here. Also call Madam to witness this important moment for generations unborn. Quick, Dandy boy!' And he shooed Dandy out of the room. Dandy exchanged looks with Segi.

Dandy did not go in search of Josco and Alali. He went directly upstairs to Madam's apartment and breathlessly told her, 'Madam, what did I tell you?'

'Wetin you want for my house, Dandy?'

'What I told you is already happening!'

'Tell me something!' Madam said, nonplussed.

'Come downstairs to see it all for yourself.'

'Wetin be de trouble?'

'I know you gave some money to Basi towards your chieftaincy.'

'Yes, I give 'am money.'

'You know he's used the money to buy the full regalia for a Princess and has made Segi a Princess?'

'Impo!' Madam said, stamping her foot on the floor.

'Well, he even asked me to invite you and others to witness the investiture.'

'Tell me something!'

'Seriously, Madam.'

'Basi is mad! He is mad!'

'You always said so.'

'I come give 'am my money too, like foolish person.'

'I always said so.'

'I go show 'am pepper. Pepper! Proper pepper!' shouted Madam. And strengthening the tuck of her loin cloth, she ran downstairs, with Dandy close on her heels.

Basi was busy flattering Segi in his "Palace", meanwhile.

'You look really gorgeous, Princess Segi,' he said.

'Thanks, Basi.'

'I'm sure everyone will be here soon and we'll conclude the ceremony. Then we can hold a little celebration, you and I, Alali, Josco and, with a bit of luck, Madam.'

Josco and Alali burst into the room and seeing Segi in regalia, fell to congratulating her.

'She looks regal,' said Alali.

'A real Princess,' said Josco. 'I hope she paid for the title, Mr B?'

'Oh no. Segi's special. The Street deserves a Princess and Segi's been specially chosen.'

'Fantastic!' said Alali. 'How d'you think Madam will take this?'

'Oh, she's happy as a sandboy about her chieftaincy title. She'll see this as a big rehearsal,' Basi replied.

'Madam's vicious and unpredictable,' Alali warned.

'Leave that to me, Al. I can always take care of Madam.'

At the mention of her name, Madam flies into the room like a spirit and assails Basi.

'You fit take care of me, eh? Na so, Basi?'

Basi is taken aback and screams, 'Madam!'

Madam is relentless. 'So you take my money go give dis young gal wey no get work only to go from one man to anoder.'

'Madam!' pleads Basi.

'And na him go be Princess and myself common chief. Which one more important, *wayo* man, Princess or Chief? Ehn? Which one more important. You tink I no sabi anytin? Princess no be daughter of Queen or King? And chief no be common chief? And na me dey pay for everytin. I go show you pepper today, *wuruwuru* man.'

'Madam, the chieftaincy title is . . .'

'No be title I want. Na my money. My rent. Na him I want. Which kain nonsense. You just dey play *wayo* every time. No respect for your mama sef. Give me de money I bin give you.'

'Madam, I used the money for the regalia.'

'Regalia. Regalia. For Chief or for Princess, ehn? Answer me dat one, *wayo* man. Come on, give me my money, now now!'

'I spent it already, Ma . . .'

'Okay. I go take all dese beads and de nonsense you take my money buy. But you must return every kobo after. Foolish man. You dey sell princess and chief. Just wait for me. I go show you pepper. After dis, you no go take anoder woman make *ye-ye*.' And she took everything Basi had bought, including what beads Segi still had on her person.

As for Dandy, he was enjoying Basi's discomfiture. Watching Madam give Basi "pepper" treatment was always a pleasure, and he stood back now, egging Madam on. 'Show him! Show him! Show him!' he cheered her on. When Madam had seized all the beads and feathers and it looked as though she had run out of steam and venom, Dandy said, 'Seize the mattress! Seize the mattress!'

Madam rounded up on him with a 'Shut up, you bungling bum of a barkeeper!'

Such unexpected poetry tripping off Madam's tongue was enough to win her the loud ovation with which the company, including Basi, greeted her closing performance as she swept regally out of the room, her palms glittering with chieftaincy paraphernalia.

Curtain call.

The Contract

Madam's failure to get the chieftaincy title owed a lot to her pride. She did not lie back to bemoan her failure. She preferred the set-back to the loss of any bit of her dignity and of her assessment of herself in her own eyes.

It may be asked why she did not get just any other person to give her a title, take the photographs and have the fact advertised in the newspapers for public consumption. The truth is that Basi was the only man on the Street who had the courage to sell titles. And he was the only one who had sufficient credibility in the eyes of the residents to make a title given locally have requisite respectability.

It soon began to be noised abroad that Madam's failure to obtain the title had severely damaged her chances of winning the end-of-financial-year supply contract for which everyone had been waiting.

It was what everyone referred to as a "megacontract", running, as it did, into almost ten million naira and covering a wide variety of goods, including spare parts for aircraft, tractors, furniture, drilling rigs, pins, clips and toilet rolls. It was the sort of contract which Ministries awarded at the end of the financial year to mop up all unused funds in the Budget – it being a cardinal principle of all civil servants not to allow voted monies to lapse unutilized. If that happened, the Budget for the following year would be slashed, since the Ministry would have demonstrated its total inability to spend money, especially borrowed money. Such a contract was normally awarded in a great hurry, which meant that the conditions for awarding it were fairly haphazard, and normal procedures did not have to be followed to the letter. It was the type of contract officials loved to award, and Amerdolians to get.

The gentleman who had responsibility for preparing the contract papers as well as receiving and vetting the tenders was a Principal Secretary in the Ministry. He was a very powerful man, much in demand and very much courted by all, especially the proud members of the American Dollar Club. Several Amerdolians were often seen in resplendent dresses, shiny shoes and great headties waiting in his outer office. They often waited for hours on end while he negotiated at great length on his telephone or spoke to other young ladies at lengthy meetings in his office. What he discussed was never really known; whom he trusted was his cherished secret; his business partner was entirely his choice. He had a number of them, and they varied from contract to contract. He was a powerful man.

It must be said that Madam was one of his favourite people. Madam was accordingly never seen in his outer office. And he avoided Madam's apartment at No. 7 Adetola Street like the plague. That is not to say that they did not meet. They did. In secret. At a place known to only both of them. What they discussed was always a secret closely guarded by both of them. What else they did at their meetings, no one knows. But Madam was a spinster, extremely attractive and of the best graces. She was ambitious too and the Principal Secretary was not blind.

The only fact which may be released was that he informed Madam that the "megacontract" was likely to be won by a titled person – a chief. No one knows why a chief was preferred that particular year. Government predilections and policies were as seasonal as the weather, as changeable as the weather vane. Chiefs happened to be in season. Maybe that is why all inhabitants of Lagos were buying or assuming chieftaincies at breakneck speed. It certainly accounted for Madam's attempt to purchase a title from Basi.

When that attempt crumbled at the feet of Madam's injured dignity and pride, the Principal Secretary was duly informed of it. In tears and moans. He did not hesitate to ask her to dry her tears. Indeed, he dried her tears himself with kisses and embraces, when she proved too distraught to do it herself. He assured her that they would win the contract. "They" referred to the partnership between himself and herself – if only she met the minimal conditions as advertised. Madam thereupon dried her tears and read the newspapers with necessary attention to detail.

Just as Basi did.

One night as he sat in the "Palace" scanning the newspapers while Alali filled in football coupons, he suddenly jumped up excitedly.

The Contract

'At last, Al. At long last! It's happened,' he shouted.

'What now?' asked Alali.

'The contract to end all contracts. All ten million naira of it. Supply of spare parts for aircraft, tractors, drilling rigs, pins and clips, furniture, toilet rolls. Oh, my God!' he exclaimed rapturously.

Alali was not moved by Basi's expressions of delight. He continued to fill in his football coupons.

'Did they advertise the contract in the newspapers?' he asked quietly.

'Yes,' said Basi, thrusting the particular page of the newspaper under Alali's nose. 'Look, here it is.'

'Forget it, then.' Alali pushed the newspaper gently away. 'The contract's been awarded already.'

'Nonsense!' said Basi, sitting next to Alali. 'It's all here. The forms to be filled in, the requirements, the conditions. How can it have been awarded?' he asked.

'It's all eyewash, man,' Alali said firmly.

'I'm going to win the contract, man. The conditions and terms appear to have been tailored for me. Fill in the forms correctly, produce a Tax Certificate and Certificate of Proficiency in Mathematical Calculations. How many of these idiotic contractors around here can fulfil these hard terms?'

'I bet they can all either produce them or forge them. Who's going to ask?' Alali was adamant; he seemed sure of what he was saying.

'Go to hell!' Basi cursed. 'Your brain's full of football coupons. I'm filling in the contract forms. There are millions to be made, man. Win the contract, sell it immediately, rake in the commission. Ten per cent of ten million and you have a million.'

Alali was not listening any more. Basi went to his bed and settled down either to work or dream.

Madam's voice sailed in from upstairs. 'Al! Al dear! Al!' she called.

They were not sure whether to go into hiding or answer her.

'You heard that? Madam wants me,' Alali said uncertainly.

'What's she up to?' Basi wondered.

'I bet she needs my help. She never said "Al dear" to me ever before. She can't be asking for her rent. Should I go to see her?'

'I don't see what harm that would do. Any idea why she wants you?'

'Maybe she's seen the contract advertisement too,' Alali suggested mischievously.

'She won't dare apply for it. Where's she going to get a Certificate of Proficiency in Mathematical Calculations from? Where will she obtain a Tax Certificate? She'd be silly to apply.'

'I'm sure she'll apply,' said Alali, getting up from his seat. 'And she'll probably win.' He put away the football coupons in the food cupboard.

'Over my dead body,' Basi vowed.

The door flung open and Madam stepped gingerly into the room. She had been eavesdropping on them as usual.

'Your dead body, Basi?' she asked half-humorously. 'Na who go chop all dose millions of naira wey you get?'

'Not you, anyway,' Basi said in an unfriendly tone.

'Thank God. Because na so so debt you go leave behind. *Wayo* man!' She laughed, then turning to Alali, said, 'You no hear I dey call you?'

'I did,' replied Alali.

'Why you no answer now?'

'Madam, you're not my friend,' replied Alali in a surly voice.

'Not your friend? Why? You don forget? No be me dey give you money when you dey make "one-man-contractor" for Adetola Street here? Abi you don forget? Or you tink say I no remember you?'

It was indeed true. Madam it was who had stretched forth her bejewelled hands once from her car and given Alali the five naira note which had elicited from him the joyful shout of "Madam de Director".

Those were in the days before he found sanctuary with Basi. Alali remembered.

Basi wished he did not. 'That's exactly how Eve got the better of Adam,' he said beneath his breath.

Madam heard him faintly. 'No mind Basi, Al,' she said. 'Make we go my house go talk,' she coaxed Alali, passing a friendly arm round his shoulders.

'I'm very hungry,' said Alali.

'Never mind,' replied Madam in a voice that suggested she was going to feed him. Alali appeared to have got the message.

'What is it you want from Alali anyway?' Basi asked.

'Na me and him. Which one be your own?'

'You now want to instigate him against me?'

'By how?' asked Madam. 'You tink you are very important, Basi?'

'I am. A millionaire-on-the-make . . .'

Madam interrupted him. She was getting quite impatient.

'Oh, come on, Al. Make we go. No mind Basi. 'E too dream. Every time, million, million. Kobo sef 'e no get. Dreamer!' And she sighed.

'I? A dreamer? You wait until I get the millions. Just you wait.'

Madam was not waiting. She took Alali by the hand and nipped smartly out of the room. Basi lay back in his bed, preoccupied with his contract forms.

When they got upstairs to her apartment, Madam dipped her hands into her bra and took out a letter which she handed over to Alali. The latter read it and whistled.

'Interesting!' said he.

Madam told him there was a minor problem. Alali quickly guessed it. The Tax Certificate, the Certificate of Proficiency in Mathematical Calculations and the forms. Madam was surprised as to how he knew it. Alali said he had seen the contract advertised in the day's newspaper. He told Madam Basi would be tendering and he was sure to win.

'Ha! ha! ha!' laughed Madam. 'Basi no fit win dis contract.'

Alali insisted he would. Madam dismissed the idea with a wave of the hand. Finally, she appealed to Alali to help her fill in the forms. She gave him a pre-prepared quotation indicating the acceptable prices of the various items. She had obtained the quotations from her partner at the Ministry the previous night.

'Go fill de form for me, you hear,' Madam said.

'And what do I get for my efforts?' asked Alali.

'I go pay you well, no worry. I go give you better chop with wine. Trust me.'

Alali was satisfied and returned to the "Palace" with the papers. He told Basi all that had happened and showed him the confidential figures which Madam had given him on trust. Basi spent the night copying them out on his tender papers. Alali worked hard all night perfecting Madam's papers.

With the forms out of the way, Madam was now faced with the more difficult problems of the Tax Certificate and the Certificate of Proficiency in Mathematical Calculations. Her way round both problems lay with Dandy and Josco, and she duly sent for them the very next day.

Josco was the first to turn up. Past events had made it clear that Madam was not to be trifled with – that her wishes were commands. She told him of the requirement for the contract – the presentation of a tax receipt.

'Easy,' said Josco.

'Wait, my friend,' Madam said. 'Who tell you say 'e easy?'

'You haven't been paying your taxes?'

'Which one concern you inside dat?' asked Madam angrily.

'Sorry, Madam.'

'Better mind your business.'

'What's my business?'

'Anytin wey I tell you to do.'

'Right, Madam. So what d'you want me to do?'

'I want Certificate of Proficiency in Mathematical Calculations.' Madam pronounced it absolutely correctly. She had gone over the name several times with her friend, the Principal Secretary. Just to be sure she had it right.

'You'll like me to fetch you the certificate?' asked Josco with keen interest.

'You see, if I have that certificate . . .' Madam prevaricated.

'The Tax Certificate or the Proficiency Certificate?' interrupted Josco.

'Wetin you tink? I get my Tax Certificate. I dey pay my tax always. Go get me de Proficiency Certificate, *jowo*.'

'It will cost money, Madam,' Josco said.

'It's a matter of cash! Get it quickly.'

'The quicker, the more expensive.'

'It's a matter of cash!'

That being concluded, Josco went on his way to accomplish the delicate task he had undertaken. He met Dandy on the stairs on his way to answer Madam's invitation. They exchanged pleasantries and parted company.

Dandy's meeting with Madam was brisk and to the point. Madam asked Dandy to get her a Tax Certificate.

'Why do the rich always evade payment of taxes?' asked Dandy. Madam ignored the question and pressed on Dandy the urgency of the situation.

'Get me de certificate as you dey get your own, I beg. I know say you no dey pay tax. Still you dey show certificate before you get liquor licence.'

'It costs money,' Dandy warned.

'It's a matter of cash!' said Madam.

'It costs a lot of money. Even more than the tax itself.'

'It's a matter of cash!' replied Madam.

'And you have to pay in advance.'

'No-oh. I no go pay till I see de certificate.'

'Then you'll pay whatever I demand.'

'It's a matter of cash!'

Dandy got suspicious. What was it that made Madam so willing to pay out huge sums of money? She was even willing to pay more money for a forged Tax Certificate than she would have paid to obtain a genuine certificate. Admittedly, the latter would have been a slow, laborious process. No matter. Dandy nurtured his suspicions.

'Is there some big deal going?' he asked.

'Yes,' replied Madam truthfully. 'Big big contract. Many millions.'

'Hell, I should have known that!' yelled Dandy. 'Give me a piece of the action, Madam,' he pleaded.

'When I get de Tax Certificate, you get de action.'
'It's a deal,' said Dandy, simpering with delight.
'I want de proper certificate-oh. I tink you understand?'
'No problem, Madam.'
Dandy went straight to The Man on the Street whose responsibility it was to obtain such certificates from government quarters. The Man was a well-known man, very popular too. He frequented the Bar for drinks and had done well for himself and his family. He was building a new house on the Street, and already had a mansion somewhere in the village of his birth. All his children were in school. God had blessed him. Dandy paid for his services in advance. The Man was a good businessman. He always delivered. On time. His price was not negotiable. In this particular case, he did deliver post-haste. After all, Madam had said it was only a matter of cash. Dandy was sure she would pay for everything, including his commission.

For a time, there was excitement on the Street, on the part of the Company. Whenever there was big money around, there was bound to be increased expectation. Basi was busy finding his way round the problems demanded by the contract. He had his contacts, and although he never ever paid his taxes, was able to meet all the conditions laid down by government for tenderers.

However, he was in for the shock of his life. He told the story to Alali as they sat in the "Palace" in the dark, one night. One of the numerous power cuts had happened. They had no money for candles, and they had decided to go to bed. But it was so hot, they could not sleep. Basi was not only physically uncomfortable. He was in mental agony.

'This place's gone to the dogs, Al,' he said in the gloom.
'Which dogs?' asked Al.
'Dirty, stupid, mad dogs.'
No dogs barked in the eerie darkness. There was only the great silence broken by a singing mosquito darting past Basi's ears.

'I went to submit my tender for the contract this afternoon,' Basi said after a while.

'The megacontract for the supply of aircraft spares, pins and clips, drilling rigs and toilet rolls?'

'The self-same. I fill in the forms, fulfil all the conditions, and I go to submit my bid to the Tenders Board. Know what happens? The Secretary turns me away. Says I'm late. Late! And the contract was advertised only a few days ago,' said Basi, sounding hurt.

'That's what I said. They award the contracts in secret and then advertise. It's all eyewash,' replied Alali.

The mosquitoes sang on in the darkness. Basi and Alali could not see each other. Basi swatted a mosquito and turned round in his bed.

'I'm not going to sit here and see all those millions go into useless hands,' said Basi after a while.

'Useless hands?' asked Alali uncertainly. 'Whose hands?'

'All hands that are not mine.'

A long silence again followed. Even the mosquitoes appeared to be listening now.

'Madam's in on the deal, Mr B,' said Alali after a while.

'Has she submitted her tender papers yet?'

'I don't think so. But she's confident of winning.'

'I'm sure she's behind my failure. I see her finger in it.'

'I think she'll win that contract.'

'How d'you know? Can she meet all the conditions?'

'Looks like,' Alali said.

'Impossible! She can't add two and three. She doesn't pay her taxes. She can't even fill in the forms.'

'I've filled in the forms for her. And she ordered the certificates from Dandy and Josco. And although you are already late, she's still not submitted her tender.'

'I smell a rat. I smell a rat,' said Basi ruefully.

'You can't trust these civil servants. They're up to all sorts of tricks. I bet the Amerdolians know what's happening better than we can ever do.'

'Damn the Amerdolians! As for Madam, just you wait. I'll fix the greedy, arrogant, double-crossing woman! . . . You haven't given her the forms yet?'

'No.'

'Don't give them to her until she's paid you.'

'I won't.'

No more was said that night. Basi slept fitfully all night. He had lost millions that day and felt unusually uncomfortable.

Early the next morning, Alali went to see Madam to submit the forms he had undertaken to fill in for her. Shortly after he had gone, Josco stopped by at Basi's "Palace" on his way to Madam's apartment.

'There are millions in the air, Mr B,' he said.

Basi touched his cap. 'I know. I should know,' he replied. 'Are you in on the deal?'

'Oh yes,' said Joseo excitedly. 'Madam's at the centre of the deal. Asked me for a Certificate of Proficiency in Mathematical Calculations.'

'You've obliged her?'

'For a fee. Yes.'

'Did she pay you in advance?'

'No.'

'She won't pay you.'
'Why not? I worked hard at it.'
'She won't pay you,' Basi said firmly.
'She will.'
'Right.' Basi stopped arguing with him. 'But make sure you don't part with the certificate until she's paid you.'
'Fair enough,' said Josco, gripping the certificate more firmly. And he went off to Madam's apartment.

Where Alali was at that moment in conversation with Madam over the forms he had filled in at her request.

'My dear Al,' she says, 'you don complete de forms?'
'Yes.'
'I hope no mistake-oh?'
'None whatsoever. I went over them with a fine toothcomb twice.'
'Let me see, Al dear,' and she stretches forward her hand to take the forms from Alali. 'Dat's a good boy, a really good boy,' she says as she puts the forms away in her bra.

Alali tries in vain to reach for them, saying, 'They're my property until you pay me.'
'Behave!' glowers Madam. 'You no dey respect your senior?'
'You have to feed me for filling in the forms.'
'After I don win de contract.'
'Before.'
'After.'
'Before.'
'After.'
'That's not fair, Madam.'
'Respect your senior! Commot.'

And Josco enters just in time to hear Alali's next words: 'You will pay for this, Madam!'

'But of course, my dear Al! Hello, Josco. Welcome. Sit down.' And Alali leaves, distraught, for the "Palace" where Dandy had been seeking Basi's professional advice.

'How much do I charge Madam for getting her a Tax Certificate?'
'I knew she couldn't have a certificate,' Basi had exulted.
'She's in on the biggest contract in town. She's going to supply . . .'
'Aircraft spare parts, drilling rigs, tractors, pins and clips, toilet rolls,' Basi interrupted.
'She's given you a piece of the action?' Dandy asked.
'Oh no. She's done everything to keep me away from the contract. That woman!'
'How much do I charge her?'

'A huge chunk of the contract value. Without you, she couldn't make it, could she?'

'Hell, I should have known that!' sang Dandy.

'Don't give her the certificate until she's paid you. You know how greedy and arrogant she is. D'you hear me?'

'Loud and clear,' said Dandy as he set off for Madam's apartment.

He enters the lounge in time to hear Josco telling Madam, 'You will pay for this!' To which she answers, 'But of course, my dear Josco.'

The gravamen of their discussion is that Madam has told Josco she will not pay for the Certificate of Mathematical Calculations until the Tenders Board has accepted it and she has won the contract. All of which drives Josco to the wall. Madam is unmoved by his anger and is happy to see him go. He is too angry to say a word to Dandy.

Dandy fares no better than both Alali and Josco. Madam's last words to Josco have served to disarm Dandy and he is in exuberant mood.

'The task is done,' he announces proudly to Madam.

'Wonderful! Show me.'

'You have to pay me first,' Dandy says.

'Yes, I go pay you. I no for pay you? You sef! Dem write my name on de certificate?'

'Sure! Your name's right there. See!' says he, pointing to her name on the certificate which he still holds firmly.

'From de Internal Revenue Office?'

'Sure!'

'Make I see am. Sweet Dandy. You do well-oh! Make I see am, I beg.'

Dandy gives it to her. 'Look at it, Madam. But you must give it back to me. It's my property until you pay for it.'

Madam takes it, looks at it and seizes it. She promises to pay Dandy after the Tenders Board shall have accepted it and she shall have won the contract. A quarrel develops, but Madam has all the stakes on her side. Dandy leaves her quite disgruntled.

He returns to Basi's "Palace" to find the others mumbling, grumbling and groaning their discontent aloud.

'Pushed me out of her lounge!' grumbles Alali.

'Seized the certificate, put it in her bra and told me to respect my elders,' groans Josco.

'A bad woman, arrogant and mean,' moans Dandy.

'Mean and dirty. I knew she'd refuse to pay,' Basi draws upon his bile.

What to do? None of them appears sure. They are lost. Finally, Basi takes it upon himself to act. 'Right, boys, take it easy. I'll see what I can do. I'll sort her out.'

A week passed and nothing happened. Basi tried to glean as much information as he could as to Madam's intentions. Finally, he gathered that Madam was due to be interviewed at the Tenders Board. The morning of the interview, he called on Madam.

'Come in if you're handsome and rich!' Madam answered in reply to his knock at her door. As soon as Madam saw him, she said: 'You come pay your rent, Basi?'

'It's bad enough bribing the Secretary of the Tenders Board to refuse my tender . . .'

'Wetin you dey talk?' Madam asked.

'. . . But to refuse to pay the boys who've worked so hard for you is criminal.'

'Criminal. Wetin be criminal, you *wuruwuru* man. Look, no waste my time. I get better tin to do dis morning. I get important interview for Tenders Board.'

'And you think the deal is in the bag, right?'

'Oh yes. I sure. Will happen will happen. I finish everytin last night.'

'Last night. I see. You're mighty sure of yourself.'

'It's a matter of cash! Basi. I get better friends, my dear.' And she giggled like a schoolgirl.

'Will you let me in on the deal?' asked Basi in conciliatory tone.

'By how?' asked Madam.

'I'm going to put things fair and square to you,' said Basi. 'For the effort of the boys and myself, I demand a payment of one million naira!'

'One million naira! For doing what?'

'You would not obtain the contract without Al filling in the forms, Josco and Dandy supplying the important certificates, and my supporting them.'

Madam laughed derisively. '*Wayo* man, you too like *jibiti*. Na money go kill you. Commot for my face make I see road, *boh*!'

'You're playing with fire, Madam!'

'Fire. Fire.' And Madam laughed again. 'Your fire don quench. I pour water for am long ago. Long time. Commot. *Wuruwuru* man.'

'I'll show you. As to that contract, you won't get it while I live.'

'You don die finish, Basi. You be proper dead body. If you interfere with my business, I show you pepper. I show you say my name be Madam!' Then, true to herself, she turned an electric smile on Basi. 'If you jus keep quiet till I get the contract, I go give you sometin wey you go like, sweet Basi!'

Basi was not impressed. He went to Dandy's Bar where Dandy, Josco and Alali were waiting for him. He walked in, his face screwed up in disgust. Alali noted his frustration.

'You didn't make any progress with her,' he divined.

'No. She's mean, dirty and arrogant.'

'A double-crosser!' added Dandy, and he spat his disgust to the floor.

'I haven't finished with her yet. Now, what are the facts of the case? She's tendered for the contract with forged papers,' said Basi.

'So they'll find her out. And she won't win the contract.'

'Nonsense!' said Basi. 'You know as well as I do that everyone tendering has forged one paper or the other.'

'I suspect she's done a deal with the Secretary of the Tenders Board. Once he says her papers are right, she'll be on her way to winning the contract,' Josco said.

'And you know what? She told me the deal was wrapped up last night.'

'Hear that?' Dandy asked. 'Wrapped up. Last night. See? Last night. That's the type of woman she is. She'll do anything for money. Anything!' And he spat his spite on the floor.

Certainly, Madam appeared very confident of victory and she dressed accordingly for the interview. This confidence was interpreted on the Street in a way to support Dandy's assertions to his friends at the Bar. My uncle, for one, agreed with Dandy that Madam would willingly do anything for money. But that was the ethos on Adetola Street. Madam had only outsmarted everyone else. Or had she?

She dressed up gorgeously and drove into the premises of the Tenders Board. At the sight of her, the security men and messengers drew smartly to attention and volunteered to show her the way to the Board room. Madam smiled her gratitude to them. Her make-up was perfect, the varnish on her nails matching her shoes, handbag and head-tie. Her blouse was snow-white and her loin-cloth was wine embroidered with gold. So dressed, she surmised that the Tenders Board, the contract itself, would not dare refuse her.

It was a cardinal policy of the business class of Lagos that the contracts you won were directly proportional to the way you dressed and the car you drove. For this reason, most businessmen and women invested heavily on such capital items as clothes, cars and jewellery. Some made sure their offices, if they had them, were also heavily furnished with refrigerators, stocked full with alcohol, and even stereo sets. All other things came after these items. And truly, there was not much else. Because it would have been held foolish of any businessman or woman worth his or her weight in gold, to invest in men and material. Supply contracts, heavily loaded in favour of the contractor and aimed to short-change the government, were the order of the day. And the contractor did not bother to dirty his hands in performance of the contract. He sold it as soon as he had obtained it, creamed off the profit and applied for the next contract or deal. Madam was as familiar with it all, as she was sure that, the financial year ending that very day, the contract would have to be awarded that same day.

No wonder she smiled so happily and waved so gaily to Segi whom she saw on her way to the offices of the Tenders Board. Segi had been out of town and did not quite know what was happening. She repaired to Dandy's Bar to find out.

Psalm 31 lumbered past her as she walked to Dandy's Bar.

The assembled company she met at the Bar was gloomy and distraught. They sat disconsolately, leaving their glasses untouched.

'Why are you all so gloomy today?' asked she.

'There's trouble,' replied Dandy.

'And Madam's ever so breezy, well-dressed and full of smiles!'

'Where did you see her?' asked Dandy.

'Near the offices of the Tenders Board.'

'See what I said?' Basi asked.

'Exactly what is the problem?' Segi insisted.

'Looks like Madam is about to win a multi-million naira contract,' Dandy explained.

'And what's so bad about that?'

Basi was bitter. 'She used everyone here to get there. And just dropped them like toilet paper into the lavatory cistern,' he said.

'Basi!' chastised Segi.

'He can't help himself when the millions slip through his fingers,' said Alali to the amusement of the company.

'What makes you so sure Madam's going to win?' Segi asked after the laughter had died down.

'She's fulfilled all the conditions. Al filled in the forms correctly for her, and she got both a Tax Certificate and a Certificate of Proficiency in Mathematical Calculations.'

'How on earth!' Segi said in total disbelief. 'Madam can barely read and write. And she's a born tax dodger.'

'Sure!' said Alali.

'So how did she get the certificates?'

There was silence in the Bar. Josco and Dandy resorted immediately to their glasses. Alali looked at the ceiling, Basi at the floor. After what seemed like eternity, Dandy said:

'Zosco sorted her out.'

'Josco!' reprimanded Segi, fixing him with a hard stare.

'She didn't pay me, nor did she pay Dandy,' Josco said into his glass.

Segi asked what Dandy supplied. Dandy confessed to having made the Tax Certificate available to Madam.

'You both have a case to answer. But Madam must not be allowed to profit by her trickery.'

'Precisely!' said Basi radiantly.

'But she's definitely made a deal with the Secretary of the Board,' Dandy said. 'And the contract will be awarded today.'

Segi knew exactly what to do, and recognised the essence of speed in the matter. She invited Alali out and they both left the Bar. *Psalm 31* was available and they boarded her to a secret destination.

The company was mollified by Segi's attention, and they would have been quite happy if Josco had not raised a niggling question.

'Suppose they ask who forged Madam's certificates?' he asked.

'They won't ask,' Dandy opined.

'Why not?' inquired Josco.

'Because they are thick as bricks at the Board. Corrupt to the teeth. Anyway, we can always lay it at Madam's door. She ought to know how to wriggle out. Spideress!' said Basi.

'Hell, I should have known that!' Dandy cheered. 'Madam's in the soup!'

They dispersed on that note. Basi invited them over to his place for the evening when he expected there would be news from the Tenders Board. He thought they should be together when Madam returned from her interview.

Madam's interview went extremely well. It turned out that she was the only one whose papers were in order and she was the only interviewee. The questions had been properly rehearsed and she fielded the answers expertly. Everyone present was impressed by her thorough knowledge of import procedures, supply procedures and by the availability to her of funds. Oh yes, she would supply the goods, and did not mind waiting the necessary six months before the slow wheels of government would turn towards the honouring of her invoice. She was consequently awarded the contract.

The sun shone brighter as she walked out of the offices of the Tenders Board, the letter of award in her handbag. The Principal Secretary, her business partner, had ensured that the letter was typed and signed that same day before closing hours. Madam drove back to her apartment with a heart full of song and cheer. She did not notice the potholes on the road. She did not notice the purulent drains. Her world was one happy, sunny afternoon that day. She soon arrived home.

As agreed, Dandy and Josco had repaired to Basi's to await Madam's return. They were all full of hope that Segi's intervention would lead to Madam's disqualification. As Madam passed Basi's "Palace" on her way upstairs, she noticed that Basi had company. On seeing them, she stopped by to pay her respects.

'Great souls,' she piped happily, 'how can I thank you all?'
'For what?' they all asked simultaneously.
'For helping me win the multi-million naira contract.'
'You have won the contract?' asked Basi incredulously.
'Hands down,' replied Madam gaily.
'Advertised yesterday, entry closed the previous day, interview today and you have already won?' Basi mocked cynically.
'Yes. Is all in the bag.' And she waved the letter of award under Basi's nose.

Basi took the letter and read it aloud.

'Fantastic!' said Dandy after the letter had been read.

'And as lady of honour concerned, and winner of multi-million naira contract, I must thank you all for helping me. One good turn deserves another.'

'Great soul!' said Josco.

'Make I go my house go get some cash for all una,' said Madam in her usual pidgin as she turned to go.

Dandy, impressed, flattered her with a 'Madam the Madam!'

'It's a matter of cash!' she replied, and walked majestically out.

Alas! Would it were only a matter of cash! For at about the same time, Segi's letter was hand-delivered by Alali to the Secretary of the Tenders Board. The letter spoke of forgeries and unpaid taxes and mentioned the name of Madam. The Secretary would have paid no attention to the letter had he not seen that copies were sent to the Chairman of the Tenders Board who also happened to be a Minister of State, to other members of the Board and to the newspapers. Upon which he quickly dictated a letter, expressly addressed to Madam informing her that the contract awarded her that same day had been cancelled for certain unspecified reasons. It may be assumed that he did not bother to verify the facts in Segi's letter because he already knew them well. He gave his letter to Alali to deliver to Madam.

Alali waited for some time for *Psalm 31* to turn up. It did not. So he ran the distance back to the "Palace", arriving even as Dandy was praising Madam as a great lady and Basi was bemoaning the fact that she could now afford to be generous. Alali had run a great race, and was out of breath.

'I've submitted the letter,' he said. 'Madam's finished.'

'Finished?' asked Basi. 'Go back, Al, and withdraw the letter immediately.'

'Why? . . . What's the . . .' stammered Alali.

'Don't argue,' commanded Dandy. 'Go and withdraw the letter.'

'Can't be done,' Alali said. 'As soon as I submitted Segi's letter, the

Secretary read it, and quickly wrote a letter cancelling the contract award.'

'Wharahell!' shouted Dandy, holding his head in agony.

'The contract is cancelled?' asked Josco in anguish.

'Yes. Here's the letter of cancellation. It's addressed to Madam,' said Alali, showing everyone the letter.

As Madam's footsteps were heard outside, Basi said to Alali: 'Pocket that letter in the name of God. Madam must not see it!'

Madam breezed into the room and distributed little brown envelopes to everyone.

'Here is the money I promised you all,' she said.

Eagerly, they tore open the envelopes. And seeing that each envelope contained but five naira, they exchanged bitter glances.

'Holy Moses!' exclaimed Basi. 'Al, hand her the letter.'

'What letter?' asked Madam.

'It's from the Tenders Board,' said Alali, handing it to her.

Madam read the letter and collapsed on the spot. Basi and his friends pelted her with her brown envelopes.

And one more great hope on Adetola Street fell on its proud face.

The Bank Loan

'The only reason they speak so glibly about the millions is because they do not understand money. There is no money culture here. We are largely a subsistence economy. Besides, numeracy is a long way away. Few appreciate what a million of anything is, or what it can do, or what can be done with it.'

The voice of my uncle. A voice crying in the wilderness. I did not understand him; no one on the Street would have thought that what he was saying was important. They could not have understood him. No one had ever conceived of a million of any money as something an individual could own, keep and use. My uncle shouted louder to no effect.

He was drowned, in any case, by the voice of government heard regularly on radio and television which proclaimed oil to be a wasting asset. The proceeds from oil were to be invested in agriculture. They ran into hundreds of millions, those proceeds. So said the voice. The people listened, mesmerized. Agriculture. The millions. Hundreds of millions.

The Bank Loan

This was immediately interpreted on the Street to mean that everyone had to be gentlemen farmers. Live on the Street, say you own a piece of land somewhere in the provinces and the banks would pour money on you. Oil was a wasting asset; money in agriculture would make the country prosperous for all time. Many cashed in on the fad, including foreigners. Gentlemen farmers sprang up like *okro* plants in a vegetable plot after the first rains of the year.

It soon became known that Basi was about to obtain a multi-million naira loan from the Bank. No one said what bank. He had formed what was popularly known as a "consortium" of all his friends and they were about to hit it "big, real big".

I met Basi himself one day as we waited for *Psalm 31* at the Bus Stop. This was a very rare occurrence, because our paths never ever crossed. I was going to central Lagos to pursue the formalities for my entry into the University later that year. I do not know where Basi was going to. But he was at the Bus Stop. It was not much of a Bus Stop. There was nothing to indicate that it was a stop. People just stood in a heap between a puddle and the open drain; if there were enough of them pressing to go into one of the yellow buses, that was a Bus Stop. As soon as the bus stopped, they clamoured, fought and battled their way into it, streams of sweat running down their faces and necks in reward for their valiant effort. So many were the people on the Street, so few the buses, that successful bus-riders went into popular lore. The Bus Stop Man was a hero among us.

That morning as we stood at the Bus Stop, you would not have thought that anyone on the Street knew Basi, in spite of his outstanding red singlet with the sobriquet "To be a Millionaire, think like a millionaire", and his blue "Mr B" cap. Yet all the whispers were about him.

When *Psalm 31* drove up, the conductor, dressed in rags, kept up a regular chant of 'Waaf, waaf, waaf', indicating that the bus was on its way to the wharf. We hastily clambered into it. It was while we sat in the bus as it wound its perilous way towards the wharf that Basi and I fell into conversation. Maybe I should not call it a conversation, because Basi spoke all the time or almost all the time!

'I'm lying in bed one morning when my man, Al, comes up to me all dressed and ready to go out. He asks me to lend him a naira. I don't like to lend my millions or any part of it to anyone. So I ask him what he's going to use the money for. He says he has to attend an interview. I think it's one of his interminable searches for a job so I ask him to scram. But when he tells me the interview has to do with millions of money in local and foreign currency, I sit up in bed and prick my ears.

' "Millions," I say, "and you didn't tell me about it all this time?"

105

' "Well, it's a kind of not matured yet," Al says.

' "Not matured yet! Who cares for mature millions?" I ask. "I want to be there when they're conceived and hatched."

'I'm sure Al had wanted to surprise me. But the cat gets out of the bag and he's forced to tell me about a Mr Da Silva.

' "Mr Da Silva," I say. "That's as close to gold as you can get. "What about him?" I ask.

' "He's up to his teeth in money," Al says.

'I don't understand how such a man could be around and I do not know him while Al, my disciple, does. And apparently it's Josco who has introduced him to Mr Da Silva. I'm predictably mad at both Al and Josco. I turn the heat on Al.

' "Why do you hate me so?" I ask.

' "Who said I hated you?" replies Al, visibly hurt.

' "If you don't hate me, how come you hear about millions of money, indeed billions, lurking with a man and I don't know the man?"

' "It's not my fault," Al pleads rather lamely.

'I apply the heat. "How not? Millions are my business, aren't they?" I have now driven the facts home to Alali. He smiles and says, "To be a millionaire . . ."

' "Think like a millionaire!" I complete my favourite slogan for him.

'I know now that Al is on my side. That when he sees Da Silva, he'll be speaking on my behalf. That he will not undercut me. You have to be careful, you see. Because in my line of trade, people undercut you quite easily. On Adetola Street where I live, you cannot trust anyone, not even your closest friend. But Al has justified the confidence I have in him. Since I took him from the Street into my Palace, he has been an asset; in my struggles with Madam over rent, in my general business. He is my ear and my eye. And he respects me too. Which is more than you can say for most friends. So I find him the one naira he needs for his journey to Mr Da Silva's. "Thanks a million," says he.

'Boy, do I like to hear the sound of that word? "Al, I like that," I say to him and I wish him a lucky trip. He goes off and I lie back in my bed to think. But I am too excited by the thought of the ultimate result of Al's trip to rest in bed. I get up, put on my shoes. My shoes are worn now; there is a hole in the sole of the right foot. I will buy a new pair as soon as the millions roll in.

'By the time I've finished dressing up, Josco comes into the Palace. He has come in search of Al, he says. To take him to Mr Da Silva. We shake hands with each other.

'Josco is a pal of mine. The first time he came to the Palace, he was out to trick me and Al. We nailed him and since then he's been with us. He

The Bank Loan

lives under Eko Bridge and is in touch with Lagos life. An invaluable man. But he has to be closely watched. He drinks a lot and is a compulsive liar. But he comes in handy most times. Trust him to know who has come into town with new wealth or new ideas.

' "How's the underworld?" I ask him.

' "Underworld?" he repeats after me, not quite sure what I mean.

' "I mean the world under the Eko Bridge."

' "I've been a bit out of touch with that section of humanity," he says proudly.

' "So what's your new fancy?" I ask him.

' "Mr Da Silva whom I met the other day," he answers.

'I offer him a chair. I have to pry the facts out of him.

' "Well, yes, I did hear you are with him. What's new?"

' "He's big in the banking world."

' "Exactly what does he do?"

' "He's a big financier and consultant."

' "Holy Moses!" I say to myself. Then to Josco I say aloud, "Financier and Consultant! What does he finance and whom does he consult?"

' "You know the new government budget is heavily into agriculture."

' "So I hear. But I'm not interested in agriculture," I say.

' "Why not?" Josco asks.

' "Where do I practise agriculture? In this single, God-forsaken room I hired from Madam?"

' "You must have land in the village."

' "I don't."

' "You could buy land some place around Lagos."

' "Where?"

' "Near Ikorodu, for instance."

' "Does Mr Da Silva have a particular interest in Ikorodu?"

' "No. He's Brazillian," says Josco.

' "So is he going to help me buy land in Brazil?"

' "No,' says Josco. "That's not how Mr Da Silva operates."

'We are getting to the facts now. "How does he operate?" I ask.

'Josco now speaks confidentially. "Listen, Mr B," he says. Everyone calls me Mr B, except Madam. I like the name. Sounds better than Basi, don't you think? And B stands for brains which you need to survive in Lagos. "Listen, Mr B," Josco repeats. "This is top secret."

' "Before you start, let me warn you," I tell him. "I hope this is none of your usual hair-brained schemes." When a man starts telling you something is top secret, you have to be on your guard. When that man is Josco, you need your armour. Josco assures me he is being honest. All he is doing, he says, is assist Mr Da Silva promote his business. That is not unusual. So I take Josco at his word. I ask him to fire ahead.

' "I think Mr Da Silva understands how things work around here. He's in league with some big shots in the big banks," Josco says.

' "Yes?"

' "And counting on government's partiality for agriculture, he prepares feasibility reports for agricultural projects."

' "Good."

' "It works out this way: the would-be borrower gets Mr Da Silva to prepare a feasibility report for a small fee. Mr Da Silva takes the report to the Bank. The Bank is normally happy with Mr Da Silva's reports. They approve the loan. The client gets his millions, Mr Da Silva his commission."

' "And everyone is happy," I say.

' "Cool!" replies Josco, his small eyes darting about the room.

' "So why does Mr Da Silva not write the reports for himself and get the loans?" I ask.

' "He's a foreigner; he cannot borrow money locally. And he's interested in consulting work, not in agriculture. He represents an international financing organization which lends money to the local banks. Mr Da Silva is a complex man, Mr B," Josco says.

' "I see . . . Now, having got the loan through Mr Da Silva, what happens?"

'Josco is scandalized. "Mr B! Do you ask me what to do with money?"

' "I know I can spend it," I say, "but how do I repay?"

' "Repay whom?"

' "The bank which lent me the money."

' "Who repays banks? Never heard of bad debts, Mr B? How do bad debts arise?"

' "On agricultural loans arranged by Mr Da Silva?" I essay.

' "You said it, Mr B," Josco tells me. And he chuckles.

'Josco is incapable of a genuine laugh from the heart. He always chuckles in his throat. I don't find him amusing. But I admire him.

' "Boy Josco! You're a genius. I didn't know there was so much learning going on under Eko Bridge!"

'Josco smiles in self-satisfaction. He likes to be praised. He thanks me.

' "I've been in the thick of things in Lagos for long and I didn't know there was this really easy way to the millions," I say.

' "And many more," Josco replies.

' "You should be very rich soon, Josco."

' "Cool!" he replies and smiles.

' "Now as to the Da Silva man, how does he sort me out?"

' "If you will let me have five naira, I'll fix things."

The Bank Loan

' "Five naira? Is that a fee, a loan or what?"

' "Just my taxi fare to Mr Da Silva and back."

' "You favour expensive modes of transportation these days," I say.

' "It's not my fault," replies Josco earnestly. "Mr Da Silva demands it."

' "I'll pay. Tell Mr Da Silva I require a loan of ten million naira."

' "Yes, boss," replies Josco.

' "And mark you, no tricks. Either from you or from Mr Da Silva. It's in everyone's interest to play fair with me. Otherwise, I'll cut someone's throat!"

'I make no bones of my intentions. You have to be hard or people will take you for a ride. You understand? I give Josco the money he wants and he takes leave of me. It's been a good morning for me, and I am quite happy with myself.'

There was a glint in Basi's eyes as he spoke. *Psalm 31* made slow progress up the Street, unskilfully negotiating the potholes and puddles of water, the street hawkers and idle pedestrians. Sometimes we stopped moving completely, stuck in the snarling traffic. The day was humid, the sun shone brightly and the inside of *Psalm 31* steamed like a swamp. Squashed together on the seats, we sweated. Yet the conductor of *Psalm 31* insisted on finding more passengers. He hung precariously on the rear door which stood half-open to let in the dust and flies and yelled "Waaf, waaf, waaf".

In response to his call, some more unfortunate men and women came to join us. Basi kept everyone entranced, so entertaining was his story. And did the people of Adetola Street like to hear stories! You could see that Basi was basking in the glow of their admiration.

After a short pause, Basi resumed his story.

'Later that day, I went to see my pal, Dandy. You know, the proprietor of Dandy's Bar. Good guy when all's said and done. Former seaman. A real character. Could run the Bar better if he had business sense and stopped looking for other things to do. I don't mind that, though. Makes him want to invest in my ventures. He's forever looking for a piece of the action. Pays readily too. Good man. As soon as he sees me, he greets me excitedly:

' "Mr B!"

' "Good old Dandy!" I answer back. We shake hands. "How's life treating you?"

' "I'm down, not out," says he. "The Bar's empty."

' "Hard times, I'm afraid."

' "It's biting me pretty bad."

' "Not to worry. All will be well."

'Dandy likes that message of hope. It cheers him and when I ask for a shot of my usual, he gladly obliges me. Now because business is not so brisk, he asks for payment. That is unusual between us, but I'm in a cheerful mood and I pay willingly. Dandy serves me his best gin, although I cannot say he does that always to every customer. He genuinely respects me, you know.

'I take a sip of the gin and smack my lips with pleasure. Dandy is watching me keenly and as I put down the glass, he asks:

' "Things looking up for you, Mr B?"

' "There's a God in the Heavens. He doesn't forget his own," I say.

' "Mr B, you've gone poetic!" Dandy says.

' "Poetry is good for the soul," I reply.

'Then Dandy leans across the Bar and asks me confidentially,

' "Tell me the secret of your happiness."

' "I think I'm on my way to the millions at last," I smile.

' "Hell, I should have known that!' Dandy exclaims, adding, "How come?"

' "With the help of Josco."

' "Zosco! Haven't seen the bloke for azes."

' "He's been busy with a Mr Da Silva."

' "No wonder I haven't seen him for azes. What are they up to?"

' "They're working on agricultural loans for me."

' "For you? Do you own land?"

' "Yes and no," I reply.

'This answer does not please Dandy. He frowns, drinks from his bottle and makes faces as though the brandy were bitter. He almost chokes on it. Luckily, he doesn't. Then he says to me:

' "Man, you either own land or you don't."

' "I don't, as such," I say, "but Mr Da Silva's going to sort that out."

' "Is he a landowner?"

' "He is a friend of all the banks in Lagos. They all trust him."

' "And once he says you can have a loan . . ."

' "They give you the money. In millions."

' "Hell, I should have known that!" Dandy sings and I can see the excitement dancing in his eyes. He takes a shot of brandy, sure sign that he will soon be wanting a piece of the action – some of the loan. I'm happy at that, and smile.

' "All you do is give Mr Da Silva a percentage of the loans. And pay for the feasibility report he writes."

' "Hell, I should have known that!"

' "Want a piece of the action?"

' "Sure!" Dandy says.

The Bank Loan

' "You'll have to pay five hundred naira."
' "For what share of the loan?"
' "Well, I've applied for ten million naira. You can have the usual ten per cent of the amount."
' "One million naira!" Dandy yells into the ceiling of the Bar.
'For a moment I think his yell will bring down the roof. It doesn't. I can see that Dandy is totally sold on the idea. I bore into him some more.
' "And you need never pay the money back."
' "Why not?"
' "Because you will have used it."
' "Yes. In expanding the Bar. Buying more drinks. Better chairs and tables. More business, more profits. I can repay."
' "Why d'you have to? It can be written off after a few years."
' "And I need never repay?"
' "Never. That's how people get rich in Lagos."
' "Then I can marry four wives, buy six cars, build ten houses and zust quit this hopeless, cockroach-infested Bar."
' "Take a chieftaincy title . . ." I urge him on.
' "And become a true millionaire at long last!"
'And now Dandy is actually dancing, his way of expressing joy. He twists and turns and gives me five hundred naira, extracted from his right sock which is where he keeps his money. I pocket the money and have a drink. I'm thinking how the thought of earning the million naira has set Dandy dancing. I suppose he wants to be like me. Of course, he can't be. To be a millionaire, he has to think like a millionaire . . . That's easier said than done. However, if he is with me, he'll be alright!'

Basi laughed, child-like, touching his cap. Everyone on the bus was now fully engrossed with his story. And when he paused, they all sighed and chuckled, as though to say, "What a man!"

Unlike Basi, *Psalm 31* is not making much progress up the Street. Indeed, it has not moved at all in fifteen minutes. We are at a loss as to what might be the reason for this. It transpires that a herd of cattle is in front of the long line of vehicles and is taking its time to arrive at its destination. Everyone curses, sitting in their cars or buses, but no one does anything about it. That is quite usual on the Street. When it happens, the leading vehicle tries to find a way, its way, past one of the cattle. This is according to the ethos of the Street, where self-interest, even on the part of vehicles, is the reigning attribute.

The conductor of *Psalm 31* is not worried by the lack of progress. He is pleased by it. It gives him time to fill the bus beyond its allowed capacity. He descends from the bus and keeps up a constant chant of "Waaf, wa. .af, wa. .a. .ff". One or two unwary passengers happy to be rid of the unrelenting hot sun and dust, stray into the bus to the consternation of those of us who are already baking in it. However, each person grumbles secretly. No one challenges the conductor. He has power and is free to do as he pleases until he drops dead. According to the ethos of Adetola Street.

Basi resumes his story. He is as delighted in telling it as we are in hearing him out. He is under the distinct impression that we all admire him. And he appears to cherish that.

'Having concluded the deal with Dandy, I return to my Palace. Al is not yet back and that worries me some. I am pacing the room and looking out through the window at intervals when suddenly, Al bursts into the room. He is looking so cheerful, I do not bother to ask him how he's fared with Mr Da Silva. Something tells me we've hit it big this time. Al confirms my joy. He says Mr Da Silva is dying to see me. Holy Moses! I say I'll go to see him immediately. But Al reminds me I'll need the one thousand naira fee for Mr Da Silva's feasibility studies.

'That poses a little problem. But then I remember Madam, my landlady. She's in the habit of calling on me daily, on the pretext that she wants her rent. She is bound to come in at some point during the day. And I feel certain she will want a juicy piece of the action.

'Al suggests that I contact Segi and appeal to her to speak on my behalf to the Directors of Saros Bank which Mr Da Silva has chosen for my particular loan. Apparently, without Segi saying certain things to them, making them certain promises, the loan might take some time to approve. To save time, I ask Al to go and see Segi. I feel sure she will oblige me. She's a good girl, likes to assist me. Alali leaves on the instant.'

Basi stops talking for a moment, looks round for the bus conductor and says, 'Will you tell the driver I have an interview to attend? We're crawling. If I miss my appointment, there'll be real trouble for both of you.'

'Sorry sah. No be my fault-oh. No be my fault. To God. Na all dis *malu. Malu* jus block road since. Dem go turn now now go dem own and we go move. Sorry sah,' the hapless driver replies.

Basi looks at his watch, mumbles 'Time is money', turns to me with a faint smile and resumes his story.

'I pace my Palace wondering if I should go up to Madam or wait for her to come down. She arrives and starts raising her usual hell about rent paid and unpaid. She orders me upstairs to explain myself. Clever spideress. She wants my company and won't say so honestly. If I know her, she has probably been eavesdropping on us and has heard us speak of my many millions and wants to share in them. Indeed I'm to find out that that is the case.

'I run upstairs after her. And you should have seen her the moment I spoke about Mr Da Silva. Her eyes widened, their pupils dilating orgasmically.

' "Have you heard of him?" I ask her.

' "Yes. Dem speak of am during last meeting of American Dollar Club," she answers.

' "I'm fully involved with him."

' "Impo," asserts Madam.

' "Why?" I ask.

' "Mr Da Silva no dey see person wey no be millionaire."

' "Well, my man Al has held an interview with him on my behalf already. And Josco has gone to fix an appointment for me."

' "Nah so?"

' "It is so," I say.

' "Basi, Basi, 'e get anytin wey you no fit do?"

'I can see that she is impressed. I impress her the more.

' "Mr Da Silva is arranging a loan of ten million naira for me."

' "An agricultural loan?" Madam asks.

' "Oh yes."

' "Do you have land?"

' "I don't," I say. "But you do, Madam, don't you?"

' "Yes. I have a lot of land at Ikorodu," she answers.

'I know then that Madam has indeed been eavesdropping on my recent conversations – with both Alali and Josco. The vixen. She'll want a part of the loan – the better part, I know. More so as she knows we will not be repaying it. I'd be happy to keep her out. But I need her contribution to make up the one thousand naira which Mr Da Silva requires as his fees. So I ask her to join the consortium I've set up. She doesn't trust me and hesitates, probing me with endless questions. She doesn't believe that loans can be obtained so easily. I give her several examples of men who got such easy loans – facts I've got from my friends. She knows the women – members of the American Dollar Club – who have become paper farmers too. What really makes her pay up is when she hears that Dandy has paid and that Alali, Josco and Segi are contributing in kind. But as usual, she demands majority shares.

' "What d'you want?" I ask her.

' "Eighty per cent of de loan," she says.

' "Holy Moses!" I say.

' "And I go pay cash," she says. "No moless."

' "Madam the Madam!" I flatter her.

' "It's a matter of cash!" she says, and pulls out a wad of notes from the folds of her dress. She hands over five hundred naira to me with a warning not to misuse it. I like the feel of the notes in my hand.

' "I love your style, Madam," I say. "When the millions roll in, you and I will celebrate properly."

' "Remember, I wan eighty per cent of de loan," Madam says.

' "Madam the Madam!" I flatter her once again.

' "It's a matter of cash!" she replies.

'Just at that moment, Josco arrives and tells me Mr Da Silva is ready to interview me. I say goodbye to Madam and she wishes me the best of luck.'

Psalm 31 is now mercifully ploughing its dusty way towards the wharf, the herd of cattle having at last left the major road. There is no bus route, so *Psalm 31* takes the longest possible way, dropping off and picking up passengers as it goes. Its exhaust is broken and it makes the most atrocious noises. But no matter. We are on our way. Basi pursues his story to my delight.

'I met Mr Da Silva. A wonderful man. He had a suite at the Eko Holiday Inn. He entertained me well too, with drinks and stories. You could tell that he knows Lagos well. There is not an important name in government, business and social circles he did not reel off the tip of his tongue. And he knew more about them than they knew about themselves. I was very impressed with him. A handsome, well-dressed man of the world. In the end, I gave him his fees of a thousand naira and he made me fill in application forms for a loan of ten million naira from Saros Bank. I signed on the dotted lines, so to speak, and he gave me a copy of the feasibility studies for Basi Farms. We parted on the best of terms.

'For a month or so nothing happened. Segi confirmed he had seen the people at the Bank, yet nothing happened. Segi kept saying that the procedures for getting the loan are normally slow and cumbersome. I had to be patient. All the shareholders in the consortium too. Especially Madam, who was constantly at my throat for her five hundred naira. You'd have thought she had given me five hundred thousand naira, the way she kept at it! I waited, nonetheless.'

'Make sure you stop me opposite the headquarters of Saros Bank,' Basi shouted to the conductor.

'Yes, oga,' replied the conductor.

Psalm 31 laboured on towards the "waa-a-f". Basi pursued his tale. Now there was excitement in his voice. I did not know whether it was because we were getting closer to Saros Bank or because he was getting to the climax of his story.

'Finally, Segi turned up at the Palace. Yesterday. And said she had had a chat with the Chairman of Saros Bank. You know, that girl is really something. There's hardly a place she cannot get to in Lagos; hardly a personality into whose office she does not have admission. At first, I did not believe her.

' "You saw the Chairman himself?" I asked.

' "Yes."

' "What did he say?"

' "The Board have already considered the proposal for Basi Farms," she answered.

' "You don't say?"

' "And approved it in principle," she said in a matter-of-fact tone.

' "Approved it!" I almost jumped from my seat. Yes, I jumped from my seat.

' "Here's the letter of approval," said Segi, handing me the letter.

'I took it and looked at it fondly. It actually bore the logo of Saros Bank. An elegant 'S' written in a globe. And then I read the glorious words. Ten million naira loan approved. Ten million naira! All that remained was for me to have word with the Managing Director of the Bank. To dot the eyes and cross the tees. I fell on my knees and thanked God. Yes, I did. Then I went off to Madam's and showed her the letter. Then to Dandy's. We celebrated all night. I didn't sleep at all. And now here I am, on the way to the office of the Managing Director of Saros Bank and . . .'

Psalm 31 screeches to a halt as Basi is speaking. He gets up and says to me, 'Can you give me ten naira?' Without thinking, I open my handbag and give him a ten naira note. He thanks me and threads his way through legs and knees to the door. The conductor bars his way, asking for the bus fare. I can see Basi point to me. 'She will pay,' he says, and steps gingerly down. He blows me a kiss. As he walks away, I read the letters on the back of his singlet: "Think like a millionaire". Basi's slogan. *Psalm 31* moves off. The conductor demands Basi's bus fare. And I pay.

The rest of the story is fairly well-known by all those who should know it. That afternoon, Segi is the first to arrive at Basi's "Palace". Alali is alone at home, and when she sees Segi, rushes forward to embrace her. There are tears of joy in his eyes. 'At last my tribulations in this city of sin are at an end!' he cries.

'How beautiful!' says Segi sympathetically.

'I'm going to buy myself a Mercedes, have a really good meal, go on a trip round the world, buy myself some lovely suits, and . . .'

Dandy bursts into the "Palace", bottles of spirit under his armpit. He has drunk himself into delirium tremens and barely stands on his feet. 'I heard you, Alali,' he drawls. 'If you get a Mercedes, I'll buy a Rolls. And I'm going to quit that cockroach-infested Bar once and for all; build myself a beautiful house and sleep for six months.'

Close on his heels is Josco. He vows that he will no longer live under Eko Bridge.

'You heard already?' Segi asks him.

'Yes. Mr Da Silva told me. And you know, he's demanding only twenty per cent of the loan.'

'Twenty per cent?' asks Alali. 'Let him have fifty!'

'Ten million! We'll need some trucks to carry all that money from the Bank,' adds Dandy.

'And a football field in which to sit and share it,' concludes Josco.

The applause which follows Josco's words is only stilled by the entry of Madam. She is cheered in raucously with the words 'Madam the Madam', to which she replies as usual, 'It's a matter of cash!'.

'The whole town dey sing wit de news. Members of de American Dollar Club don send me solidarity message tire.'

They celebrated and toasted each other to the endless repetition of Basi's eternal slogan, "To be a millionaire, think like a millionaire". They danced and danced to song after song. They were in such high spirits, they did not know when Basi slipped into the room, his buoyancy of the early afternoon considerably deflated.

At sight of him, Alali shouted merrily, 'Gorgeous B! We made it at long last!' and went to shake hands with him. Dandy came up and offered him a glass of brandy. Madam, Josco and Segi came crowding round him.

With an enigmatic smile on his face, Basi quietly drew Alali aside and whispered into his ear, 'Sorry, mate, there's no loan.'

'No loan?' asked Alali aloud, disbelief registering as loud in his face as there was disappointment in his voice.

'No loan!' echoed everyone in unison.

'No,' said Basi weakly in a low, mournful voice.

'What happened?' asked Madam after a while.

'The Bank wants a collateral.'

'Collateral!' they all shouted.

'What's a collateral?' Dandy asked before Basi could reply.

'Apparently before the bank lends you money, they require that you have more than double what they're going to lend you.'

'Hell, I should have known that!' said Dandy.

'So now they want either one half of the houses on swank Victoria Island or twenty million naira in a deposit account in their Bank.' He almost spat out the last two words, in his bitterness.

The silence which pervaded the room was deafening. While Basi sat on his bed, the others remained on the spot where they stood, transfixed.

'Some people can be mean,' said Josco finally.

Basi shook his head sadly and said, 'To hell with their loans, overdrafts, bad debts and collaterals. What I want is a clean, cool million!'

But what he wanted did not matter to Adetola Street. His words on *Psalm 31* that morning went round very quickly and it was soon said everywhere that Basi had obtained a ten million naira loan from the Bank. His stock rose even higher on the Street. And the number who wanted to be like him increased dramatically. His folk-hero status was definitely in the ascendancy.

When my uncle heard the full details of the story, he said a number of things puzzled him. Who was Mr Da Silva? Was he actually a foreigner or was he a local man working with Josco? But why did not Basi and his friends know that loans needed collateral? Or did they?

But above all, he could not understand how I had ended up not only lending Basi money, but also paying his bus fare!

How could he understand? He had not been on *Psalm 31* with us, had he?

Countertrade

Basi's failure to secure the ten million naira agricultural loan hurt, but it was immediately set aside as one of the exigencies of business. He had lost nothing himself beyond the small sums he had given to Alali and Josco – replaced, no doubt, by the money he had "borrowed" from me on our journey on *Psalm 31*.

Madam was not as mad as she might have been in the circumstances. She was quite unpredictable in these matters. She contented herself with adding the loss to the debts which Basi owed her.

Not so Dandy, for whom the loss of five hundred naira was quite a disaster. It meant that he had lost a huge chunk of his trading capital. And that was no laughing matter. He could hardly replenish his stock, more so as, following a government ban on the importation of spirit, available brandy from smugglers was costing a fortune.

He mulled over his loss for weeks. Determined to drown his sorrows, he sat at the Bar vacantly and had incessant recourse to his favourite drink, brandy.

Josco stayed away from Adetola Street for a long time. He had to, because he did not want to be held responsible for the losses his friends had suffered. Although Mr Da Silva could be said to have fulfilled his part of the bargain, Josco knew that some evil people might suspect him of foul play. He could have earned a commission from Mr Da Silva; Mr Da Silva might have been one of his cronies – a man who led people up the garden path of their stupidity, knowing that in the end, the Bank would ask for collateral security over and above the mere ownership of land, surveyed or not. There were many other possibilities that could have arisen. To keep away from questions being asked was wisdom.

He turned up eventually, at a time when he felt sure that the past would be readily forgotten in the excitement of new, golden and promising proposals. A Greek ship had just berthed at the ports, and if it did not exactly bear gifts, it bore business, multi-million naira business. Which was bound to excite the proud inhabitants of Adetola Street. Josco knew the Captain of the ship, either directly or by proxy, and knew too what sort of business the gentleman was interested in. He decided to share the knowledge with his friends.

Josco stopped by at the Bar one afternoon. Dandy was fairly besotted and hummed deliriously to himself.

'Dandy, Dandy!' greeted Josco cheerfully. 'You're in low spirits.'

'Yeah, the Bar's low on spirit,' replied Dandy.

'You've spirited it down your long throat,' joked Josco.

'No way, Zosco. There's no spirit in town. None. Everything's banned.'

Josco sat on a stool directly opposite Dandy and watched him put the bottle to his lips, and swallow the liquid with a scowl.

'I've got news for you, Dandy. The *Spartacus* has berthed. From Greece. I saw the captain, Mr Spiropoulos. He's got a lot of spirit on board. It's worth two million dollars U.S.'

'Hell, I should have known that!' squawked Dandy. Is he selling on credit?'

'I don't think so. I shouldn't think so.'

'Boy Zosco, go tell Mr Spiropoulos Dandy will buy all the spirit on board the *Spartacus*. All the spirit. On credit.'

'Mr Spiropoulos sells for cash, man.'

'Tell him to sell to Dandy on credit.'

'Mr Spiropoulos will not sell on credit. He may make the offer to Mr B and he will make the millions instead of you.'

'Basi! Impossible! I am the owner of the Bar. I have a licence to sell spirit.'

'Well then, you must make an offer to Mr Spiropoulos,' Josco urged.

'Oh yes. I want to get those millions. Not Basi . . . Will make arranzements . . . You have any samples?'

'Yes.' Josco produced a bottle of cognac from his trouser pocket.

The bottle had an electric effect on Dandy. He sprang to life, clasped the bottle to his chest, raised it against the dim electric bulb and yelled, 'Hell, I should have known that!'

Josco smiled. 'It's going for two naira. And you can sell it for thirty or more.'

'Yeah. That's my type of business!' Dandy kissed the bottle.

'Dandy, Dandy!' shouted Josco, his eyes twinkling mirthfully.

'Yeah!' Dandy replied, and began to stroll round the Bar like a peacock. A myriad possibilities passed before him as he saw himself the proud possessor of the shipload of brandy.

Josco left him in his trance and walked briskly to No. 7 Adetola Street.

It was a bright day and the Street bustled with activity. Pedestrians in flowing robes slouched past, covering their eyes from the billowing dust raised by passing traffic. The market was alive with music, laughter and quarrels. The shops were littered with all sorts of goods imported from different parts of the world, thanks to the easy availability of oil money.

Coincidentally, it was oil Josco thought about as he wended his way to Basi's "Palace" that afternoon. For he had been told that Captain Spiropoulos wanted bunker fuel. And he knew what that meant. Wealth. He knew where to get bunker fuel from – stolen bunker fuel – only he did not have the funds with which to buy it. And Captain Spiropoulos would not pay in advance of the receipt of the fuel. Nor would he advance money, no matter how small a sum, towards the purchase of the goods. He insisted on paying upon delivery. Josco therefore needed Basi and his ingenuity.

Basi was at home patiently listening to Alali's moans and groans of the harshness of their lives.

'All I hear about is the oil boom. But where is it? Boom! boom! boom! but not around the "Palace" here,' grumbled Alali.

'I'm fed up,' confessed Basi. 'But I tell you, one of these days, things are going to boom around here, and we'll be in the millions.'

Basi could be expected to look on the bright side of life, and to spread his infectious optimism to his pupil. Alali caught it instantly.

'To be a millionaire . . .' he shouted gleefully.

'Think like a millionaire!' Basi answered. 'All over Lagos people are making it real big on oil. My nose tells me something's going to turn up pretty soon!'

'How d'you know?' Alali asked seriously.

'Intuition, man, intuition!'

Something did turn up. In the shape of Josco. His cap fixed on his head, his trousers drawn up by suspenders up to his navel, and a rather cautious smile on his lips. He had not forgotten about Mr Da Silva. He hoped that Basi would have forgotten.

'Good Mr B!' he called as soon as he entered the room.

'Boy Josco! Long time no see. What's new?'

Josco was happy. Basi's cheerful greeting was a signal that their friendship had not flagged. And his questioning after novelties meant that Josco's proposals would certainly receive attention. He made the proposals directly, putting it in as palatable a form as possible.

'Care to make a few millions in hard currency?' he asked, settling into one of the two chairs in the room.

Basi did not answer immediately. He turned to Alali and said, 'Hear that, Al? Do I care to make a few millions?'

Alali got up, walked over to where Josco sat and gave him a friendly tap on the shoulder. 'What d'you think Mr B lives for? he asked, a certain note of pride in his voice.

'Well then, here goes,' said Josco, shifting forward in his seat as though he wanted to be as close as possible to Basi. 'Mr Spiropoulos, Captain of the *Spartacus*, a Greek ship which berthed yesterday, needs bunker fuel . . .'

'He can get that from the National Oil Corporation,' interrupted Alali.

'No way! He'd pay through his nose. He wants to buy it on the black market. And he'll pay in dollars, American dollars.'

'Holy Moses!' whooped Basi.

'He needs one thousand barrels of the stuff. One thousand dollars the barrel.'

'A million dollars!' Alali calculated.

'Holy Moses!' yelled Basi.

'And all it costs us to buy it through the back door is fifty thousand naira,' said Josco.

'Holy Moses!' whooped Basi.

'Will you play, Mr B?' asked Josco.

'Play? I'm captain of the team, the winning team.'

'To be a millionaire . . .' cheered Alali.

'Think like a millionaire!' Basi replied, as he did a pirouette.

'So, what do I tell Mr Spiropoulos?' inquired Josco.

'Tell him Mr B is in on the deal. He'll have his thousand barrels of bunker fuel in no time. I'll sort it out. I'll talk to Madam.'

'Good Mr B!' chanted Josco flatteringly.

'That's me!' Basi replied, striking a pose. Then turning to Alali, he said, 'See what I said, Al? . . . To be a millionaire . . .'

'Think like a millionaire!' Alali replied with a loud laugh.

And they fell to congratulating each other with backslaps and handshakes as though they had actually come into the millions. In their estimation, they had.

Cheered by Basi's enthusiasm, Josco retraced his steps to the port to inform Captain Spriopoulos that he had top businessmen on the line to purchase his entire stock of brandy and supply all the bunker fuel he required. On the way, he saw Dandy hurrying towards No. 7 Adetola Street. He was mumbling to himself; his mind, it appeared, fixed on something deep.

When he knocked on Madam's door, she was at breakfast.

'Come in if you are handsome and rich!' said Madam through a morsel of food.

'Madam the Madam!' greeted Dandy.

'It's a matter of cash!' replied she.

'There's a real fast deal going. Millions are involved in it,' Dandy announced.

'Tell me something!' Madam kept her cutlery on her plates and pricked her ears up.

'There's this ship, *Spartacus*. And its Captain, Mr Spiropoulos.'

'*Spartacus*. Spiropoulos. Ridiculous,' said Madam.

'No, Madam. It's "fantabulous". You see, there is no spirit in town. And Mr Spiropoulos has a shipload of spirit. We can earn millions . . .'

'Tell me something!' interrupted Madam, pleased at the thought of the millions.

'. . . if you provide money for buying the entire consignment.'

'And wetin you go provide?' asked Madam.

'I'll sell the goods.'

'Suppose say you use de money? Or you come sell de drink for credit to your friends? Or suppose say you come drink everytin by yourself?' Madam returned to her meal.

'How can I drink up a whole shipload of brandy?' Dandy asked.

'You fit. You be proper boozeman.'

'Madam, the deal is worth millions. Millions,' he emphasized the word. 'It's not a joke.'

'I know. But I no want am.'

'Don't you trust me?'

'At all, at all.'

'Do you want me to make the offer to someone else?'

'You fit.'

'I can't believe my ears,' said Dandy incredulously.

'Dat na your *toro*,' replied Madam, chewing away.

'You are too sure of yourself, woman!' Dandy said with a tinge of anger.

'Na me you dey call "woman"?' asked Madam, getting up from her seat.

'You are a woman indeed and your middle name is "unpredictable". Fancy refusing to earn millions,' said Dandy, thoroughly worked up.

'I no fit do business with boozeman like you. You no know any business at all, at all. Boozeman!'

Dandy got up. The bile rose up in him. He felt insulted, but so full of anger was he, he found no words beyond a flat 'I'll have the last laugh.'

Madam laughed hilariously, got up from her seat, opened her front door and, motioning to Dandy, said, 'Commot for my house, boozeman!' Then she laughed to his face again.

Dandy walked out like a beaten dog, with his tail between his legs. At the door, face to face with Madam, he stared fully at her and emitted a loud 'Get out!'

The smell of brandy hit Madam hard in the face and she turned away, holding up her nose. Dandy slouched off.

Madam had not recovered from Dandy's visit when Basi came in. He had seen Dandy on the stairs, greeted him, but received a stony silence for his troubles. Madam said she was not surprised, and she narrated what had transpired between Dandy and herself. Asked if she had come to an arrangement with Dandy, she laughed and said:

'I dey put food for my nose wey I go do business with boozeman like Dandy?'

'Great soul! Proud Amerdolian! I'm happy you refused to go with him. Because I have a much better offer.'

'More millions dan Dandy?' asked Madam sarcastically.

'Certainly!' replied Basi, taking her at her words. 'And in this case, you don't muck around with goods. As you would say, it's a matter of cash.'

'Tell me something!' said Madam, impressed. The word "cash" always had an effect on her. It turned her on, so to say, unfailingly.

'Captain Spiropoulos needs bunker fuel for his ship. One thousand barrels. And he'll pay one thousand dollars the barrel.'

At the mention of the word "dollars" the proud member of the American Dollar Club started to dance. 'Dollars? American dollars?' she asked as she danced away.

'American dollars. Convertible currency. Can you beat that, proud Amerdolian?' Basi asked, watching Madam with great delight as that worthy wiggled her waist to the sound of dollars rustling in her ears.

'American dollars. Wey dat Captain Spiropoulos sef?' Madam asked, after her dance was completed.

'Right here. In my pockets. He and I are the best of pals.'
'Mr B! You too sabi important person. You be better tenant-oh.'
'Trust me, Madam!'
'Oh yes. I trust you. Why not? American dollars.'
'Madam the Madam!' cheered Basi.
'It's a matter of cash!' replied she.
Dandy re-entered the room and was amazed to find such hilarity in the room he had left stained with bitterness and hatred a while earlier.
'Ah, keeper and leader of the Bar, what brings you back?' asked Basi.
'I've been looking for you,' Dandy replied.
'But I passed you on the stairs just now.'
'I was thinking of other things.'
'Boozeman,' said Madam, and she sighed contemptuously.
'Madam, why are you treating me so harshly?' Dandy asked.
'No ask me stupid question. Why you go come my house come insult me. I be your mate?'
'Insult Madam? Oh, Dandy, you shouldn't do that. You've been naughty,' rebuked Basi.
'Not me. I made her proposals . . .'
'Proposed to Madam?' asked Basi mischievously.
'De man just dey insult me,' hissed Madam.
'I didn't propose to her; I made business proposals,' said the hapless Dandy, feeling himself driven against a wall of hostility.
'A proposal is a proposal,' said Basi, rubbing salt into Dandy's wounds. 'You should know your limits, man. Madam is a proud Amerdolian, you know. She shouldn't be trifled with.'
'Tell am, Basi. Tell de boozeman something.'
Dandy was taken aback completely. 'So what's the new chumminess between you two? Has Basi paid you all he owes?'
'Will you mind your business,' said Basi, advancing on him.
Dandy stood his ground. 'That's exactly what I'm doing,' he replied, staring Basi in the face. Then turning to Madam, he said, 'Madam . . .'
'I don tell you say I no wan do business wit you. Basi and myself we dey supply bunker oil for Captain Spiropoulos. 'E go pay us American dollars.'
'Instead of accepting cash from the Captain, why not accept the spirit from him?' Dandy asked.
'That's countertrade,' said Basi. He had read about countertrade somewhere in the newspapers. He used the term to confuse Dandy, who refused to yield.
'Yes. Countertrade. Everyone's doing it. Let's do it,' Dandy suggested.

'I no trade. I no count. I no counter no trade. I no like boozeman,' said Madam firmly.

'What d'you say, Basi?' asked Dandy.

'I say exactly what my precious landlady says. Countertrade is the pastime of boozemen. I hate it.'

Dandy was thoroughly deflated. He felt frustrated. There was silence in the room for a while as he looked from Basi to Madam and then back to Basi. Then he said limply:

'So you won't go with me?'

'That is the message,' replied Basi firmly.

Dandy turned on his heels and walked slowly out of the room. Loud peals of derisive laughter from Madam and Basi followed him down the stairs – into Adetola Street. *Psalm 31* grunted past in similar fashion.

When Dandy had gone, Basi turned to Madam and said:

'Now to the business in hand. We'll need some money to purchase the fuel.'

'It's a matter of cash!' said Madam as she dug into the cushion of her settee for some wads of currency notes. From behind the mirror which was a central part of the furniture in the lounge, she extricated a shopping bag containing more wads of currency notes. Then from the chest of drawers in the dining room sideboard. She undid the tuck of her loin-cloth, and from a cloth bag which hung down her thighs, she got yet more money. Finally, she dipped her hand into her bra and found more money. She handed the money to Basi who had watched the proceedings first with amusement, then with amazement and finally with great respect for the resourceful woman.

It was a cardinal point with the members of the American Dollar Club that they should never be found without money at home. In that way, no business deal could escape them at any time of day or night. They disdained the use of banks which were an unnecessary impediment in the way of fast deals, the metier of the Amerdolians.

'I tink de money do?' asked Madam after she had handed over the wads of notes to Basi.

'You didn't even count it,' observed Basi.

'No worry. It's a matter of cash!' Madam replied.

'That's my type of woman. And as I always say, to be a millionaire, think like a millionaire!' Basi was beside himself with joy.

'I go surprise de members of American Dollar Club,' vowed Madam.

'Proud Amerdolian!' This from Basi.

'It's a matter of cash!'

'See you soon.' And he floated on air back to his vaunted Palace.

No one could truly understand what power Basi had over his landlady.

Normal people would naturally presume that after the failure of the agricultural loan escapade, Madam would not ever trust her money to Basi. But there she was, yielding more than easily to a proposal that was as light as gossamer. My uncle held that Madam was a thoroughly brainless woman, driven by greed and tormented by her arrogance. If she financially survived all the foolish schemes she had undertaken, it was only because she had the support of such men as the Principal Secretary at the Ministry of Works who constantly plied her with minor supply contracts in return for her feminine favours. But then my uncle had his grouse against her. He could be trusted to discredit Madam who, it must be said, was quite a success on our Street. At least in the eyes of a majority of the residents of the Street, who admired her intrepidity: her ability to use what she had to get what she wanted, as they said.

When Basi got into his "Palace", he found Alali waiting anxiously for him. He reported his signal success and asked Alali to go to the port and check if there was a boat called the *Spartacus* captained by a Mr Spiropoulos in berth. Alali hired a taxi with funds supplied by Basi and soon returned to say that both boat and Captain were real.

As Basi sat in his "Palace" to count the money Madam had given him, Dandy sat disconsolately at the Bar, bleary-eyed and distraught, seeking solace in brandy which he gulped from the bottle.

Josco, having given certain assurances to Captain Spiropoulos, returned to the Bar to find out how Dandy had fared.

'How far?' asked he of Dandy.

'No way!' Dandy replied.

'What do I tell Mr Spiropoulos?'

'Tell him I'm still making arranzements.'

'The ship could sail any moment now. She's almost completed discharging her cargo.'

'It can't sail without bunker fuel.' Then he asked hopefully, 'Or have you supplied the fuel?'

'Not yet,' replied Josco.

'Basi must be waiting for you. He and Madam are in on the deal. Hasn't Basi told you?'

'Not yet.'

Basi walked into the Bar at the mention of his name. He was in high spirits. There was a well-wrapped bundle under his precious armpit. At the sight of Josco, he let out a surprised shout: 'Ah, Boy Josco, so how's our good friend Mr Spiropoulos?'

'He's anxious to leave. He needs his bunker fuel immediately.'

'Well, that's why I've been looking for you. Madam and I are into the deal in a real big way.' Then, prying deep into Josco's soul, he added,

'Now, we're relying on you absolutely.'

'Trust me,' pleaded Josco.

'I would not normally trust you. But I know you won't like to go to jail once again.'

'Not at all. Not at all,' Josco said hastily, his eyes darting about.

'So you won't play any tricks . . . Make sure Mr Spiropoulos doesn't pull a fast one on you, either. You can't trust a Greek sailor, captain, midshipman or whatever.'

'Oh no,' replied Josco.

'There is actually a Mr Spiropoulos?' Basi eyed Josco thoroughly.

Josco went on his knees and lifted his hands to the ceiling.

'I swear before God and man!' he said.

'You may swear a thousand times, I'd still not believe you. However, I had Alali check everything. It's all okay.'

'Cool!' said Josco, relieved.

'So here's the money for the fuel. And be sure you return with the million dollars before the *Spartacus* sails,' said Basi, handing over the bundle of money to Josco.

'Cool!' said Josco as he received the money.

'To be a millionaire . . .' said Basi.

'Think like a millionaire!' replied Josco.

Basi smiled with self-assurance and complete satisfaction. He did not want to leave without a swipe at Dandy whose discomfiture he was enjoying. It was an important principle on Adetola Street that you rejoiced in the misfortune of your friends.

'Well, Dandy, you missed out on this one. Too bad,' Basi shook his head sadly. Then he quickly added, 'By the way, Josco, what's Spiropoulos going to do with all that drink?'

'He'll sell it to someone else.'

'Too bad, Dandy, too bad. I should sell the Bar if I were you. The shelves are empty, the patrons are all gone, cockroaches have taken over; soon the spiders will weave a web around you. Too bad, man. So long.' And touching his cap in mock respect, he walked in his characteristic way out of the Bar.

To all Basi's taunts, Dandy had said not one word. He sat behind the bar, downcast, resting his chin on the palm of his hand, and staring transfixed into space. He was not exactly the fool Basi thought him to be. He, too, had a few tricks up his sleeves, and when brandy permitted, could be trusted to pull some of them from the bag.

He had been thinking, while Basi and Josco discussed. And from somewhere deep in his brains now resurrected the idea he had earlier placed before Madam and Basi, an idea which had been rejected off the cuff.

'Boy Zosco, have a drink,' he said, knowing that Josco would never refuse it.

'Thanks, brother, thanks.' Josco took the glass of beer Dandy offered and had a long draught. He smacked his lips in grateful appreciation.

'Tell you what. You don't have to receive money from Captain Spiropoulos.'

'Why not?' asked Josco in disquiet.

'Take the spirit in esanze for the bunker fuel.' "Exchange" proved difficult to pronounce.

'How do I pay Mr B?'

'We'll pay him after I've sold the drinks.'

'But I have to pay Mr B in American dollars.'

Dandy thought over that for a moment. The answer came to him in a flash. 'I'll sell the drinks for American dollars. Two million dollars. We'll give Mr B one million and split the balance.'

'Cool!' cried Josco.

'How's that with you?'

'I buy the idea,' said Josco. Some other idea came to him and he said slowly, 'But it will take you some time to sell the drinks. Mr B won't wait long for his money.'

'No problem. We'll give him a carton of special dollars first,' replied Dandy, placing enigmatic emphasis on the word "special". 'That will keep him happy until we've sold the goods out and we then pay him in full. I'll give you the cartons of special dollars as soon as you produce a part of the consignment, okay?'

Josco considered the proposal for a moment. He called upon another glass of beer for assistance and having found it, rewarded Dandy with an 'Okay. You've given me some new ideas. It's all right. I'll sort things out. I'll deliver the drinks tomorrow.'

Dandy was so happy, he almost jumped out of the Bar. 'Boy Zosco!' he cried. 'Give me a few hours. By the time you return to the Bar, Mr B's money will be ready.'

'Cool!' said Josco.

It was already night. There were no street lights on Adetola Street. One of the interminable power cuts which were a regular feature of Lagos had come on and it was quite difficult for a pedestrian to pick his way through the potholes and garbage heaps which adorned the Street.

Josco was determined to deliver the money he had received from Basi into safe hands. He was not going to take risks with the money. He did not want to take it to his place of abode beneath Eko Bridge. There were enough bandits there to kill him if they once suspected he had some money on his person or in his house. Nor was Adetola Street without its terrors. Josco took every precaution.

He put the bundle of money between his body and his shirt, tucked the shirt into his trousers and belted up properly. Satisfied that anyone who wanted the money would first have to take his life, he stepped into the darkness, walking swiftly by the headlamps of the vehicles and headed for Segi's apartment on the Street.

As he walked, he looked round, flicking his neck from side to side to ensure that he was not being followed. He prayed that Segi might be home when he arrived.

He soon arrived at Segi's and heaved a sigh of relief. Segi was surprised that he should call on her so late. Josco had never before been to her apartment. Indeed, no member of the circle had ever called on her. She did not ever encourage them to do so. She did not invite Josco in, merely answering him through the parted curtains of a barricaded window. All windows had to be properly protected against robbers and housebreakers. As power was suddenly restored, Segi took the further precaution of switching on the security light which immediately bathed Josco in recognition, his small, wiry frame blown out of proportion by the money he had on his person. Segi was predictably wary of him.

'Segi, the lady with the beautiful eyes! I'd like to see you,' said Josco.

'Any problem?' inquired the lady and her beautiful eyes.

'D'you mind keeping some money for me?'

'Where did you get it from?'

'A cousin of mine sent it. I have no bank account, as you know. And I can't keep the money in my place under the Bridge.'

'Why not?'

'Money and the Bridge are not good friends. I'm speaking from experience. Besides, it's night and anything could happen before I get home.'

'How much is it?'

'I haven't counted it. But my cousin said it's about a hundred thousand naira.'

Segi whistled. 'A hundred thousand naira! Jesus! He must be rich.'

'Very rich!' asserted Josco.

'And he can entrust all that to you?'

'I don't understand money. I wouldn't even know what to do with all that money. So he can afford to trust me. Same as I trust you, Segi.'

Segi was hesitant but Josco's further earnest pleas convinced her he had not stolen the money. She made him parcel it properly and received it from him with a warning that he would have to take back the parcel the following day. Josco promised to call the next afternoon to collect it in person. He might, he said, even call in the company of his cousin, the one who had given him the money for safekeeping.

'Sounds okay,' said Segi. 'I think you are an honourable man, Josco, being so scrupulous with your cousin's money. I wonder why the Police ever locked you up.'

'Justice is blind, Segi. But I'm not complaining.'

'Good night, Josco.'

'Good night, Segi.'

It was a peculiar night for members of the Company. Madam and Basi had a particularly delightful night. For as soon as Basi returned from Dandy's Bar, he went up to Madam and told her that Josco had taken the money and undertaken to deliver on his promises the following day.

'How much 'e go give us?' Madam asked.

'One million American dollars.'

'Wonderful! You trust Josco?'

'Yes. He can't afford to disappoint me. The fear of the Police alone keeps him on the right track.'

'Good. After dis, I tink I must go to America, de house of de dollars. What you tink, Basi?'

To which Basi gave the only answer possible: 'Madam the Madam! Queen of the American Dollar Club!'

'It's a matter of cash!' Madam concluded proudly.

And they celebrated their new hopes with drinks and idle chatter. Even in his dreams, Basi saw the millions assuredly "rolling" into his "Palace".

Dandy did not rest. He went round his cronies asking if they had old dollar notes which they could spare for a while. He was able to get some quantity which, added to the substantial number he had himself, sufficed for his purposes. He then proceeded to assemble all the blank papers of dollar size which he always kept. He made neat, little bundles of the blanks, placed genuine dollar notes first and last in each bundle, and thus assembled two cartons of ostensible dollars. He had little sleep that night.

Josco, for his part, did not sleep at all. As soon as he had deposited the money given him with Segi, he found his way back to his shack under Eko Bridge where he told one of his many friends that everything had gone well. It was safe to deliver the barrels of fuel to Captain Spiropoulos.

'Have you got the money?' his friend asked.

'Yes. I had to leave it at Adetola Street for fear of bandits.'

'Good. Make sure you get it here tomorrow.'

'Cool!' replied Josco.

Had they wanted to, they would have found bunker fuel quite easily on the unofficial market. The men whose duty it was to sell bunker fuel from the government-owned refinery were keener on lining their pockets than enriching an already more-than-rich government. So they normally siphoned off the fuel and sold it at less than a quarter of its official price to the likes of Josco and his friends. The channels of this trade were well-known. But Josco and his friend had a healthy disdain for such tricks.

They had long decided how to deal with Captain Spiropoulos. Having already assembled the requisite barrels, they had filled them with water and then topped them with a little bunker fuel so that the unwary might presume them filled with bunker fuel.

They hired a lorry and laboured all night to have the fuel delivered to Captain Spiropoulos. In return, Spiropoulos gave them almost all the cartons of brandy he had on board the *Spartacus*. They took them to a warehouse, from which Josco took a number of cartons to Dandy's Bar.

By the time this complex operation was completed, day had dawned. Dandy was delighted to have his drinks.

'Boy Zosco, you're wonderful!' he congratulated Josco.

'Thanks, brother, thanks,' replied he.

'I didn't believe you could do it!'

'I knew I'd pull it off easily. Captain Spiropoulos co-operated with me all the way.'

'Is he gone?'

'Yes.'

'When's he returning to port?'

'Before the end of next month. Says Lagos offers him roaring business.'

'Let him roar back immediately. He'll make Dandy a multi-millionaire next trip,' said Dandy.

'Cool! Dandy, you have to sell the drinks fast so we pay Madam and Mr B their dollars.'

'No problem. The big buyers will pay in dollars and collect the stuff. How many cartons in all are there?'

'Five thousand.'

'I'll sell all except those I'm reserving for the Bar before the week runs out. We'll have the dollars ready.'

'Cool! Dandy, Dandy!'

'Yeah! I'll show Madam and Basi what stuff I'm made of.'

'What about the initial dollars to keep Basi happy?' asked Josco.

Dandy took up the specially prepared cartons containing the blanks.

'It's all in here,' said Dandy, giving the cartons to Josco. 'The first and last notes are genuine. The rest are blanks. I bet Basi will be so excited at the sight of the real thing, he'll not bother to check the rest.'

'Leader of the Bar!' shouted Josco, admiringly.

'Yeah . . . Of course by the time he is ready to spend the money, we'll send him genuine money and say our first payment was made in error.'

'Cool!'

'I'm going off right now to see the big buyers. See you soon, Zosco.'

Josco, armed with the two cartons of "special dollars" was already on his way to Basi's "Palace" where, at the rising of the sun, Basi unaccustomedly woke up from sleep. He felt himself tingling with vitality, so hopeful was he that the day would bring to fruition his many ambitions and hopes of the years. He had every reason to believe that the deal he had struck with Josco would succeed. The *Spartacus* was in port, it needed bunker fuel and Josco was in a position to supply it. Madam had given the money for the purchase of the fuel. All was bound to be well. For, in Basi's world, nothing ever went wrong, until it had gone wrong. That was the fashion on Adetola Street.

Alali shared his friend's high hopes and inquired after them loyally.

'Any news of Josco, Mr B?' he asked, as though Basi was bound to have received such news by telepathy or in his dreams.

'I expect him here soon. One million dollars, Al. One million American dollars. Can you believe it?'

'To be a millionaire . . .'

'Think like a millionaire!'

Suddenly the door flung open, and in walked Josco, two cartons on his head. He placed the cartons under his foot and said, 'Mr B, I've brought your wealth!'

Basi was too stunned to speak. But when he finally found his voice, all he said was, 'Great, man, great! I knew you'd perform.'

'Mr Spiropoulos is a man of honour,' said Josco.

Basi opened the carton, took out a bundle, sniffed it, and said, 'This smells nice.' Then he replaced the bundle in the carton and danced round the room. After which he clasped Josco in an embrace and said, 'I could love you for this, man. All my life, I've been waiting for this moment. I knew it would come. I knew! Boy Josco! You're great! Madam should see this right away. Al, go and get Madam.'

'Let's meet at Dandy's later to . . .'

'The right place to celebrate . . . Al, ask Madam to come to Dandy's Bar to collect her millions from me, Mr B.'

Alali darted out of the room and up the stairs with feet of light. Josco darted back to Dandy's. He had not wanted to ask Basi to come immediately. But the latter had chosen to do so in his usual hurry. Josco sensed trouble. Because Basi might ask for the remainder of his money. He might even find out the trick Dandy had played. He panicked right to the door of the Bar. Dandy was in.

'Have you made arrangements to sell off the brandy?' he asked in tremulous tones.

'Yes. Why?'

'Basi and Madam are coming to receive the balance of their money.'

'Really? Why so soon?'

'You know Basi. He wants his money quickly.'

Dandy was silent for a while. Josco's mind darted to the money he had left with Segi. His friend of the Eko Bridge would already be worried that he had not showed up with the money as he had promised. Now his problems were multiplying. He thought of going to get the money from Segi, returning to his Eko Bridge shack and then returning to Dandy's Bar. But just as he made up his mind to do so, in came Basi, Alali and Madam.

Basi bore the cartons which Josco had just given him. They sang and danced to an old song used by the magicians of Adetola Street:

>Come and see America wonder
>Come and see America wonder!

Once they entered the Bar, Basi walked up to Josco and placing his hand on Josco's shoulder, said to Madam, 'Here is the genius of a man. Boy Josco!'

'Cool!' replied Josco, recovering possession of himself.

'How did you feel carrying all that money?'

'I wished it all belonged to me!' said Josco, smiling.

'You no for sabi how to use de money,' Madam intervened.

Dandy stepped into the situation. 'It's a great day for all of us,' he said. 'Look at my Bar. I never had so much drink in all my life.'

Seeing the cartons stacked to the ceiling of the Bar, Basi got suspicious.

'Where did you get all the drinks from?' he asked.

'Mr Spiropoulos did a deal with him,' replied Josco quickly.

'Really?' asked Basi.

'Oh yes. He had to create space in his ship for some bags of cocoa. He was about to throw the drinks into the sea when Dandy offered to take up the stuff . . .'

'He sold it to me for a song,' asserted Dandy.

'A beautiful, soft song that!'

'I can't say I wasn't happy, lady and zentlemen. So why don't we celebrate? The Bar was never so full! And I tell you, when the *Spartacus* returns to port next month, I will be celebrating another million!'

Basi was so impressed by that claim that he let out the loudest 'To be a millionaire . . .' anyone ever heard on Adetola Street. To which they all replied in one voice, 'Think like a millionaire!'

'Let's have the drinks, Dandy. On my account,' ordered Basi.

'Have it on the house! On the house, Mr B!' And he opened one of the cartons delivered by Josco and emptied it of its bottles of brandy.

He was interrupted in his task by the entry of Segi.

'You're all celebrating,' she said in surprise as soon as she saw them.

'Sure, Segi,' answered Dandy. 'Come on, zoin us! Zoin us!'

'What are you celebrating?'

'Madam and Mr B just earned a million dollars and Dandy a million naira,' Alali told her.

Segi frowned. 'Josco gave me a huge sum of money he didn't even bother to count. If I may ask, to what do you all owe such extraordinary fortune?'

'The *Spartacus*, Segi. Captain Spiropoulos,' Alali said.

'That dupe?'

Dandy cut her short. He had poured out the drinks and given everyone a glass. He didn't want Segi to tell stories of dupes and similar reptiles. 'Oh come on, chaps, let's have a drink on the house,' he said.

They raised cheers to the *Spartacus* and her intrepid Captain. Then they raised the drinks to their lips. And all spluttered instantly.

'Holy Moses! What sort of . . .' shouted Basi.

'Coloured water!' howled Alali.

'Poison!' growled Madam.

'Zosco, what did the man give you?' demanded Dandy.

'Dandy, it's brandy,' said Josco.

'Brandy, Dandy? It's poison. Coloured water . . . Mr Spiropoulos . . . You sure? . . . And the money . . .' Basi was incoherent. Several thoughts darted through his mind. He tore open the carton of money Josco had given him earlier and investigated the bundles closely. Then he found the truth. 'It's all blanks! Blanks! Josco, what's the meaning of this?' He held Josco by the throat.

'No, no, Mr B. Please. I'll explain,' Josco squeaked.

Basi had lifted him off his feet. Now he put him on the counter of the Bar and said, 'Quick, quick. Before I throttle you, you blackguard.'

Josco shivered with fright. His lips trembled, his hands shook uncontrollably. 'Dandy's idea,' he croaked. 'I got the blanks from Dandy. We were to sell the drinks given by Mr Spiropoulos and give you the proceeds.'

'He gave you coloured water to sell?'

'I didn't know, Mr B. He tricked me. Mr Spiropoulos.'

'You mean say Mr Spiropoulos play you *wayo*, ehn? Mr. Spiropoulos?'
'Yes, Madam.'

'So Basi, wey my money? Wey my money? Wey my money?' Her voice rose higher and higher as she walked closer to Basi and held his trousers. Basi in turn held Josco by the throat.

'Come on, Josco, tell the truth before I throttle you!' as he increased his grip on Josco's throat.

'No, Mr B . . . Please . . . Please . . .' squeaked Josco, as he struggled fruitlessly against Basi's pincer-like grip on his throat. '. . . Really . . . I did not supply the fuel . . . I gave . . . him barrels of water with a layer of oil.'

'So where's the money?' Basi asked, tightening his grip.

'Segi . . . Segi . . . I gave it . . . to . . . Segi.'

Segi returned the bundle of money to Madam. But Basi was not finished with Josco, nor with Dandy.

'Josco, you blackguard. Think you can con a Greek and con me too? You met your match in the Greek. Now this is my message. Al, give him one on the nose.'

Alali did not need to be invited twice. He punched Josco heavily on the nose.

'As for you, Dandy, I'm going to teach you the lesson of your . . .' But Dandy was not waiting to be taught any lesson whatsoever. He fled into the toilet and locked himself there. Not the shouts, the screams, the threats of Basi and Alali would bring him from there.

Madam and Segi had already left the Bar. Basi and Alali followed later, leaving Josco on one of the chairs nursing his pains.

When Dandy finally essayed out of the toilet, he made for Josco who, quickly divining what was going to happen next, found his quick exit through the front door.

When I called later that night to buy a stout beer for my uncle, Dandy told me he was out of stock. And then he sat me down and told me his tale of woe. I listened attentively and with great amusement which I hid from him.

I was not surprised. I was now used to Adetola Street and its ways. I no longer needed even my uncle's assessment of events. I had begun to see how greed and foolishness could together make fiction of life.

The Candidate

There was nothing predictable on Adetola Street. Morning came as a surprise. And when dusk fell, that was a surprise too. Everyone was used to rapid, unexpected changes which were accepted as a matter of course. That was why when Shala Punta, who lived down the Street, suddenly became very rich, rode three specially-upholstered cars and became Chief Doctor Shala Punta, no one batted an eyelid. That was why no one questioned Basi's claim to be a millionaire. That was why no one expressed surprise when it became public knowledge that Dandy was contesting the seat of Governor of Lagos.

Even the fact of the election, that there was to be an election, came all of a sudden. We were used to frequent changes of government. We'd wake up of a morning and hear a crackling of noises on the radio, hear a voice proclaiming that the previous government had been dismissed for a carefully-listed catalogue of crimes against the nation, the economy and the people. And we would run on the Street, cheer, sing and dance. When six months later the same drama was enacted over again, we would run on the Street, cheer, sing and dance. The men on the stage did not matter. Anyone had a right to be there.

For some time, soldiers had been prominent on the stage. My uncle said the waste-disposal men would be next, and after them the bus drivers, then the barkeepers. Instability was the hallmark of our life. In the words of my uncle, the only stable thing on our Street was the green algaeous water which sat still in a turgid stream in the open gutter running the length of the Street to nowhere.

But stable or not, life on the Street was one long excitement as the most improbable events happened with predictable regularity. There was excitement in the blaze of the colours of the clothes we wore, in the constant cacophony of Adetola Market, in the blare of horns from the likes of *Psalm 31*, in the teeming grass which lined the roads, in the rats which scurried from the garbage mountains into our houses and back to the safety of the garbage mountains. Yes, there was excitement. And money engineered and sustained that excitement, as it sustained our hopes in a brighter tomorrow.

But there was no excitement greater than the fact that power was to be returned to the people. Not that anyone on Adetola Street knew or understood power beyond the fact that whoever had it would make a lot of money. There were enough examples to prove the point to make any doubts unnecessary.

Basi and Company

It was in the nature of Adetola Street that he who was most impecunious at the time should be the most ambitious. And the most acceptable to the people. The manner of it was in character.

After the failure of Basi to get the agricultural loan, a failure which cost Dandy a lot of money; after he had failed to recoup his losses through the countertrade deal, thanks to the smartness of Captain Spiropoulos, Dandy was predictably distressed. As were all other members of Basi's circle. As usual, they kept their counsel and did not meet for quite some time. Nothing disturbed the peace except the faint noises of the coming election. That noise did not as much as stir in Dandy's eardrums. Until Josco came breezily into the Bar one morning.

It was Josco's fashion to arrive with interesting news; such news as would immediately obliterate whatever past differences existed between him and those to whom he brought the new news. That morning, Dandy had the cockroaches in the Bar very much in his mind. He was chasing them from one dark corner to the other, tipping the chairs and tables over in the effort, when Josco came in.

'Dandy, Dandy! What's the matter?' asked he, after watching Dandy unobserved for a while.

Dandy was surprised to see him. He gathered up the chairs and tables.

'Boy Zosco, these cockroaches are too arrogant. They think they're my landlord!'

'Sell them drinks on credit and they'll leave you alone,' suggested Josco facetiously.

'There are no drinks. The Bar's finished, man. Finished!'

'You will have to change occupation.'

'What else can I do?'

'If you've survived all the cockroaches in the Bar, you can go places.' Josco moved to sit on a stool at the bar. 'Give us a drink,' he said.

'There's nothing in the Bar. Can't buy drinks, won't sell drinks,' Dandy replied and chuckled ruefully.

'Dandy, man of the people! True man of the people. Leader of the People's Bar!' Josco flattered him.

It was an unfailing ploy. Dandy fell for it. He served Josco immediately, boasting, 'Dandy's down, not out.'

'Great man! That's why we all love you!' said Josco as he downed his glass of beer in one long gulp. He smacked his lips and drawing closer to Dandy, said to him confidentially so that the walls might not hear, 'The people have decided that you should be Governor.'

'Governor!' howled Dandy incredulously. There was even a hint of alarm in his voice and in the tipping over of the miniature bottle of brandy, his constant companion.

The Candidate

'Relax, Dandy. True man of the people . . . All the boys under the Bridge, above the Bridge, at the wharf; all patrons of the Bar are behind you. They sent me.'

'How can I be Governor?' asked Dandy, still unconvinced.

'How not? Anyone can be Governor. If they win the votes.'

'Can I win the votes?' asked Dandy with some interest.

'Depends on your backers. They get you into the right Party, they put up the money for the show of a campaign, they stuff the ballot boxes, they count the votes, they declare you winner. And you are Governor. Easy.'

'Hell, I should have known that!' declared Dandy, pulling up his trousers from his waist to his navel. 'I should have known that!'

Indeed he should. Because Josco was absolutely right. Josco smiled at the progress he appeared to be making.

'And when I'm Governor?'

'That's another story altogether. Endless dinners and cocktail parties, brandy by the barrel, despatch riders. The sirens flashing past Adetola Street (and here Josco imitated the sound of sirens) frightening the likes of Madam and Mr B.'

'Hell, I should have known that!' said Dandy.

'The only thing to be is Governor. Living on other people's money . . .'

'Free drinks and no taxes.'

'And the treasury will be at your disposal. Madam's riches, all the riches of the members of the American Dollar Club, Mr B's millions. Yours, all yours.'

'I'm Governor already! Boy Zosco!'

Dandy brought out a virgin bottle of brandy from an inner cupboard and served Josco. He watched Josco drink with great satisfaction. When Josco had drained the glass, Dandy said, 'Now to the Governor business.'

'I have it in hand. I'm Campaign Manager.'

'Boy Zosco, I love you!'

'You will love me more when it's over . . . I'm recruiting Mr B and Alali . . .'

'Those bad men! How can they . . . ?'

'Careful, man, careful,' said Josco, interrupting him. 'Don't speak ill of the electorate. They're right until they've installed you in Government House.'

'But the money, who pays?'

'Madam, for instance. She'll get contracts from you afterwards. The boys too.'

'Hell, I should have known that! Madam for sure!'

'Leave it all to me. I will recruit the staff, raise the funds, register you in the Ruling Party, put your name before the Electoral Commission. I will even sign the papers on your behalf. I know how you sign your name, boss.'

'Boy Zosco! You're a zenius. If I become Governor . . .'

'If you become Governor? You're already Governor! So, speak Governor, act Governor, be Governor.'

'Boy Zosco!'

'Cool!'

'I like you!'

'Thank you, Governor.'

'Thank you, my boy.' This in a deep, officious voice.

'Can I have two bottles of brandy? . . . For the boys.'

Dandy produced the desired bottles of brandy with alacrity. There was a new light in his eyes, a new nimbleness to his limbs, a new lease to his life. Josco noticed it.

'People's Governor!' flattered Josco.

'My boy!' crooned Dandy.

Armed with the two bottles of brandy, one in each armpit, Josco left the Bar. He slipped into Adetola Street. A bright sun shone overhead; the harsh, blinding sunlight forced him to shade his eyes with his cap. There was more than the usual bustle on the Street, election fever being very much in the air. Raucous shouts of party slogans and busloads of women singing and chanting; loudspeakers mounted on open trucks blared forth meaningless messages to which no one appeared to be listening. Josco walked fast. Towards No. 7 Adetola Street.

Basi lay in his "Palace", his legs up as usual. Alali had gone to Mama Badejo's *buka* to buy some fried plantains for breakfast. He returned empty-handed. Mama Badejo was not prepared to sell to him on credit. He already owed her more than she could tolerate. When he returned, Basi, guessing what had happened, did not ask. Instead of talking about breakfast, he said, 'Hey, Al, what's all that noise outside? Won't let a man sleep.'

'It's the election campaigns. Some carnival of an election.'

'Pish for the elections!' said Basi. 'Who cares who wins? Same incompetent, corrupt fools.'

'Winner takes all. The treasury, the contracts, the licences, the girls, the madams, the taxes, the licences,' Alali reminded him.

'You have a point there, Al,' Basi said as he sat up in bed. Something had clicked somewhere in his brain.

'So you do care who wins?' Alali said.

'Sure! Could be the difference between my present millions and the future. Between paying and not paying taxes. He has my vote who abolishes taxes.'

'I'm hungry. I'll vote for who abolishes hunger.'

'House rent.'

'Who d'you think will win?' asked Alali.

'Who're contesting?'

'Don't know. Josco might. He's got a nose for such things.'

'Where's he? I haven't seen the fellow for ages.'

Josco walked into the room, an enigmatic smile on his face. He had not seen Basi since the Spiropoulos affair and was not sure how he would be received.

'Mr B!' called Josco enthusiastically.

'Boy Josco!'

Basi was as welcoming as ever. If he bore Josco a grudge, his voice did not indicate it. Basi was not one for bearing grudges, anyway. Seeing the bottles of brandy under Josco's armpits, he said, 'Your arms are full. Been having a good day under Eko Bridge?'

'Not today. Dandy's Bar's afloat.'

'Afloat?' asked Alali incredulously. 'There was nothing there a while ago.'

'There's everything there now,' Josco confirmed.

'Are the Customs people on strike or something? Where did he get the drinks from?' asked Basi.

'I don't know. All I know is that he asked me to give you these.'

Josco placed the bottles of brandy on the centre table.

Basi looked carefully at the bottles. 'Dandy send me brandy? Is he out of his mind?'

'Oh no. He sends it with his love and respects.'

'His love and respects. Hear that, Al? Dandy was always a man to be trusted. A great man.' Basi opened one of the bottles and served himself a drink. 'A great man,' he repeated.

'In every respect,' concurred Alali, as he served himself from the bottle.

'I'm happy you both think so,' said Josco. 'Because Dandy's due to be Governor.'

'Governor? Of what?' asked both Basi and Alali simultaneously.

'City Governor.'

'Dandy. City Governor?' Basi laughed and roared, fell on his bed and kicked his legs in the air. 'The joke of the year.'

'An absolute farce, if you ask me,' said Alali.

'Governor indeed! What put such a preposterous idea into you?' asked Basi of Josco.

'It's not me. It's the boys. They put up Dandy.'
'It's impossible!' said Basi, stabbing the air with his hands.
'Incredible!' said Alali.
'Everything is possible in Lagos,' Josco said simply.
'A down-and-out fellow like Dandy to contemplate being Governor!'
'The man can't even run his cockroach-infested Bar and he wants to be Governor,' Alali complained.
'It's happened before, hasn't it?'
'That a bartender became a Governor?' asked Basi.
'Worse. Court interpreters. Illiterate traders. Actors. Impecunious lawyers. Dandy's better than most,' answered Josco.
'Al, let me have a shot of brandy before I lose my senses,' Basi ordered.

He drank the brandy, then nodded several times. 'There's truth in what Josco says, you know,' he mumbled, as if to himself.

Alali who also seemed to have been thinking of Josco's speech said, 'Mr B, we better get a piece of the action before it's too late.'

'Who would want Dandy as Governor?' wondered Basi.

'All the drunks of Lagos. The patrons of the Bar. Smugglers of spirit. Drug traffickers. Dodgers of tax. Thieves. Put them together and you have more than three-quarters of the adult population of the city,' replied Josco immediately.

'Holy Moses!' Basi said.

'So, Mr B, I propose that you become one of Dandy's backers. Let's sponsor him.'

'And what do I get for my efforts?' asked Basi. This was very important on Adetola Street. You did not do anything, unless you were sure of getting something, money, for it. Josco knew that. He said laconically, 'What do kingmakers get from kings?'

Basi got the point. 'Say no more, Boy Josco, say no more. Al, from this moment onwards, Dandy is our choice for Governor.'

'Perfect,' said Alali.

'When we've made him Governor, we'll help him keep an eye on the government treasury, eh?'

'And land allocations,' said Alali.

'Import licences', added Basi.

'Taxes,' opined Josco.

'Wicked landlords and landladies,' said Basi.

'Liquor licences,' said Alali.

'I say, we shall all be millionaires! Multi-millionaires!' asserted Basi.

'To be a millionaire...' Josco said with a meaningful twitch of his lips.

'Think like a millionaire!' replied Basi.

'We have to register Dandy's papers.'

The Candidate

'Yes, yes, yes,' said Basi. Then he thought better of it and said, 'No. Hold it. I have to speak to Madam. I have to get her interested in Dandy's new career. I have to.'

They parted company. Josco, now he had received Dandy's agreement, had to go and file his papers in the Electoral Commission and to raise money on Dandy's behalf. Basi went upstairs to see Madam. Alali remained in the "Palace".

Life on Adetola Street was a nightmare. Those who lived it were not aware of the fact. But their lack of awareness did not matter. It enabled them to act out their lives, believing that they were living normally. Those who knew that they were not, my uncle, for example, worried themselves to no avail. When to this nightmare was added a dream, such as Josco had engineered in Dandy, the result for the dreamer was either ridiculous or pathetic.

Dandy had become one of the two ever since Josco spoke to him. Believing that he was already Governor as Josco had told him, and resolved to act out the role at Josco's bidding, he paced the Bar, his left hand behind his back, making speeches to an audience which included the cockroaches.

'If you do not obey me, I deal with you. Send you packing. I am the boss. The king. But if you obey, well then, you will be well-fed, well-housed, I will give you free drinks in the Bar. You won't pay tax. Oh no. No tax. And no liquor licence. If you are on my side and I like you.'

As he spoke, he gesticulated wildly, stabbing the air with his right hand, looking directly in front of him and smiling or laughing as the spirit drove him.

He was thus when Segi, on her way to central Lagos, stopped by to see him. She watched him silently for a while and then burst into laughter. Dandy, surprised, turned round hastily and fell down.

'Drunk as usual, eh?' taunted Segi.

'No way, my girl, it's the burden of office,' replied Dandy, rising from the floor.

'What burden?' What office?'

'The office of Governor, my girl.'

'Cut it. When did you start "my girling" me? And what's all this about the office of Governor?'

'You haven't heard? You've been out of town. I'll tell you . . . I'm contesting the election. I'll be Governor.'

'You? Governor of Lagos?'

'It's an open and shut case. I'll be Governor.'

'Stop dreaming, Dandy,' chastised Segi.

Dandy strutted around the Bar like a peacock. He now spoke in a special, authoritative voice summoned from somewhere in his gutturals: 'I know what I know, girl. Everyone's on the campaign trail. Basi, Alali, Josco, all the residents of Adetola Street. It's an open and shut case.'

'You've been nominated?' inquired Segi.

'Sure!' replied Dandy proudly.

'Your candidacy accepted by the Electoral Commission?'

'Better than that. It's going to be a walkover. My opponents have withdrawn. I'm unopposed.' Dandy had begun to invent.

'Dandy!' rebuked Segi.

'Ehm... Segi, don't call me Dandy anymore. It's "Your Excellency". Hope you don't mind.'

Segi took offence. Her eyes flashed fire.

' "Your Excellency", is it? You dreamer!'

'It's expensive abusing a Governor, my girl. That's why I say a woman's place is in the kitchen.'

'Ah-ha, you male chauvinist pig. I thought so. A woman's place is in the kitchen, is it? And yours in the Governor's mansion?'

'Oh yes,' replied Dandy. And he laughed.

'You don't know the power of a woman, Dandy. I'm going to teach you the lesson of your life, you lazy bartender. Just you wait!' said Segi as she swooped out of the room.

Dandy watched her go. 'Zust you wait!' he mimicked her, laughing the laugh of an all-knowing, successful, self-assured man whom no threats on earth could daunt.

Basi was in no such strong position with Madam whom he had gone to visit. As usual with him, he had not one but several plans. He hoped to get Madam interested in contesting the election. In which case, he would become her promoter. This would be better than supporting Dandy whose main backer was Josco. Clearly, Josco had stolen a march on him there, and Basi never did like to play second fiddle to anyone. If he did not succeed in persuading Madam to contest, he would then convince her to put up money for Dandy's candidature. He felt sure that Madam would agree to do so once she knew that she would win hefty contracts if Dandy became Governor. The only snag in his way was the recent failure of their countertrade deal. He could only hope that Madam had forgotten that fiasco.

When he knocked on her door, Madam invited him in with her customary 'Come in if you're handsome and rich!' As soon as he entered, she welcomed him with a 'You done come pay your rent, Basi?'

'Well... Madam... not quite,' asserted Basi.

'I for surprise, *wayo* man.'

'But there's even better news than that.'

'Tell me something!' said Madam.

'The election of the Governor,' said he.

'*Wayo* man. You don start your *wuruwuru* again. You dey look for *awoof* wey you go chop.'

'No, Madam. This time round, the proposal is foolproof.'

'Tell me something!'

'Dandy's going to be Governor of Lagos,' Basi said.

At that, Madam went into stitches. She laughed so long, Basi was forced to tell her that what he had said was not meant as a joke. Still Madam laughed.

'Oh, Madam!' pleaded Basi.

Madam finally wiped her tears of mirth and said, 'How man wey no fit chop, no get money, no dey pay tax go contest and win election?' She went into another round of laughter.

'Anywhere else, Madam, that would be the case. But Lagos is another proposition altogether.'

'Basi, you and your friends, una head no correct.'

'Madam, why not contest the elections yourself? That way, we'll have the millions to spend!'

This drove Madam decidedly round the bend. She had had enough of Basi's millions which never ever materialized.

'Millions, millions, millions! Every time million. Basi, which one you dey? *Wayo* man, no bring your *biribiri* to my house today, you hear? I don tire for your *awoof*.'

'To be a millionaire, you have to think like a millionaire,' Basi said.

'I know, *wuruwuru* man. I don tire for think like millionaire. I tire well well, you hear? When your friend don make Governor, come see me. I go join una chop de money.'

'Madam, you are missing a golden opportunity.'

'Thank you. Go get my rent. Das all I want, you hear? *Wuruwuru* man. God don punish you well well. Go get my rent!'

Basi knew he had lost. Whenever, in the course of any conversation, Madam reverted to the rent matter, there was no taking her away from it. But he was not going to leave her without firing a salvo. Backing towards the door for a quick exit should Madam turn vicious, he said, 'I didn't even think a woman would have the good sense to invest in a rosy future.'

This had the effect on Madam which he had anticipated. She was stung to the quick.

'Basi, you dey abuse me? A woman. Wetin you mean by dat nonsense? Ehn?' She beat her breast and advanced towards him. 'Woman. Myself? Good sense? Na which sense I take build my house? Ehn? Na which sense. You stay for my house without no pay rent, and you abuse me on top. Ah-ah. Woman no get sense, abi? Answer me dat one, *jibiti* man. Answer me. Ah-ah.'

Basi was not waiting to hear any more. He went out of the room in a flash and headed for Dandy's Bar. Dandy was still addressing the cockroaches in gestures and grimaces, practising a campaign speech. Basi entered the Bar and fell immediately to flattering Dandy. He got a free drink for his efforts and went on to press his claims on Dandy.

'Of course, we are all behind you,' he said.

'Thank you, citizen B,' Dandy replied.

'How much do I get?'

'Millions, man, millions. The treasury of the government will be yours.'

'Good. Madam has refused to contribute.'

'That woman! That woman! I'll deal with her.'

'We'll send her into exile, Dandy.'

'Sure!'

'I have organized all my men to work on your behalf. They will be here soon to hear from you directly. You must make them impressive promises. And remember, I'm your right hand man. Forget about Josco. He'll have to take orders from me henceforth. Our Governor!'

'Thank you, worthy citizen,' Dandy replied.

'To be a millionaire . . .' said Basi.

'Think like the Governor!'

They sealed the deal with a handshake and a drink. Basi went to search Josco out, to see how well he had perfected the arrangements for Dandy's candidacy and to organize the projected meeting of "the boys" with the Candidate.

While he was at that, a most important meeting was taking place between two very important ladies who that very day had heard women being insulted openly. Madam was at home alternatively swearing to heap coals of fire on Basi's head and going into stitches at the thought of Dandy being a Governor.

Segi met her in the latter mood.

'Good evening, Madam,' Segi greeted. 'What's so funny?'

'Basi tell me say Dandy wan be Governor.'

'Dandy tells me he is already a Governor.'

'Tell me something!' said Madam, and burst into peals of laughter.

Segi joined her, and they laughed and rolled about until they fell into each other's embrace.

'Dandy asked me to call him "Your Excellency". And he ended up insulting me and all women. "A woman's place is in the kitchen", he told me.'

'Tell me something!' Madam said.

'I stopped by in his Bar, and you should see him playing the Governor or the Candidate, addressing the cockroaches in his Bar.' Segi suited action to word and mimicked Dandy's every action. Madam had another round of laughter. Already, her sides had begun to ache.

'De man don mad well well. Him and him friends. Dem all mad.'

'And he dares to look down on women. Yet women are more than half the electorate!'

This spurred Madam's anger. She was no longer laughing. There was resolve in her voice when she spoke. Arching her brows, she softly but firmly said, 'Dandy no fit be any Governor. At all, at all. Whether Basi dey-oh, or 'e no dey for am.'

'Basi supports him?' asked Segi.

Madam told her what had transpired between Basi and herself, laying the proper emphasis on Basi's insulting remark about women and pouring her venom on his inability to pay his rent. Segi expressed her concern over what the men had planned for all women. It was enough to ruin mankind.

'Dandy no fit be Governor, whether, whether!' said Madam.

'He will be if it's left to the men of this city. There are enough drunks, debtors and tax dodgers to put him in Government House. And they are all together in one Party.'

'Which Party be dat?' asked Madam anxiously.

'The Ruling Party.'

'Ruling Party? Then I must join de Opposition Party.'

'Right,' said Segi. 'Anything to stop Dandy and Basi. Teach them never to insult women, whether they are politicians or not. I must show them the power of a woman.'

'Tell me something!'

'I'm going off now to the Electoral Commission. I'll get the Secretary to go through Dandy's registration papers with a magnifying glass. I'll help him interpret the regulations properly for once. When I've finished, I'll come to let you know how I've fared. Ciao, Madam!'

Segi wiggled out of the lounge. Madam stood transfixed for a while, pondering, no doubt, the necessity for joining the Opposition Party. Up to that moment, she had not given sufficient attention to the elections. Some Amerdolians had joined the Ruling Party. One had even become Leader of the Women's Wing. Madam had not quite liked that. Why should there have been a Women's Wing at all? A Party was a Party. And one, whether male or female, was a member as of right. She had abjured joining for that particular reason. But she had not thought of what she was losing by staying away from the Parties altogether. The contracts.

The millions. Oh, she had to become a Party person. But she was not going to be in the same Party as Dandy. It was now a battle between women and men. Between her contempt for Basi and Dandy, poor, egoistic fools, and the contempt which both men had expressed for women. She decided to join the Popular Opposition Party (POP). She did so that very day.

The procedure was simple. You walked into the local Secretariat of the Party and bought a membership card. It was just a matter of cash. There were no Party manifestoes. And nothing distinguished the various Parties beyond the Party symbols. Madam returned home that day quite satisfied with herself. She would sit back and watch political developments on the Street.

Josco, for his part, was making things happen. There was no shortage of persons willing to invest in a future Governor. There were enough illiterate or semi-literate smugglers wanting a Government that would turn a blind eye on their activity to make fund-raising a joy. Once Basi added his authoritative voice to Josco's, these men paid happily. They were not absolute fools. They paid to anyone who came around to raise funds. It was only wisdom not to put all one's eggs into one basket. Nor were they overly concerned with the Candidate, his track records, his abilities or anything that would normally conduce to the eligibility of a candidate. They knew what being a Governor was all about: disbursement of funds from government coffers to friends, relatives and associates, the award of contracts, the appointment of one's friends to lucrative jobs. That was all. One did not require particular abilities to perform these tasks. Anyone could do them. Everyone could do them. It was a free for all.

So it was that all matters connected with the candidacy of Dandy were completed, including ensuring that he was returned unopposed. Could such a task be accomplished by the likes of Josco and Basi? Everything was possible. What did it require anyway? Someone to bribe the messenger at the Electoral Office to burn the opponents' files. Enough money to fend off any policeman who dared to make inquiries into the "disappearance" of the opponents' papers. Some more money to ensure that if the miscreant was charged to court, the case file similarly disappeared. There were so many other permutations and combinations, all of them original to Adetola Street, as to make the angels weep.

Now, having, as they thought, ensured that Dandy was returned unopposed, Basi, Josco, Alali and a host of lesser denizens repaired to Dandy's Bar where the eminent gentleman was luxuriating in his newfound powers of eloquence and drama. He welcomed them with a ready smile and open arms.

The Candidate

'Your Excellency!' greeted Basi.
'Welcome, honoured citizens and countrymen,' replied he.
'How's His Excellency today?' asked Basi.
'In great shape. God bless you, distinguished citizens.'
'How's it like being First Citizen?'
'Oh, it's a great responsibility. A great responsibility,' in guttural tones.
'You have our blessing, our support.'
'Thank you, fellow countrymen!'
'You heard the good news of course?' asked Josco.
'Yes?' replied Dandy, not having heard the good news.
'About your being returned unopposed.'
'Oh yes. That was always on the books.'
'And his is the only name . . .'
'Of course. What did you expect?' Dandy was in full flow.
'And once you are Governor, we'll take this city in our hands and transform it.'
'There will be no more taxes!' Dandy decreed.
'Yeah!' cheered everyone in the Bar.
'Salaries will double!'
'Yeah!'
'There will be free education!'
'Yeah!'
'Free medical services.'
'Your Excellency!' shouted everyone in full voice.
'All unemployed people will be paid!'
'Governor! People's Governor!'
'New transport systems, electric trains!' And he paused for a while, looked round for effect and added, 'We will air-condition the streets of Lagos, starting with Adetola Street!'
'Our man! Our Governor! Power to the people!' cheered the assembled group variously.
'Citizen Basi, you will be in charge of all contracts!'
'My lord and master!' said Basi with a bow.
'Boy Josco, you will be my deputy!'
'As Your Excellency pleases!' said Josco, going on his knees before Dandy.
'Alali, you will take charge of all hotels and food.'
'Call on me, sir, at all times!' said Alali, doing obeisance.
They lifted Dandy shoulder-high and took him out of the Bar, chanting as they went along Adetola Street, 'Power, Power!' 'Power, Power!' A number of residents seeing the group in celebratory mood, left all they

were doing and joined them with bottles, drums and anything which could make music. Hawkers, traders, bus drivers and bus conductors joined the impromptu carnival. The carnival went the length of Adetola Street, through the entire length and breadth of Adetola Market and returned to the Bar, where there was considerable drinking and dancing until the early hours of the morning.

In due course, Dandy got invited to the office of the Electoral Commissioner. The Commissioner wanted to see the great man who had been returned unopposed. Dandy repaired there in a hurry and what transpired between them will remain a secret for all time. But it must be said that the Commissioner was keen on reminding the Governor-elect that he had "helped" the great man to his new situation. Because on Adetola Street, no one did a job. Everyone was out to "help" the other, and therefore to have recompense in cash or kind in the ripeness of time.

Soon the news was all over the Street that Dandy had been returned unopposed as Governor, officially. This was in spite of the fact that no official announcement had been made. Congratulations poured in to Dandy at the Bar in the thousands. Everyone reminded him of the important role they had played in "helping" him to the new job.

Basi, Alali and Josco had enough time too to savour their extraordinary luck. The "Palace" was a beehive of activity. On one occasion, as Basi returned from a trip to central Lagos, he was heartily welcomed by Alali who was looking forward to his role as the giver of all licences:

'Mr B!' he called, as Basi walked into the room.

'That's me!' answered he, proudly pounding his chest.

'Looks like we've landed in a gold mine this time.'

'Yeah. Gold-digging is my first love.'

'Do you think Dandy will fulfil his promises?'

'Sure! If he does not, someone will have his throat cut. Oh yes. We're in the millions already!'

'To be a millionaire . . .' cheered Alali.

'Think like a millionaire!' Basi replied.

Josco turned up at the "Palace" with a smile and a carton of beer.

'Good Mr B! Hi, Al!' he greeted.

'Boy Josco!' replied Basi. 'How's His Excellency?'

'He's in full flow at the Bar. Says this is the last week of the Bar on Adetola Street. Next week, the Bar moves to Government House. As soon as his election has been officially announced.'

'Yeah!' roared Basi and Alali, setting up quite a commotion which drew the attention and ire of Madam.

She swooped into Basi's "Palace" and demanded silence.

'Which one una dey disturb me like dis?'

'Our candidate has won, Madam,' replied Basi joyfully.
'So?' asked Madam.
'We're celebrating, as you can see,' said Alali.
'Nonsense! Nonsense! Una no sabi anytin.'
'Everything's okay, Madam,' replied Josco. 'Dandy won't forget you,' he teased.
'Shurrup, you! Wey dat your Dandy sef?'
'Don't call him Dandy anymore. He is "Your Excellency",' Basi interposed.
'Commot for my face. Wetin be Excellency? Make I warn una. If I hear more noise, I go drive all of una from my house ... You Basi, you no fit pay your rent till now; na only *wahala* you fit make, *jibiti* man.'

She left the room, quite flustered. She had expected that Segi would have voided Dandy's candidature. As she had not seen Segi for some time, the rumours of Dandy's easy election filled her with foreboding.

But she did not have to worry. Segi was saving her blow for the moment when it would hurt most. Two days before the official announcement of Dandy's election was due to be made, she called on the Electoral Commissioner and firmly demanded to be shown Dandy's registration papers.

The Commissioner was completely taken aback. No one in Lagos dared exercise this right. They were too frightened of authority to demand their rights. But the young woman who sat in front of him appeared quite adamant. And her mesmerizing beauty demanded that he attend to her.

He brought out Dandy's file from his drawer.

'He's been returned unopposed. The announcement will be made in two days.'

'Are all his papers in order?' asked Segi, fixing the Commissioner with eyes of steel.

'Yes,' said the Commissioner, shifting uneasily in his seat.

'I don't think so,' said Segi firmly.

'How d'you know?' asked the Commissioner, leafing through the files absent-mindedly.

'I'm sure of it. I'm sure he does not have a Tax Certificate.'

'Tax Certificate? Tax Certificate?' The Commissioner turned the pages of the file over and over again. He began to sweat. 'I thought ... I thought ... No, it's not here. I thought ...'

'Never mind what you thought, Mr. Commissioner. I'm now going to leave you to do what you should do. And please, no tricks.'

With that, she got up and walked silently out of the room. The

Commissioner called his subordinates and gave them definitive instructions.

The day prior to the date of the announcement of Dandy's election finally arrived to considerable merriment and noise making on Adetola Street. An elaborate binge had been planned to take place in Basi's "Palace" in honour of the Governor-elect. Basi had made sure that Madam and Segi were invited.

The party started well enough, with Basi, Josco and Alali in the best of spirits. Others soon joined them. Before the party, Segi called on Madam and assured her that she had made the Electoral Commission scrutinize Dandy's registration papers and that a Tax Certificate not being among the papers, and it being mandatory that all candidates file such certificates to indicate a minimal responsible citizenship, she was sure his candidacy would be voided that evening at the latest. Madam therefore turned up at the party in the company of Segi.

Dandy made a dramatic entry, dressed in his best suit and in his usual bowler hat. He was in excellent spirits. His presence in the "Palace" was greeted by shouts of "Excellency! Excellency!!" He acknowledged the greetings with a victory sign.

'Come on, Gov, have a drink with us,' said Basi, pressing a glass into his hands. Then he raised his glass and said, 'To the health of the Governor!'

'Yeah!' shouted the crowd.

'Thank you, ladies and gentlemen,' said Dandy after the cheers had died down. 'Thank you. Tomorrow, I leave for Government House. I promise you, as Governor, I will run an open government. Open government!' He smiled and received the cheers gracefully. Then calling for silence, he announced, 'Josco, Basi and Alali will be Ministers.'

This was greeted with loud cheers, laughter and aplomb. The three Ministers-to-be received congratulations all round and drinks were passed round.

On this happy scene there now intruded an unknown face.

'Mr. Dandy, sah,' the face said.

'Yes. Come in, my boy!' invited Dandy.

'A letter from the Electoral Commission, sah,' said the face, handing over the envelope to him.

'Thank you,' said Dandy. 'That's my Certificate of Election. The Commissioner was to send it. Alali, read it,' he said, handing him the envelope.

Alali tore it open and read the letter. His face immediately soured.

'Your Excellency,' he called softly, turning to Dandy.

'Go on, read it aloud. I run an open government. Read it to everyone's hearing. It's a people's government.'

This remarkable speech was cheered with shouts of "Power! Power!!"

Alali read aloud. ' "Mr Dandy of Dandy's Bar, I am directed to inform you that one condition for contesting the election is the presentation of a Tax Certificate . . ." '

'Tax Certificate!' echoed Basi and Josco together.

Madam and Segi exchanged glances.

Alali read on. ' "We have now discovered that you did not file a Tax Certificate. Nor is your name on the Tax Register . . ." '

'Holy Moses!' bellowed Basi. He knew the implications of the "discovery".

' "In the event, we have no option but to annul your candidature until we have evidence to the contrary." '

Dandy collapsed spastically in a heap on the floor of the "Palace". He had to be revived with his favourite brandy. Madam and Segi exchanged broad smiles. The crowd gradually thinned out of the "Palace". Dandy sat up. When he spoke, his voice was low and trembled with emotion.

'They want a Tax Certificate, Zosco,' he said, looking miserably at Josco.

'So it seems,' Josco replied, equally miserably.

'I cannot borrow one from you, Mr B?'

'No.'

'Nor you, Alali?'

'I'm jobless, Dandy, I don't pay taxes.'

The two ladies giggled.

'How about you, Zosco?' asked Dandy.

'I don't pay taxes,' Josco replied.

'So that's it, gentlemen. We will fight another day.'

The two ladies laughed.

'It's back to the Bar, Dandy,' said Segi triumphantly. 'You're down, man.'

'Down, but not out . . .' said Dandy, getting up from the floor and wiping the dust off his clothes. 'Who cares to be Governor? All that trouble and hard work. Men and women telling you lies all the time. Who cares? It's better to run the Bar.'

'Dat cockroach Bar,' said Madam, as she and Segi walked provocatively past Dandy and out of the "Palace".

'Get out!' howled Dandy in a voice that could be heard miles away.

Basi, Alali and Josco remained silent, tongue-tied.

The Party Secretary

Dandy's failure to win the gubernatorial election did not make waves on the Street. My uncle had watched the improbability with deep misgivings. He was relieved when, as he had wished, Dandy crashed out of the race. Segi's intervention may have ruined Dandy and his friends. Worse men were indeed elected to become Governors elsewhere. Some of them could not read and write. No one thought it incongruous.

Basi, for his part, did not take the defeat lying down. In his inimitable style, he was up and about early, looking for alternatives. The Street sympathised with him. It was unusual for a millionaire's candidate to be worsted at an election for not having his tax papers correct. How many candidates paid taxes?

Basi was not interested in answering that question. The National Elections were still to be held and Basi did not see any reason why he should not profit by them. The most important point was to ensure that he eliminated all such errors as had led to Dandy's failure. He set about doing that meticulously.

He took *Psalm 31* one early morning to the library at Yaba and borrowed dusty, stained books which had lain on the shelves untouched for decades. One of them was *Ethics in African Politics* by Okli Sendemende. The other was *Success in African Politics* by James Kariuki Nelson. And also *Wealth and Politics in Africa* by Tedum Tambari. Basi returned to the "Palace".

He spent the next three days poring over the books from cover to cover. He made copious notes. Whenever he was reading at night and one of the city's power cuts brought darkness, he bought a candle and read on. Alali was surprised at his mentor's newly-acquired keenness for books. Basi normally read newspapers, not books. When Alali questioned him about his new habit, he did not answer.

After he had satisfied himself with the books, he walked over one day to the Headquarters of the Ruling Party and said he wanted a membership card.

'You want to be a member?' asked the Secretary-General of the Party.

'Yes,' answered Basi.

'Good. Where do you live?'

'Adetola Street. No. 7 Adetola Street. In the Palace.'

'You have a palace there?'

'Yes.'

'Then you are a rich man.'

'Yes,' said Basi, touching his cap.

'What's your name?'

'Basi. My admirers call me Mr B.'

'Ah, Mr B. Of course, of course. We've heard about you. Millionaire. You were also Dandy's right hand man, the gubernatorial candidate who was disqualified at the last moment.'

'Unfortunately.'

'Oh yes. That was most unfortunate. Anyway, these things happen . . . So why do you want a membership card? You can't be just a member of the Party. Let me see . . . Let me see . . .' And the Secretary-General turned over the pages of a big file leisurely. 'Yes. We don't have a Secretary for the Adetola Street area. Would you like to be Party Secretary over there?'

'Oh yes,' replied Basi gladly.

'It's not often we have a millionaire as Party Secretary. Yes, we'll be pleased to have you. I don't need to tell you what are your duties. I'm sure you already know them. But just to be on the safe side, I'll brief you.'

The Secretary-General lit himself a cigarette and offered Basi another. Then he drew himself up on his chair and, between puffs on his cigarette, said, 'You have to drum up membership, for a start. Secondly, you must find campaign contributors. Of course all those who contribute now will be duly rewarded. And future rewards will be directly proportional to present contributions. Ha! ha!' The Secretary-General puffed away on his cigarette.

'We do not pay local Secretaries . . . You don't need the money, of course. However, after we've won the elections, and the government treasury comes under our control, there are, shall we say, rewarding contracts for all Secretaries . . . You understand all that, of course, as a man of the world. Ha! ha!' The Secretary-General emitted smoke from his cigarette. 'As for the election itself, we have to win, you know. The Ruling Party has to rule, ha! ha!' The Secretary-General extinguished his cigarette, threw it on the floor, and lit another cigarette.

'When the time comes, you will be given specific instructions. Which you must obey. Ha! ha!'

Basi listened carefully to the Secretary-General. When he had finished, he thanked him and promised to work very hard in the interest of the Party.

'And in your interest too, man. We shall enjoy,' concluded the Secretary-General, chuckling.

Basi got up from his seat, shook hands with the Secretary-General and sauntered out of the room. The Secretary-General watched him go, congratulated himself on so important a catch, and made notes in his notebook.

For his part, Basi walked proudly out of the office. It was raining heavily and he stood in the veranda of the building for a long time. He had no money and was at a loss how to get back to his "Palace".

News that he was in the building had gone the rounds of the idle desks in each office and the occupiers of the desks came pouring forth to congratulate him on his wise decision to join the Ruling Party. They were sure, they said, that his entry into the elections would alter the fate of the Party nationwide.

Basi took their felicitations with a quizzical smile. It was not for him to acknowledge public acclaim enthusiastically lest his public esteem be dented.

He seized the opportunity, though, to cadge a lift from one of the many drivers of the Party's fleet of cars. The young man, dressed in print trousers and jumpers of similar material with a skull cap on his head, was only too willing to oblige the famed millionaire.

'I teenk I drop you at your Palace, sah,' says he.

'Oh yeah,' replies Basi, sinking deeper into the cushions in the rear seat of the car.

Driving through the heavy downpour was quite an ordeal, as sheets of rain obscured the vision through the windscreen. The wipers were powerless as the car lurched from one pothole into another, and negotiated puddle after puddle. Basi did not particularly worry. It was not often that he rode in a chauffeur-driven car. If what he was going through at that time was a sign of things to come, he did not care if the heavens wept tears of blood.

The car soon arrived at No. 7 Adetola Street and Basi ordered the driver to stop.

'Dis na your Palace?' asked the driver, grinding the brakes to bring the car to a halt.

'Yeah,' replies Basi in a dignified voice. He opens the door of the car and steps into a puddle of water. He pretends as though that is natural. He bangs the door and walks away without a word to the driver who stares at his disappearing back with undisguised admiration.

Basi arrives home in high spirits. He is singing in full voice when he opens the door and informs Alali that he's become Organizing Secretary of the Ruling Party for Adetola Street area. Alali cannot believe his ears.

'So that's why you've been studying these books?' Alali asks. 'Did you have to pass an examination?'

'No. But I know one or two things about politics now. Thanks to the books.'

'Such as?'
'That the quickest way to wealth in Africa is through politics.'
'That's nothing new, Mr B. Everyone knows that.'
'Well, I didn't.'
'What difference would it have made?'
'I'd not have wasted my time hanging around all sorts of money-making ideas. I'd have joined the Party from the beginning.'
'You're right there now.'
'About time too.'
'What are you supposed to do?' asks Alali.
Basi gives him a knowing look, his eyes wide open. 'Drum up membership. And whatever else my fertile imagination may call up in the interest of the Party.'
'I bet you'll want to earn money.'
'Naturally,' replies Basi. 'That's what the books say. Politics is the quickest and surest way to wealth in Africa.' He takes up Okli Sendemende's book and shows Alali the page where it's written. 'I mean, talent is not even needed. All you do is get there,' here he snaps his fingers, 'and you're made! As sure as there is hell fire!'
'The way you put it, everyone should be in politics.'
'Sure! Al, I'm going to enrol you into the Ruling Party right away. Any objections?'
'None,' Al replies, quite pleased with his official membership of the Ruling Party.
Basi writes his name in an exercise book which he takes from the centre table. 'Who else can you think of immediately?'
'Josco, Dandy, Segi,' Alali replies on the instant.
'Definitely. When they hear there's money in it and no work to do, they'll enrol. I'm not even charging an enrolment fee.'
'Why not?'
'Instruction from Party Headquarters.'
'So how do they pay you?'
'They don't pay at all. Organizing Secretaries are not paid. But after the election is won, the national treasury just belches the money bags and we all help ourselves to our hearts' desire.'
'Fantastic!' exults Alali, looking at Basi with adoring eyes. His boss appears to have hit the bull's eye this time.
'Yeah, man. Just what I've been waiting for. Al, at last we're going to be rich. I can already see the millions dancing in my direction.' He pauses for effect . . . His eyes dance with joy. Then he brags. 'To be a millionaire . . .'
'Think like a millionaire!' Alali replies.

There is euphoria in the "Palace" as Basi paces the room, savouring his new power and wealth. All of a sudden, an idea hits him between the eyes. 'Know what, we didn't include Madam among the new Party members,' he says.

'A serious omission . . . D'you think she'll agree to membership?'
'Why not?'
'I think she's a leading member of the Opposition Party.'

This is correct. When it appeared as though Dandy would become Governor, Madam had enrolled on the opposite side, just to let him know. This bothers Basi for a moment.

'Madam was bound to make the wrong choice,' he says. But his distress is short-lived. 'Anyway, once I tell her, she'll cross carpet.'

This was to be expected on Adetola Street where ideals did not matter. Money was the name of the game. Alali is not absolutely sure, though. He asks if Basi is sure that Madam will change parties.

'Of course. Unless she's a fool, which she's not . . . Put it this way, Madam stands on one bank of the river. There, there's as much starvation as you will find in most developing countries in Africa. Children and mothers are dying everyday. Madam looks across the river to the other bank where everyone's having constipation because they're overfed. She's invited to cross the river on a magic carpet. What d'you think she'll do?'

'Swim across the river to the rich bank without waiting for the magic carpet. That's what I'd do,' replies Alali.

'That's what Madam will do,' asserts Basi. 'And she won't want to know that the river is full of crocodiles.'

'You bet,' Alali laughs. 'To be a millionaire . . .'
'Think like a millionaire!'

Basi hurriedly packs up his voluminous books, tells Alali he's going to see Madam and asks him to go and intimate Dandy, Josco and Segi of his new situation as Organizing Secretary and his desire that they all help him win more members to the Ruling Party. He ambles out of the room, weighed down by his books.

Madam is at home working on her gorgeous headties, trying to knot them into various shapes. When Basi knocks, she ushers him in with her customary 'Come in if you're handsome and rich!' Without looking up from her chores, she bullies Basi.

'Basi, you still dey for house by dis time? You no dey tink how you go pay rent.'

'That's all I ever think of, Madam. Morning, noon and night. Just how I can pay my rent so you're off my neck. Because I'm sick and tired of your . . .' Rent-paying is a sore point with Basi.

'Basi!' roars Madam in rebuke.

'My apologies, Madam,' he meekly replies, going down on his knees.

But Madam is already incensed. 'I tink time don reach wey you go commot for my house. Ah-ah. As your rent dey increase na so you dey insult me. Wetin?'

'Madam, I'm sure you'll be sorry to see me go.'

'Nonsense!' asserts Madam testily as she knots a headtie.

'If only you knew the good things I've got for you today!'

'Wetin you fit give person?' Madam asks, screwing up her face.

'This one's great. See here. Books and books and books. I've read myself blind.' Basi is now in his element. Madam is willing to listen to him.

'And na wetin you dey read sef?' Madam asks.

'Politics.'

'Politics?'

'Yes, Madam. I'm tired of being ruled by mediocres, preached to by hypocrites and taught by buffoons. Since I can't beat them, I've decided to join them.'

' 'E good say you dey learn am for book. You go do de politics well well.'

'Oh yes. In fact, I've been appointed Organizing Secretary of the Ruling Party for Adetola Street . . .'

'Basi!' calls Madam sternly.

'Madam!' replies he, shocked at the tone of Madam's voice.

'You for join my Party. Opposition. Basi, I see say you no like me at all, at all. Even, no be say you no like me. You no like yourself. How you no go join Opposition Party when me I dey inside am?'

Basi holds up the Okli Sendemende book. 'Madam, this book says poor people cannot afford to be in the opposition in Africa.'

'But na we go form de government next time.'

'That is if there's going to be a next time. Chapter 4 of this book says, "In African politics, there never is a next time. By the next time, the treasury is empty, the nation is dead, the robbers are on the street, and the soldiers are out on the shooting range". That's what the book says.'

'If next time no dey for book any time na de right time.'

'That's correct only in songs . . .' Basi asserts. And to show that he does know the song, he sings it: "Any time is the right time . . . do, do, do, do, do dat, dat, dat . . .", accompanying it with a jig.

Madam goes into stitches. Basi immediately capitalizes on the fact that he has been able at last to put her in good humour. He knows that half the battle is won. Madam is as wax in his hands from that moment.

Many have wondered why Basi has always been able to get virtually everything he wants from Madam. How could so astute a lady be that gullible? The secret will never be known in full. Madam herself guards it jealously. But there can be no doubt that Basi's charm, his honeyed tongue, his poetic way of putting his case, his self-assurance, erudition and winning ways lie behind it. As much as Madam's greed and her gullibility.

After he has let Madam have her bellyful of laughs, Basi turns his charm on her. 'I've a proposal to make to you, Madam. In your interest. In our general interest.'

This excites Madam. 'Tell me something!' she says.

'I invite you to join the Ruling Party.'

This is poison to Madam's ears. 'God no gree bad tin,' she says.

'Hold on, Madam. Hold on. Be patient.' Basi consults another volume of his books and comes up with a quotation which he reads to Madam's hearing: ' "Never be hasty in politics. Time is on the side of the patient politician". That's a fact, Madam. Consider it, politician.' And then he says with a flourish, 'I invite you to join our Party as Leader of the Women's Wing!'

'Leader of Women Wing!' repeats Madam enthusiastically, if incorrectly.

'Yes, my dear lady, the position has been waiting for you! And more!'

'Tell me something!'

'There will be contracts galore.' He says the last word in a way to emphasize its amplitude and the great blessing it confers. 'Contracts!'

Madam is in the high heavens. Contracts, she has always wanted. She will do anything to get them. Basi knows as much and now he puts a gloss on them.

'Yes. Not some minor grade B contracts which you have to chase from office to office. Oh no. These contracts are delivered to you at home, signed and sealed. After you have performed, the cheque and payment voucher are delivered on the same day to your residence. And if you don't want to take the trouble to go to the Bank, the Bank Manager himself will come here to collect the cheque. Because it is drawn on the Central Bank itself. See?'

The last word is drawn out on the lips, just to impress. Madam cannot resist it all. She is convinced that Basi is right, and accepts the offer. Besides, there is nothing wrong in holding the membership card of every available Party. All one's eggs must not be put in a single basket.

'Na me be Woman Leader,' she asserts.

'You see, Madam. If you had been in the Ruling Party all this time, you'd not be spending your time chasing impecunious tenants.'

'Tell me something!'

'However, now you are in the Party, everything's alright. You will be richer, I will be rich. Alali will be rich. Josco will be rich. Dandy will be rich. Segi will be rich. We will all be very rich!'

'It's a matter of cash!' Madam exults.

They both laugh heartily. The laughter has not died down when Basi returns to the track.

'One little matter though, Madam. People like you who are known to have money must contribute to the Party.'

'Why?' Madam hates to be asked to pay money to other people.

'We have to win the elections. And as you would say, "It's a matter of cash." '

'So na because you wan money na him you come call me?'

'Yes and no,' Basi replies.

'*Jibiti* man, you don come again? Which one be "yes" and which one be "no"?'

'Yes, I'm looking for campaign contributors, no, I didn't call on you for that reason.'

'So why you come call me?'

'I've told you already. I want you to be richer. I owe you a lot of money. I'm anxious to repay you.'

Three wonderful reasons, all of them very acceptable to Madam, very pleasant to her ears.

'Okay, I no mind. I like am.'

'And you'd better pay up soon because the elections are due any time from now.'

She pricks her ears. That is news to her as indeed to all members of her Party who are not aware that a date has been fixed for the elections. Basi is not particularly sure either. The General Secretary had not told him when the elections were going to be held. He had only said they would be held soon. Basi, in his inimitable way, put his own construction on the General Secretary's words. When Madam protested that the Opposition Party did not know the elections would be held so soon, Basi said:

'You are no longer of the Opposition, Madam. That's why you now know.'

'So una no dey tell Opposition de time of elections?'

'No, Madam. We could not afford to forewarn our enemies. To be forewarned is to be forearmed, they say.'

There were no opponents in Lagos politics. Only "enemies" out to eliminate or be eliminated. It was a matter of life and death. Basi understood that. The stakes were high, so also the risks.

'Are you sending your contributions?' he asks after a while.

'It's a matter of cash!' replies Madam.

Basi glows with satisfaction. He has won the first battle. 'Thanks, our Woman Leader,' he puffs. 'And please make sure it's a hefty contribution, as the contracts we get in future will be directly proportional to the payments we make now.'

'I go send the cheque to the Party direct,' Madam replies.

'Great! I see you still do not trust me.'

'How I go trust *wuruwuru* man like you? If I give you de money you go chop am. You no go send am to de Party. I go give my money to de Party.'

'Fair enough, our gracious Woman Leader. Actually, I prefer to rob the national treasury like most people do. My conscience stops me from robbing you.'

'Conscience!' laughs Madam. 'Basi, you get conscience?'

'Oh yes, I do.'

'Na war for you, Basi. Anyway, make you and your conscience stay. Me, I get work to do.'

'Our Woman Leader! We shall enjoy!' flatters Basi.

'It's a matter of cash!' replies Madam as she returns to her battles with her headties.

Basi packs up his voluminous books and leaves the room with a last, lingering look at Madam. Once again, he has won a signal war. He thanks his stars. He hopes and prays that Madam will send a cheque of at least thirty to fifty thousand naira to Party Headquarters.

It is a very busy period for Basi. He goes to the mosque on Fridays, wearing the badge of the Ruling Party on his cap. He is in church on Sundays, the first man by the door and he remains there until the service begins. At the end of church service, he is the first man by the door, shaking hands and greeting everyone, including children, graciously. The children flock around him. He tells them how wonderful the Ruling Party is, and how they must make sure their parents vote for the Party.

He is a frequent visitor to Adetola Market where, armed with a bell, he rings the beauties of the Ruling Party into the ears of the market women and their customers. He urges everyone to vote for the Party because it is sure to bring to everyone what he fondly calls "life more abundant". The details are not necessary, and he does not supply any. No one asks him either. They listen to him, half-resignedly, as though he is only doing what he has been paid to do.

In the evening, he is at the various gaming machines where gamblers seek their fortunes in the jangling of metal. He does not gamble, of course, because he has no money. But he assures all those who are busy at games, that they will have more money with which to gamble once the Ruling Party wins the election.

The Party Secretary

The layabouts on the Street are the raw materials of which electoral victories are made. Basi organizes them into a fighting front. Their task is to strike terror into the heart and mind of the enemy. They are not paid, naturally. They all hope that once the election is won, jobs will be provided for them. Basi has promised as much, and they trust him. After all, he is a millionaire and money talks. When money talks, unemployed, penniless people have to listen. Basi ensures that his terror squad establish their presence on the Street. They sing, dance and romp through the Street three times a day. The lesson is not lost on the residents of the Street. They ride *Psalm 31* gratis. The driver is pleased to oblige them. *Psalm 31* is behind on payments of hire purchase instalments. Election favours to the winners might help the next payment.

Meanwhile, Basi keeps an eye on events at Party Headquarters. He knows when Madam sends her cheque for fifty thousand naira to the Party. His stock immediately rises at the Secretariat. Madam's donation is one of the heftiest so far. Everyone agrees it could not be otherwise. Where a millionaire is Party Secretary, members are apt to donate unimaginable sums. Basi flaunts his colours all over the Secretariat. He is doing well. One thing remains: he still needs to establish the allegiance of Dandy, Josco and Segi.

For they are in a position to thwart him at any time, or perhaps place a block of stumble in his path. And he cannot afford that event. He has already sent Alali to speak to them on a number of occasions. Alali has assured him that they are all on the side of the Ruling Party. But he does not believe Alali. He has to hear them swear allegiance to him. Because they are all as mean as the residents of Adetola Street, as Adetola Street itself. Basi asks Alali to summon them to the "Palace".

After several tries, Alali is able to assemble them and together they troop into the "Palace" as Basi is busy calculating the millions he will earn after the election is won.

'Everyone's here now, Mr B,' Alali says when they have all settled in. Segi sits in one of the chairs, the others stand around.

'Welcome, my dear friends, welcome,' Basi says. Then turning to Alali, he asks, 'Have they all agreed to be loyal members of the Party?'

'In principle, yes,' Alali replies. 'But there are one or two problems. They'd like to hear from the horse's mouth, for one.'

'Well, the old war-horse himself is here now. Fire ahead, lady and gentlemen,' beams Basi, rubbing his palms together.

Dandy speaks first. 'Basi, I hope this is not one of your usual tricks.'

'Tricks? No.' Basi is scandalized. 'This is business, Dandy.'

'And you say there's money in it?' asks Dandy.

'Millions!' explodes Basi. 'Millions. We'll be stinking rich. It's like you're locked up in the vaults of the Central Bank and are told to please yourself before daybreak.'

Basi looks round to see the effect of his words on the audience. They are devastating. They all mull over Basi's words for a minute. Segi finds her voice first.

'You see, we don't believe that if there was money in it, you'd invite us all.'

'You're right,' Basi replies. 'If it was some small sum of money, I'd certainly not invite you. But the amount of money involved in this is so huge, it boggles the mind. It's too much even for my greed.'

'Exactly how much is it?' Josco cuts in quickly.

Alali loses his temper. 'What's the point of all these questions? The boss has already said it's like being locked up in the vaults of the Central Bank.'

'So he's already "the boss"? And the money hasn't come in yet. What will happen when the money arrives?' asks Dandy testily.

Alali goes for him; Dandy squares up, ready for a fight; only the timely intervention of Josco and Basi prevents a bloodbath. Alali glares at Dandy who stands on the spot, breathing like a grampus. The embers of hot fire die down gradually.

'Lady and gentlemen,' says Basi, 'there is no need to fight. We are all going to be stinking rich. Let us grab the opportunity now it's come knocking on our very door. There is hardly time to waste. There is no work involved in it. All you have to do is shut your eyes . . . yes, shut your eyes to whatever happens on this Street on election day . . . Whatever happens, do nothing. Absolutely nothing. Am I understood?'

'Yeah!' they all chorus, pleased, no doubt, by the prospect of earning huge sums of money simply by shutting their eyes. What bliss!

But Basi is not finished yet. He informs Josco he will be needed as soon as the elections are over. There are one or two things Josco must help sort out. Josco says he is at Basi's service – to be used as "the boss" pleases.

'As soon as our victory is announced, go to Party Headquarters and collect a letter addressed to me.

'Yes, boss,' Josco answers.

'How are we going to share the proceeds from our enterprise?' Segi asks.

'What do you want?' thunders Basi impatiently. 'The way things are designed, even if you have one per cent of it all, you're rich for the rest of your life. What share do you want?'

'I suggest we split everything equally, the five of us.'

The Party Secretary

'You've forgotten Madam.'

'Ah, Madam!'

'She's the main campaign contributor. And Leader of the Women's Wing.'

'So that makes six of us,' says Segi. 'Equal shares.'

'Agreed?' asks Basi of Josco and Dandy. He's sure Alali will accept whatever he has decreed.

'Sure!' chorus Josco and Dandy.

'This is so easy, I'm becoming suspicious,' says Segi.

Alali quickly allays her fears. Going close to her, he says pointedly, 'The best things in life are simple, Segi.'

Basi supports him. Taking up Okli Sendemende's book, he turns over the pages rapidly. Finding the particular paragraph he has been looking for, he reads excitedly, as the others crowd round him. ' "In Africa, the easiest and shortest way to wealth is through politics." ' Then he drops the book on the centre table, as though to say, "You heard it all now".

Dandy picks up the book, turns it over, upside down, and flicks the pages clumsily.

'Hell, I should have known that!' he says.

And that concludes the matter. Once again, Basi has won. It is an important victory for him. It means that come election day, there will be no blocks of stumble in his way. The lady and men whom he has just won over constitute the most troublesome, most envious, most vicious, untrustworthy spoilsports God ever placed together in one place at one time since creation. Uniting them behind one is no mean feat. Basi knows that. But he knows they have to be watched. Because they are changeable.

'Good, lady and gentlemen,' he addresses them grandly. 'Our meeting will be after the elections. In the meantime, please take orders from Alali . . . Josco, remember to go to Party Headquarters as soon as the announcement is made. And please all of you, shut your eyes on election day.'

'Yes, sir,' answers Josco.

'Goodbye,' says Basi.

They answer severally, 'Goodbye', 'wish you luck', 'best wishes', 'happy elections', 'sweet victory', and depart in a group.

Basi is left alone in his "Palace" to savour his latest victory, as Alali has gone to Mama Badejo's *buka* to angle for some food. He lies in bed dreaming of the new wealth which he sees dancing into his "Palace". It is a dream he has often had. This time round, he thinks success is at his fingertips. All the signs appear to favour him. He is in the good books of the Secretary-General of the Party. Madam has sent a campaign contribution of fifty thousand naira which is said to be one of the heftiest contributions by a single individual. All that is left is victory at the polls for the Ruling Party and Basi will have achieved his life-long ambition.

However, upstairs, in Madam's flat, a strange conversation is going on between its lovely occupant and an even lovelier, gorgeous, gossipy female by the name of Segi. She cannot restrain herself at the thought of sharing the proceeds from the campaign equally with everyone else on the Street. She congratulates Madam on her wisdom in "crossing carpets" from the Opposition to the Ruling Party and on making a generous contribution to the coffers of the Party. More so as the contribution is going to bring more than fair returns. Returns which will be shared equally between the six of them. The word "equally" maddens Madam. Because she's a major contributor and expects a major share of profits. Segi speaks on.

Madam hears her out patiently, intervening from time to time with a quizzical "Tell me something". The anger in her flashes fire in her eyes. But all of it is lost on Segi. They part on even terms, and the Ruling Party retains its two proud females happily.

The Party's name has been carefully chosen. The idea is that it must never be out of power. That condition would spell disaster for the leaders and members of the Party. It cannot be tolerated. So, everything has to be done to ensure that power is retained. And the electoral votes have to be greater than on previous occasions. The last election had seen the Ruling Party romp home with ninety per cent of the votes cast. The decision now is that the Party must score ninety-nine point nine zero per cent of votes cast. So that the opposition can be flattened with rabbit punches and left reeling on the ropes, gnashing its teeth in pain in a permanent coma.

To this laudable end, brilliant plans are hatched and rehearsed at nocturnal meetings of the ideologues of the Party whose main metier is their ability to spring a surprise. They have reviewed the campaigns; they have dined and wined the members of the Electoral Commission; they have surveyed all returning officers and found them of a suitable cast of mind. Those who are not have been replaced. All is well.

Basi is not seized of all the facts. Facts which have to be closely guarded lest they should slip to the enemy. So he lives on hope. He hopes that the majority of the people on Adetola Street are members or sympathisers of the Ruling Party. He hopes that no matter how the people vote, the Party will win.

His hopes are justified by the great confidence on display at Party Headquarters. Everyone says it's going to be a Technical Knock Out (TKO).

The Party Secretary

Everyone knows about the knockout. No one is telling what will be the technique.

Some tin shacks are hurriedly put up one week in two or three spots on Adetola Street. A contract worth hundreds of millions has been awarded to have these shacks constructed. Lanterns worth tens of millions have been ordered from the Far East to help in the counting of votes by night. Another contract worth hundreds of millions has been awarded to several individuals for the supply of ballot boxes. The news is abroad that some of the boxes being ordered have false bottoms which will allow fake ballot papers to be planted in the boxes even before voting commences.

The Street is full of activity and rumours. Enemies are bred as maggots in rotting fish. Recrimination is mutual. Each accuses the other of vote-buying, of bribery and corruption, murder and arson. The promise remains of life more abundant for the victors. And for the losers, eternal damnation. Thus, life on the Street, for weeks and weeks.

For Basi, they are weeks of torment. But he continues to work hard for the Party. Through Alali, he ensures that Dandy, Josco and Segi remain on line. Madam is strangely quiet. But since her money is deeply invested in the Party, he feels sure she will not do anything unexpected. Which is the reason why when he sees her in her Bank one morning, waiting to see the Branch Manager, he does not give a thought to what she might be up to.

Madam is a particular woman and she gives particular instructions to the Bank Manager who requests her to put it in writing.

'Write it by yourself,' Madam says.

Then it strikes the Manager she might not be able to read and write. He writes a note and asks Madam to sign. She reads it and signs with a firm hand. Strange woman. So she can read and write. She gets up and walks firmly away, her gorgeous headtie sitting pretty on top of her head and billowing away in the air thick with election rumours and election happenings. Strange woman.

Even more confusion is in store as it is suddenly announced that the elections will be held within three days. On the third day, everything is in its rightful place, the voters are at the booth, on long queues. But before they have cast votes, before votes are counted, there is a voice on the radio announcing that the Ruling Party has scored an overwhelming victory at the just concluded elections. The Party scored ninety-nine point nine zero per cent of the votes cast. Magic!

The voters are completely confused and confounded. Some eat up the ballot papers in their hands, others make a dash for the zinc sheets which have been used in constructing the polling booths – they need them to complete the living quarters they are building; others return home wearily wondering exactly what is happening; some are happy at the turn of events and slip into bars to celebrate with drinks.

Among these latter are Dandy, Josco, Alali and Segi who see in the miraculous events, the road to their ultimate salvation. Indeed, no sooner is the Ruling Party's victory announced than Josco picks up his cap and jacket, and leaves, as instructed, for the Headquarters of the Ruling Party.

Basi, who has been out on the final trail of votes, returns to his "Palace" giddy with joy and excitement. No sooner is he seated on his bed than Madam comes in to check if she's heard right about the victory of the Ruling Party.

'Just as I said,' replies Basi.

'Dem fast-oh. Wonderful. Dem no vote sef. Jus announce by radio. Wonderful. No vote at all.' Madam is slightly upset, but Basi does not notice.

'I knew there would be no need to vote. This is what we call a Technical Knockout. The opposition withdrew knowing it was going to lose. Madam, it was no use voting ... Now I hope Josco remembers to obey my instructions.'

'You send am message?' Madam asks quizzically.

'Yes. If he gets to Headquarters early, he will find certain papers meant for all Organizing Secretaries whose areas made donations to the Party.'

'Dem get de money wey I dash de Party?' There is a slight hint of irony in her tone.

'Oh yes, I'm told it was one of the heftiest donations. And you know what that means?' Here Basi begins to pace the room excitedly, grinning, smiling and chuckling by turns. Looking keenly at Madam, he says, 'Some really big contracts and import licences are on the way. Supply contracts, building contracts, visible and invisible contracts, cleaning contracts, instant contracts, timeless contracts. Money in the millions. Madam, you have made it. We have made it. To be a millionaire, think like a millionaire!'

Madam is strangely silent, fixing Basi with an amused look.

'That's what I always say!' Basi shouts, then he looks out through the window and says with a tinge of anxiety in his voice, 'Oh where is that Josco of a fellow?'

Just as he asks the question, Dandy, Alali and Segi come in to congratulate Basi who welcomes them with firm handshakes.

'Zentleman Basi! Looks like the Good Lord is smiling on you at long last!' says Dandy when they have all settled down.

'About time too!' croons Basi. 'God knows I've waited long enough.'

'Declaring for the Party was a real stroke of zenius,' Dandy asserts.

'Not at all. Not in the least. It's all in the books. We should have been reading the books instead of trudging the streets in search of jobs and business.'

'I bet you'll throw away the books now that the millions have started to roll in,' Dandy teases, to general merriment.

'We'll see how things go in the next week or two.'

'Madam, you must be happy you backed Basi with your abundant cash!' Segi says.

'It's a matter of cash!' Madam replies unenthusiastically.

'Al, did you see Josco at all?' asks Basi.

'He went off to Party Headquarters as soon as he heard the announcement. I think he should be on his way back any minute now,' Alali volunteers gladly.

A knock is heard at the door and Josco barges into the room, tripping over Madam's legs and almost destroying the centre table. He is in a state of high excitement. His hands tremble slightly as he hands over the envelope to Bàsi.

'What did I say? Madam, what did I say! Look at this! Look at this! Our very first envelope!' Basi shouts as he tears the envelope open. They all, except Madam, crowd round him, curious to know what the envelope contains. Basi reads the contents aloud in a voice thick with happiness. 'It's a Local Purchase Order for furnishing the offices of the Party. It's worth two hundred and fifty thousand naira!'

'Yeah!' A loud cheer goes up.

'Did you hear that?' Basi asks of no one in particular. 'Two hundred and fifty thousand naira! And that's only the "victory contract", as we call it. More will follow!'

'Wonderful!' says Madam.

'Incredible!' Al shouts.

'Unbelievable!' says Dandy.

'Unforgettable!' agrees Segi.

'Cool cash!' asserts Josco.

'Madam, the ball is in your court now,' says Basi.

'Which court? Una get case? Una wan take me go court? Wetin I do?'

'I meant, Madam, that the Local Purchase Order is in your name.'

'Tell me something!'

'Yes, Madam. You made the campaign contribution. The contract is in your name. But it is addressed to me. The money passes through you to all of us.'

'Basi, Basi, you na wonderful man.' Madam begins to wonder about the instructions she had given her Bank Manager.

'I've always told you to give me a chance. *Da mihi locum standi et terram movebo*,' says Basi, striding about the "Palace" proudly.

'What's that?' asks Segi.

'Latin,' Basi replies, and everyone, except Madam, stands up to give him a standing ovation. 'It means, "Give me a place to stand and I will shake the world." '

There follows another round of applause for Basi. The fact that he can speak Latin impresses them beyond words.

'Mr B's in his best possible mood today,' says Alali appreciatively.

'And why not? He's made. So are we all,' replies Dandy.

'To be a millionaire . . .' exults Alali.

'Think like a millionaire!' replies Basi.

If Madam is suspicious, she doesn't show it. She throws up leading questions, noting the answers carefully.

'How we go supply de furniture?' she asks. 'As I see am 'e go cost more dan two hundred thousand naira to supply wetin dem want.'

'Two hundred thousand naira? No way. Let me see.' Basi brings out a pocket calculator and does a quick calculation. When he is through he tells Madam, 'By my calculation, we should invest no more than fifty thousand naira.'

''E go take long time before bank go give you dat kind money.'

'Will it?'

'Yes now,' replies Madam.

'Well, I can't afford to wait. Neither can the Party, if you see what I mean. Josco, you and I have to talk.'

He invites them to withdraw for a while as he wishes to have a tête-a-tête with Josco. They part with handshakes all round. Basi sees them all to the door and returns to the room, his face grim, determination written into his eyes.

'Josco, you've got to put on your thinking cap now,' he says.

Josco, unthinking, touches his cap and says, 'So long as there's money in it.'

'Huge sums of money, man. Millions. Don't talk about money anymore. Sounds vulgar to me. I mean, we're practically swimming in the commodity, aren't we?' He glares at Josco and then dismisses him and his anxiety over money from his mind. He returns to the point at issue. 'Look, this matter of furnishing the offices of the Party. We don't have to mess around with carpets, blinds, curtains, do we?'

'No sir, we don't.' Josco has to be humble before the money bags. Show sufficient respect. Hence the "sir".

'But the papers have to be signed by the storekeeper.'

'I understand, sir.'

'Can you make him sign as having received the goods?'

'I will, sir,' Josco replies.

'You know what to tell him? What to promise him? Or what to do if he proves difficult?'

'Yes, sir.'

'I'd have done it myself, but, really, there has to be division of labour. After all, we're together in this matter. And this is right up your street,' Basi says with a knowing wink.

'I agree, sir,' Josco replies with a sly smile.

'So you will have the waybill duly signed by the storekeeper and report back to me.'

'In no time at all, sir.' Josco pulls up his wiry frame and is through the door like the wind before Basi can say goodbye.

Basi believes that Josco will perform his assignment successfully. It is not a strange assignment by any means. Getting an official to sign for goods that have not been delivered is as common as getting a certificate of illness from an Adetola Street doctor. All you have to do is pay money or promise to pay on demand. Basi knows that Josco can even go one better. He can forge the storekeeper's signature and present the fake document to the Secretary-General, who will authorize payment without knowing what has happened. He decides to go and inform Madam of the progress he has made in supplying the furniture. He knows he will still need her to endorse the cheque to him for collection.

He might as well have saved himself the trouble. Madam, as usual, has eavesdropped on his conversation with Josco and is fully aware of their plans. She is waiting for him in her lounge when he appears. She is anxious to drive a nail into his heart, to assuage her wounded Amerdolian pride.

'Basi, you na wonderful man,' she says.

'Thank you, Madam. Josco should be back soon with some news.'

'Him don go deliver de furniture?'

'Yes, Madam. He'll return with the waybill duly signed.'

'How did you raise the money for the purchase of the goods?'

'That's my secret, Madam. I've got powerful friends in the right places, you know.'

'Why dem no help you pay your rent?'

A question which rightly irks Basi. 'Madam, that song's now out of tune. I can now pay not only rent; I'll buy all the houses on Adetola Street, for cash, hard cash!'

'My new millionaire!' Madam says, the sarcasm in her voice undisguised.

'Yeah!' replies Basi, pleased that Madam has recognized his new status.

He excuses himself and ambles out of the room, wriggling like a worm. No sooner has he arrived in his "Palace" than Josco barges in again in a state of high excitement, yelling, 'Mr B! Mr B!'

'Boy Josco! Has everything gone well?' Basi replies.

'Cool!'

'The waybill is signed?' Basi asks with a wink.

'Yes. The waybill's signed. And the cheque's being prepared. Will be ready soon.'

Madam enters the room. She is looking rather glum, to Basi's surprise. Basi welcomes her back to the "Palace" respectfully, offers her a seat, and turns his attention to Josco.

'Why didn't you wait for the cheque?' he asks Josco.

'I came to give you a situation report.'

'Ah, great. But you must go back to collect the cheque. In these matters, time is of the essence. I don't want the man who's supposed to sign the cheque to have a heart attack before he's signed it. So, go back now and see that you return with the cheque... Ask Alali and the rest of the gang to come and see me immediately.'

'Right, boss,' answers Josco as he takes his leave.

'Basi, everything good dey happen for you dese days,' Madam flatters.

'I can't complain, Madam. And when the money is in my hands, I'll show Adetola Street what a home-bred millionaire can do.'

At that moment, Alali, Dandy and Segi come into the room. There is ample evidence on their breath that they have been having a good time.

'Where've you guys been?' Basi asks.

'We've been celebrating,' Alali says.

'You shouldn't have left me for so long,' Basi rebukes them mildly.

'Josco's told you what happened?'

'Yes,' replies Segi.

'I expect he'll be back soon with the cheque. A cheque for – what do you know – a quarter of a million naira. I should be writing a few fat cheques for each of you thereafter.'

He has no bank account, and no cheque book, but that is of no consequence to most of his audience. Dandy is definitely star-struck.

'Boy, you've really hit it big!' he says.

'Real big!' asserts Alali.

'You ain't seen nothing yet. Just give me some more time,' brags Basi, pacing the "Palace" like an emperor.

'I'm sure you will want to marry soon,' Segi says half-seriously.

Basi moves close to the chair on which she's sitting, and says he never really thought of it. 'But I should, I should,' he says wistfully. Then moving over to Madam's chair, he asks, 'Madam, what do you say?'

'Dat na your own *toro*,' Madam replies laconically.

They burst into laughter at her words. Basi positively exudes confidence and radiant happiness. His happiness is compounded when Josco rushes into the room. Basi anxiously asks him if he has obtained the cheque.

'Yes. Here's the cheque. It's in Madam's name though.'

'Fantastic!' Basi exclaims. And holding up the cheque so everyone can see it, he says, 'Ladies and gentlemen, the cheque is here! The whole cheque! Heavens, this is something! I think we should celebrate!'

Alali reminds him that there is no drink in the "Palace".

'Oh, no drinks . . . Madam, you better endorse the cheque to Alali. Alali and Josco, you two go to the bank and cash the cheque. Quick! Quick!'

Madam endorses the cheque as they all crowd round her. As she signs, Basi yells, 'What a signature!' Alali grabs the cheque, pockets it, and he and Josco run out of the room.

Basi is cock-a-hoop with joy. 'Whew!' whistles he. 'Some event on some day.' And he mops the sweat of excitement from his brows with a handkerchief.

'How d'you feel now as an approximate millionaire?' asks Dandy.

'Just you wait till I hold the cash in my hands . . . Where are Alali and Josco then?'

'But they've only just gone,' Segi replies. 'It will take some time to get to the bank, cash the cheque and count such a huge sum of money. And I guess they should need a truck to bring it down.'

'A truck to bring it down! I like the sound of that, Segi . . . I can't wait to hold the notes in my hand. Madam, you'll be glad you gave me shelter when things were bad! What's that I hear?'

He looks through the window in the expectation that the truck bringing Josco, Alali and the money is around. His ears have deceived him.

Madam sits nonchalantly through it all. Her mind is at the Bank. She wonders if her wishes have been carried out. She prays there should have been no mistake. Strange woman. When her pride is pricked, she will even forgo her love of "abundant cash".

Alali and Josco race to the Bank. When they get there, there is a crowd waiting at the cashier's desk. Some have been waiting for over an hour. It is a laborious process withdrawing money from any Bank in Lagos. The cheques have to be verified by three or four persons at the Bank because forged cheques are a normal staple. Besides, people who have no money write cheques to others.

Alali and Josco are kept on their heels for a long time. Eventually, a clerk yells out Alali's name. He moves forward with a smile. But the cashier is not smiling. He has brought back two cheques and hands them to Alali. On both is written, "Cheque countermanded". Alali does not understand what that means. He is not in the business of cashing cheques. He asks for an explanation.

The cashier tells him that whoever wrote the cheque has ordered that it should not be honoured. Alali is flabbergasted. He demands further explanation. The cashier says that the Secretary-General of the Ruling Party has found that a cheque emanating from Adetola Street has been countermanded. Consequently, the Party cheque to the Secretary of the Adetola Street chapter of the Ruling Party cannot be honoured. The cashier says he has been on the lookout for the writer of the first cheque whom the Secretary-General has been unable to trace. He asks if Alali will deliver the particular cheque to its owner. Alali agrees to do so and is thanked by the cashier. He and Josco leave the Bank with scowls on their faces. They walk back leisurely to Adetola Street, the two cheques in Alali's pocket.

Dandy, who has been keeping steady watch at the window, is the first to see them. He informs the group that Alali and Josco are back. Segi rushes to the window to see them.

'What? Returned so soon? And where's the truck that was to bring the money?' Basi asks.

'There's no truck, Mr B,' Segi says, returning from the window.

Alali and Josco enter the room with leaden steps.

'Ah, my friends, you're back. Where's the money?' cries Basi.

'We brought back two cheques,' explains Alali.

'Yeah!' cheer Basi and Dandy.

'Two cheques!' says Basi. 'Hear that?'

They clap.

'There's no money,' Alali says matter-of-factly. 'We brought back two cheques instead.'

'Two cheques? Why?' Are you teasing, Al?' Basi asks.

'No, Mr B. Here are the cheques. One is the cheque which Madam gave to the Party, the other the cheque the Party gave to Madam,' Alali says, as he hands over the cheques, to Basi.

Basi is confused. The two cheques are glued to his fingers.

'What does this mean?' he asks.

'Well, I think Madam's cheque bounced. "Cheque countermanded" is written on it. So the Party's cheque was countermanded as well.'

'Impossible! Impossible!' whines Basi. Then turning to Madam he asks plaintively, 'Madam, what happened? Tell me what happened. Somebody's trying to ruin me. Madam!'

Madam is already on her feet, happy that what she ordered has been properly obeyed. She replies to Basi's question quite hastily. 'You see, when you ask me to give the money to your Party, I 'gree. But I won't give my money to useless Party. I am leading member of Opposition Party. And you know it!'

'But you agreed to cross carpet?' whines Basi.

'No, not me,' answers Madam. 'I no do dat kain thing. How una come talk equal share when na me make all de contribution? Ehn? Which one una dey? You can't assault me like dat. You can't. I no be your mate. My name is Madam. Even sef, you no supply de furniture. Why dem go pay you? Foolish man! You tink na so to get money?'

As she storms out of the room, Basi follows after her, dejectedly, shouting, 'Madam... you've ruined me... Ruined me... Ruined me!' But Madam is not listening. She is a determined woman, and once again, she has had her way.

Alali, Josco and Dandy break into tears, loudly bemoaning the loss of their share of the booty. They swear to have their own back on Madam at the earliest opportunity. Her greed, arrogance and meanness are that day confirmed in their eyes, if such confirmation was needed.

As for Basi, his face is a study in disappointment. He suddenly sees himself back in his miserable "Palace", all the hard work of the past months dissolving into nothingness before his eyes, his very pride hurt to the core. He is for a moment a rump of a man, humiliated by a woman, and as he turns unseeing into the room, he collides with Alali. He gathers himself up slowly, picks up the Okli Sendemende book from the centre table, opens it at a random page and slumps into bed with the open book lying across his chest, weakly asking the book, as it were, 'Where did I go wrong?'

The rats in the ceiling squeak in reply.

An Efficient Company

Political failures almost always ended up in business. Which made my uncle describe business as the dumping ground of failed politicians. He said it had to be, since business was so very wide in definition. Anything passed as business on our Street. The woman who sold disused tins and empty bottles in the market, was as much a businesswoman as Mama Badejo in her famed *buka*; the man who sold old newspapers in an uncovered corner of the market was as much a businessman as Mr Quickpenny of the motor spares stores or Mr Finecountry who was a financial consultant and analyst.

Much was not known of who was a financial consultant and analyst, or what he did beyond the fact that Mr Finecountry was, most impressively, a financial consultant and analyst. As usual, rumours started flying all over the Street. It was said that he was a middleman. This was a man who dressed well, did nothing beyond making people shake hands with each other and made a lot of money from both handshakers. Each handshaker was pleased to pay Mr Finecountry for making it possible for him to meet another handshaker. If one handshaker happened to be a top civil servant and the other handshaker a foreigner with a lot of goods to sell, Mr Finecountry did extremely well indeed.

Mr Finecountry had built a house in the style of one he had seen in the Bahamas. Now he had built a house in the Bahamian style, it was left for everyone to see how important a middleman was to the business of government. He was the envy of all on the Street. He even had another house in the Bahamas too. He normally locked up the house on Adetola Street. The house was properly protected from all intruders by barbed wires and concrete walls.

Along with Chief Doctor Shala Punta, Mr Finecountry showed that everything was possible on the Street. That stories of men who rose from rags to riches did not only happen in books. They happened on Adetola Street, right under the nose of Basi and his friends.

After the loss of money occasioned by Madam's treachery during the elections, Basi did not spend his time bemoaning the fact. He had a bad night's sleep all right, but when he woke up the next morning and beheld the splendour of the morning sun and Mr Finecountry's house basking in that sun, he knew that all was not lost. All he had to do was try again.

He had acquired a bad name at Headquarters and there was no point trying a return to politics. Millionaires are not supposed to have friends whose cheques are countermanded. No one was accepting excuses, more so as the election had been "won" and it was time to share the booty. Basi found consolation in the fact that he was only one of several people who had gone away empty-handed from the elections. He was a part of the huge majority. He was not in bad company.

Not so Alali, who spent the days lamenting the fact that all his hard work during the elections came to nought. He made open plans to return to his village, angry that he had wasted his time in Lagos, achieving virtually nothing. His relationship with Basi was considerably strained. Basi had to go out of his way to find the reasons which would convince Alali to stay with him. He needed Alali for an aide. He had come to value his company. For two days, he went out on secret missions without telling Alali what he was doing. Alali was sulking, anyway, and did not want to speak with him. Three days after the fiasco of an election campaign, Basi was busy seducing Alali once more. It was noon, and they were still at home licking their wounds.

'I won't be persuaded this time,' Alali said as he turned over the pages of a magazine lazily.

'Is that so?' yawned Basi.

'Days have stretched to months and months to years and still . . .'

'It's the same old story, the same hunger.' Thus Basi, laconically.

'The same joblessness.'

'Your usual singsong.'

'So I'm returning to the village.'

Basi got up, as though stung. 'Well then, goodbye, sonny. Who wants you in Lagos, anyway?' He drew on his trousers.

'Seriously, Mr B, I've got to leave.'

'So there won't be hunger in the village? And jobs go begging there, eh?'

'At least there isn't a Basi to get on my nerves, no Madam taunting me day and night, no Dandy ready for a fight and . . .'

'Come on, Al. Lagos is crawling with opportunity.'

'It hasn't crawled up to me.'

'You walk up to it, pick it up,' Basi said.

'The same old story . . .'

'The usual singsong.'

'And I'm tired and sick of it. Sick, sick, sick,' said Alali, hitting the arm of the chair on which he sat several times.

'Tired. Sick . . . In the land of opportunity. No wonder you are poor.'

'And you are crawling in wealth, aren't you?'

'Hey, Al, be careful how you talk to a millionaire-on-the-make.'

'You've been on-the-make so long, I think you're overcooked. Burnt out.'

Basi refused to take offence. He said tamely, 'You don't know me, Al.'

'No wonder no one'll give you a job.' Alali was being deliberately provocative.

'Who wants a job? You won't catch me looking for one.'

'Why not?'

'Because if you look carefully at the magazine in your hands, you'll read that the richest people on earth are the self-employed.'

'It's in the books. So was the matter of politics. Remember Okli Sendemende and his book on African Politics? Did it make us millionaires?'

'Forget about the past, Al. We've learnt our lesson. We must look forward to the future. The future is most important.'

'So?'

'I've decided that you and I are going to self-employ.'

Alali chuckled. 'Doing what?' he asked.

'Everything.'

'No one can do everything.'

'We will.'

'We have no money.'

'I'm a millionaire-on-the-make, remember.'

'Until you make the million, you're not made.'

At least Alali is no longer mulishly antagonistic. Basi sees that he is beginning to win. He refuses to get angry with his assistant, using on him all his guile, all his power of persuasion. 'We'll make it, Al,' he assures him.

'But we have no investment money.'

Basi lights a cigarette, and puffs away, buying time while he thinks. He comes up with an idea.

'The man who stuffs things into the back of a lorry all day, how much does he earn?'

'A lot of money,' Alali essays.

'Wrong. He earns little or nothing.'

'No?'

'Just enough to keep body and soul together . . . And the driver of a ten-ton truck?'

'He's rich.'

'No, Al. What about the owner of the lorry?'

'He must be filthy rich.'

'No, no. The really rich one is he who takes no risks, does no work. The middleman. He connects lorry and driver to the hirer. He renders a service all right, but it's easy work, Al.'

'That's smart,' Al says. His eyes shine with interest and excitement.

'It's crystal clear; to make the millions, don't invest. Take no risks.'

'Be a middleman.'

'Right you are! Dream up ideas and the millions will roll in.'

'To be a millionaire . . .'

'Think like a millionaire!'

Basi sees that Alali is out of the doldrums. He is winning. He now goes for the kill.

'So what have you dreamt up?' Alali asks.

'Money-earning ideas. We're going to be stinking rich.'

'I can't wait, Mr B. I need the money.'

An Efficient Company

'When the money starts rolling in, you won't know how to spend it.'
'When will it start rolling in?'
'Soon. All we do is print a complimentary card.'
'Just that?'
'Yes. Basi and Company. Importers, Exporters, Distributors, Commission Agents, Security Agents, Land-Clearing, Surveying, Party Chairs for Rent, Moon Exploration, Gold Mining, General Supplies.'
'Fantastic!' yells Alali.
'And you drop the cards wherever you go.'
'Who'll believe us?'
'The people of Lagos are gullible, man. They trust the man who sells charms in Adetola Market; they trust the hypocrite who preaches in the one-room church; they trust Ndu the native doctor with his dangerous potions. Why won't they trust our complimentary card?'
'Sure they will.'
'Good. Here, some cards. I already printed them. And I've been distributing them all over the Street and beyond.' Basi gives the cards. They are printed in several colours, for effect.
Alali is impressed. 'Mr B!' calls he, admiringly.
'That's me!' replies Basi with a winning smile. 'To be a millionaire . . .'
'Think like a millionaire!' Alali replies.
'I say, we'll soon be inundated with requests from people wanting to do business with us. They will come knocking at the door of the Palace, begging us to do business with them and . . .'
At that moment, there was a rap on the door. 'See? It's already happening,' Basi says.
Before he could move to open the door, Madam had entered the room, one of Basi's complimentary cards in her hand. By instinct, sheer force of habit, Basi dived under the bed while Alali dashed behind the food cupboard.
'No use, Basi. Is too late.'
'Madam!' called Basi, emerging from his hiding place.
'You no fit hide from me dis time.'
'Who said I've been hiding from you?'
'Na me. Every month-end, na him you go pretend say you travel. You hide return when you tink say I dey sleep.'
'Hide. Return . . . Into my own Palace. Madam, you don't know what you're saying. You know I've been busy with the elections.'
'Elections don end since long time, *wayo* man.'
'Since then, I've been busy at work.'
'Which work? You no go die if you work any work even for one day?'

'What's a day's work when I'm busy the year round?'

Madam was incensed at this claim. Dismissing them, she roundly rebuked Basi for printing a complimentary card which made claims that were manifestly false. She pooh-poohed Basi's claim to be able to do security work. And she revealed that she had been sending away callers asking for a false organization called *Basi and Company*.

'People have been coming?'

'I jus turn dem back, one time!'

'Just why do you hate me so much?' Basi asked. 'Why are you so jealous of my success?'

'Jealous. Success. Basi, na dream you dey dream. Come back and pay your rent, you hear?'

'Each time I complete arrangements to pay you off, you are there to ruin me. That's how you stopped me from making money from the elections.'

Madam was not listening to him. She warned him to ensure that no strange faces were seen around the premises as she was making arrangements to host members of the famous American Dollar Club. She did not want people to steal the goods she had prepared for her party.

'You can hire my Company to do your security work.'

'*Jibiti* man. You wan tief my property. *Yeye* man!'

'Madam, I think you're too cocky.'

'Cock, hen, turkey or chicken. Make I warn you. If you dey tell people say you get company wey you no get, I go report you to Police. You hear?'

'Are you threatening me, Madam?'

'No. I jus tell you wetin I go do. Das all.'

'Alright. We'll see.'

Madam stalked out of the room, banging the door behind her. Alali reappeared from his place behind the food cupboard. Basi stood there, gnashing his teeth, promising to give as good as he got.

'Just wait. She thinks my company is fake. I'll show her what metal I'm made of.'

'You're hard as stone.'

'Thank you very much,' Basi replied. 'Get ready, Al. We'll go to Dandy's, have a drop and perhaps I'll send Dandy and Josco on an errand.'

Madam went shopping in preparation for the meeting of the American Dollar Club which she was going to host. Meetings of the Club were always extraordinary occasions. There was always a lot to drink and even more to eat. The Amerdolians prided themselves on their ability to demolish whole chickens each and cartons of beer and spirit. They

An Efficient Company

dressed to outdress one another with clothes imported from all nooks and corners of the world. They wore jewellery in abundance, large ornamental pieces gaudily crafted in great, big sizes. As for their florid headties, they screamed aloud colourfully, and rose from feminine heads to the high heavens. The chatter of their meetings was idle, consisting largely of the cost of clothing, jewellery and perfume in Hong Kong, New York, Rome or London. The Amerdolians were a show-off, a lasting testimony to the over-abundance of easy money in the city of Lagos. Preparing to host them meant for Madam the purchase of drinks, cooking of food, and the hire of party clothes from Madam Adekunle. Because, although Madam owned enough apparel to wear herself, she could not be really sure. She had to be better dressed than everyone else, and to change three or four times in the course of the meeting. Besides, she might have to show to inquisitive Amerdolians, the whole extent of her wardrobe. Indeed, that is an understatement. For Madam owned not just a wardrobe, but an array of trunk boxes each filled to the brim with headties, lace blouses, loin-cloth, shoes and jewellery. To each item, one two or three trunk boxes.

In the circumstances, her desire for peace and quiet, for non-intrusion of strange faces into the premises was understandable.

These preparations for the party were unknown to Dandy and Josco who sat at Dandy's Bar drinking, as usual. Their thoughts went to Basi, naturally. He was a common point of reference.

'Boy Zosco, seen Mr. B lately?' Dandy asked.

'No,' replied Josco. 'Things have been rather quiet at No. 7 lately.'

'Everything seems to be going wrong for him. Haven't heard of his millions since after the elections.'

'You know Mr B. He'll bounce back to life soon. The man's tough! I bet he destroys Madam for spoiling his election act.'

'Madam's something else. You wouldn't have thought she'd pull such a fast one on us all,' said Dandy.

'Pulled the rug from under Mr B's feet. He'll settle with her when he gets his millions.'

'He'll never get them,' said Dandy. 'But if he does, he'll crush Madam to the dust.'

The subject of this conversation was at the door. He strolled confidently into the room, Alali in his trail.

'Mr B!' greeted Josco enthusiastically.

'Boy Josco! Dandy! How are you? Haven't seen you guys for quite a while.' Thus Basi, breezily, engagingly.

'That's what we've zust been saying,' replied Dandy.

'How's business?' asked Basi, sitting on a stool by the counter.

'Business is bad,' Dandy said.
'I don't believe you, Dandy.'
'Why not?'
'Because you should have told me. When things get bad, I'm always at your disposal.'
'Things have been quiet down your end lately.'
Basi guffawed at that. Beckoning to Alali who was in a corner chatting up Josco, he said, 'Al, did you hear that? Dandy says things have been quiet at our end.'
'He doesn't know what we've been up to, I guess.'
'Tell them,' ordered Basi.
'We've formed a new Company.'
'A new Company? What name?' demanded Josco.
'What else but *Basi and Company*?'
'What do you do?' Dandy asked.
'Everything,' Basi readily answered, and then paused to see what effect that would have on the listeners. Then he sallied forth. 'Import and Export, Security work, Clearing of Land, Surveys, Gold Mining, the lot.'
'Sounds like you want to corner everything in sight,' Dandy joked.
'It's an emporium. A million dollar baby,' Basi said proudly, a twinkle in his eyes. Then, suddenly hardening his features, he said, 'I mean, we should have been rolling in wealth now if Madam had not been turning back our clients . . .'
'And putting blocks of stumble in our way,' added Alali.
'She dared to call the emporium a fake,' said Basi, thumping the table.
'That's mean!' Josco declared.
'And silly!' Dandy was not to be outdone in the matter of castigating Madam.
'In the midst of all that, she and her friends of the American Dollar Club are busy celebrating, drinking, dancing, showing off their wealth!'
'While we can't find money for a meal,' added Alali bitterly.
'I think she's overdue for a lesson,' said Dandy.
'Right. That's what I say. And what I came to see you guys about.'
'Just tell us what you want us to do, Mr B,' Josco said.
Basi outlined his plans to them. He said he wanted to teach Madam a tiny little lesson. Just to prove to her that there was nothing fake about *Basi and Company*. They would have to get Segi out of the way because, according to Basi, being a woman, her middle name was "Unpredictable". Once she knew what they were up to, she might tell on them. Al was despatched to go and take care of Segi.
With Segi out of the way, they would have to arrange to ruin Madam's preparations for the meeting of the Amerdolians. Basi proposed that

An Efficient Company

Josco and Dandy go up to Madam's room to remove some of the goods she had purchased for the party. Madam would be stunned by the disappearance of her goods, then the Security Division of *Basi and Company* would step in to find the goods. Once the goods were found, Madam would not only eat her words of the morning, she would be forced to hire the Company to protect her wealth for all time. And, as soon as Madam had hired them on a permanent basis, he was sure all the members of the American Dollar Club, anxious never to be outdone, would hire them too. 'That way, the millions will start pouring in!' Basi added finally.

Josco was impressed by the plan. He said as much when he shouted, 'To be a millionaire . . .'

'Think like a millionaire!' replied Basi.

As to when they would start, Basi suggested that they do so immediately. Madam had been shopping wildly for some days, and was at that very moment away on a spree. He asked Dandy and Josco to go into her apartment and remove anything that struck their fancy. 'Take them into the Bar here and await my further instructions,' he ordered.

'But isn't that against the law?' Dandy asked. 'I don't want to go to zail,' he said, with a look at Josco whose teeth had begun to chatter.

'It's only a practical joke. We won't keep the goods for long . . . Be sure you don't lose any of the things you take away. Remember, Madam's my landlady.'

Promising to keep a bright lookout lest Madam should return and take them unawares, he set them on their way. However, Dandy would not proceed without promise of shares in *Basi and Company*.

'Will I have a piece of the Company action?' he asked.

'Sure!' replied Basi. 'You can have several pieces of the action, Dandy.'

Fortified by this assurance, Dandy and Josco set out for No. 7. As Basi had said, Madam was absent. They knew that she was in the habit of leaving the key to the front door beneath the footmat. Only Madam knew why she preferred to keep the key there instead of carrying it on her person. Dandy lifted the footmat, obtained the key, opened the front door and gained access to the apartment. The lounge was stacked up with cartons of beer, bottles of brandy, whisky and crates of soft drinks. Dandy and Josco proceeded to cart them away. And not without mishap as the cartons kept falling down.

Basi kept anxious watch from his room, looking out of the window of his room to see if Madam would return. She did not until Dandy and Josco emerged from her apartment bearing some of her property to Dandy's Bar. Basi felt elated.

When Alali arrived in the "Palace" to inform him that Segi was out of town, Basi believed that the gods were on his side.

'How are things going over here?' asked Alali.

'Okay,' Basi confirmed. 'Madam should get a fright when she returns. Did you see her on the way?'

'Nope,' said Alali.

'Josco and Dandy have fixed her up, I should think.'

'Great!'

'She'll be retaining a Security Company next. And we should win the retainership. The money will flow, Al. We'll be very rich. To be a millionaire . . .'

'Think like a millionaire!'

As they spoke, Madam walked past their window and up the stairs. In her hand was a bundle of clothes. Basi watched her walk upstairs and asked Alali to go to Dandy's Bar to inform Dandy and Josco to report to Madam's lounge and take away the bundle of clothes Madam had just brought in. Alali dashed out of the room.

Madam walked towards her apartment to be confronted by the sight of an open door. Surprise. When she entered her lounge, shock waves passed over her as she realized she had been robbed. The realization did not come immediately. First was the idea that something had gone wrong – the disorderliness of the room induced that feeling. Next, the surprise. And finally the shock at the meaning of it all.

She dropped the bundle of clothes she had in her hand, stood still for a minute, and then raised a loud cry of distress mingled with anger. She dashed out of the room, flew down the stairs and irrupted into Basi's room, shouting, 'Teeves! Teeves!!' Basi went towards her and held her firmly.

'My life don spoil-oh, my life don spoil,' howled Madam disconsolately.

'What's the matter?' asked Basi.

'Everytin for my house. Everytin! Oh God, wetin I go do-oh. I don die. I don die today.'

'Hold yourself, Madam. What's the matter?'

'Dem broke my house, enter, take everytin. Everytin!'

'Holy Moses!'

'Everytin eh!' moaned Madam. 'Abi dem no dey here?'

'What?'

'All de tins for my party. Abi dem dey here?'

'No! You can search the room.'

She did so frantically. She looked under the bed, in the food cupboard, behind it; among the clothes on the rack, and beneath the chairs. In her confusion, she did not realize that cartons of beer could not be hidden beneath chairs. She thrashed about the room whispering, 'Nuttin. Nuttin,' like one demented.

Madam was disconsolate. 'Teeves, teeves!' she moaned. 'Wetin I go do-eh? My party . . . my party . . . Basi, you and Alali go see sometin. If una no see sometin know say my name no be Madam . . . Eh, eh, eh. Everytin for my house. Everytin.' She held both arms over her head, pointing heavenwards.

Weeping loudly, she shuffled out of the room, briskly ran up the stairs, only to find that there were more surprises waiting for her. For while she was downstairs berating Basi, Dandy and Josco had returned to her flat as suggested by Basi and taken away the bundle of clothes she had dropped in her shock at the disorderly state of her lounge.

Dandy and Josco had obeyed Basi to the letter and Alali who had seen to it now returned to the "Palace" to inform his mentor that their mission had been successful. There was no doubt about that, for upstairs, on discovering her further losses, and especially of clothes she had rented from Madam Adekunle, she howled like a lioness in pain.

Hearing her howls from his "Palace", Basi began to boast to his friend. 'Al,' he said, 'we've got Madam precisely where we want her.'

'I can hear her screaming.'

'Good for her. She'll be back soon to complain about her further losses.'

'And then you can make her a proposal she dare not refuse.'

'Go and ask Dandy and Josco to return the goods to me forthwith. We'll be millionaires soon.'

'Will do. See you soon, millionaire.' Alali strode out of the room and out into Adetola Street, towards Dandy's Bar.

Madam, afflicted by the second theft of her property in one day, returned to Basi's "Palace". She was in tears.

'Basi, Basi, you know say de time wey I dey talk to you, de teeves come enter my house again, tief Madam Adekunle him cloth?'

'So you can see Alali and I had nothing to do with it.'

'Oh Gawd, wetin I go do? Wetin I go do – eh?'

'My Security Company can assist trace the goods.'

'True?'

'Yes. We're part of a national network. All I need do is get on the radio and the goods will be traced.'

'*Shay* no be una tief my property?'

'Madam, you don't have to hire my Company, if that's the way you feel.'

'I beg helep me, Basi. Help me.'

'I'm trying to help. If only you'll let me. Will you hire the security services of *Basi and Company*?'

'How much you go charge? Eh, my property-oh. My party! How much you want?'

'Twelve thousand naira per month. And you must promise to get the one hundred members of your Club to hire us too. That will make a cool million each year.'

'It's a matter of cash! Make I go my house go bring de cash.'

Madam left. Basi paced his "Palace", his eyes shining in expectation. He had achieved far more success than he had imagined. Once again, he had scored a signal victory over his cocky landlady. He had his stars to thank.

Alali had reached Dandy's Bar and told both Dandy and Josco to return Madam's goods to the "Palace". He returned to inform Basi that he had delivered his message and that Dandy and Josco were on their way.

'Madam returned to the Palace. She's retained our services.'

'Really?' marvelled Alali.

'Oh yes. Twelve thousand cool. And a hundred members of the American Dollar Club in the same amount. A cool million, I tell you.'

'To be a millionaire . . .'

'Think like a millionaire!'

Alali sat in the lounge chair, sampling their easy victory.

'This is simply brilliant,' he said.

'She'll be pleased when she returns to find all her goods here. She'll know that we are an efficient company. And the news will be all over the city in no time. We're made. Multi-millionaires.'

They shook hands in self-congratulation, back-slapped each other and whooped round the room excitedly. Basi looked out of the window to see if Dandy and Josco were on their way.

They were not. For, as Alali left the Bar and they prepared to send Madam's goods to Basi, who should turn up but Segi? She was surprised to find the Bar piled up unusually with cartons of beer, bottles of alcohol and wine, and a bundle of feminine clothes.

'What's happening, Dandy?' she asked suspiciously.

'Nothing,' Dandy replied.

'What d'you mean, nothing? From where are these cartons of beer? The bottles of wine?'

'What a question to ask a barkeeper?' chirped Josco.

'And the bundle of clothes?' asked Segi.

'What's your business?' Josco asked testily.

'My business is to keep you on the right side of the law. What have you two been up to?'

'Nothing. It's zust a zoke,' replied Dandy sheepishly.

'What joke? Come let me see.' Segi opened out the bundle of clothes and examined each item carefully. 'These are the clothes Madam just hired from Madam Adekunle for her party. How did you come by them?'

'It's none of your business!' Josco declared.

'Oh really? Well now, Josco, I think you had it coming to you a long time. The Police . . .'

Josco was frightened. He did not ever want to hear about the Police. He trembled like a leaf, his teeth chattering.

'Not the Police, Segi. Please! . . .' Then walking over to where Dandy stood, he whispered to him, 'You better tell her the truth.'

'Basi sent us to take them from Madam's place,' Dandy mumbled.

'Whatever for?' Segi asked.

'Madam's been at him all morning. And he wants her to hire his new Company's security services,' Dandy said.

'Security services! Basi's gone mad. So the best way to secure work from Madam is to rob her?' demanded Segi.

'It's no robbery. He means to return the items. After all, we've not used or sold any of them. They're all here,' Josco said.

'If I know you, Josco, you'll be hawking these things on the Bridge at daybreak.'

'No, no, no,' demurred he. 'Segi, honest, it's just a joke.'

'And a very expensive joke at that. You better send everything back to Madam's before I set the Police on you and your jokes.'

'And what do we tell Madam?' asked Dandy.

'Your business, not mine,' Segi snapped.

'This is not fair,' said Josco.

'I'm glad you think so. In any case, I'm going to No. 7 Adetola Street right away to wise Madam up about you. Ciao!'

Leaving Dandy and Josco with a load of problems on their hands, Segi kept her promise and went directly to Madam's flat. She found Madam dreamily trying to restore order to her lounge. Madam took fright at her entry. She turned round and on seeing her asked, 'Segi, na you?'

'Yes. Your lounge is a real mess.'

'Dem tief all my party drink plus de cloth wey I jus hire from Madam Adekunle.'

'What are you doing about it?'

'I don hire security to catch de teeves and return my property.'

'Basi's new Company, no doubt.'

'How you come know?'

'Because Basi masterminded the robbery.'

'Why?'

'To make you hire his Company.'

'So 'e know where my property dey?'

'Of course! They are in Dandy's Bar. I saw them there a few minutes ago.'

Madam was quite a sight. The anger welled up in her. Her pride was pricked. Basi had tried once again to play on her intelligence, to impose on her. She did and undid her headtie. She tied and retied her loin-cloth. 'Na so, ehn? I for talk. Dis Basi man. I go show am pepper today. I go show am pepper. *Jibiti* man. *Wuruwuru wayo* tief. Make 'e wait for me. Security Service. *Basi and Company*. 'E go see fire today.' She ran down the stairs, Segi in her wake, and irrupted into Basi's "Palace" just as Dandy and Josco set down all her goods before Basi.

At sight of her, Basi, unaware of what had transpired between Josco, Dandy and Segi at the Bar, announced proudly, 'We've found your goods, Madam.'

'You don find dem, ehn? Na you tief dem. Na you find dem.'

'What . . .' said Basi.

'Shurrup your lie lie mouth!' thundered Madam, as her eyes flashed lightning. 'You hire Dandy and Josco to tief my property so I go hire your security service, not so? *Jibiti* man. *Wuruwuru, wayo* tief. Security Service. I go secure you for prison. I tink you like *awoof*. You go see fire today. All of una. Prison!'

'Madam, please. I don't want to go to prison,' pleaded Josco.

'I go teach all of una. No be play play. Nonsense!'

'It was only a zoke, Madam,' dawdled Dandy.

'Una wan take me make ye-ye, ehn? Una look me, tink say I be de kind person useless people fit take play play?'

'Madam!' pleaded Basi.

Madam walked up to Basi and fixed him with eyes of steel.

'*Jibiti* man. I go punish you, *helele*. I go show you wetin you never see since your Mama born you. You, plus your Security Company. Importers and Exporters, Land Clearing, Security, Gold digging. I go bury you inside your gold mine. Today. *Shay* you sabi make fake Company? Wait and see!'

'The Company is real, Madam!' whined Basi helplessly.

'E-ehen! Na better Company? Good. Awright. De American Dollar Club members dey come my house tomorrow. Na your Company go make security for dem, you hear? Una go make sure say dem no tief dem tyres and dem cars. Awright?'

Basi was delighted. So Madam was about to hire the services of his Company after all. 'Hear! hear!' he cheered.

'Great!' said Alali, finding his speech at long last.

'We're back to business!' said Basi, smiling.
'Una go do am by *fosa*.'
'By *fosa*?' screamed Basi.
'Yes. Free of charge.'
'Nonsense!' Basi said.
'No be nonsense. If una no gree, I report una to Police for de tief una tief from my house. You must do the work by *fosa*.'
'Oh!' grumbled the group.

But Madam was not listening to them anymore. She was determined as ever to humiliate them.

'Send my property to my house!' she ordered.

And as they stooped slowly to pick up the cartons, she yelled, 'Quick!' They obeyed her. Finally she said in a loud voice, 'Security officers, Attention. Forward march!'

Basi and his friends trooped dejectedly out of the room, cartons, bottles and crates on their tired shoulders.

When the Amerdolians did arrive, Basi and his friends were on hand to render them the very essential service of watching over their cars, ensuring that they lost neither tyres nor whole cars. So enthusiastic were they, so thorough in execution, the fact was not lost on the proud Amerdolians. Madam earned fulsome praise as the owner of a very efficient Company with loyal, honest workers – a Lagos rarity.

The Ghost Workers

The elections over, it was time to share the booty. Many had obtained positions in government and settled down to the loot of the treasury – through contracts of inflated value which were not meant to be executed and did not get executed, although they were paid for in full; through loans which the banks were asked to make to favoured party members on the understanding that they were not to be repaid; and through other devious means as yet unknown to the book of tricks.

Perhaps none was more thorough, more brazen than that by which the payrolls of various government institutions and parastatal organizations were inflated to overblown sizes, leading to alarming amounts of money being filched out of government coffers. The newspapers were full of stories of huge armies of paper soldiers, paper messengers, paper clerks, paper nurses, paper mailmen, paper cooks, paper gardeners. They were known by the generic term "ghost workers".

And ghosts they were indeed. For they did no work, were not seen and yet they haunted the establishments and the city, causing nightmares to such as my uncle, one of the few who bothered about such minor irritations.

Basi was late to catch the fad and latch on to it. He came to know about it in an appropriately rather bizarre manner as he lay in bed, his feet up, his eyes fixed to the ceiling, in a vacant, dreamy stare. Alali was leafing through a newspaper. The failure of their security company had set him on his interminable search for a job. Doing the rounds of the offices, he had been introduced to ghost-working. Although he had "ghost-worked", that is, put his and Basi's names on several payrolls, he had not believed it until he read about it in the newspapers. That day's edition of the *Lagos Messenger* reconfirmed his information. He laughed excitedly, reading about it.

The sudden laugh surprised Basi. It woke him from his reverie. He sat bolt upright and asked, 'What's the matter?'

'Ghosts,' Alali replied and guffawed.

Basi took fright. 'Ghosts? Where? How? Ghosts? Here in the Palace? . . . My God, ghosts? Al?'

'Cool it, Mr B. Cool it.'

'Cool the ghosts? What d'you mean?' Basi trembled with fright.

Alali laughed heartily. 'I never saw you so frightened. Why, you're shaking from head to toe. What's the matter?'

'What did you say about ghosts?' Basi remained scared.

'Oh, the ghosts,' answered Alali carelessly.

Basi was in a different world. A world of his imagination, peopled by ghosts and ghouls. 'Ghosts, Al? Oh, my God, this must be Madam's doing. She's sent ghosts to hound me out of my Palace.' And he made to run out of the room. Alali stopped him.

'Cool it, man, cool it. It's only a news item in the papers.'

'Ghosts are only an item in the papers?' asked Basi.

'Yes.'

'You frightened me well enough, numskull,' said Basi.

'Mr B, I think you're a coward.'

Basi lunged at him. 'Al, are you gone crazy or something? You talking to me like that? You're growing familiar, too familiar. I don't take that from you or anybody. You dare call me names?'

Seeing that Basi was angry, Alali apologised profusely. Mollified after a while, Basi demanded and got the newspaper which Alali had been reading. He flipped through it quickly and came to the page with the ghost story. He read it frowning, and broke into a broad smile.

'I see, I see,' said he. 'There are ghosts on the payroll of the government.'

'Ghosts all over the place!' Alali replied.

'What's so exciting about that?'

'There's money in it. Millions!'

'Ghosts carry millions around?'

'Oh no. The payrolls are stuffed with names. These names are called "ghost workers". Come the end of the month, all workers are to be paid. Whoever has his name on the roll gets paid, whether he's worked or not. In this way, government pays millions each month.'

'Holy Moses!' wondered Basi. 'Is there anything people won't do for money in this God-forsaken city?'

'So how do you feel?'

'Rotten, Al, rotten.'

'Why?'

'All that easy money's been around and I never got my hands on it. Millions upon millions. Holy Moses!'

Alali told him he had in the past week organized to have their names on the payrolls of all the Ministries and parastatals. This pleased Basi beyond description. There was great excitement in his voice when he spoke:

'Holy Moses! Come the end of the month and all we're doing is dashing from one cashier to another; one building to another. If we do the same throughout the country, we become truly national figures.'

He embraced Alali, telling him how proud of him he was, adding, 'Have you calculated exactly how much we're going to make this month from ghost working?'

'It's frightful, man. Frightful. Millions! To be a millionaire . . .'

'Think like a millionaire!'

Basi had raised his voice beyond normal in his excitement and invited the attention of Madam as she sat upstairs in her apartment at a sumptuous lunch. Irked by Basi's noise, she abandoned her repast and arming herself with a screwdriver, repaired hastily downstairs. Her hurried footsteps on the stairs were unmistakable. When she arrived at the door like a wind, Basi and Alali quickly dived for cover. Madam entered, looked round and called Basi. Receiving no answer, but convinced that he was in the room alright, she started to remove the hinges of the door to Basi's room. Alali got up from his hiding place behind the food cupboard, rushed past Madam and fled through the door. Surprised, Madam stopped working at the hinges for a moment, then she resumed her work. Basi emerged from hiding and called to Madam.

'*Wuruwuru* man!' shouted she.

'What are you doing to my Palace?'

'Your "Palace"! I dey remove de door. You no see?'

'Leave the door alone,' pleaded Basi as he moved to restrain her.

'Commot, *jibiti* man!' And she returned to the door.

'Madam, what's the matter?'

'Why you dey disturb me everytime for my house? I no go hear sometin because you and your friend dey shout. To be a millionaire, think like a millionaire. Which kind millionaire you be sef? Rent you no pay, chop you no get. Still everytime million, million. If you no pay my rent, I remove de door.'

'I will pay. I'll pay. Everything. Soon.'

'Nonsense! You no fit pay. Which work you get?'

'Madam, believe me, I'm not unemployed. On the contrary, I'm overworked. I have more than thirty jobs.'

'More dan thirty jobs!' laughed Madam. 'More dan thirty jobs. Na your ghost dey work for thirty places de same time?' And she laughed again.

'You are right, Madam.'

'Na for night you dey do de work? After all you no dey commot for house for morning. Soso sleep na him you dey sleep.'

'Ghosts are all over the place.'

'True?'

'And ghosts work only at night.'

The repeated mention of the word "ghost" got Madam as worried as Basi when first he had heard Alali mention it. She went one better. She shut her eyes, dropped the screwdriver, and screamed, 'Ghosts! Ghosts!'

'You didn't see any ghosts, did you, Madam?' asked Basi half-seriously.

Madam did not wait to answer. She staggered out of the room and out into the Street. A light drizzle was falling, but Madam did not notice. She did not appear to know where she was going.

At Dandy's Bar, Dandy and Josco were drinking and chatting.

'Need an extra hand in the Bar?' asked Josco.

'What for? No one comes here these days.'

'Too many unemployed people. Yet government spends a lot on salaries.'

'To whom do they pay those salaries?' wondered Dandy, as he put his miniature bottle to his lips.

Presto, Madam came in trembling with fear. She was in quite a state.

'You see anytin for Adetola Street?' she whispered.

'Yes,' replied Dandy.

'Wetin?' asked Madam, drawing nearer him.

'Well, it's stranze,' Dandy said.
'Wetin be strange?'
'What he sees on the Street,' Josco joked.
'Like?'
'Madam walking into my Bar to ask for things unusual.' Dandy was enjoying himself. He winked knowingly at Josco who returned the compliment.

But Madam was in earnest. 'Una no see ghost for Adetola Street?' she asked.

'Ghosts?' asked Josco and Dandy simultaneously. Fear crept into their eyes.

'Yes. Basi say ghost plenty for Adetola, especially by night. Abi una see any ghost?'

Madam had planted the idea in them. It was surprising how the idea took root in their minds almost immediately.

'Now you talk of ghosts,' said Dandy, 'I did wonder how my money and my drinks keep disappearing.'

'And I get chased at night under the Bridge,' Josco said.
'Ghosts dey for Street!' Madam screamed.
'Ghosts are on the Street!' yelled Josco.
'Ghosts are on the Street,' piped Dandy.

Madam began to tremble uncontrollably. She ran out of the Bar. When she was gone, Dandy asked Josco if he actually thought there were ghosts on the Street? Josco said he did not think so.

Dandy opined that Basi had devised a scheme by which he would frighten Madam out of her wits with tall tales of ghosts – just to keep her from demanding her rent. They agreed to find out more about the ghosts from Basi. After a few more drinks, they set out for No. 7 Adetola Street.

Back at the "Palace", Alali had returned and Basi was regaling him with tales of his triumph over Madam. He recounted how the moment he told her he was ghost-working, she began to see ghosts.

'If she knew how much money there is in it, she would love ghost-work,' laughed Alali.

Walking over to Basi's "Palace", Dandy had convinced himself that Basi was at his usual tricks. He had seen no ghosts on the Street as he walked along, had never seen ghosts. It was all in Madam's imagination. Basi had set her up beautifully. And he had to be doing it for money. Dandy figured he wanted some of the money for himself.

Alali welcomed them cheerfully to the "Palace". Dandy went straight to the point combatively.

'Basi, what's all this about ghosts?' he asked.

'What's your business?' demanded Basi.

'Madam is scared stiff,' Josco said.

'About time too,' replied Basi testily. There was granite in his voice as he spoke. 'You know she came here armed with a screwdriver ready to remove the door to the Palace?'

'Hell, I should have known that!' Dandy blurted out.

'And then the ghosts caught up with her,' Alali chuckled away.

'If you're with the ghosts, Basi, there must be money with them,' Dandy essayed.

'Oh yeah.'

'Easy money,' Dandy said.

'Tons and tons of the commodity,' bragged Basi as usual.

'Can I have a piece of the action?' Dandy had finally arrived.

'Oh no,' replied Alali. 'The ghosts will eat you up, Dandy. You're nice, juicy and fat.'

'Watch it, young man,' Dandy said as he lunged at Alali. Josco came between them to stop a fight developing.

'Leave him alone, Al', Basi admonished his protégé.

'Thanks, Mr B,' Dandy said. 'But will you give me a piece of the action?'

'The action's in only one piece, Dandy. We mean to keep it that way,' Basi said.

Dandy was upset. He motioned to Josco with a flick of the neck that they leave. As the door shut behind him, he heard Basi say derisively, 'A piece of the action. Always!' As though that were some invitation, Dandy turned on his heels, opened the door and said, 'Let's have a piece of the action, Mr B.'

'Sorry, mate,' replied Basi, 'the action's in only one piece.'

Dandy shut the door and stayed outside long enough to hear Basi remind Alali that the month would soon end. 'The millions should roll in soon,' he laughed. To be a millionaire . . .'

'Think like a millionaire!' cried Alali joyfully.

Dandy did not return to the Bar. He went upstairs to Madam's apartment. Madam was in jitters. At the slightest sound, she imagined that ghosts were after her. She had been unable to get rid of the absurd fears which Basi had planted at the back of her mind. When Dandy knocked at the door, she jumped with fright, and sought refuge behind the dining table.

'Madam the Madam!' called Dandy.

'Who be dat?' Madam asked in a hoarse whisper.

'It's me,' replied Dandy.

'You na man or ghost?'

'Dandy in the flesh, Madam, Dandy himself.'

But Madam had already made up her mind what to do.

'Ghosts! Ghosts! Help! Help!!' she screamed, louder and louder until Dandy, unable to bear it, ran off.

The next few days were days of torture for Madam. But they were days of exultation for Basi and Alali as they luxuriated in the power which the fear they had spread on the Street gave them. Madam did not call at the "Palace". Whenever she went downstairs, she tiptoed miserably past Basi's door.

Dandy, angry with Basi for denying him a piece of the action in the ghost scheme, and unable to approach Madam, sat in frustration at the Bar, drinking down his upset. Josco called on him one day and met Segi at the door. They sat down to a drink and a chat while Dandy snored away.

'Dandy's been mad at Basi and Alali,' Josco confided in Segi.

'Why?'

'They won't give him a piece of the action.'

'What action?'

'Well, there's this thing about ghosts on the Street. And as I understand it, there's a lot of money in it.'

Dandy opened his eyes as though the mention of a lot of money had awakened him. He drawled out, 'Lots of money. Yeah.'

'Good morning, Dandy,' teased Segi.

Dandy rubbed his eyes. 'I dozed off, Segi,' he said. 'It's a hard life at the Bar. And now Basi's found the easy way out, he won't give me a piece of the action.'

'Exactly what is this action?' probed Segi with a smile.

'Has to do with ghosts carrying heavy money bags. Mr B's helping them. He is now a ghost-worker. He will get rich.' And he sighed with envy.

'You believe that?'

'He sure does,' replied Josco. 'Went to discuss it with Madam.'

'Madam saw the ghosts while I was at her place.'

'What did she do?' asked Segi.

'Screamed. Yelled. Called for help,' replied Dandy.

'And what did you do?'

'Found my way out. Fast as I could make it.'

'Did you find any money bags on the way?'

'Hell, no!'

'Any ghosts?'

Dandy hesitated for a while. 'Well, I think so. Yes. I saw the ghosts... I did,' he said, a far-away look in his eyes.

Segi laughed. She could guess what had happened. Basi was taking advantage of Madam. She would have to advise Madam. She took leave of Dandy after inviting him and Josco to Madam's place. Shortly after her departure, Josco emptied his glass and went into the toilet. Dandy had dozed off. He opened his eyes only when he heard his name shouted loud by Basi who had just entered. 'Ghost! Ghost! Help! Help!' he screamed. Josco returned to the Bar.

Basi ran off, as Dandy hid behind the Bar, an absurd fear of ghosts leaving him trembling like a leaf in the wind. Basi returned to his "Palace" greatly excited, an impish smile on his face.

'Everyone's scared stiff of ghosts on the Street now,' he told Alali.

'You should hear Dandy screaming the moment he saw me. "Ghosts! Ghosts! Ghosts! Help! Help!" ' he told Alali.

'Madam's completely shattered too.'

'She won't have time to ask for her rent, now.'

'Gives us a breathing space before the money starts rolling in.'

'When's pay day?'

'The day after tomorrow.'

'We have to make some money before then. Some chicken change to keep body and soul together.'

And so a plan was hatched to conjure ghosts away from the Street for the benefit of Madam and Dandy and all those who had fallen prey to ghost stories. Basi swore he would earn "baby millions" from his new venture and went into ecstasies calculating how much each victim would pay him to have the ghosts exorcised.

Unfortunately for him, he had not counted on Segi. She stopped by at Madam's. Madam lay prostrate on her sofa, her eyes glazed and fixed on the ceiling as her lips moved in silent prayer. She jumped up as soon as she heard Segi's footsteps.

'It's me, Madam,' Segi announced.

'Oh, Segi, I happy say you come. I dey fear for . . .'

'There are no ghosts on Adetola Street,' she said to allay her fears.

'No call dem name at all, at all or I go begin see . . .'

'But Madam, it's all in Basi's imagination.'

'Tell me something!'

Dandy and Josco came into the lounge and sat down.

'Well, Basi and Alali have found a way of earning easy money. They have put their names on the payrolls of all the Ministries and parastatals. They do no work, but hope to be paid at the end of the month. They are called ghost-workers.'

'Hell, I should have known that!' Dandy yelled. 'Josco, let's go.'

He got up, left the room. Josco followed him.

'Wetin dem want do now?' Madam asked.
'Dandy is so foolish, I feel sorry for him.'
Regaining her composure and self-assurance, Madam thanked Segi for getting her out of the scare of ghosts which Basi had engineered in her. She knew now what to do, although she was not in a hurry to do it. She would take her revenge in her own time.

Dandy and Josco had gone to the Bar to fortify themselves for the confrontation with Basi which Dandy planned once Segi had introduced him to Basi's scheme. Madam however preceded them at Basi's.

Basi was counting his riches when Madam called on him.

'Each department gives one thousand, one thousand departments will yield a million. Oh, I've made it! I've made it! I'm rich. Rich!'

'Na so,' said Madam derisively.

'Ah, Madam! The ghosts are beginning to yield their fruit.'

'Tell me something!'

'Oh yes. And I wanted to tell you, I can conjure away all those ghosts who've been haunting you.'

'Na him.'

'It will cost some money.'

'It's a matter of cash!'

'When do I start?'

'Now, now. *Wayo* man. *Jibiti* man. *Wuruwuru* tief. You tink say I no go know? You too like *awoof*. You wan tief government money, ehn? I don catch you. Water don pass *gari*.'

Basi went on his knees immediately. He pleaded fervently with Madam. 'I didn't start it. I'm only doing as others,' he said.

'Na him,' Madam replied sarcastically.

'Madam, everyone's doing it.'

'I hear.' Thus Madam, derisively.

'Honestly, Madam. Everyone.'

'So why you begin frighten me by talk of ghost and no ghost?'

'It was only a joke, Madam. A practical joke.'

'*Shay* you go get plenty money by de ghost work?'

'Millions, Madam, millions.'

'Good. If you no give me some of dat money, I send you to prison. One time!'

'Please, Madam, please. What d'you want?'

'If you get ten naira, you give me eight.'

'Oh, Madam.'

'Oderwise, I send you to prison, useless, *wayo* man.'

'Alright then,' agreed Basi. He knew Madam would act true to her word, if he dared demur.

'Plus you go clean all de gutters round de house.'
'Why?' asked Basi.
'Because government dey pay you. Abi, not so?'
Basi was dumbstruck. Madam dug into him.
'When de ghosts begin work, we go get plenty money. You and me ... To be a millionaire, tink like millionaire.' And she swaggered out of the room.

Basi watched her go. He was helpless in the situation. He was still thus when Dandy and Josco called on him. Dandy's self-assured steps told Basi that he too knew the truth about ghosts.

'So how are the ghosts?' asked Dandy.
'They're working, working, working.'
'And when they come marching in?'
'Alali, Madam and I will smile.'
'So Madam has joined you?'
'Oh yes. She has eighty per cent.'
'You will keep me out as usual?'
'Course you're out. Clean out. I won't do business with you. You're a fool!'
'Not this time, Mr B. Oh no. Josco and I are on the payrolls already.'
'You put your names there?'
'Oh no,' Josco answered. 'We shall be Basi and Alali.'
'That's dishonest,' Basi asserted vehemently. 'I warn you against impersonation. It's a criminal offence.'
'Thank you, Mr B,' Dandy answered coolly.
'I'll report you to the Police,' Basi threatened.
'Suit yourself,' Dandy replied.

Basi was stuck. He knew that he could not report to the Police. He had to manoeuvre out of what was essentially a tight corner. He could not afford to lose to Dandy.

'Right, Dandy,' he said. And extending a hand to him, he said, 'We're friends. You have a sure piece of the action. After all, Alali and I couldn't be in all those places at once on pay day. Yes, you can both represent us in some of the departments.'

'Cool!' exulted Josco.
'And you will help clean the gutters around the premises here.'
'Why?' interposed Dandy testily.
'Madam demands it.'
'What's she got to do with it?' demanded Josco.
'She's got a huge piece of the action.'
'No way!' asserted Dandy.
'What d'you mean, no way?' asked Basi.

'There's no how she can go from office to office claiming to be Basi or Alali. So how can she earn money when she's done no work?'

Basi smiled triumphantly. 'But that's what ghost-work is about. And that's why we've all settled for it.'

Dandy was disturbed. He paced the room restlessly. He did not see why he should clean Madam's gutters, go round collecting the salaries and let Madam share in the booty.

'Look, Mr B, you give in too much, too often to that cantakerous, greedy woman.'

'She's my landlady and I owe her a lot of money.'

'Oh well,' said Dandy, surrendering. But not without a struggle. 'I don't have to clean her gutters, anyway.'

'Would you rather she reported us to the Police? She's threatened to do so.'

Josco did not want to hear about the Police under any circumstances. 'Say no more, Mr. B,' he pleaded instantly. 'I'll clean the gutters.'

Basi was winning. His accustomed cheerfulness returned and he began to give instructions. 'Now then, tomorrow is the day. Dandy, you'll work from the east; Josco, from the west. I'll work from the north and Alali from the south. We'll meet here at the centre. In my Palace. With the money bags ... The millions are waiting for us, boys. Get ready to spend cash, hard cash.'

His optimism infected Dandy. 'Great!' shouted the latter.

He paced the room, rubbing his palms together.

'To be a millionaire ...' he smiled.

'Think like a millionaire!' replied Basi and Josco simultaneously. There were handshakes all round and they congratulated one another on their extraordinary fortune.

They were about to take leave of each other when Madam reappeared, spade in hand to remind Basi of his promise to clean the gutters around the premises. She merely handed over the spade to Basi and turned on her arrogant heels.

All that evening, the residents of Adetola Street were surprised, indeed shocked, to find Alali, Dandy and Josco cleaning Madam's filthy gutters. Basi stood up, supervising and cheering them. As no one ever cleaned the gutters on Adetola Street, the labours of Basi and his friends were regarded as odd. Some began to wonder if the four men had gone mad or tipsy or both. Many who heard of what was happening came to see for themselves. They registered their shocked disbelief in ohs and ahs. 'They are mad! They are mad!' all the residents of the Street said, as little mounds of green debris piled up between the gutter and the road.

They were completely fatigued by the time they were done, and even

Madam who watched from a vantage point on her balcony, felt that they had surpassed themselves. They parted in excellent spirits, though, Basi inviting them all to the "Palace" for seven-thirty the following morning.

It must be supposed that they slept well that night and that Dandy whose Bar was a centre of gossip did not hear the news which had started to do the rounds on the Street.

It was Segi who brought the news early the following morning to Madam who, having had a hearty breakfast, was preparing to go out. Madam was happy to see Segi who had not only freed her from her absurd fear of ghosts, but had given her the opportunity to have her own back on Basi. Now the gutters around her house were spick and span, although she felt sure they would soon get back to their accustomed filthy state. She embraced Segi.

'Welcome, Segi. I happy say you tell me wetin Basi bin dey plan.'

'Basi is a con man,' Segi said.

'Proper *wayo* man. Anyway, dem don clean my gutter well well, and any money dem get from dat ghost work, na me go chop all. All!'

'So you have joined their dishonest scheme?'

Madam was taken aback. She looked carefully at Segi and seeing disapproval in her face, decided to backtrack. 'Ah, no-oh. I bin tell dem make dem clean my gutter. Dem say I must to join to do ghost-work. Na him I 'gree,' Madam lied.

'So now they've cleaned the gutters you won't work with them?'

'At all, at all,' Madam said emphatically.

'Well, I'm happy you are not with them because you know Basi is a crook.'

'Na war for Basi. Every time money, money, money. Million. Many many million. Still 'e no fit pay rent.'

'I think I'll deal with him this time,' Segi said.

Madam thought about that for a while. In the true tradition of Adetola Street, she decided to ditch Basi.

'Show am pepper, my sister,' she said. 'Make we go Basi him house. I know say 'e never wake, *wayo* man.'

They walked leisurely downstairs.

Basi and Alali had just woken up simultaneously. There was a cheeriness about them as they completed their morning toilette, that could only have been accounted for by the knowledge that it was a special day. Their conversation showed as much.

'This is the day, Mr B,' said Alali.

'Yeah. The millions come marching in today.'

'I dreamt of it last night.'

'So did I. I lay there on that miserable bed. And the millions came to wake me up. "Up, up, millionaire Basi. Take us in your arms. Embrace us. Kiss us. Love us. Millionaire!" '

'To be a millionaire . . .'

'Think like a millionaire! . . . Now, Al, you know I've had to sell a part of the business to Madam, Dandy and Josco. Bad people. Vicious and greedy. You must keep an eye on them. They may try to trick us out of the millions. Keep your ear to the ground. Watch out for Segi too. She may be used against us. Understood?'

'Yes, Mr B.'

'Wonderful! Let me just get my hands on those millions.'

'What are you going to do with all that money?'

That amused Basi no end. What was he going to do with all that money? He burst into loud peals of laughter. He was still laughing when Dandy and Josco walked into the room.

'Welcome, gentlemen, welcome,' he said through his laugh. 'Did you hear Al?'

'Oh no. What did he say?'

' "What are you going to do with all that money?" he asks. Well, Al, I will . . . enjoy it.'

'Super!' cheered Josco.

'Good, good, good,' said Basi, rubbing his palms gleefully. It's all go now. And we'll all meet at the centre here in my Palace, remember. Good, shall we then?'

Madam and Segi sauntered into the room. Basi eyed Alali and he slipped out.

'Hey, ladies, what brings you to my Palace so early on God's best morning of the year?'

'What makes it the best morning of the year?' asked Segi.

'It's pay-day today,' said Basi.

'Pay-day for a chronically jobless man?'

'Oh, you don't know, Segi. Al, Dandy, Josco and I have been working very hard. We are now on the payrolls of the government.'

'Payrolls of the government?'

'Yes!' answered Josco, Dandy and Basi together.

'Bad news, mates,' Segi announced.

'What?' asked Basi, missing a heartbeat.

'Well, government has just discovered that they've been paying too many workers. Now they won't pay unless workers show a proper letter of engagement, a passport photograph and evidence of work done.'

'Holy Moses!' shouted Basi, disappointment boldly stamped on his face.

'Dirty dozen!' said Josco.

'Shurrup!' Madam ordered him.

'And the Police are on the trail of ghost-workers.'

Josco went on his knees. He trembled like a reed in the tide. 'Mercy, Segi, mercy,' he pleaded. 'We haven't received any money. Not a kobo.' He began to whimper.

Dandy walked up to him and pulled him up. 'Get up, Zosco,' he said. 'It's not your name that's on the payrolls. Zust Basi and Alali, the clever dicks. Millionaires on-the-make. Now face the music, Mr B. Ghost-worker!'

He motioned to Josco with a flick of his neck to leave the room. They walked away triumphantly, without as much as a look in the direction of Basi.

Basi was not to be put down. 'Right,' says he. 'So I lost a million this time. Big deal! There are other millions to make.'

'From whom?' asked Segi.

'Madam will, for one, pay me for cleaning the gutters of the premises,' he said.

'At all, at all,' replied Madam. 'I tink you be ghost-worker? Dem dey pay ghost if 'e no work. If 'e work, dem no pay am. Abi, no be so?'

'You're mean, Madam!' Basi cursed.

'Abi, you dey curse me? *Wuruwuru, wayo* man. You curse me? I go remove de door of dis room, now now! If you talk again, I show you pepper . . . Wey my rent? Give me my rent, *jibiti* man.'

'Madam, I just lost one thousand jobs. How do you expect me to pay your rent?'

'I no care. I no busy. If you no pay de rent now now, I remove de door.'

'We cleaned the gutters already, Madam,' pleaded Basi.

'I no care. I no busy. Dat na ghost work. Ghost no dey . . .'

Madam was already at the door, holding and shaking it as if to tear it away from the hinges. In the same moment, there irrupted into the room a figure dressed in whites, as a ghost. Madam and Segi took fright. Yelling 'Ghost! Ghost!' they fled from the room. Basi was at their heels. But he felt a pair of hands hold him back, wrestle him to the floor.

Alali threw off the white bedsheet and stood in the centre of the room laughing.

'Al!' called Basi, pleasantly surprised.

'Mr B!' replied Alali.

'To be a millionaire . . .'

'Think like a millionaire!'

They sat in the room, laughing out their ribs, their failure behind them, as though it had not happened.

The successful ghost workers, whose activities had alerted the goverment, were not so easily beaten. They rested for a while but also returned – after the government had lowered its guard. They continued to haunt their victim for a long time. Which was no surprise to my uncle.

The Proposal

Watching Basi and his friends over the months, I thought they had exhausted all the avenues to wealth which Adetola Street offered. My uncle had decidedly given up on them. They no longer featured in the conversation of our household. As far as he was concerned, they were a blot on the landscape and best ignored since he could not remove them with a flick of his fingers. So he dismissed them from his mind, calling them "jokers", "clowns" and "childish idiots".

Quite on the contrary, I had a feeling that Basi was perhaps the most serious man on the Street. At least he took himself seriously and pursued his aims with a singlemindedness which was really quite uncharacteristic of the men of my acquaintance. I do not know how often I hoped that Basi would finally find the key, the missing link that would enable him make his millions, just to show the residents of the Street that nothing was beyond our dreams. And perhaps I was not alone in wishing him well. Otherwise, why was he so popular on the Street? Why did the children love him so much? Why did they run after him, fondly calling him "Mr B"? Why did the adults adore him, though secretly? Or were they all foolish?

My interest in Basi had certainly opened my eyes to the way we were on Adetola Street. I did not quite need my uncle and the interpretation he put on Basi and his friends. I could now draw the conclusions myself, based upon my observation of Basi's ways and exploits. What was phenomenal about him was the way he seemed to understand everything about the ways of men, and how he sought to subordinate these ways to his will, to his benefit. Although he had not succeeded, he had come near to success more than once; somewhere at the back of my mind, I felt that he would succeed one day. I longed for that day, even more than he appeared to hunger for it.

He reminded me ever so powerfully of the Tortoise, the hero of all the folktales of my childhood, an archetypal figure, the eternal trickster who, from story to story, was only temporarily bested, never defeated. If so, Basi had not exhausted himself. He would still offer me a lot more to enjoy, a lot more to ponder upon. I waited anxiously.

My time on the Street was drawing to an end. I was about to go into University and I did want to leave Adetola Street without fond memories. I was not to be disappointed. For, at my age, love is important. And the last escapade of Basi and his friends, which I was privileged to witness before my exit from the Street, had to do with love.

I did wonder from time to time why none of the famous six on the Street was married. Did they not know about love? Did they not wish "to settle down", as my uncle normally described marriage? The events of my final days on the Street were to prove that this was as much on their minds as it was on mine.

It all started, as the story is told, as Segi and Madam chatted one day in Madam's lounge. Segi sat puffing away at her cigarette while Madam sipped her favourite wine. They chatted about marriage and Madam spoke as to how marriage did not matter when one was young, but as one grew older, it became, if not an obsession, at least an important matter.

'No be say I old-oh,' she said. 'De tin be say . . .'

'Of course you're not old,' replied Segi as she puffed away at her cigarette.

'Last week, some members of American Dollar Club tell me say I still dey look young.'

'That's true.'

'One of dem come call me "sweet sixteen." '

The way she said it, you could tell she was enamoured of the term.

'Really?' asked Segi, rolling her lovely eyes archly.

'Yes. Dat day, as I return, I come look for my mirror well well. I no dey boast-oh. But I like de tin wey I see.'

'How nice!'

'You tink de woman wey call me "sweet sixteen" dey talk true?'

'Sure!'

'Make 'e no be say you dey flatter me-oh?'

'Not at all,' replied Segi with a smile.

Madam got up and stood before the large mirror in the lounge. She made faces, touched the wrinkles on her face, felt her breasts, her stomach and her upper arm. She declared that her face had a few wrinkles, her breasts had grown a little flabby, she had a bit more flesh on her stomach and upper arm but then added quickly that exercise would soon bring her back to shape. She did a few exercises. A bend, a lifting of both arms. And she felt better.

Segi suggested that make-up would help. Madam agreed with her, then declared herself alright, regretting though that it appeared only women noticed the fact, not men.

The Proposal

'Men,' hissed Segi, 'they don't know what's good for them. I don't give a damn for them.'

'Tell me something!' replied Madam.

'I don't give a hoot for men.'

'When woman young, men go chase am. When 'e old small, men go just look am, greet am. When 'e don old dem no look am, no greet am. Na so woman life dey.'

'Men!' hissed Segi.

'But old men go dey follow young girl-oh.'

'Young men prefer mature women, I'm told.'

'Tell me something!'

'Yes, Madam. Which penniless, homeless man would not be excited by a woman who can feed, clothe, house and mother him?'

'Na true-oh.'

'You should think about that seriously.'

'You know anybody like dat?'

Segi thought for a while and came up with a bright idea.

'Well, come to think of it, how about Basi?'

'Basi?'

'He's not married, is he?'

'No.'

'Why can't you buy his love and attention?'

Madam collapsed into a chair and laughed hilariously. Laughter-induced tears welled up in her eyes. She wiped her eyes and laughed again, uncontrollably.

'Basi! Ha! ha! Wetin you mean? Basi! Ha! ha! ha!'

'What's wrong with him? He's handsome . . .'

'Proper *jibiti* man. 'E no get common kobo, ha! ha!'

'That will make him obey your smallest wish.'

'Basi!' And Madam laughed again. 'How person fit marry Basi? 'E go kill person with dat him million talk. To be millionaire, tink like millionaire! Ha! ha!' And she mimicked a Basi-style walk.

'If you won't have Basi, there must be someone else.'

'I never see de person wey I fit marry.'

'Why not write to the newspapers?'

Madam listened attentively as Segi outlined how to set about it. The way she put it, it sounded quite easy. Place an advertisement in the papers. Rich, unmarried, marriageable woman in her early thirties looking for a young, handsome, cultured husband. Professional preferred. Or something like that. Applicants to report in person to a selected rendezvous. That would do the trick. Madam was not quite sure. She could not sign such an advertisement. Segi advised that she did not have to sign her name. A pseudonym would do. A friend of hers had got the cutest husband in town the same way. It was amazing how many shy, well-groomed young men could not find the right type of woman to marry!

Madam promised to think about it. Preening herself before the mirror, she said she could do with a nice, handsome, young husband, more so as she thought herself still quite young and good-looking.

Madam was not one to waste words or let a beautiful opportunity pass her by. Her conversation with Segi was an eye-opener and she meant to benefit by it.

As often happens, in fiction as in real-life, that very day a letter had arrived in Basi's "Palace" as Alali and Basi sat together doing nothing, as usual. It will not be quite correct to suggest that they were idling. Alali was smoking the very end of a cigarette, determined to draw the last whiff of tobacco from it. Basi sat reading the letter which had just been delivered. From time to time, he looked away from the letter at his pupil, struggling with the butt of a cigarette. When he saw danger threaten, he raised an alarm:

'Hey, Al, that cigarette's finished. You're going to burn your lips.'

'I'm hungry, Mr B,' Alali casually replied and finally abandoned the cigarette, eyeing it sadly as it burnt itself out on the cement floor.

'Hunger is a common condition, Al. Here's what someone back home says. "I'm hungry. Please help me. Send some money. After ten years in Lagos, you must have money, a good wife and children." See, Al?'

Alali laughed, saying, 'They must be dreaming out there in the bush.'

'Money's no problem. The millions are bound to roll in soon.'

Such optimism always spurred Alali to greater things. The words were no sooner out of Basi's lips than Alali trumpeted their great slogan, 'To be a millionaire . . .' To which, inevitably, Basi answered, 'Think like a millionaire!' They allowed the sentiments to seep down the "Palace" walls. Then Alali primed his mentor further. 'But a good wife and children?'

'Well, those don't just roll in.'

'They could come after the millions. I mean, no woman likes to marry a poor, down-and-out-fellow . . .'

'Like Dandy.'

'Or me.'

Basi got up, paced the room, deep in thought. 'You've given me an idea, Al,' he said after a while.

'What?'

'Suppose instead of the wife and children following the millions it was the other way round?'

'Impossible!'

'What's impossible?'

'Money doesn't go after women; women go where there's money.'

Dismissing that, Basi said, 'In Lagos, everything is possible.' He continued to pace the room in thought. Suddenly facing Alali, he asked, 'Listen Al, you agree I'm handsome?'

'Sure.'

'Tall?'

'Yes.'

'Personable?'

'Perfectly so.'

'What makes a man a more eligible bachelor?' Basi asked.

'Money in his pockets. If a man with the face of a chimp, or the size of a midget has money, he'll find a beauty queen to marry.'

'Well, alright,' conceded Basi grudgingly. 'But, this city is crawling with a variety of women – rich traders, wealthy professionals, divorcees, widows – all dying for excitement.'

'What sort of excitement?'

'The type money cannot buy . . . Company, good company.'

'What for?'

'For parties, shows, dances, dinners, you name it. A rich woman walks single into a party and the riff-raff come along and ask for a dance. Insulting?'

'Yeah.'

'But if the same woman had a husband by her side, she'd adorn the party. Lagosians hate unaccompanied, independent women. And somewhere in this city, there are such women.'

'Yeah.'

'The only thing to do is find them.'

'You need not just one, but several?'

'Well, one must have a choice in these matters. Establish a fall-back situation . . . If one lets you down, you go to the next.'

'Brilliant,' said Alali. 'What do we do?'

'What d'you mean, "we"?'

'I'm personable too, am I not? And am not short? So what stops me?'

Basi was genuinely angry. 'Al, you think too much of yourself sometimes, you know. You want to enjoy all senior jokes.'

'So it's a joke?'

'Who said? I'm in search of a wife. A wife whose pretty face will set the millions dancing my way.'

The mention of the word "millions" brought the slogan 'To be a millionaire . . .'

'Think like a millionaire!' shouted Basi.
'What will you do?' asked Alali.
'I think I'll place an advertisement in the papers.'
'Good idea.'
'Personable, young, millionaire-on-the-make . . . I like that . . . millionaire-on-the-make, desires in marriage a mature, beautiful, even-tempered lady. Must be a professional and or wealthy.'
'No woman could refuse so inviting a call.'
'The bit about the millionaire-on-the-make must entice them,' said Basi.
'Oh yeah. Birds of the same feather flock . . . you know . . .'
'That's the idea. A rich woman for a rich man, eh, Al?'
'Good idea, Mr B.'

Basi sat down to write out the advertisement. He wrote quickly; the words flowed easily. Alali leaned over his shoulders and read as he wrote. Soon, Basi was done. He read it over carefully.
'That should do it,' he said.
'Yes. Except you have some loonies replying to the advertisement.'
'Loonies? Who are loonies?'
'Mad men, mad women.'
'And why should they reply to my advert?' Basi asked testily.

He glared at Alali who immediately found refuge in humility.
'I didn't mean it that way.'
'Al, you better watch it, understand? Because one of these days you'll get what's been coming to you for a long time.'
'Yes, Mr B,' said Alali, avoiding Basi's lunge at him.
'Thanks a million,' said Basi.
'To be a millionaire . . .'
'Think like a millionaire!'

Peace was made; Basi felt good. He said he would go to place the advertisement in the newspaper. He perked himself up and was soon ready to leave.
'See that none of this gets out to the goons on the Street. Because once they know, there'll be trouble.'
'Yes, Mr B.'
'If this gets out, I'll hold you fully responsible. Because you're the only one who knows.'
'Unless Madam has been eavesdropping on us through the keyhole as usual.'
'She has not.'

And with a "bye for now", Basi left the room.
Odeco Nigeria Limited was a well-known establishment on the Street.

The Proposal

Its signboard was, as usual, unmistakable. It rose from a long pole above a corrugated iron sheet wall and told the world that *Odeco* received advertisements for all the newspapers in Lagos and elsewhere. "Put your adverteesement in all newspaper," it admonished passers-by. "Seeing is believing". Only those who needed its services knew what the office looked like. Barricaded behind the rusty corrugated iron sheets, it hid itself in a building lot, among cement blocks, cement mixers, iron rods and planks. Its Managing Director was a Storekeeper, with the responsibility of ensuring that none of the property of the developer disappeared at night with thieves of whom there was an abundance, or in the day with the workers of whom there was an equal abundance. To fulfil this onerous responsibility, the Storekeeper made the building lot his home, cooking, eating and sleeping there. It was not known where he performed his ablutions. What was known is that he received advertisements for all national newspapers on the side.

Odeco was, in truth, his main business. The storekeeping job he did on the side. He had been using the empty lot unauthorisedly for the *Odeco* business and when the owner of the lot wanted to evict him, he offered his services as Storekeeper. He charged minimally for these services, having extracted a promise from the landlord to have the garage in the new building reserved for the use of *Odeco*.

As Managing Director of *Odeco*, he held a very powerful position on the Street, as the custodian of red-hot information on obituaries, marriages, changes of name for whatever reason, jobs wanted, situations vacant, houses to let and so on and so forth.

It was to him that both Madam and Basi repaired to place their advertisements. And he it was who advised both parties which newspaper would publish their announcement earliest. Needless to say, both advertisements appeared on the same day in the same newspaper. And the facts were common property to a favoured few even before the newspaper published them. But that is another story.

Suffice it to say that Josco bought the newspaper in which the facts were published on the day as he paid his usual visit to Dandy's Bar. He turned over the pages leisurely as he drank his favourite beer. The advertisement column caught his attention. He read something which tickled him mightily and he went into stitches.

'Boy Zosco, what's so funny? asked Dandy who was busy adulterating drinks at the Bar.

'Some of these Lagos characters have gone crazy,' replied Josco.

'The city's full of them. Gutter men. Down-and-out people.'

'Like you?' teased Josco.

'Dandy's down, not out,' he snapped.

'I see. Well, these ones in the newspaper today seem to be on the rise. Listen. This woman wants a husband and advertises for one.'

'That's usual, these days. She didn't include her photograph, did she?'

'She might look a cross between a sheep and a cat and who'd want her then?'

Dandy laughed. 'Is she rich?' he asked.

'So the advertisement says.'

'Young?'

'Early thirties.'

'Even if she looks like a pig, she'll find a husband.'

'Would you marry her?'

'Why not?'

'D'you care to answer the advertisement then?'

'Does it say she wants a man like me?'

'She wants a young, handsome, cultured husband. Preferably a professional.'

Dandy chewed over that for a moment. Then he said, 'Yes, I'm young, handsome, cultured. And I have the equipment for a husband... But the professional bit, well, barkeeping is a profession, isn't it?'

'Sure it is. I think you should answer the advert, man.'

'Boy Zosco, I don't think I can stick a wise Lagos woman.'

'If you marry her, you'll be rich.'

'No. What I need is a young girl from the village. One I can order around. Who'll help me in the Bar. I hate your Lagos madams. But who knows...'

'Suppose the advertiser should turn out to be Madam, Mr B's landlady?'

'Or someone like her?'

'That should be something!'

'The garrulous, ancient hag will kill me in one week of marriage.'

'She'll treat you like a slave.'

'Ask me to do her laundry, sweep her floor. Taunt me day in, day out with her riches.' And he fell to acting out a scene with Madam softly calling "Dandy dear, serve me breakfast". "Dandy dear, fetch my shoes". "Dandy dear, it's a matter of cash". They laughed.

Dandy said, 'No, Boy Zosco, I won't marry a Lagos madam,' and returned to his chores while Josco read his newspaper.

After a while, Dandy said, 'Boy Zosco, no one comes to the Bar these days.'

'Not even Basi?'

'He's so broke, he can only drink on credit.'

'He'll pay when his millions start rolling in.'

Dandy laughed. 'When's that?' he asked.

'He alone knows ... Look, Dandy, here's another advert. This time from someone on-the-make.'

'On-the-make? What does that mean?'

'I'll read it in full,' said Josco. 'Young millionaire on-the-make desires in marriage a mature, beautiful, even-tempered lady. Must be a professional and or wealthy.'

'Where's the young millionaire going to get that sort of creature?'

'God alone knows,' Josco replied.

'If she's beautiful, she won't be even-tempered. And if she's a professional, she can't be wealthy.'

'That's true.'

'I say, the city is crawling with a lot of cranks.'

There was silence for a while as Josco digested Dandy's words.

Suddenly, he said, 'Say, Dandy, the idea of the young millionaire-on-the-make rings a familiar bell?'

'Sounds like Basi to me.'

'I didn't think there was another Basi in town.'

'Oh yes. Lagos practically creeps with his type.'

'I've got an idea, Dandy,' Josco said quickly.

'Not one of those mad practical zokes of yours?'

'I mean, I could make the lady meet the young millionaire-on-the-make.'

'By sending each of them a reply.'

'Sure. And if they met here in the Bar with their friends, you would sell more beer and spirits than you've done in the past year!'

'Interesting!' Dandy said.

'They're both stinking rich. They'll be wanting to show off.'

'The rich don't drink, Zosco, and they don't show off.'

'Not in Lagos. Who holds the night parties, blocking the roads and streets? Who throws money on the faces of singers and dancers? Dandy, the Bar must come alive for once.'

Dandy said he would go along with Josco.

'Stock the Bar with champagne, brandy and beer. The lady and the millionaire-on-the-make are going to meet here. I'm going to invite them.' He told Dandy exactly what he proposed to do.

He wasted no time in carrying out his resolve. The imp in him flourished as he sent the letters off, both letters signed "Hibiscus". In both letters, he named a date, the Saturday following and prayed, hoped and waited. He took Dandy into his confidence. He was not to be disappointed.

The Managing Director of *Odeco Nigeria Limited* received both letters, opened and read them discreetly, re-sealed and despatched them. It was his custom. And so it happened that Madam received a reply to her advertisement.

She shared the news with Segi as soon as she got it.

'I told you it would happen, didn't I?' Segi said.

'Tell me something!'

'It's happened just as in the case of my friend. Her lover signed his letter "Allamanda". Yours has signed his "Hibiscus." '

'Dem like flower.'

'Flowers are a sign of love and purity, Madam.'

'Hibiscus. I like de name. I like am plenty.'

'And you are to meet him at Dandy's Bar.'

'De man sabi sometin. Sometime 'e don know my house sef. Na him 'e come say make him meet me near am. So we go reach home quick after de meeting.'

Madam was over the moon. In her ecstasy, she did not stop to think. She did not for once suspect that anyone close to her might have answered the advertisement. She did not even suspect that someone might be pulling her legs. On Adetola Street, everything in a newspaper was taken at face value. Madam was as gullible as they come, and the way to her desires was a one-way street.

'I beg, Segi, make you come on Saturday. Make we go Dandy's Bar together. You go help me dress, you hear?'

Segi promised.

'I go put hibiscus for my dress. Make de man know say me I know dat flower be wetin you call am, Segi . . . sign of love and purity.'

The euphoria in Madam's lounge was matched by that in Basi's "Palace" downstairs. Alali passing by *Odeco Nigeria Limited* had been halted by the discreet Managing Director of that worthy establishment who gave him a letter meant for Basi's eyes only. Alali carrying the letter home excitedly called Basi from the doorway.

'Mr B, there's news for you.'

Basi was lying in bed, day-dreaming as usual. He sat up on hearing Alali's words. 'Good news? Bad news?' he asked.

'It's a letter.'

Basi's face fell. He lay back in bed. 'Must be someone from the village asking for a loan,' he said in a low voice.

'Nope. This one bears a Lagos postmark.'

'A Lagos postmark? It's impossible.'

'It is from Lagos.' He gave the letter to Basi.

Basi took it, looked at the postmark. 'So I see . . . So I see . . .,' said he, and ripping the envelope open, asked, 'Who in Lagos remembers good old Basi today?'

'Could be the taxman.'

'That's not funny, Al,' replied Basi, giving him a dark look.

'A lover?'

Basi had torn the envelope open and was reading the letter.

'What d'you know?' whooped he.

'What?'

'The letter's from a lover . . . Al, it's the reply to my paid advert.'

'Fantastic! What does it say?'

'It's signed by "Hibiscus." '

'How romantic! Who's "Hibiscus"?'

'Al, whoever she is, I say, I like her style.'

'And what does "Hibiscus" want?'

'She's a mature, intelligent, beautiful, even-tempered lady who's been dying to marry a millionaire-on-the-make.'

'And she's found the answer in you?'

'Looks like,' Basi replied proudly. 'It's not a bad choice, eh. She's chosen well, I should say.'

'Oh yes,' agreed Alali.

'And now, Al, I'm at last going to show Madam what stuff I'm made of. I'll stuff her rent arrears down her throat in brand new currency notes.'

'Mr B!' cheered Alali.

'I'll pack out of this hell-hole with the speed of lightning, to the safe haven of my darling.'

'I bet her home is surrounded by lots and lots of hibiscus.'

Basi smiled, as though he had considered that possibility and welcomed it. He said, 'Hibiscus mutabilis. White in the morning, purple at noon and bright red in the evening. Oh, it should be paradise.'

'Suppose she turns out to be some old hag fit only to be hung on a peg like second-hand clothing?'

'Then I'll hang her on a peg.'

'Or should there be no "Hibiscus" at all except in the imagination of a joker?'

'Al, you're either mad or jealous.'

Alali took the hint. 'I'm sure she's a rich, powerful woman,' he said.

'Now you're talking!' Basi smiled. 'She's got to be. How many Lagos women know the name of a flower called Hibiscus?'

'Very few.'

'And I've got the best of them.'

'Mr B!' Alali cheered.

'That's me!' Basi exulted. 'I'm sure she's tall, elegant, luscious. Oh, I'll hold her tenderly in my arms, embrace her, do elegant turns with her on the dance floor . . . waltzes, quick-steps, highlife.' He suited action to the words, dancing round the room crazily. 'And she will shower me with money, currency notes, brand new currency notes!'

'Mr B!' shouted Alali characteristically.

'That's me!'

'She proposes to meet you in Dandy's Bar,' said Alali, reading the letter.

'Clever girl! She's researched me out and proposes we meet close to my Palace.'

'With a bunch of hibiscus flowers for easy identification.'

'Al, you're a genius. Why, I never thought of that. I'll go all over Lagos to fetch the reddest of hibiscus flowers.'

'Tomorrow is the date, Mr B!'

'And tomorrow I say goodbye to Madam and this rat-hole.'

The rest of that day and a part of the next witnessed a flurry of activity at No. 7 Adetola Street. Madam went in search of hibiscus flowers. As did Basi. Basi went borrowing a suit. Madam got her best wear from its storage at the bottom of a valued trunk box. Basi laughed and did little jigs in his "Palace". Madam sang, whistled, danced and drank in her apartment. Basi dreamed. As did Madam. None knew what the other was doing. Neither of them foresaw what would happen later that day. When, early in the evening, Segi arrived to assist Madam with her preparations, Alali had already made sure that Basi looked his best.

Over at Dandy's Bar, the stage was set. The endeavours of the Managing Director of *Odeco Nigeria Limited* were not in vain. The Bar was full to capacity. Dandy was himself surprised to see the crowd that had gathered. He made money, and smiled happily as he served the crowd. He smiled even more when the author of his fortune arrived.

'Boy Zosco!' he greeted him.

'Cool!' replied Josco.

'There's going to be quite a show tonight.'

'Cool!' I expect the city's lost some hibiscus flowers, ha! ha!'

Dandy laughed too. 'Mr B's said to be in high spirits. Ordered a new suit of clothes. On credit.'

'Madam too. She's done her hair up in a new style called "Eko Bridge". And I hear her headtie for today is as tall as the skyscraper of the External Telecoms Service.'

A ripple of laughter passed over the room. The Managing Director of *Odeco Nigeria Limited* and his friends drank their beer and heard nothing.

But when Basi walked proudly into the room with Alali soon afterwards, an involuntary gasp escaped the assembled group.

'Mr B!' greeted Dandy and Josco simultaneously.

Basi looked round the Bar nervously and smiled sheepishly.

'Dandy, Dandy!' he called, 'the Bar's full tonight. Anything special?'

'No,' answered Dandy. 'A new consignment just came in by boat. I found the best drinks in town on board.'

'I see,' said Basi.

'What's special, Mr B?' asked Josco. 'Why the hibiscus flowers?'

The Bar fell silent. You could have heard a pin drop. Basi looked at the bunch of hibiscus flowers in his hand and said, 'Oh, the hibiscus flowers,' as though he was not aware he had them. 'They're in season. Lovely, aren't they?' he asked.

'Perfect,' replied Alali.

Dandy walked up to him and ran his hand over the lapel of his jacket. 'A new suit too. Have you hit the zackpot at last?' he demanded.

'Ah, the jackpot,' Basi replied. 'A good description.' He paused for a while, then asked almost confidentially, 'Has any lovely lady called here tonight?'

'Oh no. No lady has called. Expecting one?'

'Not at all. I was just asking, kind of. Since there are so many gentlemen here tonight, I thought the ladies might come too.'

'Looks a bit too early,' Alali said. 'Why don't we have a drink?'

'Yes. Let's have a drink. Dandy, a drink,' Basi said.

Dandy served them. After a while, Basi suggested to Alali that they go outside to see what was happening. Alali demurred; he did not want to go into the light drizzle that had begun to fall. Basi insisted, and they left the Bar.

They were gone but a few minutes when Madam and Segi turned up. Madam was gorgeously dressed in a yellow lace blouse and a colourful, embroidered loin-cloth reaching to her ankle. On her head was a heavy damask headtie done up in knots on her forehead. She wore heavy coral beads and her ears glittered with diamonds. Her bangle was made of gold and on her left breast sat a huge shiny brooch and a bright red hibiscus flower. She looked disdainfully around the Bar.

'Dandy, Dandy!' called Segi as soon as they entered the room.

'Segi of the lovely eyeballs!' Dandy replied.

'Boy Josco!' Segi called to Josco.

'Cool!' replied Josco.

'Ah, Madam, you're looking cute,' said Dandy.

Madam turned up her nose. 'Dis your cockroach Bar too smell!'

'We'll clean it with hibiscus flowers,' replied Dandy.

Another ripple of laughter passed through the Bar. Madam glared at everyone.

'Das why I no dey like dis Bar,' said she, spiritedly.

There was immediate silence.

'So what are you doing here with a red hibiscus flower?'

'Hibiscus,' Madam repeated and smiled. 'Oh hibiscus.'

The Bar burst into laughter. When the laughter had died down, Madam asked, 'You don see one gentleman wey . . .'

'Sorry, no gentleman has come here. Expecting someone?'

'At all, at all,' replied Madam. 'I jus dey ask.'

'Have a drink, Madam.'

'Your glass dirty too much,' Madam replied.

'We'll clean it with hibiscus flowers,' laughed Dandy.

Madam fidgeted with her headtie, then invited Segi to help her do it up firmly. They disappeared into the ladies room beyond.

The Bar filled up with noise and merriment. It was still thus when Basi and Alali re-entered.

'A horrible drizzle,' Basi complained.

'Ruined your suit,' observed Alali, trying to flick off the raindrops.

'Not to worry . . . Any news, Dandy?' he asked, turning to the barkeeper.

'What news?' Dandy asked.

'Has an elegant, mature, intelligent, beautiful, even-tempered lady been here?'

'Oh yes,' Josco quickly interposed. 'Gone to the ladies to sort out her gorgeous headtie.'

'She's elegant?'

'Ravishing,' replied Dandy. 'She asked after a zentleman.'

'She did! Holy Moses! And am all wet. Come on, Al. Let's go and change.' Then turning to Dandy, he said, 'If she comes again, detain her here. Right?'

'Will do,' Dandy replied as Basi and Alali went through the door.

A few moments later, Madam and Segi returned to the Bar.

''E never come?' asked Madam looking round.

'Who, Madam?' asked Josco.

'One tall, rich, handsome, young man . . .'

'Oh yes. Someone like that did call to ask for an elegant, mature, intellizent, beautiful, even-tempered lady.' Thus, Dandy.

'Wetin you tell am?'

'That no one like that had called.'

'Wetin him do den?'

Dandy said the gentleman stepped out of the Bar, saying he would return later. Madam sighed. Then declaring that she had to do up her headtie, repaired once again to the rooms beyond. As she walked past Josco, the latter said, 'Are you the elegant, mature, intelligent, beautiful . . .'

'Shurrup you mouth,' snapped Madam. And she swaggered off.

When Basi returned to the Bar, he had new clothes, a fresh bundle of hibiscus flowers, and there was apprehension on his face.

'She's not out of the ladies yet?' he asked of Dandy.

'She was here while you were out,' Dandy replied.

'Says to call her when you come in,' Josco added.

'But I asked you to detain her here . . .'

'How could I detain such a beautiful lady with a lovely hibiscus flower pinned to her gorzeous dress?'

'Oh, Dandy!' moaned Basi. 'Call the lady. Say I'm here.'

Josco went to the door and piped, 'Sweet lady, he's here.' He returned quickly to the Bar and took a vantage seat on one of the high stools.

Everyone could see that Basi was highly excited. He fidgeted with his dress, touched his hair, looked at his shoes. He was still at this activity when Madam walked majestically into the Bar. There was loud laughter from the clientele as Basi lifted his eyes from his shoes and came face to face with Madam.

At sight of Basi, Madam stood petrified, rooted to the spot. She fainted and fell backwards into Segi's arms. And the Bar rocked with loud, long, derisive laughter.

*　　*　　*

I was due to leave Adetola Street the next day for Ibadan to begin my studies at the University. That night, before I went to bed, my uncle spoke at length to me about the need to work hard and to be proud, strong and fair to others. I listened to him politely and thanked him. In my heart of hearts, I knew that I was grateful to him not so much for that night's lecture, as for the opportunity he had offered me to be a part of Adetola Street.

The next morning, I stood by the roadside waiting for *Psalm 31*. It duly drew up through the potholes, trailing a cloud of dust and smoke. I clambered into it, sat down and waved my uncle goodbye. *Psalm 31* drove off with a loud noise, past Dandy's Bar, past No. 7 Adetola Street and soon we had left the energy, the noise and the laughter of the Street behind us.

But the faces of the best citizens of the Street, of Basi, Madam, Alali, Josco, Segi and Dandy stuck indelibly to my memory. And I knew I would return to Adetola Street to share in the laughter they made, if not in their lives.

Psalm 31 screeched in agreement!

THE END

Glossary

wuruwuru wayo man (p.31) trickster
wayo (p.31) trick
shebi (p.45) I think, suppose
mumu (p.59) foolish, stupid
akamu (p.59) lazy, lousy
Your *shakara* full my belly (p.64) I am fed up with your arrogance, bluff
your *jibiti* full the house (p.64) your tricks are legion
wuruwuru (p.64) trickery
biribiri (p.64) hustling
lai-lai (p.69) forever, at all
take anoder woman make *ye-ye* (p.88) fool another woman
show you pepper (p.88) teach you a lesson
jowo (p.94) please; I beg you
boh (p.99) my friend
malu (p.112) cattle
toro (p.121) business
wahala (p.149) trouble
shay (p.183) I hope
helele (p.186) severely
by *fosa* (p.187) free of charge
Water don pass *gari* (p.195) You are in trouble; your situation is hopeless